All's Fair, Mrs. Biddle

A Byblos Foretold Trilogy

Babes at Sea

Peddlers All

Dames Engaged

The Byblos Foretold Novaplex

Trilogies

All's Fair, Mrs. Biddle

Novellas

Babes at Sea

Peddlers All

Dames Engaged

Supernumeraries

The Fly Maiden's Book of Virtues

ByblosForetold.com

All's Fair, Mrs. Biddle

M.E. Meegs

Lycophos Press

Northampton, Mass.

First Print Edition, February 2016

Lycophos Press
Northampton, Mass.

ISBN: 978-1-938710-17-9

To Susie

Contents

Babes at Sea

The First Novella

1

The muffled clatter of rain on slate infused the grubby attic room of the grubby inn with a palpable gloom, while the relentless drip caught by a cracked chamber pot provided an unnecessary reminder of the wretchedness of her state... *plic... plic... plic...*.

For five days, Mrs. Biddle had waited for word. For five days, tension waxed as food and money waned—just as it had throughout the long, wet French spring... *plic... plic... plic...*.

Eight months on the Pas-de-Calais, the last three in another leaking attic room, where for the first time in her life Mrs. Biddle had been compelled to accept charity. And that she resented most of all. Resented the fact of it, if not the cause. Now, in this last week of May, she had come to Cherbourg on a vague promise from a dubious man. And for five days and nights, she waited... *plic... plic... plic...*.

Her mood, never one that could be judged sunny, had turned as foul as the weather. Still, as she sponged herself before the few remaining shards of a shattered mirror, Mrs. Biddle took solace in the resplendent, if intermittent, view. She had recovered nicely from her long infirmity. And what was privation to a woman who fed on adversity as lesser women feed on pastry? Tension for her was simply the unavoidable precursor to action. In this she resembled nothing so much as a coiled spring. A rather good-looking coiled spring, to be sure. Few others sported so statuesque a figure, so clear a complexion, or so blonde and lush a mane. As frequently happened, Mrs. Biddle was cheered by her own superiority. But, speaking honestly, she couldn't deny she was a coiled spring in dire need of a good bath.

She had just finished dressing when there was a knock.

"*Un message, madame.*"

Mrs. Biddle opened the door and took a handwritten note

from a boy in an ill-fitting uniform. As she read, he waited. She looked down at him in disgust.

"*Va-t'en!*" she shouted.

He made a face, then spat back over his shoulder, "*Gadoue!*"

It was with the slamming of the door that the fruit of Mrs. Biddle's recent infirmity announced herself from her makeshift cradle—a small drawer suspended by cord from the peak of a dormer. Her mother picked her up and brought her to the bed. Then hoped against hope that the well had not yet run dry. For like her mother, Eugenia was not one to give up easily.

The name—meaning as it does *well-born*—was chosen as testament to Mrs. Biddle's own opinion of herself. How could her daughter be otherwise? She did, of course, resent the encumbrance on a life which had been kept scrupulously free of encumbrances. Not even marriage was allowed to impinge upon Mrs. Biddle's devotion to self. But here, at her breast, was an extension of that self, and even if she loved the child only half so much as she loved herself—a daughter's chromosomal entitlement—it would still be far more than any self-abnegating genetrix could muster.

"*Bonjour*, little sister!"

A petite girl—no older than seventeen, but last called ingénue at twelve—entered the room bearing a baguette and two pots. She set these on the table, then pulled an orange from one pocket of her jacket and a parcel of soft cheese from the other.

"Where did you spend the night?" Mrs. Biddle asked bitterly.

"Making sure baby sister has some breakfast beside the milk of a witch," the girl answered in a thick French accent, but nearly correct grammar.

After throwing off her jacket, she tied her russet hair into a loose knot, then pried the baby from her mother—the latter making no protest. She sat down at the table and dunked a finger in the pot of milky chocolate, then let the baby curled in her arm suckle it. Mrs. Biddle rose and rebuttoned her blouse before the broken mirror.

"This is for you to eat," the girl said, nodding toward the

food but not looking upon the woman at the mirror. "I've well eaten."

"Your belly full, is it? Have a care, girl, or soon you'll find yourself with your own little sister. Or the pox."

"That makes nothing to me," the girl told her as she waved the small bottle of holy water she wore on a string about her neck and depended on as spiritual prophylactic.

"Simple peasant. You think that protection enough when you spend the night passing yourself about?"

"I *do not* pass myself about!" the girl shouted back indignantly. Realizing her tone had unsettled Eugenia, she softened it. "I was with a... *éminent* man, the husband of the mistress of the mayor."

"He told you the mayor beds his wife?"

"Yes. And why not? It is a... *honneur?*"

"Honor. So, I have the mayor's cuckold to thank for my breakfast?" Her pride temporarily subdued by the aroma of cheese and coffee, Mrs. Biddle took a place at the table.

"No. This is for baby sister—you are the cow it must go through first."

"Then I suppose I must eat my grass."

"And say *meuh!*" the girl added for the benefit of her little sister.

"I'm an American cow," Mrs. Biddle corrected. Then, in a display that would have shocked any who knew her in the prenatal past, she gave her child a spirited "*moo-oo!*"

"So the cows talk different also?" the girl asked.

"Yes, and the roosters."

"No *cocorico?*"

"*Cockadoodledoo!*"

While her elders went through their bilingual bestiary, Eugenia, quite reasonably, looked on in stupefaction. Barely three weeks out of the womb, she had not yet learned an infant must pay for her keep by lavishing signs of amusement on her caretakers whenever they chose to degrade themselves. She *was* grateful for the chocolate her benefactress had provided, but surely she had adequately expressed her appreciation by not immediately regurgitating it upon the girl's blouse.

In truth, the girl—Mélisande, she called herself—was not even ten years younger than her "little sister's" mother. Though her exact role was a matter of continuous debate, she was an adjunct acquired during the previous winter. She had arrived in Étaples sometime before Christmas and Mrs. Biddle had made occasional use of her as factotum, with the girl wanting no payment beyond lessons in English. It was, she claimed, with that objective that she had come to the colony of Anglophones on the Pas-de-Calais.

When the money ran low and Mrs. Biddle economized by moving to the hostel's attic, the artful girl attended her more frequently—like the others at Étaples, she was convinced that sooner or later the proud woman would wire home for passage. For her own part, Mrs. Biddle knew full well the girl was merely ingratiating herself in the hope of securing a berth on the inevitable return voyage to New York. And Mélisande knew that Mrs. Biddle knew.

When spring arrived and the pregnancy proved difficult, Mélisande took on the duties of nurse, and her self-serving motives were mildly diluted with something resembling compassion. But the birth of Eugenia changed everything. Mrs. Biddle was completely dependent on the girl for two weeks, by the end of which Mélisande's devotion to her "little sister" had become fact.

As a nearby bell struck one, the insufferably precious game ended when neither patron nor retainer could remember the call of a rhinoceros. Her dignified demeanor restored, Mrs. Biddle rose from the table and announced they would be sailing that evening.

Mélisande was ecstatic. Six months of attending this contumelious shrew had worn thin even her good humor. Now, at last, she was sailing to New York. And not as an ignorant provincial likely to end up the exotic in some tenderloin house of sport. She had used her time in Étaples wisely, mingling freely with the expatriate poets and artists—in some cases quite freely—and would arrive in New York thoroughly fly.

"I must go off to make arrangements," Mrs. Biddle told her. "You'll need to start packing. We catch a boat from the Gare Maritime at five."

On picking up her jacket, Mrs. Biddle displaced that of the girl. The gold fob of a watch peeked out from a pocket. With a subtle grace born of careful breeding, Mrs. Biddle palmed the watch and slid it into her bag.

Down below, she negotiated her way through the damp, narrow lane, past the broken glass, half-eaten fruit, and filthy progeny of the slum, trying in vain to ignore the over-powering stench of urine. When an inebriated sailor slouching in a doorway made a suggestion she thought demeaning, Mrs. Biddle spat on him without turning her head. Though few would guess it to look at her—especially those unacquainted with her expectorial marksmanship—Mrs. Biddle was no stranger to her milieu. Her first memories were of a street indistinguishable from this in all its essentials, if not its particulars. The drunken sailor, for instance, who now stumbled from his haunt and challenged her with insulting gibes, would have been wearing the uniform of the U.S. Navy rather than that of the French. But if the menace was universal, the methodology employed in confronting it was quite personal. Mrs. Biddle lowered her arm and shook her sleeve. A straight razor fell into her palm.

Today, however, there would be no need for threatening gestures. Just ahead a sergeant of police turned onto the block, followed by two gendarmes. As they passed, Mrs. Biddle acknowledged the sergeant's suggestive smile with a stern look of reproach. When the sailor made a complaint against her, the already annoyed policeman shoved him to the street without slackening his pace.

II

Ten minutes later, Mrs. Biddle was in the lobby of the Hôtel de l'Aigle. But it was five minutes more before the other made his appearance. She knew that no matter what time she arrived, he would materialize some minutes later. He was a man of petty habits. The type of man who would hide himself in a corner of a hotel lobby behind a newspaper he couldn't read.

"I'm sorry I'm late, my dear," the man currently calling himself Dowling proffered.

Mrs. Biddle said nothing, simply smiled contemptuously at the copy of *Le Figaro* he'd placed on a table. There was no need for her to embarrass him further by inquiring in her perfect French what he'd gleaned from his reading. He averted his gaze, needlessly patting his thin grey hair. Mrs. Biddle had drawn first blood.

"Why no word for five days?" she demanded.

"There was no word to send, my dear. When he didn't board the *Deutschland*, it became a game of wait and see. It was only this morning I heard he'd be sailing on the *Kronprinz Wilhelm*. They should have left Southampton an hour ago."

"And who is 'he'?"

"'He' is the perfect dupe, a jay-town rube as wealthy as Midas. Name's Dexter. Timothy Dexter. He's on his way home. With Archie Cobb as his valet. Do you remember Archie?"

"A bald Englishman? Favored the drop game?"

"Yes, but he has other talents," Dowling assured her.

"And he's the one who spotted this Dexter?"

"That was another Englishman, a friend of Archie's. This fellow had some elaborate game going that went off the track. When it was over, all he had to show for it was the rusting hulk of a steamer stuck in the mud near the mouth of the Thames. Not only was it worthless, he'd been enjoined to have it towed off. Well, he meets this Dexter while loitering about the Métropole, sees he's an easy mark, and by the next morning he's sold him the wreck for ten thousand dollars, *cash*."

"How much more does he have?"

"From what he's heard, Archie thinks there must be fifty thousand more."

"And my share?"

"A full twenty percent."

"And you and Cobb? Forty each?"

"He's put a lot of work into this, and I've put up quite a bit of capital. Securing cabins at the last minute doesn't come cheap. It's only fair."

"Twenty-five."

"Well, it will have to come from mine... but I guess I can't deny you that," Dowling acquiesced, then added with affected beneficence, "I always was soft on you."

A slight, upward curl appeared on Mrs. Biddle's upper lip. Those of her acquaintances familiar with it took it as a signal to seek safer quarters. Dowling examined the crease of his trousers.

But Mrs. Biddle knew she had lost the round. His ready compliance meant that he'd probably offered Cobb a twenty percent share, saying *she* was getting forty. Then agreed to raise Cobb's portion to twenty-five out of feigned friendship. Now the old man would be taking a full half for himself. It wasn't the first time she had allowed him to cheat her. But she swore it would be the last.

"Just what do you have in mind?" she asked.

"We sell him the deed to an underwater duchy."

"An underwater duchy?"

"Yes. You see, there's a fictional syndicate with plans to build a railway tunnel under the channel, Dover to Calais. And you are the heiress of a duchy that became submerged about the time of the Norman Conquest. The syndicate needs the deed to complete the tunnel."

"Are you serious?"

"Perfectly. I grant it's a little baroque, but that's what you need for a fellow like this. I'll be posing as agent for the syndicate, following you across to get the deed. Archie convinces Dexter he can clean up by getting in front of me, then selling it to the syndicate for a healthy profit."

"What deed?"

"Well, grant, more properly."

He produced an antiqued document written in monastic calligraphy on brittle parchment. Writ large across the top were the two words *Ducatus Aquatiquus,* and affixed at the bottom was the wax seal of Charlemagne—conveniently rendered in modern nomenclature. The text between began, *"Osculetur me osculo oris sui,"* which Mrs. Biddle recognized as the offering of a kiss that opens the Song of Solomon. On the reverse was a crude map demarcating the borders of the duchy—a geographic pustule rising from the epidermis of northern France.

"You are Lady Eleanor Marsouin of Aquatique," Dowling went on. "Traveling incognito, of course, posing as an American, Elsbeth Duncan. That way, if your accent fails you, there's a ready excuse. Though I doubt Dexter would notice one way or the other."

Mrs. Biddle bristled at the suggestion any aspect of her being could fail her.

"I'll need two hundred francs and the same amount in dollars," she told him. However dubious the scheme, if it got her to New York with even a modest amount of cash, she would be content.

"What for? Your cabin's paid for, *with a bath.* Do you have any idea what that costs?"

Mrs. Biddle said nothing, simply sat stone-faced until the other took out his wallet and placed two hundred francs on the table.

"That's all I have with me," he told her. In fact, he could easily have produced the two hundred dollars. But he had no intention of insulating her from failure. "One other thing, my dear. I've arranged to have a woman travel as your maid. There's plenty of room in your cabin, and it will lend credibility to your story."

"Who?"

"Her name's Céleste. She's top-notch, helped me through a difficult night in Trouville."

Mrs. Biddle smiled at his revelation. "I have my own maid," she told him. "Your paramour can travel in your own cabin."

"Leave yours behind. Or send her steerage," the old man told her. "I'm sorry, my dear, but on this I must insist."

Sensing Dowling's resolve could more easily be circumvented than assaulted frontally, Mrs. Biddle silently gathered the banknotes from the table and placed them in her bag.

"So I'll see you at five o'clock?" the other asked. On Mrs. Biddle's nod, he added, "Céleste will be on the tender but standing apart. She'll approach you."

Outside, Mrs. Biddle for the first time connected the sergeant of police with the watch she'd taken from Mélisande's jacket. She took it out and read the inscription carved on the case, *À M. Bouc, de son cher ami M. Cocufieur, le maire de Cherbourg*. Many were the ways of the French that irritated Mrs. Biddle, but she felt obliged to admire the frankness with which they approached matters of the heart. It was difficult to imagine an American cuckold accepting a commemorative gold watch from his wife's lover.

Eugenia! Mrs. Biddle, still unaccustomed to troubling herself over another being, picked up her pace. At the inn's street door, a gendarme stood chatting with a working girl. Mrs. Biddle passed them and upstairs encountered the second gendarme with his ear to the door of her room. He made a feeble attempt to stop her, but she pushed him aside.

The queer scene that greeted her prompted a strange sense of relief. Eugenia was flying about the room in the hands of a prancing police sergeant, naked from the waist down, while Mélisande watched bare-breasted from the bed, shrieking encouragement. At the sound of the door the sergeant instinctively covered his modesty with the only shield at hand. Mrs. Biddle took her child from him, and while he hurriedly dressed, spoke to him in French.

"You came for the watch of Monsieur Bouc?"

"Yes, madame. But...," he nodded toward Mélisande.

"Yes, I see you've been paid. But it would be to your advantage to have the watch as well, *n'est-ce pas?*"

"You have it, madame?"

"Be at the Gare Maritime at five o'clock this afternoon, where the boat for the Lloyd line docks. You will see a woman approach me. Wait until I nod—she will have the watch. You may not be able to charge her, but hold her until the boat departs."

"As you say, madame." He gave her a short bow and made his exit.

Mélisande, shameless as always, sang a vulgar ditty while she dressed.

"You took my watch, madame. It was a gift."

"Why must you always lie to me?" Mrs. Biddle asked. "You lie with a cuckold and steal his watch. Then you need to lie with the... *flique*. You need to give up the thieving and whoring if you want to come with me to New York."

"And the lying?"

"Yes, and the lying."

"Which lying? There *seems* to be two. One is a sin. The other a... *occase?*"

"Opportunity? What are you talking about?"

"Well, if I go to confession and I tell the priest, 'Father, I have sinned. I lied *to* my father,' he will tell me I must say thirty Ave Marias. But if the next week I say, 'Father, I have sinned. I lied *with* my uncle for a...' *franc?*"

"Two bits."

"'I lied *with* my uncle for two bits,' the holy father will tell me how I can make three bits without leaving the confessional."

"You wicked girl." Try as she might, Mrs. Biddle was unable to suppress a smile. "But you *lay* with your uncle—and you can't have three bits."

"Why can't I?"

"Bits only come in twos. So, two bits, or four bits, but not one bit, or three bits."

"That is very silly."

"Yes, best to stick with dollars and cents. Now we need to hurry and pack."

The coiled spring had sprung....

2

While Mrs. Biddle prepared her party for its evening departure aboard the S.S. *Kronprinz Wilhelm*, Tomasz Szczęsny—a distracted young man who spent a good part of his day trying to keep his tie straight, hair combed, and shirt tucked in—was leaving that ship's telegraph office with a cable for his employer.

It took very little to distract Tomasz. The weather alone—be it sunny or dreary, arid or damp—often led his thoughts astray. Place him on a bustling London thoroughfare, or even a moderately busy street in his native Łodz, and he would, within seconds, be lost in contemplation of the countless human dramas playing out before him. On one memorable autumn afternoon, the sight of a forlorn-looking rat traversing an alley sent him into an hours-long reverie that was broken only when a resident some floors above thought it an opportune moment for emptying her chamber pot.

The sad truth was, Tomasz Szczęsny had the heart of a poet. Worse still, he had the mind of a poet. But, at least in the eyes of his friends, he did have one saving grace: he did not write poetry.

Tomasz had no time for writing poetry. His domineering father had instilled in him a sense of familial duty that precluded such frivolous pursuits. For it would be up to this unassuming boy to regain some semblance of his family's former prestige. The Szczęsnys, you see, had been of the minor nobility until dispossessed during one of the eighteenth-century partitions of Poland. Tomasz was never quite sure which of the several partitions it was, or whether the family estate was lost to the Prussians or the Austrians, only that it was up to him, and him alone, to remedy the situation as best he could.

As the Polish kingdom had been dismembered into oblivion, and the doling out of aristocratic titles therefore in abeyance, it would be necessary to venture further afield. Tomasz's father set his sights on Victoria's England—seat of a sprawling empire of unimaginable wealth, and one which had demonstrated its good breeding by having never invaded Poland. He sent his son to the University of Krakow, where he could learn a passable English at modest expense, and, more recently, financed his trip to London. The goal: to marry the daughter of a duke, a marquess, or, if absolutely unavoidable, an earl. But nothing less would do, for she must bear the title of Lady. His father made it quite clear that if he returned home the son-in-law of a mere baronet, he could expect disinheritance. Rather an empty threat, as there was not much left worth inheriting. But so thoroughly had his father conditioned Tomasz that he went to England with the sincere intention of carrying out his sire's desire.

Regrettably, Tomasz arrived in England just as the vogue for marrying aristocratic issue to American millionaires was hitting its stride. What the average duke was looking for in a son-in-law was a man who could shore up the family finances with ample sums of a sound currency. Fanciful Poles residing in third-rate Chelsea boarding houses were not high on his list.

It was just after breakfast one morning at his third-rate boarding house that Tomasz was presented with what seemed a simple solution: *become* an American millionaire. He was speaking with another inmate of the house, a man named Archie Cobb, who some days earlier had been told of Tomasz's predicament. Archie informed him that he had recently taken the position of gentleman's gentleman to a wealthy American and that he had been tasked with finding a secretary to serve the same master.

"Just think of it, Tommy," Archie enthused. "You'll be privy to all the secrets of the trade. See it as an apprenticeship. In a year or two you go off on your own, make your own fortune, and quicker 'an you can say Jack Robinson, you'll have to beat back those blue bloods with a club. Why, every evening your mail will be flooded with invitations to house parties, theatre outings, fancy-dress balls. All the best hunts will be badgering you to sign on. This is an opportunity you can't afford to pass up, my boy. You know what they say—when fortune smiles, embrace her.

Then take her off to a quiet corner, that's what I say."

While it did seem odd that a man who made his living performing tricks for the theatre crowds of Covent Garden was in a
position to mete out appointments to the entourage of an American millionaire, Tomasz suppressed his skepticism and allowed
his inner poet to lay out a convincing case that led to his ac-
ceptance of the adventuresome plan. And so it was that only a few
hours before our meeting him, Tomasz had boarded the
Kronprinz Wilhelm as secretary to Timothy Dexter.

You will, dear reader, find it illustrative of how easily Tomasz could be distracted when I reveal that during my long
explication of his circumstances, he'd gotten no further than the
promenade deck, just one deck below that of the telegraph office.
While descending the stairs, he had caught sight of a charming
young woman looking back over her shoulder. Not at him, but in
his general direction. That was all it took.

Tomasz wandered after her, soon losing her in the crowd.
Then, a moment later, she emerged, now walking toward him.
She was herself distracted, reading a letter as she hastened along.
He could see at once that she was a woman of passion, the way
her lips quivered as she read, the way her eyes seemed to feed on
the words, the way she blushed at one particular passage. A man
called her from behind, and as she turned to look, she collided
with Tomasz.

"Take this for me and destroy it," she said, pushing the letter
into Tomasz's hand. She was German, scented with lavender.
"Go. Quickly!"

Never one to fail a lady in distress, Tomasz took her offering
and hurried below. When he reached the upper cabin deck, he
paused to peruse the letter. It was a billet-doux. And a particularly piquant one, at that. He was glad now that he had spent so
much time at university learning the idiomatic vocabulary of the
female anatomy in each of the languages he was assigned to
master, as the vibrant argot used in the penultimate paragraph
bore a striking resemblance to that of a pornographic novella his
German roommate had shared with him. It would be a crime to

destroy so artistic a missive. Someday, Tomasz felt sure, he would need to come up with just this sort of communiqué. He put it in his pocket, pushed his unruly black hair out of his eyes, and knocked on the door of his employer's cabin.

"You may come forth," Timothy Dexter called from within.

"I have the cable, sir," Tomasz informed him, tucking in his shirt tail as he did so.

"Read it, boy. Read it."

"Sir, we have received what we believe a very generous offer of six hundred pounds for the S.S. *Oblinibat* from a reputable scrap dealer, buyer to bear all costs. Please send instructions. Signed, Nye, Clare & Co."

"Six hundred pounds, sterling! That's three thousand dollars, boy. A comely, buxom profit." As he so often was, Timothy Dexter was excited. And when Timothy Dexter became excited, his snow-white eyebrows hopped about his forehead like a pair of rabbits performing a synchronized ballet.

"Is this the steamship that is broken in the Thames?"

"One and the same. I had a feeling it would be worth something as scrap. Price of iron was due for a rise."

"How could you be sure?" Tomasz asked, hoping to glean his first piece of financial acumen.

"Never sure, boy. Never sure. Just felt it. Then I meet a fellow without leaving my hotel willing to sell the title to five thousand tons of iron, and I know the gods want me to buy." The right eyebrow did a solo pirouette.

"For how much did you buy it?"

"A mere ten thousand."

"Ten thousand dollars?"

"Yes, ten thousand of the genuine article."

This confused Tomasz a good deal. He freely admitted the market economy was a closed book to him. Still, how could selling for three thousand dollars what you bought for ten thousand be profitable? It would, he feared, be a long apprenticeship....

"Shall I take a letter in reply?" Tomasz asked. "I should be able to mail it when we reach Cherbourg."

"Good thinking, boy. Yes, take a letter." Dexter rummaged through one of the several stacks of paper lying on the floor until he found one with the address of the firm. "To Nye, Clare & Co., 88, Bishops Gate Within," he read, then stopped. "Within what?" he asked.

"Perhaps it means they have offices at that address, but no sign outside," Tomasz suggested.

"Very shrewd, boy, very shrewd. Well, let's get back to it. Sirs, have received your cable and answer it with esteemed affirmation."

"Does that mean they should sell it?" Tomasz asked.

"Yes, sell the damn thing, and send payment to my solicitors." There was another pause while Dexter again searched his piles of papers.

"Perhaps it would be helpful if I were to organize your correspondence?"

"Let *you* have my papers? Never, boy. Never. Ah, here it is. Send payment to my solicitors, Crowders, Vizard, Oldham & Co., 51, Lincoln's Inn Fields. Yours benevolently, Timothy Dexter."

"I will type this immediately, sir, and bring it back for your signature."

"Sound plan, boy. And send Archie around."

Tomasz made a slight bow and went off to the cabin he shared with Archie Cobb, thus interrupting what had been a very thorough—and thoroughly fruitless—search of his belongings.

"How's the old man?" Cobb asked.

"Oh, very happy. Though I don't understand it. You know that steamship he bought?"

"The one stuck in the mud?" Cobb smiled.

"Yes. He's sold it for three thousand dollars and says it is a nice profit. How can that be when he paid ten thousand of the genuine article for it?"

"Did he use the term 'genuine article'?" Archie Cobb swallowed hard.

"Yes. Is that better than banknotes?"

"It depends which side of the transaction you're on." A note of despondency colored Archie's voice. In his circles, the term "genuine article" was used only ironically, to refer to currency of private manufacture. Had his old friend Len Bailey sold his steamship for a pile of counterfeit bills? Seemed impossible. No, more likely Dexter had used the term not knowing its meaning to the cognoscenti.

"There can't have been a profit," Archie insisted. "He's mad. Knew it from the moment I laid eyes on him. From what I've heard, all these American millionaires are as mad as hatters. We just have to humor him. If he says he made a profit, there's nothing for it but to congratulate him."

"I see," Tomasz said. But something new troubled him. "Do you think it will be necessary for me to go mad if I'm to be a millionaire?"

"As sure as eggs is eggs, but what will it matter? You'll always have people about telling you what a genius you are, at least as long as the money holds out."

"And the blue bloods? They won't mind me marrying one of their daughters?"

"Them? They're even battier—all that inbreeding."

"Ah," Tomasz said, relieved. He took out his Blickenderfer Model 7, the odd-looking typewriter his new employer had provided, and placed it on the tiny table. "Oh, by the way. The old man wants to see you."

"All right. I don't suppose he's given you a key to his cabin?"

"Key? No, he won't even trust me with his papers. How can I be his secretary if I can't see his papers?"

"Just remember, he's rich, and we're not."

II

Archie Cobb was a man of vague middle age, forty-five at least, but not yet sixty, by no means svelte, but not particularly fat, with a bald, round pate that led directly to an equally round forehead. The latter of which was currently covered in a thin layer of moisture born of concern. Moments earlier he had quelled his anxiety over the authenticity of Dexter's store of cash, but dark doubts now clouded his conviction.

For himself, he didn't mind in the least being employed by a man who made his fortune passing the queer. What did worry him was the reaction of his accomplice, Dowling. Though generally not violent, Dowling was known to be vindictive—perhaps the most vindictive man in Archie's exceptionally wide acquaintance. It was imperative that he determine the character of Dexter's currency at the earliest possible moment. Then, if it proved only ironically genuine, Archie could disembark at Cherbourg—with luck, unseen by Dowling.

Timothy Dexter answered his knock with his customary, "You may come forth."

"I understand you have need for me, sir," Archie said, then began straightening things about the cabin. When he opened the wardrobe, Dexter took hold of his shoulder and spun him around.

"What are you doing?" he demanded.

"Seeing to your apparel, sir. It *is* one of the chief concerns of a valet."

"Never mind that. You only have to play the valet until we reach New York. After that I have something else I need you to do. You ever do any acting?"

"Oh, yes, sir. I feel, sometimes, that my life has been one long performance."

"Good. Then this should be easy for you. I need you to play an English lord."

"Of any particular station?"

"Station?"

"I mean, shall I be a duke? An earl?"

"Doesn't matter, just so people have to call you Lord."

"Then I suggest a viscount—more difficult to check up on. The Viscount of Abernethy. My mother's people are from Abernethy. For whose benefit will I be performing this role?"

"It's to satisfy my wife. I told her I'd bring back a lord for our daughter to marry. But the real ones ran too dear. I can't see spending good money to buy myself a son-in-law that's more tapeworm than man."

"I see. You wish me to marry your daughter." Archie had seen a photograph of Felicia Dexter, and though the prospect of matrimony had never before appealed, he was more than willing to explore the subject with the curvaceous young lady in question. "You are wise to close the matter forthwith. Daughters and dead fish are no keeping wares."

"Hell, she hasn't gone off yet. No, I don't want you to marry my daughter, just satisfy my wife. One look at you and the girl will have nothing to do with you. No offense."

"None taken. And once I've satisfied Mrs. Dexter, what becomes of me then?"

"We'll have to see about that, later."

It sounded decidedly indefinite. Archie preferred the security of hard cash. It was time to lay the groundwork for Dowling's scheme.

"Speaking of the aristocracy, I have heard, sir, that Lady Eleanor Marsouin of the lost Duchy of Aquatique will be boarding in Cherbourg."

"How'd she lose her duchy? Cards or dice?"

"The duchy was lost to the waters of time, submerged in a great earthquake some centuries back."

"Can't have much of an income from that."

"No, sir. Quite true. But the duchy is now sought after by the syndicate building the cross-channel tunnel."

"What tunnel?" Dexter asked.

"The rail tunnel which will proceed under the channel from Dover to Calais. Surely you've read about it in the financial press."

"What use have I for the financial press?"

His attitude came as a relief to Archie, but did not surprise him. Whatever means Dexter had used to acquire his fortune, there was no doubt they were of an unorthodox nature.

"It appears," Archie explained, "the drowned duchy lies in the path of the tunnel. The courts of admiralty and chancery—

both of England and of France—are in agreement: the tunnel cannot proceed without the rights to the Duchy of Aquatique."

"That so?" Dexter seemed distressingly uninterested in the fortunes of Lady Eleanor and her waterlogged dominion. "You know, I have some royal blood. A second cousin, thrice removed, Lord Timothy Dexter. I'm named for him."

"Indeed, sir? From which of England's shires?"

"Not England. Massachusetts. Newburyport, Massachusetts."

"I'd always been led to understand Americans shied from titles of nobility."

"Not this fellow. Had to give himself the title, but that was OK with him." Timothy Dexter's eyebrows echoed his amusement. "Being his namesake, I tried it on myself. But the wife and girl wouldn't go along."

"He that hath wife and children hath given hostages to fortune, for they are impediments to great enterprises."

"That's the real Sunday-school truth, that is. You have a nice way of putting things, Archie."

"Thank you, sir. Or, if I may take the liberty, *Your Lordship*."

"Yes, you may. Say, where does one get a drink on this tugboat?"

"The smoking saloon is, I believe, one deck above, and to the sternward."

"I think I'll venture forth. Tell my secretary... what the hell's the boy's name?"

"Tomasz, Your Lordship. Tomasz Szczęsny."

"Well, tell Tommy to bring me that letter there."

"Very good, Your Lordship."

There was an awkward moment while Archie attempted to remain in the cabin after the exit of his employer, but Lord Dexter's look of suspicion spooked the ersatz valet and future Viscount of Abernethy and he went off to his own cabin under the other's watchful eye.

There he found Tomasz petting his little moustache while he

checked his work—only seven errors, and none of them he thought critical.

"His lordship wants you to bring that to him in the smoking saloon," Archie informed him.

"His lordship? *He's* a lord?"

"Not a real one. Thinks he inherited the title from some ancestor more nutty than he is. He's made me a viscount. The Viscount of Abernethy."

"Should I call you both 'Your Lordship'?" Tomasz asked.

"Him only in private, me only after we reach New York."

Tomasz nodded as he left, but it was mere bravado. Things were not becoming clearer.

Once he was alone, Archie retrieved the sewing kit which also held his lock picks. He then spent a frustrating hour dodging stewards and battling a mounting anxiety as he endeavored to break into the cabin of Lord Dexter. Having failed, he returned to his own quarters and took out his flask, then drank to the eternal damnation of German craftsmanship.

And so, cherished reader, the principal players have been introduced. Our heroine, Mrs. Biddle (masquerading as Lady Eleanor Marsouin of Aquatique, but traveling as Elsbeth Duncan); her wayward attendant, Mélisande; the enigmatic Dowling, mastermind of the scheme; Tomasz, the dreamy Polish secretary; Lord Timothy Dexter, his eccentric American millionaire employer; and Archie Cobb, confederate of Dowling, valet to Lord Dexter, and only later assuming the title Viscount of Abernethy. Just six in all. Seven if we include baby Eugenia—though surely at this age more prop than player.

Rest assured, this will not be one of those excessively populated tales that so irritate the reader who strives to preserve his mind in its pristine state. There will be no long list of ancillary characters cluttering up the narrative. Police sergeants may dance about naked, and lavender-scented ladies pass all the salacious epistles they like. All will remain unnamed. Mere incidentals. On this, I give you my word.

3

With the aid of his flask, Archie Cobb regained his resolve. There could be no doubt, he reasoned, that Lord Timothy Dexter possessed an ample supply of reliable cash. Archie himself had taken the bank draft to the Lloyd line's ticket office and then been required to wait while inquiries were made at Lord Timothy's London bank—the cashiers of German steamship lines being as annoyingly painstaking as their locksmiths. With first-class cabins for both his lordship and his servants, not to mention the several dozen crates of newly acquired curios in the hold below, the total had come to nearly two hundred pounds sterling. No, there could be no doubt about it. Somehow—almost certainly by pure luck—Lord Dexter had come into the stuff.

It was now four o'clock and time for Archie to set the stage for the arrival of his compatriots. He went about the promenade deck listening for American accents, and when he found them, entered into friendly conversation. Sometimes he began by commenting on the weather, sometimes by offering a witty observation on the cramped accommodations. But he always ended by asking, sotto voce, if his listeners were aware that Lady Eleanor Marsouin would be boarding in Cherbourg.

"Of course, not under her real name," he confided. "Calling herself Elsbeth Duncan, pretending to be a Yank. I have that from the purser himself."

"What's this Lady Eleanor look like exactly?"

"Oh, you must have seen her photograph. Tall, blonde. The real raspberry jam, she is. No mistaking *her*."

But Archie left off all mention of the Duchy of Aquatique. There was a limit, he suspected, to even an American tourist's gullibility.

At ten minutes to five, Mrs. Biddle and her party arrived at Cherbourg's Gare Maritime, the railroad depot which occupied a large pier projecting into the harbor. She placed what remained of the two hundred francs into an envelope and mailed it to the hostel in Étaples. Once she had brought Mélisande to New York, all her debts would be paid. But unless the scheme went off, she herself would arrive destitute.

As they neared the Lloyd line's tender—the small steamboat that would shuttle them to the *Kronprinz Wilhelm*—she gave Mélisande her instructions.

"A woman will approach me. It's her you must plant the watch on."

"*My* watch?"

"She means to take your place on the boat. Keep the watch, or come to New York. It's your choice."

Mélisande shrugged a reluctant assent. "What does she look like?"

"I don't know, but she will come towards me. Can you do this while carrying the baby?"

"*Mais oui*, she will make it easier."

"Once we separate here, stay as far from me as possible. Try not to even look in my direction. You board the boat first. The woman will be looking for me, but I won't board until I've drawn her off. You must plant the watch before she leaves the boat. Once she does, I will nod and your sergeant will arrest her. When we get out to the steamship, I will board first. A small, grey-haired man with a beard will be watching me. After he boards, you may. We'll meet in the cabin, that of Elsbeth Duncan. But I don't want anyone to realize we're together for as long as possible."

As she boarded the tender, Mélisande had an inspiration of her own. She began fussing over Eugenia in the obnoxious manner of a proud mother. As she expected, this drew the attention of the other passengers. All except one—a plump young woman whose eyes remained fixed on the gangplank. Mélisande began pacing, as if to pacify the child, then stumbled into the woman. Mrs. Biddle, who had only just started up the gangplank, looked back over her shoulder as if having forgotten to attend to something, then returned to the dock. The woman now bearing the watch of M. Bouc disembarked as if to follow her.

"Miss Duncan!" she called.

Mrs. Biddle stopped, turned toward her, then nodded. On cue, Eugenia's dancing partner emerged from the shadows and pulled the plump woman aside. Mrs. Biddle now boarded the tender and made her way to the bow. All in all, a perfectly timed bit of choreography.

Halfway to the roadstead and the rendezvous with the *Kronprinz Wilhelm*, the man calling himself Dowling sidled up beside her.

"That wasn't playing fair, my dear," he complained.

Mrs. Biddle said nothing, simply stared out to sea.

"Poor Céleste," he went on. "What was it you told the police?"

"I don't know what you're talking about. But if you're worried for your lady friend, take the tender back. I'm sure Cobb and I can get along."

"With no seed money? I think you flatter yourself, my dear." It was meant as a slight, but he was the one left feeling the discomfort.

As the tender came alongside the steamship, dozens of heads leaned over the rails above, each hoping for a glimpse of the renowned Lady Eleanor. Then, when Mrs. Biddle graced them with a glance in their direction, Archie Cobb led her new converts in a rousing cheer. There was no mistaking true aristocratic blood.

Aware now that they were in the presence of a celebrity, the other passengers on the tender made way. According to the natural order, Lady Eleanor must be the first to board. Dowling, meanwhile, stood back and watched, hoping to ascertain who among the others was the maid of whom Mrs. Biddle had spoken.

The purser didn't recognize the name Elsbeth Duncan, nor had he heard the rumor she was really Lady Eleanor. But his refined sense of self-preservation told him this was a woman who would demand coddling, and no one could coddle like a purser of the Lloyd line. He personally saw her to her cabin.

Throughout dinner that evening, all eyes watched for the arrival of Lady Eleanor. But all eyes watched in vain. Mrs. Biddle and her party had their meal in their cabin, where they took turns enjoying their private bath. Later, the faux duchess gave her servant a detailed description of the scheme. Perhaps too detailed. Though by no means unintelligent, Mélisande's exposure to complex con games involving false imperial land grants and imaginary aristocrats had been limited. At the lecture's conclusion, she wasn't entirely sure whether her patron was pretending to be an American who happened to come into an underwater duchy, or a natatorial duchess emigrating to America. But it seemed a minor point and not worth suffering the inevitable sardonic remark by asking for clarification.

II

At midnight, with her daughter fed and Mélisande given explicit orders not to leave the cabin, Mrs. Biddle went off for a prearranged meeting. At 12:02, her contumacious retainer wrapped the infant in a blanket and carried her up to the boat deck, where they could both experience the open ocean for the first time.

They stood facing into a cool breeze—the girl laughing, the newborn, as usual, dumbstruck. A mere dozen feet away stood another passenger enjoying his first night on the open sea. Until their arrival, Tomasz had lost himself in the clear night sky, fashioning constellations of his own imagining. Now he turned his sights on Mélisande. Within minutes he constructed a rough outline of her life, and was filling in the blanks of what promised to be a three-volume Victorian novel when he was abruptly interrupted.

Mélisande had been swinging the baby about in a manner Tomasz thought cavalier for a mother and he was busily revising chapter seven to account for this odd behavior when the blanket loosened and Eugenia was launched into flight. Tomasz tossed aside his psychic pen and dove beneath the airborne child. Miraculously, he caught her just inches away from what looked like a lethal steel projection. Sadly, his own skull kept the appointment for her.

When he came to, Mélisande had his head in her lap and was stroking it tenderly. And the baby, which he still held to his chest, was staring up at him in a way that might have reminded those who knew him of Tomasz's own customary expression. He would have been content to remain locked in mutual wonderment with the child for as long as its mother stroked him, but a German officer coming upon the scene thought it too intimate for public display. He helped Tomasz up, and Mélisande took back her charge. When the officer had passed on, she thanked the child's savior for his timely assistance.

"Oh, I was pleased to help," he told her. "So thoughtful a baby."

"She thinks of only the one thing, her mama's milk."

Tomasz followed her look to where the baby was nestled and blushed.

"You're American, aren't you?" he asked, looking up.

"Yes, we come from... Pittsbourg." Thank goodness she'd paid attention when the Americans at Étaples spoke of home. "Pittsbourg, Philadelphia."

"Is Philadelphia a state?"

"Why not?"

"And your husband, he awaits you there?"

"No, he is dead. The Indians come and burn him up."

"How horrible."

"Yes, they are very mean, the Indians."

"So you travel to forget...." Tomasz was writing out loud.

"Forget what?"

"The cruel death of your baby's father...."

"Oh, yes. Very sad. But now we must go, or the witch will be angry."

"Witch?"

Mélisande gave him a kiss and vanished. Tomasz found a deck chair and sat down. He had a long night of revisions before him.

While her servant was giving the vacant Pole a lesson on

American life, Mrs. Biddle conferred with Archie Cobb and the man currently calling himself Dowling in the latter's cabin.

"Why in heaven's name did you miss dinner?" Dowling asked sharply. "We need to work fast—we have just five days."

"I decided it was better to heighten anticipation. Dexter must come to me, after all."

"She's right," Cobb agreed. "Even he couldn't miss all the talk of Lady Eleanor."

"Can you describe him so I'll recognize him?" Mrs. Biddle asked.

"You won't have any trouble with that. Tall and thin as Banbury cheese, with snow-white hair down to his shoulders. Looks like your Uncle Sam—only, clean-shaven."

"Have you found out exactly how much he has?" Dowling asked him.

"No, won't let me near his things."

"I thought you were his valet?" Mrs. Biddle asked.

"So did I. Seems he mainly wants me to do some play acting when we get to New York, says he needs an English lord to impress his wife. And there's another bit of a complication. He had me hire him a secretary the day before we sailed."

"Damn! Why didn't you wire me?" Dowling demanded. "I could have called the whole thing off."

Archie chose not to admit that was precisely why he hadn't wired. What neither he nor Mrs. Biddle knew was that Dowling was bluffing. For his own reasons, he couldn't afford to call the scheme off.

"It's not as bad as it seems," Archie assured them. "He left the hiring to me. His secretary is a Polish kid, as green as a leek. Knows nothing about money or business. And Dexter doesn't trust him either. Still, we might want to keep him occupied."

"I'll take care of that," Mrs. Biddle told them. They both looked at her as if awaiting elaboration. But she offered none. "So, how do we play it out?" she asked Dowling.

"Archie tells him about my role as buyer for the syndicate. We'll make sure Dexter sees me pestering you to sell, and sees some of the bundle I'm carrying. I'll get him in a card game and let him win some. Let him think I'm a dullard. In the meantime, you keep happening to bump into him. Then you confide in him."

"And the endgame?" she asked.

"An auction on the last night at sea. He and I bidding, and we make sure he can beat my last bid. So we must know exactly how much he has." He looked hard at Archie.

"Don't worry, I'll get in to see it one way or another."

"How much do you have?" Mrs. Biddle asked Dowling.

"After all the expenses, just over four thousand. During the auction, I'll agree that his man, Archie, hold the money. He can look through the bag, showing just enough to maintain the illusion. Dexter wins, you give him his deed, we make our split, and then go our separate ways. Agreed?"

Mrs. Biddle nodded, then left the cabin without another word. Dowling rose and poured out two large brandies.

"She's a hard one," Archie said. "And the way she talks to you? Can't seem to spare a kind word for her own father."

Good lord! Her own father? Well, treasured reader, no one is more surprised at this revelation than myself. But please understand, I am not the source of this chronicle, only its assembler. (A fuller explanation will be provided when time allows.) In order to preserve the story's freshness, I write as I glean. And it's only just now that I've gleaned this item of interest. In fairness, we all should have suspected they were family from the degree of loathing she's shown for him.

Mélisande returned to the cabin sometime after her mistress, and once Eugenia had been placed in her cradle, Mrs. Biddle slapped the defiant girl hard.

"*Never* take her from the cabin!"

"As you wish, madame. But why shouldn't little sister enjoy the air outside?"

Mrs. Biddle made as if to slap her again, but Mélisande stopped her, clasping her wrist in a surprisingly strong grip.

"Be careful, *madame*, or someday I will slap you back. And you will feel it for a very long time."

Mrs. Biddle knew she had gone too far in hitting the girl she still depended on. And the protest it had elicited reminded her of one she herself had made years ago in very similar circumstances. But there was no apologizing.

That night, Eugenia found herself unable to sleep and considered it a sound strategy to share the experience. At three o'clock, Mélisande put her finger on the problem. She went into the bath and opened each of the cocks just enough to provide a steady drip. Of course, this being a German ship, it was a *tropf... tropf... tropf...* that lulled Eugenia to sleep and not the *plic... plic... plic...* to which she'd grown accustomed during her stay in France. Thankfully, the young are free of linguistic prejudice.

III

The next morning after breakfast, Archie accompanied Lord Timothy Dexter to his cabin. Once again, he began straightening up. But whenever he neared the wardrobe, his lordship warned him off.

"Watch yourself, mister. Watch yourself."

Archie felt confident that he had at least ascertained where Dexter kept his loot. He now began setting up the next stage of the scheme.

"Wasn't Lady Eleanor looking radiant this morning, Your Lordship?"

"Radiant?"

"Aglow. Such a stunning woman. Yet one could see she was troubled. Something in her eye."

"Cinder?"

"Apprehension, I think, Your Lordship. She's being hounded by that syndicate we spoke of yesterday. Did you notice that man with the grey beard speaking with her?"

"Little fellow?"

"Yes, that's the one. He represents the syndicate planning to build the tunnel. He's made offers for her duchy, but she is clearly of a divided mind."

"Why's that? Why not take what she can get—can't be doing her any good at the bottom of the sea."

"True, sir. But perhaps the lady fears that the price offered is not commensurate with the deed's value to the syndicate—that this agent hopes to profit at her expense. One can't help but wonder if there isn't an opportunity here for a third party. Someone with both capital and a proper appreciation for the nuances of commercial dealings."

"You mean, get ahead of the syndicate's man and buy the deed from her, then sell it to them at a nice profit?"

"That is precisely my meaning, Your Lordship. Such a person would profit both monetarily and spiritually, for he would ensure that Lady Eleanor received a fair price."

"Maybe so. Maybe so. But if it's too fair a price, there won't be any profit for the third party."

His employer's reply struck Archie as too ambivalent. Even his eyebrows seemed indifferent. No doubt another dose of Lady Eleanor's charm would bring them around. And all that was needed to administer it was to persuade Lord Dexter to go for a stroll on the promenade deck.

This was rather easily accomplished, as there are very few diversions on a steamship between breakfast and the noon hour, particularly for men of a speculative temperament. It is true that some small wagers are made at the morning meal. The New York newspaperman at table twelve felt certain enough that the next person entering the room would be a woman that he placed a silver dollar on the table at even odds. And the German salesman at table five offered seven to four that the odd-looking Englishman at table six would again lose his bridgework in his coffee. But it wasn't until afternoon that the gambling would get under way in earnest.

As Lord Dexter and his manservant rounded the bow of the promenade deck, they were stopped dead in their tracks—the way blocked by a buzzing hive of American tourists.

"Where bees are, there is honey," Archie offered.

"How's that?"

"I suspect if we make our way forward, we will come upon the object of adoration."

Archie pushed through the crowd with his curious employer following directly behind. It wasn't long before Lady Eleanor and Lord Dexter, both on the tall side, caught sight of one another. She offered him a tableau of besieged virtue peppered with forlorn hope, utilizing the pose she catalogued as Melancholia #9, which included a hand raised to the brow, palm outward. It had served her well in the past and it did so again. Lord Dexter was affected. His eyebrows arched upwards at the inside corners, forming a white chevron—the signal flag of a touched soul.

"Someone should extricate the poor woman from these buzzards," Archie suggested.

Lord Dexter, pushing past him, accepted the assignment.

His work completed, Archie made his way to the boat deck for some morning sun. When he emerged at the top of the stairs, he espied Dowling not far ahead. He was carrying a small brown leather bag, the sort doctors make use of. Archie felt compelled to follow. When Dowling entered the purser's office, he listened through an open porthole.

"I'd like to have this put in your vault," Dowling told the man at the counter.

"Very well, sir." The attendant took the bag and gave Dowling a chit in return. "You can retrieve it anytime between the hours of seven a.m. and eleven p.m."

Archie wandered off to the far side of the ship. Was it out of concern for *his* trustworthiness that Dowling felt it necessary to check his stash? Or that of his own daughter? It certainly couldn't have been the crew that worried the old man. Archie had never seen such a dutiful group in all his life. In fact, the assistant purser helping Dowling was one of the most dutiful of all.

Mention was made earlier about the predilection for gambling on steamships. For those not interested in furthering their minds through reading, or buttressing their friendships through correspondence, there was little else to do. These sportsmen would bet on just about anything: cards, the weather, the ship's daily mileage, a human steeplechase, whether more people circle the promenade deck going clockwise or counter-clockwise, etc., etc. Needless to say, all this wagering opens up possibilities for men of flexible ethics. An adept can live high for a year on the take from one voyage. Such a man as the one currently calling himself Dowling.

It had been some years since he'd plied the steamship trade, and when he did, he had favored the British lines. But there had been one voyage to the Mediterranean via the Lloyd line when he was targeting a banker traveling to Nice. It was a very lucrative voyage. Unfortunately, it was also the one on which this same assistant purser had initiated his career as a steward, third class.

Though confident in his memory, the assistant purser did not feel certain enough to risk confronting a passenger. To do so and be wrong would mean the end of his employment. But he would keep an eye on the little man.

By this time, the sun had risen just high enough to cast a re-vivifying ray upon the visage of the still-sleeping Tomasz. He woke groggily, and was giving his face a good rubdown when Archie came upon him.

"So this is where you spent the night."

"I came up for some air and must have fallen asleep. I suppose breakfast is over?"

"Yes, but why don't we see what passes for elevenses in the Vienna Café," Archie suggested. "This sea air certainly sharpens the appetite."

As the two entered the nearby café, Tomasz for the first time set eyes on Mrs. Biddle. She and Lord Dexter sat at a table, alone.

"Who's that with his lordship?" he asked.

"Lady Eleanor Marsouin, Duchess of Aquatique."

"She is very beautiful."

"Beauty may have fair leaves, but bitter fruit."

"Is she married?"

"No, but don't go setting your hopes on her, Tommy. She'd skin you alive."

Tomasz nodded absently.

4

The second afternoon at sea was spent variously as follows: Archie Cobb took a long nap in a deck chair, periodically disturbed by ball-playing children who used him as a target and thereby interrupted his dreams of tossing them to the sharks below; Lord Dexter joined a motley party at the stern-end of the promenade, where they ventured on the coloration of the next seagull to land on the afterdeck, the others apparently too inebriated to notice it was the same three birds coming and going; in the smoking saloon, the man currently calling himself Dowling labored to secure his claim on a rich vein of ill-guarded wealth he'd unearthed, using nothing save his bare hands and a cold deck; ever the playful soubrette, Mélisande distracted a member of the crew in the cabin she shared with the sleeping Eugenia and her absent mother; and while the duchess herself gave an audience near the shuffleboard court, a captivated Tomasz looked on, musing upon the flawless commingling of feminine form and pater-pleasing title.

When things broke up, Archie felt only partially rested, Tomasz's soul only partially sated, and the Duchess of Aquatique entirely exasperated. She had expected to resume her enthrallment of Timothy Dexter. Instead, a riveting matinee performance was wasted on a school of simpletons who ogled her dumbly like so many gaping fish.

The other half of our entourage fared better. Dowling's dexterity netted him eighty-seven dollars, while Lord Dexter's keenness at ornithological observation gained him three hundred and twelve, plus a gold watch that displayed the phases of the moon. And Mélisande's talents... well, discretion prevents me from revealing what transpired in cabin 176. Suffice it to say, she got exactly what it was she was after.

After dressing himself for dinner, Archie Cobb retrieved his employer's tailcoat from the laundry, where it had been thoroughly sponged. At the previous evening's meal, Lord Dexter had collected an arresting assortment of sauces and vintages. It was not at all unusual for his lordship's garb to serve as a sort of culinary blotting paper, providing a rough historical record of his last meal. In this case, reading from the bottom-most layer first, dinner began with something in a sauce Alexander accompanied by hock, followed by béchamel and champagne. Generous portions of both bordelaise and claret came next, then the whole was topped with chocolate and Madeira.

On entering Dexter's cabin, Archie found his lordship dancing on his bed. The attentive valet soon determined the cause of the upheaval: a gigantic insect. It skittered about the cabin, then stopped to hover just opposite Lord Dexter's face, inspecting him with huge insect eyes while its subject signaled his rejoinder via flexing eyebrows. Archie rolled up a magazine and began swinging.

"Stop, you fool!" Lord Dexter cried. "Can't you see that's a darning needle?"

"Darning needle, Your Lordship?"

Lord Dexter was referring to an insect of the suborder Anisoptera, more commonly known as the dragonfly. Archie's knowledge of entomology was, in the main, limited to the bedbugs, cockroaches, and houseflies of his native London. Though once, some twenty years before, he had been stung by a bee, or wasp, while visiting a cousin—his first and last excursion to the rural districts.

In due course, the insect made its own way out the open porthole, Lord Dexter peering after it.

"Am I to understand, Your Lordship, that these bugs hold some special place in your heart?"

"The first Timothy Dexter promised he'd come back as a darning needle."

"Ah, he was a theosophist, then?"

"How's that?"

"He believed in the mystical," Archie elaborated, while helping Lord Dexter into his tailcoat.

"I suppose you could say that. Had his own fortune-teller."

"Indeed?" Archie saw possibilities for the future. "He is wise that is ware."

"Where is he?"

"The other ware, Your Lordship, meaning vigilant."

"I see. Yes, I see," Lord Dexter fibbed.

Archie's thoughts now returned to the concerns of the present. He still needed to find Lord Dexter's stash. Once again, he tried to remain behind in the cabin on his employer's exit. And once again he was thwarted. More drastic steps would need to be taken after dinner.

Against his better judgment, Archie finished his entree quickly and skipped his dessert completely. He knew the result would be dyspepsia coupled with misery—for Archie truly relished his pudding. But he also knew this would be the ideal time to force his way into his employer's sanctum. He went to his own room, where he'd removed a steel brace from his cabin mate's bed. It was flat, with angled ends, and looked almost as if it had been intended to serve double duty as a jimmy. Archie pushed it up his sleeve, then crept toward his objective.

He had just positioned his makeshift crowbar for maximum effect when he heard something fall to the floor inside the cabin. He listened closely... silence... then someone moving about... then what sounded like the wardrobe being forced open.... Good God! Some freebooter was pirating the loot!

Instinctively, Archie banged on the cabin door with his jimmy. But not being a brave man, he returned his tool to his sleeve and ran off to summon a ship's officer. He found the assistant purser not far away looking already concerned.

"Come quick!" Archie shouted. "Burglary!"

When they reached the cabin, the door stood open. They entered cautiously—but too late. The culprit had fled.

"Is this your cabin?" the officer inquired.

"No, that of my employer, Lor... eh, Mr. Dexter."

"Can you say what might be missing?"

Archie looked about. "Some silver cuff links, I believe. And a ruby tie-pin."

"Wait here—I will go for the purser."

Once the officer had left, Archie went to the wardrobe and pulled open the door. At the bottom, beside an eclectic collection of footwear, was a small carpetbag. It had the simple sort of lock easily opened with the bit of wire men of Archie's persuasion always have about them. He reached in and pulled out a banknote. Examining the bag more closely, he found it reassuringly stuffed with others. He now estimated Lord Dexter's funds in excess of one hundred thousand dollars.

It was only a few minutes more before Lord Dexter himself arrived, just long enough for Archie to have finished stuffing his socks with banknotes before quickly closing the bag.

"Caught!" his lordship shouted.

"Oh, no, sir. It was I who interrupted the thief."

Fortunately for Archie, the assistant purser arrived with his superior and verified his story. Lord Dexter made an inventory and noted that in addition to the silver cuff links and ruby tie-pin, a diamond bracelet of Parisian design and costing $5,000 had been taken. Had the others been looking his way, they would have seen the assistant purser swallow hard at this news—and then swallow hard again when the locksmith announced the door had been opened with a key.

It was Archie whom Lord Dexter had his eye on. He insisted his servant turn out his pockets and remove his jacket so the lining could be examined. It was then the makeshift jimmy fell to the floor.

"Came off the bed in my cabin," Archie explained. "I'd just gone off to tell the steward when I heard noises in here."

Lord Dexter said nothing, but his eyebrows spoke volumes.

II

The assistant purser accompanied Archie back to his cabin to look into the broken bunk. He was delightfully devoid of suspicion, offering to send round the ship's carpenter to make repairs. A few minutes later, a not-at-all-unsuspicious Lord

Dexter arrived and insisted on searching the cabin. When he had gone, Archie sat down, wiped his brow, and pulled out the sheaf of banknotes that circled his left ankle. Seven one-hundred-dollar bills, and six more circled his right. The question now was, were they authentic? This was a matter outside Archie's expertise. Had they been British banknotes, he'd know just what to look for. But he seldom came across American greenbacks.

There were, however, two aspects of these greenbacks that concerned him. First, they weren't particularly green—in fact, not green at all, more of a pale apricot. And second, the ornate writing across the midsection read, "Confederate States of America." Though no student of political geography, this struck Archie as somehow anachronistic. He was beginning to comprehend the arithmetic that allowed Lord Dexter to turn a profit selling for three thousand dollars a steamboat for which he'd paid ten thousand.

Archie returned the notes to his stockings and took out his flask. He took a long draught and thought. Then he took a second, longer, draught and thought harder. What he needed was a plan. A plan that would allow him to maintain his cozy position with Lord Dexter, yet protect him from the vengeful Dowling. With the third draught, the solution seemed obvious: betray his confederates. But, and this was key, betray them without exposing himself. To do that, he would need a third party to act as his involuntary agent. Someone gullible enough to be easily manipulated, and yet someone Dowling would accept as a believable antagonist. Yes, of course. Tomasz. Tomasz must expose the plot. Then Dowling and his daughter would be content simply to avoid prosecution. They would be free to proceed to their next affair and Archie could go on to play the Viscount of Abernethy.

The great weakness in Dowling's scheme had always been the ludicrous conceit on which it was based. If it was made clear that the duchy was purely imaginary, the plan would collapse. Tomasz must be made to discover—for himself—that Mrs. Biddle was a fraud.

While Archie went off looking for the vacant Pole, Lord Dexter entered the smoking saloon and began assessing which of the card games would prove the most profitable. He saw the little man he knew to represent the well-financed, tunnel-building syndicate sitting behind a tall mound of chips. The snow-white eyebrows danced a celebratory gigue.

Dowling rose and invited the simple-looking gentleman to join them. The others at the table readily acceded—millionaire eccentrics were always welcome, and Timothy Dexter was by now known to be both.

Over the next three hours, Dowling played the bumbler—making foolish bets, exposing his hands with transparent emotions, even misdealing. His intimidating mound of chips was reduced to a vulnerable ant hill. Meanwhile, Lord Dexter, in spite of his tell-tale eyebrows, seemed unstoppable.

But enough was enough. Dowling was determined, for a very sound reason, that the profits of the afternoon game not be sacrificed. He began playing in earnest. For the next half hour, he did himself well. But then, somewhere about the seventh whiskey and soda, Lord Dexter's eyebrows became cunning. They exhibited excitement at a pair of twos, and indifference at a flush. Instead of winning, Dowling was soon delving into the eighty-seven dollars he'd won in the afternoon session.

What made his lordship's eyebrows appear so cunning was that they had completely lost interest in the game. They had reached that state of inebriation where half-remembered anecdotes are exchanged to exaggerated amusement, and minor disputes quickly lead to harsh exchanges. It's oft said, an intoxicated eyebrow is an unpredictable eyebrow. And an unpredictable eyebrow is the poker player's friend.

As Dowling's stack shrank before him, behind his back Archie Cobb was endeavoring to betray him.

Archie found Tomasz observing the night sky from a deck chair and hailed him.

"Ah, there you are. I've been looking for you everywhere."

"Does his lordship need me?" Tomasz sat up and for the twenty-ninth time that day straightened his tie.

"If you mean, did he ask for you, no. But he needs you, my boy. He most assuredly needs you."

"What are you talking about?"

"I strongly suspect his lordship is being set up by a pair of confidence tricksters."

"Confidence tricksters?"

"Charlatans bent on relieving him of his money."

"Who?"

"For one, that phony duchess."

"Lady Eleanor? No, that I do not believe."

"I don't think there can be much doubt. You see, there is no Duchy of Aquatique."

"Who says there is no duchy?" Tomasz asked indignantly. "Since she is a duchess, there *must* be a duchy."

"Yes, but that's what I'm telling you. She is no duchess."

"Liar!" Tomasz rose and moved close to Archie. "And if you repeat that slander, I must insist we meet on the field of honor."

With that, Tomasz stomped off.

Archie sat down and wiped his brow. The foolish Slav had allowed his infatuation to cloud his thinking. And it seemed unlikely there was time enough to get the boy to see reason without provoking him to violence. Assuming he was capable of seeing reason at all.

By morning, the sea had turned rough and attendance at breakfast was sparse. Most of the passengers were staying as still as possible in their cabins. Hunger, and a bit of calm, brought many of them to the dining room for lunch. But then the weather worsened and back to their cabins they fled.

At three o'clock, Mélisande, who found the atmosphere of the cabin stifling when shared with her irritable mistress for any length of time, ventured to the reading room with the book that comprised her personal library, *The Girl Proposition*. Authored by a man named George Ade, and subtitled *A Bunch of He and She Fables*, it had been a parting gift from one of the American artists at Étaples. Study it well, he had told her, for Ade is to America what La Fontaine is to France. Mélisande had no idea what La Fontaine was to France, but she treasured the gift just the same.

She opened the book to the next lesson, or fable, which began: *Once there was a Social Fizzle named Homer Splivens. He was the dampest Fire-Cracker that ever tried to Pop.* Not only was Mélisande learning much about American rituals of courtship and marriage, she was also expanding her ready vocabulary.

III

While Mélisande read, Archie Cobb—who'd spent the morning and half the afternoon brooding over his dilemma—came to a decision. He would go to Dowling's daughter, bare his soul, and make a proposal.

Mrs. Biddle answered his knock by opening the door just wide enough to converse.

"It's rather important we have a little talk," he said.

She left him to wait in the passageway while she slid the cradle and the sleeping Eugenia into the bath. Only when she was satisfied that all trace of the child had been hidden did she allow Archie Cobb to enter. Her hard look did not make his task any easier.

"Might we sit down?" he asked.

"If you want." She cleared off two chairs.

"First, I'd like to ask about your relationship with your father."

"That's no concern of yours."

"No, certainly not. I only wish to know, are you acting for yourself, or for him?"

Mrs. Biddle made a little half-smile. "If you are asking, am I willing to sell out my father if it is to my advantage, the answer is a definite yes. You may rest assured, I can be every bit as venal as he is."

Though it was the answer he'd hoped for, Archie nevertheless felt chilled by the ease with which she gave it.

"Well, I suppose I need to begin by making a confession," he said nervously. "I've found Dexter's stash."

From his stocking, he drew one of the apricot-toned banknotes he'd taken from the carpetbag and handed it to Mrs. Biddle. Having seen from whence it came, she took it gingerly by a corner.

Her face hardened. Then, in a deliberate, ice-cold voice, she asked, "Are you telling me *this* is what he used to buy that steamship?"

"I fear so, yes." Archie was wondering if he hadn't made a mistake in thinking the daughter would be more sympathetic than her father. "My friend who sold it, Len Bailey, his eyesight isn't what it used to be. And besides, Len's always kept his mind on his business, never had much time for the politics of former colonies."

Much to Archie's relief, Mrs. Biddle laughed—a barely audible laugh, but a laugh nonetheless.

"This is priceless," she said. "I can't wait to see the old fool's face when he finds out."

"I was hoping we could see a way to avoid telling him, at least until we're off the boat."

"Yes, of course. But surely Dexter has *some* money with him. He wins every game he enters."

"He's got the goods, all right. I'm sure of that. But the old fox isn't easily snared. It might be easier to let him share it with us."

"How so? You aren't planning to remain his servant?"

"Serving him consists mostly of humoring him. He's not the sort who demands a lot of fussing. And there may be a position for you."

"What position?"

"He's the descendant of another Timothy Dexter. Lived in Massachusetts, sometime in the past."

"Of course, Lord Timothy Dexter."

"You've heard of him?"

"He was a celebrity around the turn of the last century. Wrote an absurd little book, *A Pickle for the Knowing Ones*. He spelled phonetically and made no use of punctuation at all. Until the second edition, when he added a page of marks at the end,"

Mrs. Biddle interrupted herself with another barely audible laugh, "then told the reader to salt and pepper them about as he wished."

"How quaint." Unlike Mélisande, Archie cared little for literature written in the American vernacular. "Well, our Dexter has likewise taken to calling himself Lord. Thinks his forebear visits him in the form of a giant insect. And yesterday he told me the first Lord Dexter had his own fortune-teller."

"Are you suggesting I offer him my services as soothsayer?"

"I was thinking of something more grand—say, court theosophist."

"I suppose that might be amusing. But I have my own plans."

"And landing without capital won't inconvenience you?"

"It would inconvenience me a great deal, were I to allow that situation to occur." Mrs. Biddle became thoughtful. "There is another source available, especially if you and I are pooling our efforts...."

"Your father's four thousand?"

"Why not? He'd do the same to either of us, wouldn't he?"

"Yes, I suppose he would," Archie agreed. "But I think he already suspects. Yesterday I saw him check a bag with the purser. Asked that it be put in the vault."

"That doesn't matter. All we need do is turn the auction around. Make sure *he* wins instead of Dexter. I take his four thousand, split it with you, and off we go."

"You don't think your old papa will sit still for that, do you? He must have iron nails who scratches a bear."

"We'll need to find some way to keep him in check. But we can work out the details later. For now, we should just make as if all is going according to plan. Tell him you've seen the money. How much was it?"

"Of this? A hundred thousand, at least," Archie told her. "I must say, I feel a great sense of relief from our talk."

Mrs. Biddle was about to respond when she was summoned to the bath by her daughter.

The secret revealed, she returned with the child in her arms.

"Not a word about her to anyone, particularly *him*. Understood?" Mrs. Biddle demanded.

"Yes, if that's how you want it. Well, good-bye, and good luck to us both."

Archie was not a sentimentalist, but there was something disheartening about a daughter wanting to hide her baby from its grandfather. Though in this case, perhaps, the caution was not unwarranted.

That evening, Mrs. Biddle set Mélisande onto the task of distracting Tomasz—a not too difficult undertaking given his disposition and the girl's complementary talents. She described the vacant Pole and Mélisande assured her she knew the young man—but wisely made no mention of their encounter on the boat deck two nights before.

"A very innocent boy," she said. "He reminds me of the virgin priest I won."

"What virgin priest did you win?" Mrs. Biddle asked.

"The only virgin priest we ever met. We, the girls of my town, drew lots for him. I won, so that night…"

"You tell such tales."

"It is no tale, madame. I don't see what's so strange about it—the priests drew lots for the girls when they came of age."

Mrs. Biddle shook her head, trying to hide a smile. "Where is it that you met all these lecherous priests, Thélème?"

"No, in Arras. I don't know why you should not believe it," Mélisande went on. "When I told Jimmy Egan, he told me in Chicago the priests draw lots for the boys—only, they don't wait."

5

Throughout the voyage, Mrs. Biddle and her handmaiden alternated attending meals in the dining room. When one dined publicly, the other ate in the cabin. In this way the baby was never left alone.

The third morning at sea, Mélisande went off to breakfast bearing a note for Tomasz. She passed it to a waiter and requested it be delivered anonymously. The smitten Pole wasted no time in opening the envelope that bore the scent he recognized as that of the Duchess of Aquatique.

M. Szczęsny,
I hope you will forgive my presumption in contacting you in this way. However, I feel I am at risk, and find myself without friends. There is one aboard who wishes me harm. For safety's sake, I dare not write more, but perhaps you could visit me in my cabin at ten o'clock this morning.
Yours, in desperation,
Lady Eleanor

Tomasz felt he had a very good idea as to the identity of the Cretan bull to whom Lady Eleanor alluded. The man sitting just beside him, Archie Cobb. Though it was only half past eight, and his meal barely begun, Tomasz left the room lest his emotions get the best of him. This was not the time to strike, but to prepare for the trial ahead. And for Tomasz, preparing for any sort of trial involved a lengthy mulling of probabilities. So he went now to the boat deck and mulled.

At nine o'clock, Mélisande returned from breakfast and Mrs. Biddle went off to a prearranged meeting in Dowling's cabin. She found him already in conference with Cobb.

"Archie's confirmed that Dexter has at least a hundred thousand in cash," the man currently calling himself Dowling told her.

"And it's certain none are queer?" Mrs. Biddle asked.

Archie felt sure she was merely deflecting Dowling's suspicions with a display of her customary skepticism, but he would have preferred that it not come accompanied by her customary piercing stare.

"Yes, yes, of course," he stammered. "Absolutely."

"I saw a good deal of it last night at the card table," Dowling said. "It was real enough. How far have you gotten with him?"

"Only just started," Mrs. Biddle replied. "I've told him you've offered me ten thousand, but that I think it's worth more."

"Keep at him. Tell him I've raised the offer to twenty."

"Where's he now?" she asked Archie.

"In his cabin. Having the lock changed, for the third time."

"Lock changed? Does he suspect you?" Dowling asked.

"He suspects everyone, the wily old coot. But Thursday evening he was burglarized."

Archie hadn't intended to reveal this news, but having mentioned the repeated changing of the lock, an explanation was required.

"And the money not taken?" Mrs. Biddle asked incredulously, thereby causing Archie to wish anew that her thespian ambitions were more modest.

"I interrupted the thief. He only had time to take some jewelry."

"Who was it?" Dowling asked.

"Got away while I was fetching an officer."

"You're sure this burglar hadn't time to see the money?" Mrs. Biddle asked.

"Yes, the bag was locked. I had to pick it open," Archie explained.

"Go now and keep Dexter in the cabin," she told him. "It will be much easier if I can corner him there."

When Archie had gone, and his daughter had risen to do likewise, Dowling stopped her.

"I've determined who your maid is."

"That couldn't have been much of a challenge given that we share a cabin."

"Better keep an eye on that girl," he said.

"Are you attempting to menace me, old man?"

"Only some friendly advice. I saw her flirting with an officer the other afternoon. A girl like that can be trouble."

His last sentence was delivered to the closing door.

Back in her own cabin, Mrs. Biddle instructed Mélisande to keep the appointment with the Polish secretary and see that he remained until at least eleven, but not past noon.

Archie, meanwhile, had found Lord Dexter in his cabin speaking with the assistant purser, while supervising the replacement of the lock.

"It's that man Dowling, sir," the officer said. "I've noticed you have been gambling with him. I feel I've seen him before. Under a different name, and under circumstances that do him no credit."

"You think it was him that broke in?" his lordship asked.

"No, I fear... ah, no, that is not likely. But I do think he is the same card sharp who made off with a large sum of money belonging to another American on a voyage some years back. It may be I am wrong, but I thought it my duty to caution you."

To the bewilderment of the assistant purser, Lord Dexter smiled, while above, his eyebrows performed a lively courante. The officer made a short bow and exited with the locksmith.

Archie tried to repair the damage.

"Doesn't it seem rather improbable, Your Lordship, that the same man who plies steamships as a card sharp would be hired by a syndicate of moneyed Londoners for so delicate a task?"

"You're asking me if a gang of swindlers would hire a smooth-talking charlatan to bamboozle a lady out of her property? Think about it, man. Think about it."

His valet was relieved by Lord Dexter's interpretation and was about to voice approval when interrupted by a knock. He opened the door to Mrs. Biddle, announced Lady Eleanor, then discreetly left the cabin.

Interestingly, our heroine herself had not yet determined which part she would be playing. What she did know was that she could not get Dexter to the auction by executing the original scenario. For if she *did* manage to gain his sympathy, he would hardly be likely to do something so unsympathetic as offer bogus money for her deed.

She had devised two alternative strategies. Both would require the collaboration of the fickle Lord Dexter. And both would end with the impoverishment of Dowling—an outcome she'd only first considered the day before, but one which had grown so far in her affection it had become a prerequisite.

The first strategy was to reveal the scheme in its entirety—including her own part in it—and then suggest she and Dexter collude to defraud Dowling. This plan held one minor inconvenience and one major risk. The minor inconvenience was that it would mean betraying the betrayal she had arranged with Cobb the previous afternoon. The major risk was that Dexter might prefer to expose them all rather than take a chance at what was likely to him a trifling sum.

The second strategy was to persuade Dexter to help the destitute duchess get the better of the unscrupulous syndicate and its deceitful representative. This plan would take advantage of the groundwork already laid, but it entailed one minor inconvenience and one major leap of faith. The minor inconvenience was that it would mean *not* betraying the betrayal she had arranged with Cobb the previous afternoon—since his abetment would be essential—and therefore having to share the profits with him. The major leap of faith was the same one on which the original scheme depended: that Dexter accept the faux duchy as genuine.

To decide between the two strategies, Mrs. Biddle had settled on a simple test of his lordship's credulity. She would show him her deed.

"Forgive me for intruding. But I find myself in need of someone I can trust."

"Well, don't look for him on this boat. A damnable den of thieves."

"Have you been robbed of some valuable?"

"A bracelet I bought for my daughter. A five-thousand-dollar Par-ee-shen bracelet. And a ruby tie-pin the girl gave me as a present. And a pair of cuff links, dills."

"Dills?"

"Had pickles carved on them."

"Ah. How horribly exasperating for you," Mrs. Biddle commiserated. "Perhaps I shouldn't be bothering you about my dilemma."

"Hell, girl, my whole life is one long chain of exasperations. Nothing new about that. You go ahead and sit down and empty your soul." Lord Dexter removed a stack of papers from a chair, but himself remained standing.

"That man I've told you about, Dowling, he now tells me he will give me twenty thousand dollars."

"Doubled it that quick? Then you ought to ask for fifty," he told her.

"I could so use the money. But I can't bear to part with this, my family's legacy." She reached in her bag and brought out the antiqued deed to the Duchy of Aquatique, then handed it to Lord Dexter. If he laughed out loud, she would as well—then execute strategy number one by telling him all about the scheme.

His lordship did not laugh, but held the document tentatively, gazing upon it as he would a sacred text. He knew not a word of Latin, and the name Charlemagne brought no light of recognition. But he found the crisp, yellowed parchment and red-wax seal not just credible, but convincing. And when he sighted the geographically distorted map on the reverse, his snow-white eyebrows shot northward. Strategy number two it would be.

"I feel certain this man Dowling and the syndicate mean to take advantage of my situation," she confided. "I only wish there were a way to... I believe the expression is 'to turn the tables.'"

"Swindle the swindlers?" his lordship asked, the eyebrows temporarily inscrutable.

"I hope you won't find it presumptuous of me to suppose you might approve of such a course. It's only... I've heard a rumor, and coupled with your mention of the cuff links—dills, of course... might you be a descendant of *Lord* Timothy Dexter?"

"His namesake, even. You heard of him, have you?"

"Oh, yes, of course. The Pantagruel of the Merrimack. You may count me among those who regard his *Pickle* the American answer to *Tristram Shandy*."

"Quite so, quite so." His lordship couldn't recall the question this Tristram fellow had posed, but he preferred not to reveal his ignorance before a Knowing One. "He cut that Shandy down to size. Yes, ma'am."

"What's more, he was a man of commercial genius, and one who never hesitated to engage the hypocrites."

"Fought the hypocrites his whole life," his descendant agreed. "Not to mention the damnable bloodsuckers."

"Indeed. That's why I thought you might be receptive to helping me get the better of these... bloodsuckers."

Lord Dexter emitted a raspy cackle, while his eyebrows, having shed their apparent apathy, provided a visual accompaniment of wave-like oscillations.

Assuming this to be an answer in the affirmative, Mrs. Biddle continued. "I wonder... Forgive me if this suggestion seems a foolish one, but I wonder if it wouldn't help things along if I were to tell Dowling *you* had offered me fifty thousand dollars for the deed?"

"Bid him up?"

"Yes, but in the end, through some sort of sleight of hand, I manage to take his money, yet keep my legacy." The lady now stopped to fan herself. "I wonder if we could continue our discussion on the promenade? It's rather airless in here."

Mrs. Biddle knew it was Dowling's habit to go for a morning walk, and it was important that he remain convinced that things were proceeding as planned. When they reached the open deck and she espied him some way off, she brought him to Lord Dexter's attention.

"Do you think we could give him a little performance? Let him hear you offer me fifty thousand dollars?"

His lordship embraced the suggestion, and then delivered a quite respectable, if somewhat overly theatrical, performance. Histrionic eyebrows are an actor's friends—but not when they step on his lines.

II

While her patroness was working her charms on Lord Dexter, Mélisande was attempting the same with Tomasz. He had arrived anticipating a private encounter with Lady Eleanor and was visibly disappointed to find instead the baby-tossing American widow he'd met that first night on the boat deck.

"Excuse me, please. I must have the wrong cabin."

"No, no." Mélisande pulled him toward her and closed the door. Then, by pressing her body against his, she herded him further into the room. Each time she sallied, he retreated. But given the confines of a steamship cabin, it took only half a dozen sallies to have him pinned beneath her on the bed.

She had met resistance before, but strength of character has little chance against animalistic urgings when a shapely young girl has one pressed beneath her and is tickling one's ear with her very capable tongue. When Tomasz broke out in a sweat, she took it as encouraging. When his face turned a purplish-red, she read it as an extreme form of passion. But when he began foaming at the mouth and moaning in a decidedly unromantic way, she recognized it as a seizure.

She fetched a glass of water and began sprinkling his face. Soon he recovered enough to stumble to the safety of a chair, and not long after, the hyperventilating abated. But each time she came within a foot of him, the moaning began anew.

"Are you sick?" she asked.

"No, I don't think so. But please, I am a *gentleman*."

Mélisande had no idea what bearing that had on the matter but was loath to show her ignorance. "Ohhh. I did not know."

"I came at the request of Lady Eleanor." He took out the note she'd sent him and handed it to Mélisande.

"Yes, yes. I know. But she asked me to see you. She is very busy."

"Are you her friend?"

Mélisande emitted a noise signaling her ambivalence. "We travel together. She's American also."

"I thought the duchy was in France?"

"Yes, but she lives in America. Her grand-papa dies, she gets her duchy."

"What about her father?"

"Dead."

"Indians?"

"Ummm, no. He shoot his self."

"Suicide? Why?"

"Because mother, she sleeps with grand-papa." Mélisande had a knack for creating biographies.

"Poor Lady Eleanor," Tomasz said, shaking his head. "Do you know who it is who threatens her?"

"Threatens her? No. Do you like her?"

"Oh, yes. Very much. She is the most beautiful-looking woman I've ever met."

"Yes," Mélisande agreed reluctantly. "But if you *only* look."

Tomasz hadn't heard her addendum. "Do you think she feels the same about me? I mean, that she likes me?"

"Oh, sure. Didn't she send you a note?"

"I'd like to send her one. Telling her how much I care for her."

"Why not?"

"Would you help me to write it?"

"Sure, OK. I am very good making love letters." She cleared a space on the small table, then set out pen, ink, and paper. "I will tell you what to write."

Tomasz had hoped to use the specimen the German lady who smelled of lavender had handed him as a template. But when he translated the first paragraph for her, Mélisande dismissed it, holding her nose while making a sound of extreme distaste.

"No, no. We do much better. Now, the object," she explained, "is to nail the girl without giving her a chance to become acquainted or investigate." This advice was taken directly from *The Girl Proposition*. She had known that someday Mr. Ade's treatise on American romance would prove useful, but never expected it to be so soon. Luckily, she had circled the choicest bits so they'd be easy to find. Now all that was needed was to string them together. "This is what you will write: *Dear Peacherette with the Kentucky Shape....*"

Here Tomasz stopped her to ask for clarification. She showed him the circled text and then they continued—she providing the vocabulary, and he adjusting the grammar—until finally arriving at this:

My Dearest Peacherette, You of the Kentucky Shape,

From the moment you crossed my pathway, I was stung in eight different places. You make Cleopatra look like Martha the sewing girl, and Venus arising from the sea, only squizzly old soap. You have a pair of incandescent headlights, a complexion like the sunset blush on a snowbank, and enough hair above for two girls your size.

Dare I crave a word from those rosebud lips, and hope for a melting glance from those starlit lamps? I would very much like to execute a clutch swing into the slow and dreamy.

The chickadees who chew gum on the trolley, and the mopey ones who wear wrappers and eat pickles, and the spindly ones in rainy day skirts, they are purty fair. But you make them look like the odds and ends of a rummage sale, in your exceptionally Gibson shirtwaist. I reach out my hot tentacles, O queen of the human race.

The love microbe is all through my system. The fires of passion have got beyond control and it is time to call out the whole department. I want you so hard I look in the porthole of your boodwar at night and gnaw the palings of the front fence. It is the essence of googoo, double strength.

Your omnibus of love...

They read it aloud to each other several times and while Mélisande insisted it was the real Latin Quarter article, Tomasz felt sure it wanted for something—the something that the lover of the lavender-scented German lady had expressed so well in his very stimulating penultimate paragraph. Too embarrassed to attempt a translation himself, he showed Mélisande the German original. When it became clear its meaning was lost on her, he tried to convey it via complex metaphor—the word "vessel" taking the place of the principal referent. What resulted, after much confused input by his coauthor, was an ode to glassware. Tomasz added it as a postscript.

"You will give this to your friend, the duchess?"

"Oh, sure. I will give it to her."

"And tell her, I am always at her service. And that I love..."

"Yes, yes." Mélisande was beginning to find his misdirected devotion vexing. It was now past the hour of noon, so she hurried him on his way.

Later that afternoon, while catching some sun on the boat deck, Mrs. Biddle encountered an anxious Dowling.

"Enter into a conversation with me," he whispered.

"Why? What's going on?"

"There's an assistant purser who's been watching me. Thrown me off my game—I had to leave the table."

"I don't see why I should assist you in fleecing your fellow passengers at the card table."

"Don't you? Well, if you want this scheme to come off..." He left his sentence unfinished, then changed the topic. "I heard Dexter offering you fifty thousand. I think it's time now to arrange the auction. I'll confront him and suggest it."

"No, it will be better if I tell him you proposed it. He needs to be handled very carefully."

An officer passed and eyed them, not at all subtly. Mrs. Biddle noticed Dowling tense.

"So that's your assistant purser? How did he know what you were up to?"

"No idea. The fools at the table seem clueless. Well, I had better get back to it."

Mrs. Biddle was now left to her thoughts, and her first thought was not a pleasant one. It dated back to Dowling's suggestion a few moments earlier that the success of the scheme somehow depended on his success at the card table. She could think of only one explanation: he did not have the four thousand dollars he had claimed or anything like that. And so, her reasoning continued, his checking of the bag wasn't to keep his bankroll safe from the others, but to keep them from learning he had no bankroll. In all likelihood, the old buzzard knew Cobb was observing him when he sent it to the vault. Now he was frantically trying to raise the seed money. The money she had set her sights on. Once again, she would need to revise her strategy.

I am sure, precious reader, that you will not be surprised to learn that Mrs. Biddle has deduced correctly. She is, after all, herself a virtuosa of deceit. And I hope you will find it in your heart to forgive me for having neglected to mention an episode that transpired three days earlier which sheds some light on the situation. It's just that it's been such a chore trying to keep it all straight. You honestly wouldn't believe what I have to contend with. But this is hardly the place to voice complaints.

It all began prior to Dowling and his lady friend, Céleste, leaving the Hôtel de l'Aigle. Céleste had never thought much of Dowling's scheme, or, indeed, of Dowling himself. But she did think a great deal of his four thousand dollars. While Dowling was meeting with Mrs. Biddle in the hotel's lobby, she was upstairs in room 517 replacing his four thousand dollars with cut-up strips of newspaper. Her plan was to board the tender with him, then exit at the last possible moment. When she had disembarked after approaching "Miss Duncan," it was her intention to keep on walking, into the Gare Maritime and onto the 5:23 express to Paris.

Because Dowling understood that Mrs. Biddle had engineered Céleste's arrest, he didn't realize that his money had been stolen until he opened his bag the next morning. And by then, they were well out to sea.

My, my, what a tangled web of intrigues....

6

It was late on a grey, but calm, Sunday morning and Archie Cobb's thoughts had fixated on the Vienna Café's pastry cart. He'd just made his way through a small knot of Calvinists indulging in a service *en plein air*, which at that moment meant fog and drizzle, when he saw a man leaving the purser's office with a small brown leather bag. A bag seemingly identical to that recently checked in by his confederate Dowling.

This one belonged to the lavender-scented German lady. She used it as a travel case for the exquisite collection of jewelry her once-devoted husband had lavished on her—the very man who had just retrieved it from the purser's vault. I say "once-devoted" because more recently suspicion had taken the place of devotion. He suspected his wife was having an affair with an artist of her acquaintance, and he further suspected written evidence of the affair had been hidden amongst her jewelry. He was correct on both counts, as he would have soon learned had he not been startled into dropping the bag by the first blast of the fog-horn.

He turned to retrieve it, but just as he did his wife called to him. She was herself suspicious and had followed him up to the boat deck, though not in time to see that he had already taken possession of the bag.

"What are you doing up here in the rain, my dear?" she asked.

"Just getting some air—feels quite refreshing, don't you think?"

"But you'll catch your death of a cold. Come back down, please. I'm so lonely by myself." She took his arm and gave him a look he'd not once resisted in seven years of marriage.

"You go, dearest, and I'll be down in a little while. Just a few minutes more."

"Then I'll stay with you...."

They had reached a stalemate. He was afraid to reveal that he suspected his fetching little wife until he was sure his suspicions were warranted, and so dared not retrieve the bag a few feet behind him. She was afraid to leave lest he reclaim the bag she thought still in the purser's vault, and her mad but doubtless transitory affair be exposed.

Archie, however, was under no such inhibitions. The fog had thickened and he crept silently toward his prey. When the horn next blew and the lavender-scented lady jumped into the arms of her husband, Archie seized both moment and bag. In a quick succession of cat-like bounds, he crossed to the far side of the boat and made his way down to the upper cabin deck.

There he came upon Mrs. Biddle just returning to her compartment. She looked down at the brown leather bag.

"Dowling's?" she asked softly.

"No, but just like it." Archie looked back over his shoulder. "Perhaps we can discuss it inside?"

She led him in and closed the door. Seeing Eugenia fast asleep in her cradle, she looked in the bath and found Mélisande immersed in the tub. They exchanged a brief word, then she closed that door and turned to Archie with a finger over her lips.

"I saw a fellow drop it up on the boat deck," he whispered. "I thought it might come in handy."

"You think the old man would fall for a switch?" she asked.

"If it's done with the proper finesse. And he has no reason to suspect it. Suppose while I have both his and Dexter's bags, I do the switch. We let Dexter win the auction, and your father leaves the room with this, thinking all's gone as planned."

"But how much time does that gain us?"

"Not much, perhaps. But if we just declare Dowling the winner, and you take his bag, well, in the heat of the moment..."

"You don't think he'd come armed?" she asked.

"It would be uncharacteristically crass, but your father's talents aren't what they were. And when men find themselves in that situation, they often resort to expediencies. Fear the worst, I say, the best will save itself."

"I suppose you're right," she agreed. "What's in the bag?"

"I haven't had time to look."

Archie set it on the floor and removed an oblong jewelry box which he placed on the table. Mrs. Biddle raised the lid, then fondled a string of perfectly matched pearls. She replaced these, then opened each of three drawers. The first held several rings and bracelets of various stones and settings, and nothing that wasn't of value; the second, a Henri Vever filigree brooch and three finely crafted pendants, at least one a Falize; and the final drawer, a dozen pairs of earrings, carefully selected to comple-ment the rest.

"Any of it real?" Archie asked.

"If I say no, you'll only assume I'm lying."

"Well, perhaps we can split them, along with the four thou-sand?"

"Yes, perhaps. In the meantime, it might be best if they re-main with me."

Archie wasn't sure that would be for the best. But as he pre-ferred not to be seen carrying the bag he'd so recently purloined, and knew there was no telling when his distrustful employer might again search his cabin, he acquiesced.

"There's something else," she said. "And it concerns the old man's four thousand. I can't be sure, but I believe he may have been boasting."

"What do you mean?"

"Just something he said. He implied he needed to win at the table for the scheme to go off."

"But then why check the bag?" Archie asked. Then it dawned on him. "Oh, I see. To keep us from finding out he was broke.... Well, at least I still have my position with Dexter. He that serves, is preserved."

"Let's not give up on Dowling yet. He may still be capable of raising a good sum if he has the proper set-up. As I recall, you used to be quite an admirable steerer."

"Fatten him for slaughter? Yes, all right. I'll see what I can do. There certainly is no shortage of rich fools on the boat. And perhaps you can keep Dexter entertained—he's been winning something fierce. The man's luck only seems to run one way."

"All right," she agreed. "I'll take care of his lordship."

II

Once Archie had gone, Mrs. Biddle lifted the jewel box to return it to the bag and discovered a letter nestled in the hollowed bottom. She'd only just removed it when she heard the bathtub draining. Quickly, she put it with the box in the brown leather bag, and then placed that in the one piece of luggage Mélisande had been ordered to keep out of. This was normally kept locked, but Mrs. Biddle had made sure her light-fingered retainer had had one opportunity to search it and so convince herself it contained nothing of value.

The baby stirred and her mother picked her up and brought her to the bed. While Eugenia dined, her provisioner noticed her diaper had been fastened with a tie-pin. A ruby tie-pin. As the meal was concluding, Mélisande entered the room buffing herself with a towel.

"Where's the bracelet?" her mistress demanded.

"What bracelet, madame?"

Mrs. Biddle placed her now-sleeping child in the cradle and removed the tie-pin. She held it up to her recalcitrant servant's face. "The one you found in the same cabin as this."

"I don't remember any bracelet."

"You little fool, you've put everything at risk. I may have no choice now but to turn you over to them."

Mélisande made her usual show of nonchalance, but she sensed that this was something more than mere threat. She sauntered playfully over to the crib. With one hand she lifted the baby to her mouth and kissed her, while the other hand retrieved a diamond bracelet buried in the linen below.

"It was a gift, for little sister."

"How'd you get a key?"

"Oh, that was very easy. My friend, Oskar. He gave it to me."

"Your friend, Oskar?"

"*Mais oui*, he is an officer."

Mélisande was still dressing when Mrs. Biddle answered a knock at the door. It was the assistant purser.

"Might I have a word, madame?"

Mélisande, still no further dressed than her undergarments, rushed forward and embraced him. "Oskar! *Mon chéri!*"

The reddened assistant purser untangled himself, then closed the door. Once again he addressed Mrs. Biddle. "I believe, madame, that on a previous visit, I lost a key in your cabin."

"Did you indeed? Might I ask the nature of that visit?"

"The young lady... she requested that I help her...."

"Never mind what she told you. And I won't ask what went on. You may have your key." Mrs. Biddle turned to Mélisande. "Give it to him."

The girl shrugged, then pulled the key from a shoe beneath her bed and handed it to a grateful Oskar. He thanked them and made to leave, but Mrs. Biddle stopped him.

"I suppose you know what use she made of it?"

Oskar had been trying very hard *not* to know what use she made of it. But the recent series of jewel thefts kept intruding on his delusion.

"I understand Mr. Dexter lost a very valuable bracelet," Mrs. Biddle went on.

"Ja, yes, that is true. Did you... That is, do you know..."

"How would you like to capture the thief?"

Oskar looked at Mélisande, and she in turn looked at her mistress.

"Forget the girl. She knows nothing. But if you cooperate, before we dock in New York, you will have the thief and the jewelry—including some that has yet to be reported missing."

"Has yet to be reported missing?"

"Yes, but it's safe. Simply do as you are told and you'll appear the hero, rather than the accomplice."

"What do I need to do, madame?"

"For now, the man Dowling, leave him alone."

"Very well, madame. And when will you give me the jewelry?"

"I will not give it to you. You will discover it on the thief. Tomorrow night. You'll receive fuller instructions later. Now you may go."

Oskar made a slight bow and exited.

Mrs. Biddle turned to her servant. "You've been lucky this time, but don't count on that luck holding. I've no experience of the French jails, but I can assure you, you would not find your stay in a New York jail pleasant. The very things that enable you to appear so clever on the outside will mark you as prey on the inside. You need to learn your limits. Now I must go."

This time Mélisande held her tongue and accepted the admonishment with a sheepish grin. Mrs. Biddle left the girl wondering how she could both despise and admire her mistress in equal measure. Though often she felt like strangling her in her sleep, she was, nonetheless, thankful to be apprenticed to so cunning a master.

She was also thankful that no mention had been made of the cloisonné brooch she'd taken from cabin number 12, or the gold earrings, each with a teardrop pearl and a tiny green stone, contributed by the resident of cabin 121. And no doubt the woman in 153 was thankful that the thief who rifled her cabin didn't favor the heavily jeweled rings she herself did.

But at that moment, it was Tomasz who was most thankful. He'd just spent the better part of an hour taking down one of Lord Dexter's incomprehensible letters. This one apparently asking a tailor in New York to prepare an admiral's uniform of unique specifications. Now, at last making his exit, Tomasz turned to find his adored duchess in the passageway.

"Lady Eleanor! I answered your request for help, but..."

"Yes, I am sorry I missed your call." The earnest secretary would need a new distraction. And why not kill two birds with one stone? "Are you still willing to help?"

"Oh, yes, of course, my lady. Anything."

Mrs. Biddle drew him into a side corridor and whispered,

"There is an officer of the ship, the assistant purser. He is an impostor. In truth, he is none other than the infamous Oskar, an anarchist, and assassin, hired by my enemies."

"They mean to do you harm?"

Consummate actress though she was, Mrs. Biddle had difficulty masking her tone of contempt. "One generally doesn't hire an assassin to spread good cheer."

"Do not fear, Lady Eleanor. I, Tomasz Szczęsny, will confront this Oskar."

"No, that would be precipitous. For now, just watch him. Don't let him out of your sight."

"Very good, madame." Tomasz bowed and began to leave, but then turned back. "Did you receive my letter?"

"Letter? No, what was it about?"

"I, er... perhaps you could ask your traveling companion? I left it with her."

Tomasz rushed off. The thought of recounting the letter directly to the object of his adoration—particularly the postscript—unnerved him.

III

Mrs. Biddle gave Lord Dexter's door a knock and was given the habitual permission to come forth. She did so.

"I'm happy to report that Dowling has taken the bait. I told him of your offer—which he had, of course, overheard—and he suggested an auction. The deed will be sold to the highest bidder."

"Auction?" Lord Dexter made no effort to hide his dislike for the word. He preferred to buy what others disdained, and then find ways to profit from their sale. Things such as steamships mired in the Thames, or the banknotes of a lost cause.

"You need have no anxiety," Mrs. Biddle went on. "Your money will never be at risk. I will tell Dowling that you have agreed, provided your valet acts as auctioneer. Both sides will put up money, but only some small portion need be visible. We will make sure you win the auction, but through a sleight of hand, your valet will have removed Dowling's money and replaced it with some worthless paper. Do you think your valet is capable of executing such a scheme?"

"Isn't a doubt. I only hired him because he's a charlatan."

"You hired him *because* he's a charlatan?"

"Needed one for my fool wife. The woman haunts me with batty notions."

"She sounds trying."

"She is trying, trying as all damnation. But she's just half my trouble. The real suffering comes from that girl of mine."

"Your daughter? You're afraid she'll be upset over the loss of the bracelet?"

"She'll raise hell about it, but that's not the worst of it. She's gotten herself engaged to some damn policeman. Already has a wife, says he's just waiting to divorce her. All the gossips in Byblos are on to it."

"You're from Byblos? Byblos, New York?" Her voice took on a slight tremor.

"All my life. But you're saying it wrong, should be *By-blows*."

So surprised was Mrs. Biddle at his revelation, she allowed the popular mispronunciation of a classical city to stand without comment, save a reflexive wince.

"Been there?" Dexter asked.

"No, I've never had that pleasure. Your daughter—is her name, by chance, Felicia?"

"Yes. That's her, Felicia."

I think, esteemed reader, we had better stop right here. There are certain details of Mrs. Biddle's life story which were left out of chapter one in the interest of brevity, but which now take on a good deal of importance.

For reasons not clear—least of all to themselves—our heroine had married a New York police detective named Biddle in early 1902. In September of that year, she insisted he give up his job and join her, at her expense, for an extended sojourn in

Europe. He, being nearly as obstinate as his wife, declined to do so. Instead, he took a position in Byblos, a small city upstate. Knowing as he did his wife's thoughts on small cities upstate, his action could only be read as a challenge.

In the early part of October, Mrs. Biddle informed her husband she would be awaiting him in Étaples. He replied with directions from the New York Central depot to the room he'd rented in Byblos. Each felt sure the other would eventually give in.

Later in that same month, Mrs. Biddle learned that she was bearing his child. Had she relayed this news, he would certainly have joined her via the first available boat. But her colossal pride would not allow her to use the child to decide a contest she was certain could be won on her own terms.

Several weeks before Eugenia's birth, a school friend let her know in a letter that Biddle had become engaged to a woman named Felicia Dexter and planned to seek a divorce. It was then that Mrs. Biddle determined she would cross the Atlantic as soon as circumstances permitted. She wouldn't demean herself by fighting the divorce, but she felt she must meet this fiancée. It was beyond her conception that there could exist a woman superior to herself.

Mrs. Biddle was still recovering from the birth when the man currently calling himself Dowling contacted her about a scheme that promised, at best, a sizable payout, and at worst, a ticket to New York. That the target of this scheme was the father of her husband's bride-to-be came as something of a shock. But there seemed little chance it was anything more than coincidence.

Lord Dexter appeared not the least bit surprised that Lady Eleanor, Duchess of Aquatique, was acquainted with his daughter. "You've met the girl?"

"No. I think someone mentioned her in a letter. This policeman—not Biddle, is it?"

"Yes, that's him. You know *him*?"

"Only enough to confirm your fears," Mrs. Biddle assured

him. "He is a bloodsucker of the first order."

"I knew it. Just after my money. They all are, but at least the others aren't such hypocrites."

"But your daughter cares for him?"

"Says she does. But who knows what goes through that girl's mind."

"It sounds as if you could use an ally."

Mrs. Biddle took Lord Dexter's arm in her own and led him up to the promenade deck for a stroll. By the end of their first circuit, she had amended Lady Eleanor's biography by explaining that her mother was Lydia Pashkov, boon companion to Madame Blavatsky, the *grande dame* of modern theosophy. By the end of the second circuit, his lordship was convinced of her familiarity with the occult. And by the conclusion of the third, she'd accepted a position in his entourage.

His new court theosopher then took leave of Lord Dexter to return to her cabin. It was one o'clock and her turn to tend the baby while Mélisande lunched in the dining room.

"That Polish boy, he told me he left a letter," she said. "Was there anything important in it?"

"No, only very silly. I threw it in the sea," Mélisande told her.

When she'd gone, Mrs. Biddle took out the letter the lavender-scented woman had hidden in her jewelry box. Though her German wasn't as proficient as Tomasz's, she was likewise impressed with the artist lover's frankness. A letter like this could be very useful....

7

Over the next twenty-four hours, Archie Cobb delivered no fewer than seventeen plump American lambs for the sacrificial rites conducted by Dowling at a card table in the smoking saloon. The future viscount was pleased to be sailing to this nation of braggarts. Unlike their tight-lipped British counterparts, these well-to-do Yankees couldn't help themselves from giving up their particulars to any stranger they thought worthy of impressing.

And apparently that encompassed anyone who could affect a middle-class English accent. Archie didn't have time to tell them about his fictional firm's shipping interests before they began reciting their annual income, the value of their property, and the generous allowances they gave their wife and children.

One Paterson mill owner helpfully provided both the name of his bank and the precise balance of his account, then bestowed his autograph as memento. Touched, Archie created a detailed record of their meeting and promised it would not be the last the Jersey gentleman heard from him.

Meanwhile, his new court theosopher diverted Lord Dexter with the myriad ways her occult powers could be put to use in thwarting his daughter's marriage to Biddle, the bloodsucking hypocrite and sometime policeman. So impressed was her liege lord that he set before Lady Eleanor other matters that troubled him, mostly prosaic concerns involving either his family or the municipal authorities of Byblos, and only one he thought requiring immediate attention—the crucifixion of an alderman.

Oskar, having been assured that the lost jewelry would be recovered and the thief brought to account, endeavored to occupy his mind with the comforting routine of his duties. And he was succeeding, at least until he became aware that his every movement was being followed by Tomasz, who, acting on information supplied by his adored Lady Eleanor, believed the assistant purser to be an assassin hired by her enemies.

And in cabin 176, the for-now-chastened Mélisande took up her pen. Several weeks earlier she had discovered her employer's secret journal and found its characterization of her wanting. What better use of her time than to right the matter by setting down some telling bits of her own autobiography?

It was just after luncheon on that last afternoon at sea that her mistress dispatched Mélisande to the cabin of the lavender-scented German woman with the request that she visit Lady Eleanor at her earliest convenience. Frau Kleinhempel demurred.

Yes, I know I promised not to name these characters of lesser import. But it really is rather tiresome to have to refer repeatedly to "the lavender-scented German woman." Besides, that rule was already undermined by Mélisande when the silly tart blurted the name Oskar. And since the matter *is* out of my hands, you may as well know her full name, Gertrud Kleinhempel, and that she lives with her husband in a well-appointed flat on Pilarstrasse in the posh Nymphenburg neighborhood of Munich. After all, this much could be gathered by a simple perusal of the envelope now in Mrs. Biddle's possession.

Like most of the more cosmopolitan Europeans on board the *Kronprinz Wilhelm*, the Kleinhempels were skeptical of Lady Eleanor's credentials. Though there were no public confrontations, there were numerous whispered exchanges that ended in poorly concealed titters. Frau Kleinhempel's only answer to the duchess's invitation was the Bavarian equivalent of a mocking guffaw, which sounds remarkably like the release of air brakes on a railway car. She had begun closing the door when Mélisande stopped her.

"It is about a letter of yours she has found...."

"Letter?"

"Yes, your friend, he writes very interesting letters. Good-bye, madame."

Frau Kleinhempel closed the door and sat on her bed. Thank God her husband (Christian name Luitpold, for those who are interested) was off in the smoking saloon.

Thinking her jewelry box still safe in the purser's vault, she assumed the faux duchess had gotten hold of the letter she had passed to the startled boy on that first afternoon at sea. He must be in league with this Lady Eleanor and now the faux duchess was blackmailing her. Having no money of her own, Frau Kleinhempel decided the only thing she could do was to offer a piece of her exquisite jewelry. Perhaps this so-called lady would settle for one of the lesser pendants....

The lavender-scented Frau Kleinhempel went up to the purser's office and asked for her brown leather bag. On checking the log, Oskar informed her that her husband had retrieved it the previous morning. A visibly troubled, but still lavender-scented, Frau Kleinhempel could only nod acknowledgment. The assistant purser offered a chair and she sat down, then tried to reason out what had happened.

Early in the voyage, she had become convinced her husband suspected there was something incriminating in the bag when he thrice suggested she retrieve it and display some of her costly trinkets in the dining room. Normally, he preferred that they be safely locked away. Then, beginning the day before, he made no more mention of the jewelry.

If he had retrieved the bag and seen the letter—and having as he did the emotions of a child—he would have found it impossible to keep his anger suppressed. And if he had retrieved it and *not* found the letter, why was he hiding her jewelry from her? Perhaps someone impersonating her husband had claimed the bag? She had just arrived at this thought when she saw through the porthole the startled boy to whom she had passed the *other* letter.

Tomasz had been keeping watch on the assassin Oskar when he saw the lavender-scented German lady arrive and subsequently swoon. Was no woman safe from this fiend?

Recognizing Tomasz as the inheritor of the letter with the piquant penultimate paragraph, Frau Kleinhempel rushed out to confront him.

"What have you done with my letter!" she shouted.

Reluctant to remain and discuss the matter, particularly since Frau Kleinhempel was wielding a parasol with a very sharp point like the master fencer she was, Tomasz sprinted off. The swordswoman, encumbered by her fashionably high-heeled footwear, could only shout after him. There was nothing to be done now but see what price this Lady Eleanor was demanding.

Having been one of the few titterers brave enough to titter to Lady Eleanor's face, it was with a good deal of trepidation that Frau Kleinhempel knocked on the door of the duchess's cabin.

"*Bonjour, Dame Eleanor.*"

Mrs. Biddle found her guest's French lacking. But the obsequious curtsey which accompanied it—so low it bordered on genuflection—had her complete approval.

"*Setzen Sie sich,*" she commanded, then continued in her quite adequate German. "We need not waste time. This letter has come into my possession."

She handed it to Frau Kleinhempel, who recognized it as the one she'd hidden in her jewelry box.

"You have my jewelry, too?"

"Let us say I know where it can be found."

"Are you proposing... to keep... to keep my jewelry in exchange for giving me back this letter?" Her emotions welling, the covetous Frau Kleinhempel could no longer keep back the tears.

"Dry your eyes," Mrs. Biddle told her. As a class, bourgeois housewives did not rank high in her esteem—and this frail specimen least of all. Still, she could be made use of. "You will have the return of your jewelry tonight. *Provided* you do as you're told."

"Oh, thank you, madame!"

"Your bag was dropped by a man on the boat deck yesterday morning and picked up by an associate of mine. Was it your husband who dropped it?"

"I believe it must have been, but he has said nothing."

"Then he hasn't seen the letter. I suggest you destroy it now."

Mrs. Biddle pointed to a bowl and matches on the nearby table and Frau Kleinhempel incinerated the incendiary letter.

"When you leave here, I will send for your husband. I will tell him I have recovered the bag that he lost and will return it if he follows my instructions. He will not know you've met with me, nor will he learn of that letter. Where is he now?"

"In the smoking saloon."

"When you next see him, you shall act as if nothing has happened. Tonight, the assistant purser will come for you to identify your jewelry. Pretend to be surprised. Now, you may go."

"Forgive me, madame. But the other letter?"

"I know of no other letter."

"The boy, he was just now watching me in the purser's office. Is he not your associate?"

"No. I know nothing about him," Mrs. Biddle assured her.

II

At twenty-five minutes past three, Herr Kleinhempel made his own pilgrimage to cabin 176. A steward had handed him Mrs. Biddle's note some ten minutes earlier—just after he'd drawn the third of three kings. Her offer of information on the missing bag had not been sufficient inducement for him to abandon so promising a hand.

Though at first greatly troubled at the loss of his wife's jewelry, Herr Kleinhempel came soon to appreciate how it could be used to his advantage. He would simply deny he'd ever withdrawn the bag from the vault. Leading the authorities, he trusted, to conclude that some clever thief had impersonated him. And, most essentially, there would be no trouble with his claim on the heavily insured ornaments, because it was his own family's firm that had written the policy.

Afterward, he would explain to his wife that the lost items would, over time, be replaced. Though not stated explicitly, it would be understood that she would need to repurchase them with new proofs of affection and fidelity. The Kleinhempels were of the mercantile caste.

He greeted his hostess politely, but with none of the abject submission displayed by his wife. Mrs. Biddle was noticeably puzzled at his indifference when told she was in a position to return the jewelry.

"I will be frank, madame," he told her. "It is a matter of little importance to me whether the jewelry is recovered, or the insurance claim paid. For myself, the latter resolution offers several advantages."

"I see. So you have already written off your marriage as a loss?"

"My marriage? What would you know of that?"

"I know that few women would tolerate so obvious a scheme to defraud them of what they'd gained through... let us say, backbreaking labors. Though I suppose Frau Kleinhempel may be unique in this regard. Perhaps I was wrong to think her collection carefully chosen by one who cared deeply for such material displays of devotion. I'm sure you know best."

Herr Kleinhempel, however, was no longer sure he did know best. This ersatz aristocrat had given him second thoughts. Her characterization of his wife was uncannily accurate. But there was one last matter to be considered.

"Might I inquire if there was anything in the bag besides the jewelry and the box that held it?" he asked.

"What is it you have in mind?"

"Oh, a letter perhaps?"

"No, there were no letters, no paper of any sort."

"And you searched it thoroughly?"

"Need I answer that, Herr Kleinhempel?"

"No, that will not be necessary. Tell me, madame, what is it you want in return for the bag?"

"Only your cooperation in catching the thief."

"You are unusually generous, madame. Might I ask why?"

"I wish this man to get what he deserves, but under circumstances of my choosing."

"So he is the man who recovered my bag?"

"Is that important?" she asked curtly.

"I think it would be to him."

"He will be getting no more than his due. These are my terms—you may accept them or not."

"I accept, madame. But only on your assurance I will not be accusing an innocent man."

"You will not need to make any accusation. Tonight, the assistant purser will come to your cabin. It might be quite late. He will tell you he has found the man who has your jewels. All you need do is identify them."

"Very well, madame."

Herr Kleinhempel made a short bow and left intending to return to his card game. But on the promenade deck, his fetching wife surprised him. She took him by the arm.

"Oh, Luitpold. Where have you been? You spend all your time away."

This time, the lavender-scented lady's irresistible look did not fail her. There was a great release of tension in the Kleinhempels' cabin that afternoon, and, after a light supper, it continued well into the evening.

At ten o'clock, Mrs. Biddle located Oskar in the purser's office and asked for his master key.

"My key, madame?"

"Do you, or do you not, want to recover the jewelry?" Oskar surrendered his key and she resumed. "At midnight, go to my cabin and the girl will give you instructions. Bring along two stewards. Understood?"

"Yes, madame."

When she emerged, Tomasz came up beside her.

"Lady Eleanor, what are you doing speaking with that assassin? You should be more careful."

"Setting a trap," she told him. "And I need your help."

"Anything at all."

"Come to my cabin at 11:30. The girl will tell you just what needs to be done."

"I will be there, madame."

Mrs. Biddle then went to the cabin of the man currently calling himself Dowling.

"It's all arranged," he told her. "Archie will have Dexter in the reading room at midnight. Do you have the key?"

She handed him Oskar's key.

"Afterwards, you and Archie and I will reassemble here to divide the winnings."

"Tonight?" she asked. "I'd think tomorrow would be soon enough."

"Yes, no doubt you would. But I think Archie and I will sleep easier if it's taken care of tonight."

"All right. I understand you've been doing well for yourself at the table."

"Yes, and I don't mind telling you now that it was essential that I did so. That damn Céleste cleaned me out." The tired old man looked at her as if asking for sympathy, and for a brief moment, his daughter almost allowed him some. But then he added, "Women have always been my Achilles' heel."

Mrs. Biddle shook her head in disgust and left him.

III

The reading room of the *Kronprinz Wilhelm* closed at exactly eleven o'clock each night. At 10:45, Mrs. Biddle entered the room carrying a brown leather bag. She placed it on the floor and sat down to read a magazine. Then, using her foot, she silently edged the bag under the skirting of a table. When the attendant rang his bell, she left for the Vienna Café and a prearranged meeting with Archie Cobb.

"When you go in, set yourself up at the table at the bow end," she told him. "The bag is already in place."

"All right. Do you think your father suspects?"

"Not that I can tell. How much did he raise?"

"Must be at least five thousand, but I only know from hearsay. Dexter has me a little worried. Never met a man so difficult to get a bead on."

"He's not so different from the typical self-made American yokel. They make a religion of individualism, but it usually amounts to little more than enshrined eccentricities."

"Enshrined eccentricities is right—man's as queer as Dick's hatband."

Mrs. Biddle was not familiar with Dick, or his proverbial hatband, but she seldom felt Archie's aphorisms worthy of exploration.

"Another cognac," she called to the waiter.

At exactly 11:30, Tomasz arrived at cabin 176.

"You cut your face," Mélisande said to him.

Touching his cheek, Tomasz only now realized that Frau Kleinhempel's parasol had drawn blood. He let the girl dab at it with a moistened handkerchief.

"It was necessary," he lied, "to protect Lady Eleanor. Is she here?"

"No, she comes later. She tells me to get you ready."

She'd removed his jacket before he could object. But when she began loosening his tie, he jumped back.

"You must stop this! I have come to help Lady Eleanor."

"Yes, yes. I know. But you see, Lady Eleanor is very lonely...."

"Has she read my letter?"

"Yes, three times she read it. It makes her very... hot."

"Hot?"

"Yes, she goes for a walk to cool down...."

"Then I should go to her."

"No, she wants you to stay here. You see, she likes you very much, but..."

"But what?"

"Well...." Mélisande brought her face to his shoulder and sniffed. "She says, she thinks maybe you need a bath."

It was true that with one thing and another Tomasz had let matters of hygiene slip from his mind. In fact, he hadn't bathed since he left his Chelsea boarding house. And for two days he'd been wearing the same clothes.

"I will see if the steward can arrange for me to use one of the baths."

"No, no. Why do that? We have a bath here."

"But..."

For ten minutes, his outsized modesty held his ardor at bay. But when Oskar arrived at midnight, Tomasz could be heard splashing lustily and singing a Polish love song.

Mélisande entered the bathroom and began picking up his clothes.

"What are you doing?" he asked.

"I will have them washed for you."

"At this time of night?"

"Yes, the laundryman is my friend. You wait here. If the baby cries, you give her the bottle. Good-bye."

"But..."

Mélisande closed the door and hid his clothes under the bed. Then she went with Oskar to fetch a thoroughly relaxed Herr Kleinhempel and his gainfully talented wife.

In the meantime, Dowling, Dexter, Mrs. Biddle, and Archie had assembled in the reading room. Both Dexter's carpetbag and Dowling's brown leather case were handed to Archie and he took them to the table nearest the bow. There he pretended to count the contents, carefully removing and replacing the same stacks of real currency repeatedly. He announced both totaled more than $100,000, with Dexter having a $3,000 advantage.

The bidding moved quickly to $90,000. But then Lord Dexter paused. He asked to see the deed again and inspected it carefully. The left eyebrow looked keen enough, but the right was unmoved. His lordship took them into private conference by approaching a window and staring out into the night.

Meanwhile, the others fidgeted in their seats. Dowling was nervous that he'd taken the bidding too high. Archie was nervous that Dowling had noticed him replacing his brown leather bag with the one that held Frau Kleinhempel's jewelry. Mrs. Biddle's fidgeting was not, of course, due to nerves, but merely to the fact she'd left the Vienna Café after three cognacs without visiting the Ladies' Toilette.

Once he was convinced he had all three squirming, Lord

Dexter returned and secured the deed by making his unbeatable maximum bid.

Dowling shrugged and offered Dexter his hand.

"Well, fair is fair, I suppose. No one can say I didn't give it my best. I will inform the syndicate that they will now need to contact you."

He picked up the brown leather bag from the table and was halfway to the door when Oskar entered, accompanied by two stewards.

"Excuse me, sir. But that bag—it has been reported stolen."

"Nonsense. I had it in the vault until this afternoon."

"Then you won't mind if we examine it?"

"I do mind."

"Forgive me, sir," Oskar told him, "but finding you in a room closed at this hour, I'm afraid I must insist." He then motioned to one of the stewards, who went to the corridor and returned with the Kleinhempels.

"Is this your bag?" he asked Herr Kleinhempel.

"It looks like it, yes."

Oskar placed it on a table and opened it, then removed the oblong jewelry box. The lavender-scented lady rushed forward and assured herself her collection was intact.

"My bag must have gotten switched with theirs," Dowling protested.

Instead of responding, Oskar removed a small bundle from the bag and unwrapped it.

"My damn daughter's bracelet!" Lord Dexter exclaimed. His eyebrows, still somewhat puzzled by the course of events, quietly signaled their satisfaction via a stately allemande.

"If it was a simple mix-up of bags, how is it that this gentleman's bracelet found its way into it as well?" Oskar asked Dowling.

Dowling looked up at the only one present capable of engineering such treachery.

"You, my dear?"

"I've no idea what you're talking about."

While Oskar had the stewards lead the culprit to his cabin with orders that he be kept under watch, Frau Kleinhempel examined the bracelet he'd just uncovered.

"Oh, Luitpold. Isn't it the most beautiful thing you've ever seen?"

Herr Kleinhempel had heard those words many times before and the outcome was nearly always the same. So it would be again. He was, after all, still feeling contrite for having wrongly suspected his wife. And certainly the affection she'd lavished that afternoon was deserving of some form of... commemoration.

Archie and Mrs. Biddle both left the room $2,700 the richer. But it was Timothy Dexter who came out on top. Herr Kleinhempel's check for $8,000 amounted to a 60% return on the bracelet. What's more, he succeeded in pocketing what he dubbed the "comely deed" without spending a dollar of Confederate currency.

8

On her way out of the reading room, Mrs. Biddle came upon Mélisande observing the scene from the shadows.

"The baby!" she reminded the girl.

"It's OK. Your lover is there, he waits for you."

Back in their cabin, they found Tomasz dressed in a flowery kimono with Eugenia in his lap, humming a lullaby.

"Lady Eleanor, at last…"

"M. Szczęsny, I'm sorry. I was detained. And now it's so very late. But I expect we will be seeing a good deal of one another. Lord Dexter has offered me a position in his court."

"A position in his court?"

"Yes, I'm to be his theosopher."

"You're coming to Byblos?"

"Yes, I am."

"That is wonderful!"

"Well, we shall see about that. But perhaps now we should all get some sleep?"

"Yes, yes, of course."

Mélisande reached under the bed and brought out his clothing in a heap. Tomasz took it up and made a short bow. Then, as he toddled happily off to his cabin, Mrs. Biddle dashed for the bathroom—the three cognacs had waited long enough.

The next morning, Mélisande asked about this "Byblos."

"It's a few hours from New York. I've never been there, but don't expect much."

"Why don't we stay in New York?" the girl asked.

"Because there is something I must see to in Byblos. If you come and help me, I will give you enough to come back to New York later."

"How long?"

"A month, maybe more, maybe less."

"How much will you give me?"

"Five hundred dollars. Agreed?"

"OK. But I will see a little of New York before we go to... Byblos?"

"Yes, but we will be taking a morning train tomorrow. There's one more thing. We must travel separately. I can't be seen with the baby. When we get to Byblos, you and she will stay elsewhere. I'll come whenever I can. Now I have something to give you." She removed a fifty-dollar bill from her bag and held it out to Mélisande. The girl grabbed it, but Mrs. Biddle had not yet released her end. "It's not a gift. You are to use this only in an emergency."

"Emergency?"

"*Dans les circonstances critiques.*" Only when the girl nodded did Mrs. Biddle release her end of the banknote. "The most important thing to remember is that you can trust no one, including my associates."

"Associates?"

"The people I'm traveling with, Cobb and Dexter."

"What about the Polish boy?"

"What about him? You haven't gone soft on him, have you?"

"Bah! No, I have not gone soft on him. But he does not seem dangerous."

"Well, he may be a danger of a different sort. Don't tell him you're going to Byblos."

"I'll tell him I'm going home to Pittsbourg."

"Yes, tell him you're going home to Pittsbourg," Mrs. Biddle smiled.

It was almost noon when the *Kronprinz Wilhelm* finally docked at the Lloyd line's Hoboken pier. Lord Dexter and his party were at the front of the queue, but this time the aristocrats were forced to give way. First off the boat would be the two New York police detectives who'd boarded with the pilot off Sandy Hook. Accompanying them was the man sometimes known as Dowling—though five weeks before, when taken into custody by the same two detectives, he had been using the name Leyland. As he passed his daughter, he stopped and addressed her, sotto voce.

"You may consider your share a christening gift for my granddaughter. But you may be sure," he went on, turning now to encompass Archie Cobb, "both of you may be sure, I'll be looking you up in your new home."

Mrs. Biddle looked over him to the policemen. "Please take that tiresome old man away." Then she looked over her shoulder at Cobb.

"I never said a word about the child," Archie quickly assured her.

The tension was broken when a grateful Oskar came forward and offered to escort Lady Eleanor off the boat. To Tomasz, still laboring under the misapprehension that the assistant purser was a hired assassin, his approach bore all the hallmarks of an assault. The misguided Pole flung himself at Oskar, but with such a complete lack of precision that he soon found himself sailing over the rail of the gangplank. As his jacket billowed in the wind, a well-thumbed page of writing paper slipped from an inside pocket and was sent skyward by a sudden updraft. Unhappily, the gust did nothing to delay Tomasz's rendezvous with the malodorous brine below.

Once he'd fished out his secretary and lied his way through Customs, Lord Dexter took his ill-equipped entourage on a shopping spree. Archie would need a wardrobe befitting the Viscount of Abernethy, Lady Eleanor the garb of a theosopher— and Tomasz something that didn't smell of Hoboken bilge water. But the first order of business was to replace the bracelet for his daughter that he'd sold to Herr Kleinhempel.

Mrs. Biddle suggested a visit to Tiffany's, and there helped him choose a replacement which compensated for its comparative lack of craftsmanship with more, and larger, diamonds. At $6,000 it came dearer than the original, but with the profit from the latter's sale and the avoidance of duty, Lord Dexter calculated that he was still ahead $3,200.

Herr Kleinhempel wasn't so lucky avoiding the duty that afternoon, there being a discrepancy between the customs form he'd carefully filled out the evening before and the contents of his wife's jewelry box. They'd spent a trying hour extricating themselves and were only now arriving at their Manhattan hotel.

While her husband paid the driver, Frau Kleinhempel descended from the cab with the help of the doorman. Just as she reached the sidewalk, a page of stationery carried by a strong breeze wafted against her face. It bore a familiar scent. She took it in her hand and read.... Mein Gott! It was the compromising letter with the piquant penultimate paragraph!

The next moment, her husband was coming toward her. "What's that, my dear?"

In one deft movement, the lavender-scented lady crumpled the page into her fist and swooned. The doorman caught her and brought her to a bench.

"Quick," he told Herr Kleinhempel, "go inside and fetch a doctor."

As soon as her husband was safely away, Frau Kleinhempel opened a wary eye and began eating the piquant letter. The doorman, of course, noticed nothing, and for three weeks he and his wife dined off of his discretion.

Meanwhile, Tomasz, still damp from his dunking and bearing a scent quite unlike lavender, had been sent to settle with Tiffany's cashier while the others of his party retired to a cozy café just down the street. He counted out sixty of the apricottoned banknotes Lord Dexter had given him and then waited for the cashier to hand him the receipt. Later that afternoon, after satisfying Tiffany & Co. with a check drawn on a New York bank, his playful employer bailed him out at the Jefferson Market Police Court.

Lady Eleanor begged off dinner that evening. She was exhausted, she told the others, and would have something brought to her. At seven o'clock, she left her room on the fifth floor of the Plaza Hotel and stole down to that of Mélisande one floor below. She came bearing gifts.

"Where have you been?" the girl asked. "I haven't seen any of New York."

"You've plenty of time. I've brought you some things."

Mrs. Biddle set the packages on the bed and one by one Mélisande opened them and donned their contents. When she had finished, she looked the part of a sophisticated American girl, though undoubtedly one of moderate means. Mrs. Biddle's generosity only went so far.

"Go down to the lobby," she instructed while adding a silver brooch to the ensemble. "A Miss Springer will meet you there. Miriam Springer. I told her you are the daughter of a French artist."

"Who is Miss Springer?"

"A friend of mine. She will show you New York." Mrs. Biddle took out another fifty dollars and handed it to Mélisande.

"Is this from my five hundred dollars?" the girl asked.

"No. This is for tonight."

"How could I spend fifty dollars in one night?"

"You've never been to New York. Remember, don't let Miss Springer out of your sight. And *do not* take up with any men. They aren't all like those boys you met in Étaples. Now go, and be back by dawn. We catch an early train."

Mélisande gave her a peck on the cheek and went off. She was very pleased, and sincerely grateful. But as she waited for the elevator, she took off the simple silver brooch and replaced it with the colorful cloisonné one the lady in cabin 12 had provided her.

That night, and for many more to follow, Eugenia slumbered to the drip... drip... drip... of American plumbing.

Thus ends the first novella. Those curious as to how Mélisande spent her evening in New York may wish to read "An Outing on Manhattan," the second tale in Mélisande's own book, The Fly Maiden's Book of Virtues, *which is available to the most devoted of readers at the ByblosForetold.com web site.*

Peddlers All

The Second Novella

Editor's Preface

My dearest, *most gracious* reader—before we rejoin the story proper I must beg some time alone with you. I have too long put off revealing what is, perhaps, the most extraordinary element of this most extraordinary saga: its origin. The only excuse I can offer is that I thought it wise to wait until we were thoroughly acquainted before putting your trust to such a test. And tested it will be, for the tale I am about to lay before you is so utterly fantastic, a less devoted companion might be excused for doubting it.

Some time ago, when we were all sailing aboard the S.S. *Kronprinz Wilhelm*, I mentioned that my role in this endeavor was that of assembler. I shied from taking the title of editor because I'd hoped to be able to limit my interventions. But, alas, that has not been the case.

Though I have every reason to believe that what I've laid before you is a true and, primarily, honest account, the disparate sources on which it is based are simply too contradictory for any one to be followed blindly for even the shortest period of time.

I suppose, beleaguered reader, it must seem to you as if I'm speaking in riddles. But have no fear, I'll not string out my story like some eighteenth-century sermonizer enamored of his own conception.

Early one frigid morning in February, 1903, I was returning to my apartment after a long evening spent with friends from college. I was living then, as now, in Brooklyn, right above Prospect Park, and had just left the streetcar as it rounded the plaza. Not surprisingly on so bitterly cold a night, I saw no one about, and, once the streetcar had gone, heard nothing. The sky was clear and a full moon illuminated the monument that dominates the plaza. Until... until it did no longer. I looked up and saw silhouetted against the starlit sky a slow-moving leviathan. In time, I recognized it for what it was—an airship of gigantic proportions.

I was, as you can well imagine, struck dumb in awe. The ship was dark, charcoal grey, and silent as the grave. It slowed further, and a minute later, halted entirely. Then, suddenly, a beam of light shone down into the park.

I suppose the inhabitants of the Earth can be neatly divided into two halves. Or, let us say the Earth's population. Otherwise, it might sound as if I'm suggesting the planet's inhabitants be cleaved each in their turn. And what a laborious enterprise *that* would be.

There are those who, on seeing a beam of light streaming from a silent airship hovering over a cold and friendless city, flee to the safety of their homes and wonder who to telephone. And then there are those who overcome their apprehensions and venture forth into the unknown. I, happily, count myself among the latter.

Some two hundred yards into the park, I could see where the beam reached the lawn. Then, as suddenly as it had appeared, it went dark. It had been eclipsed by a parachute, which drifted slowly downward until finally hitting the ground with a thud. Soon after, the beam was extinguished and the airship proceeded on its way.

Gingerly, I approached, and there, beneath the folds of the silk parachute, I found a wooden crate. The impact had detached its lid, and I could see that it held a collection of documents. I picked up one sheaf which was bound with a ribbon and brought it to a nearby streetlamp. What I read shocked me to the very core of my being.

I took up as many of the documents as I could carry and rushed to my apartment. Once I deposited those, I went back with a satchel through the still-empty streets. It seemed that I was the sole witness to the visitation. After filling the satchel with what remained, I returned home to spend a sleepless night examining my trove.

What was it that had shocked me so? That bundle which I'd

brought to the streetlamp, a thick stack of several hundred type-written pages, was topped by a sheet that read:

My Life
Eugenia B. _____
As set down in the summer of 1959

Nineteen hundred and fifty-nine! Some fifty-six years into the future. When I opened the bundle and began reading, I received a second shock. The author, whose married name I will reveal when the time is ripe, explained that she was committing her biography to paper for the benefit of her grandchildren. She began, naturally enough, with the date of her birth: May the seventh, 1903—some three months *after* the arrival of the airship!

The next day, there were accounts in several of the New York papers from others who'd observed the airship. But similar sightings had occurred with such frequency over the previous decade that no one was wont to believe them—the patronizing journalists expressing their incredulity with the barbed sarcasm which comes so easily to them. Having no interest in exposing myself to their sharpened nibs, I kept silent, and fully expected to hear no more about it. But the affair's final act had yet to play.

I was just finishing my lunch when the janitor came to the door. An assistant superintendent from Prospect Park had sent round a wooden crate. In his accompanying note, he conjectured that the crate had been stolen off an express wagon and that the thieves had abandoned it in the park on finding nothing in it but a large quantity of silk. It was, of course, the same crate from my encounter the night before, with the parachute neatly folded and laid inside. The lid had now been carefully reattached and on it was—prepare yourself, O constant reader, for yet another test of your trust, for on it was written *my own name and address!*

It all seemed so improbable. And yet, one explanation, or partial explanation, had come to light that morning while I was reading the life story of Eugenia. Midway through it, I came to a realization: I knew her parents.

I should tell you now that in the story as I've been present-ing it, I've changed most of the names, including Biddle and that of the city, Byblos. But not Eugenia. The choice of that name—from the Greek for *well-born*—so exemplifies her mother's char-acter that I thought it irreplaceable.

I have known Eugenia's mother since college, but for some time we have not been on the best of terms. Why her unborn daughter would send me her autobiography is a question which will likely never be answered. Or at least not before 1959, by which time, apparently, options for shipping parcels will have increased markedly.

The memoir itself comprises several bundled manuscripts. But also written in Eugenia's hand are several other works, which I assume to be literary efforts. These I have set aside for the present so as to concentrate on the family history.

Now let us turn to the other documents contained in the crate. Eugenia describes these as her source material, which she has used to augment her own recollections. I have examined them all, and by relating their contents to events and persons described by Eugenia, I believe I can now identify most of their authors.

The text which begins earliest is the two-volume journal of her mother. This she kept sporadically, and even then only be-tween the fall of 1902 and the spring of 1905, when it ends ab-ruptly. It is written in an off-putting style, all in the present tense, with its author speaking *at* the reader like the deity she believes herself to be.

Next is a volume by her mother's retainer, whom I've chris-tened Mélisande. It relates a number of ribald anecdotes, all told in a frank, unschooled voice and utilizing what appears a random assortment of French and American slang. These tales, she tells us in her prologue, were written for the edification of her "little sis-ter," Eugenia. And to ensure that the lessons are clear, each ends with a pair of amusing morals. Some of the more developed of these tales are reminiscent of those found in Boccaccio's *Decamer-on*, and some of the more earthy, of the medieval fabliaux.

Then there is an autobiographical sketch by Lord Dexter's secretary, Tomasz, who seems to have suffered from an acute form of introspection. If the resulting bathos were intentional, this might be thought the flawed work of a genius. But that would be a difficult case to argue. It isn't clear if this overwrought manuscript was written from memory or contemporaneously with the events it depicts, but I can't imagine why anyone would care.

The fourth item is a treatise by Lord Dexter himself, printed in Byblos at his expense and plainly meant as a sequel to his better-known relative's book, *A Pickle for the Knowing Ones*. It's a paragon of circumlocution, written in a state of confusion, and laced with vitriol throughout. Dexter himself calls it a "lit'ry gallim'fry" and I defer to his appraisal if not his spelling. No less odd than its contents is the binding: there is none. The pages have been purposely left loose and unnumbered. So what constitutes the beginning and what the end is a matter open to conjecture, particularly since it makes as much sense—or as little—in whatever order the pages are read. This volume—*A Pickle Salad for the Know-It-Alls, May Ye Choke on It!*—is indeed aptly titled.

The next three pieces are manuscripts authored by individuals not yet introduced in our story. The first is written by a hyperomniscient narrator who's given over to what Mr. Ruskin called the pathetic fallacy. In her telling, insects suffer angst and furniture flinches. Though the authoress is one of the principals in Eugenia's biography, her own account may be too whimsical to be of much use.

The second is a piece by another woman, written—if it is to be believed, and much of it begs credulity—sometime in the 1920s. Though she touches on many of the other characters, her chief concern is herself, and her own evolution from a dreamy adolescent sensualist into a *very* determined sybarite. The early part of it will be quite useful, but the later part seems nothing more than salacious fantasy. No one, save those of the most prurient curiosity, would wish to be exposed to it. But, then, one never knows....

Last is a very long letter dated 1931 and addressed to Eugenia. It was written—or, I suppose, is to be written—by a Roman Catholic priest well acquainted with her mother. The most erudite of all these sources, it fills in many of the voids left by the others—though, again, its reliability is questionable, its author having a reputation that invites doubt.

Also included were such things as ships' logs, the significance of which I have yet to determine. And scattered amongst all these were newspaper clippings, photographs, and other mementos—most undated and lacking inscriptions.

Which leads me to the final item: a collection of objects which Eugenia refers to as the Greta-paedia. It consists of a scrapbook fashioned from a bound volume of waltz scores and a small wooden box. The text, such as it is, is made up of primers, pamphlets, patent medicine almanacs, and dream books, either found complete in the box or dismembered and pasted into the scrapbook. These were meant, I assume, to provide guidance or instruction. The scrapbook also contains pictures from magazines, tradesmen's cards, and a variety of natural curiosities, and is quite thoughtfully constructed. A labor of love, surely, but one which gives new meaning to the term higgledy-piggledy.

In her autobiography, Eugenia makes clear that she has utilized these earlier sources in order to create the most accurate account possible. But *has* she? No. No, I think not. In fact, I would go so far as to say she is that most taxing of companions, the unreliable narrator.

I base this charge on two pieces of evidence. First, I know from personal experience her characterization of her mother to be demonstrably false. In her telling, her mother is an intelligent and attractive woman, but no more vain than is the norm of her species. I concede the first two points, but the last is utterly ridiculous. This woman is the very quintessence of vanity. And deceit. Why doesn't her daughter make mention of that, I wonder?

Well, the benevolent reader asks, mightn't we forgive a child her biased opinion of her parent? Forgive, yes. But not excuse.

And what about the second bit of evidence? This is perhaps the more damning of the two: she frequently overrules the firsthand accounts found in the other documents. For instance, her account of the sojourn in France and the nature of the voyage home, when she was just a weeks-old infant, bears little to no resemblance to that found in *her own mother's diary!*

After reading Eugenia's bowdlerization, I had concluded that hers was a normal, if somewhat eventful, life, peopled by normal, if somewhat colorful, characters. Of interest to her family, perhaps, but few others.

However, after surveying the underlying documents themselves, I realized I had the makings of a grand epic. All that was needed was the hand of an experienced wordsmith. What's more, I believe Eugenia herself came to this conclusion. For who but her could have sent the archive to my doorstep?

I bow to her judgment. For there seems little doubt that I, and I alone, am in a position to set this great work before the learned public. Where the sources contradict one another, I will endeavor to play the honest broker. And when, for the good of the entertainment, certain events beg elaboration, or truths need bending, I will not dither over trifling obligations or misguided fealty. For first and foremost, my loyalty abides with what I know to be the essential truth of the story.

1

Three loud bangs and Greta was jerked awake.

"Open the damn door!" Three more bangs. "I knows you're in there!"

Before she could lift her now massive body off the couch, the landlord had found his key.

"Where's Lyons?"

"Don' know. Went off last week."

"Never paid for May, an' here it's the second of June."

"Pat's comin' back. An' he'll have da money."

The landlord eyed the girl, plain to begin with and her belly now swelled to half again her size.

"No, sister, skipped on us both. Serves me right for lettin' him stay. Now, you get that thirty bucks, or you get on your way. I'll be back tonight." As he turned to leave, he saw Jack Tigue standing in the kitchen alcove with the neck of a broken bottle in his hand. "Don't make trouble for yerself, boy."

"Put it down, Jack."

But Jack didn't put it down, just stood at the ready until the landlord backed out the door and left them.

"Open a window, will ya? I can hardly breathe. Oh, wha'm I goin' ta do, Jack?"

"Find Pat."

Greta asked him to elaborate, but Jack had already plumbed the depths of his sagacity in coming up with the two words previously presented. He repeated them.

"Wus da use of tellin' me ta find Pat if ya can't say how?"

Greta's frustration was understandable, but only in so far as one accepts her reasoning that a seven-year-old street arab with three days of formal education would be a useful advisor for a mother-to-be with no means of support. Much as she dreaded the prospect, she would need to think.

After a revivifying lunch of boiled eggs—their principal sustenance since Jack had discovered how easily they could be procured from the wagon of a certain wholesaler—Greta surprised herself by arriving at a course of action. She would visit her old haunt, Palace Hall. It was at this Grand Street resort that she'd first met Pat, and she knew he still paid regular visits to what was popularly considered Brooklyn's most accommodating thirst emporium. And she also knew the craving for liquor was not the sole thirst to be slaked at the Hall. She carried the proof of it in her belly.

Greta had begun frequenting the resorts two years before, when at seventeen the woman she thought to be her widowed mother died. But like countless other girls found in literature of this ilk, her path into shame and degradation had been blazed at birth.

She had no memories of her earliest childhood, and was, no doubt, the better for it. She remembered fondly, however, the period which began with her sixth birthday and ended abruptly at her twelfth. That was when she'd been taken from school and sent to work in the Chelsea Jute Mill. From that point on, her life was one of grueling routine. Six days a week, she rose at dawn and trudged along dark streets from their miserable Meserole Avenue tenement to the dismal factory at the farthest, bleakest reach of Greenpoint, not to return until twelve long hours later....

Oh, all right, fastidious reader, I suppose it does sound a little too Dickensian. There's no getting by *you*, is there? Well, I confess, I was exaggerating for effect. The truth is, it was only five days a week that she returned twelve hours later. On Saturday the munificent owners closed the mill early, so it was just *nine* hours later. Furthermore, the hours spent at the mill can't honestly be said to have been measurably longer—speaking purely chronologically—than those spent at leisure. And finally, naming one of Greenpoint's various reaches the bleakest would be laying claim to improbable powers of discernment. Still and all, you may be sure her life was no cakewalk.

Between the few dollars a week Greta earned and what her

supposed mother made taking in laundry, they were able to satisfy their modest needs—with any surplus devoted to playing the numbers at the policy shops, and the occasional win financing an evening at a vaudeville show or, more rarely, an outing to Coney Island.

On the death of her supposed mother, Greta hoped to find work as a shop girl. But she lacked both the manners and the means for assembling the requisite wardrobe. Particularly after losing what was left of the burial insurance playing the dead-mother gig. It was only then that Greta could be persuaded that the woman was not her mother.

Amongst the neighbors, there had for several years been a lively debate on this very point and the tenement house broke neatly into two camps. The larger camp consisted of those who had always assumed as much. At its core were those who'd been around long enough to remember the girl arriving as a three-year-old, with the most cynical suspecting she'd been taken in as a sort of security against her supposed mother's old age.

The second, smaller, camp consisted of Mrs. Skowron, the elderly woman who lived in a tiny room on the top floor and who had long ago mastered the branch of philosophy known as the tarot. The cards, she had assured her neighbors, clearly signaled that Greta and her supposed mother were indeed blood relations.

Mrs. Skowron had always been held in high regard by Greta and her supposed mother, as she was the owner of the finest combination dream dictionary in all the Eastern District of Brooklyn. Not only was it highly illustrated, it was leather-bound and printed on heavy paper, and not in any way like the cheap pulp editions distributed by the patent medicine companies. Whatever the dream or event, Mrs. Skowron could, by consulting her book, provide the policy player with the proper numeric combination on which to wager.

But there were many caveats. Chief among them was the stipulation that the information provided Mrs. Skowron be wholly accurate. As she so often pointed out, failure was not the fault of the book, but of the informant. So when the winning gig for the day of the funeral was that of the washerwoman, 4-11-44, and not that of the dead-mother, 12-36-50, old Mrs. Skowron sat the girl down and explained that facts is facts. The dead woman could not have been her mother. Aunt, perhaps—but not mother.

One night soon after, a friend who'd left the mill a year before took Greta to one of the local resorts. As so often is the case, one thing led to another thing until the *worst possible* thing had found its way into her—for want of a better word—thing. Greta woke the next day a ruined girl. Though she had started not nearly so innocent as Mr. Crane's Maggie, she arrived at much the same condition. Instead of the streets, however, she worked the upstairs rooms of Palace Hall.

Greta, you may be sure, did not find the work pleasant. But neither had she found the jute mill pleasant. And, like most of the girls, she was sure something better would soon come her way.

It was early the previous fall that something better did come her way. Pat Lyons had been making tours of the rural districts with a young mother pretending to be the widow of a sailor lost on the battleship *Maine* when temptation got the better of him and he impregnated the woman whose virtue he'd been trading on.

The Remember the Maine Widows and Orphans Relief Society was in need of a new headliner and Pat visited Palace Hall to recruit one. This time, hoping to avoid a reprise, he planned to choose a girl more wholesome than winsome, finally settling for our dear Greta, who, if we're to be honest, fell well short of the mark in both categories.

Now all that was needed was a child for the newly minted widow. On the way out of town, Pat auditioned the homeless newsies working the Broadway ferry docks. Jack Tigue, young and underfed, was the natural choice. Never mind that his "mother" was just twelve years his senior.

The itinerant charity prospered until the spring. By then Greta's condition had become impossible to hide, and worse, the meddling state's attorney for Jefferson County had obtained a warrant for Pat's arrest. The gang fled back to Brooklyn, where Pat, after a contentious discussion, allowed Greta to hole up with him. Not because he believed her story that they'd had a liaison one drunken night in Chenango Forks and her forthcoming child its natural result. But because he believed her vow to testify against him otherwise.

It was one in the afternoon when Greta arrived at Palace Hall. Gus the bartender greeted her, but not in his customary friendly fashion. It wouldn't do to have such an obvious example of consequences hanging about the place.

"I need ta find Pat, Gus. He wen' off a week ago."

"That's tough, kid."

"I gotta find him."

"Can't help, kid. Ain't seen him in weeks."

"Well, look who's here!" Drunken Sal, one of only two working girls about that early—the other occupied in a small, grimy room upstairs—stumbled up from a dark corner. "It's 'ar little Gert!"

"It's Greta, Sal. An' I ain' so little jus' now."

"Oh, jeez. Poor kid. Give her a drink, Gus."

"No, I don' need no drink. I need ta find Pat Lyons, Sal. Have ya seen him?"

"He was here yesterday. Ain't that right, Gus?"

"Yesterday? Crissake, Gus, don't play me."

Gus drew a beer and handed it to the older woman. "Sit back down, Sal."

"OK. Stop by before you go, Gert."

"Sure, Sal."

When she'd gone, Gus opened the register. He took a slip of paper from below the cash drawer and handed it to Greta.

"What's this?"

"Where Pat's stayin'."

"Byblos? That's up past Albany."

"Yeah. You head up there."

"How? I ain't got enough to cross the river."

Gus went back to the register. He took out ten dollars and handed it to Greta.

"What if he ain't there? I won't have enough ta get back."

Gus didn't say so, but that was his thinking as well. "He'll be there. He took a train yesterday afternoon. There's a four o'clock express."

Greta went home and told Jack she was leaving to find Pat.

"Wha' 'bout me?"

"Sorry, Jack. I ain' got enough for two tickets."

"Whas' it cost?"

"Six, seven bucks. I'll miss ya, Jack."

Jack left the apartment without another word and Greta set about cramming her worldly possessions into two bags. These included four shirtwaists and two skirts appropriate to the season, but the only garment that fit was the hand-me-down frock she was wearing.

Last to be packed was a glass jar. It held a love philtre, concocted the week before from a recipe contained in Mrs. Skowron's dream book. Greta wrapped it in a skirt and placed it beside the scrapbook made from an album of waltz scores that an "uncle" had given her on her sixth birthday. He was one of several "uncles" who had visited them in those early years which the now more worldly Greta realized were more in the line of clients than kin.

On leaving, it was necessary for Greta to carry her bags down the three flights of narrow steps one at a time. After having left the smaller bag in the front hall unattended, she hurried back upstairs for the larger. The second trip nearly did her in, but on her return, there was Jack. He was sitting on her bag and holding up seven crumpled dollars. A rare tear showed itself in the corner of the girl's left eye.

"Oh, Jack, I'm glad yer comin'."

II

It was an anxious Greta who boarded the four o'clock express. She couldn't help but suspect that Gus the bartender had deceived her when he divulged Pat's new address so readily. But she had not been deceived. At least, not this time.

Pat had taken the same train the day before and arrived in Byblos late that evening. He had come in order to visit his twin brother, Danny, who made a very adequate living running that city's preeminent policy operation.

Pat would not have been surprised at Gus's betrayal. In fact, he anticipated it. His plan was to touch his brother for a loan and then leave Byblos as quickly as possible. If, or when, the bartender gave Greta the address in Byblos, she would arrive to find Danny. Being the simple girl she was, Greta would not be easily dissuaded that the man answering her knock was anyone other than Pat Lyons. Then she would become his brother's burden. If Danny objected, Greta would no doubt swear he was the Lyons wanted in Jefferson County. Or so Pat hoped.

Unfortunately, as he had explained that previous evening, Danny had no money to lend.

"Youse see, Pat, jus' dis mornin' a mad dog come up from da canal. He was slobberin', and yowlin', and scarin' everybodies. Den he comes up behin' ole Pete, da rag picker's nag. Pete jus' 'bout went mad hisself. Broke loose o'da halter. Den he bucked... an' ya knows what? He killt da hound! Well, alls da plungers in town put der last dime on 25-50-75. Dat's da gig for da name Pete, see. Well, jus' you guess wha' numbers come up.... Cleaned me out, Pat. I ain' got but two bits ta my name."

Pat was too well acquainted with his brother's gift for storytelling to believe his plea of poverty. But when Danny told him he could have the following day's take, he suppressed his incredulity.

The next morning, just after receiving a telephone call from a well-informed friend, Danny twisted his ankle. As an act of faith, he gave Pat instructions on making the afternoon rounds to collect the wagers. Later that evening, the number would be announced and they'd pay out the winners. Pat could have what remained for traveling money.

As Greta's train was speeding by Sing-Sing, and she and Jack were eating the last of their boiled eggs, Pat went off to make the rounds. He appreciated the opportunity his brother had given him in allowing him to make collections. But he had no intention of squandering it by paying off the winners. The pikers of Byblos would have to look after themselves. He'd be catching the first train north.

He'd just arrived at his final stop, a cigar store on Water Street, when someone tapped him on the shoulder from behind.

"Hello there, Danny."

Pat turned to find three strangers he knew at once to be plainclothes policemen. Assuming his brother had an ongoing arrangement with the local constabulary, he played it friendly.

"Hello, fellows. What's up?"

"Sorry, Danny. Got a warrant for you."

While one of the men slapped the bracelets on his wrists, and another searched him for weapons, Pat considered whether he should point out their error. He decided not. Facing a gambling charge as Danny seemed preferable to facing a grand larceny charge as Pat. And it also put him out of the reach of Greta.

As the prisoner was being led away, his brother received a phone call from the owner of the cigar store. The ruse had worked. His ankle now miraculously healed, Danny began packing a bag in expectation of leaving town later that night.

III

In room 312 of the Wahtawah County Courthouse, Arthur Biddle sat with his feet propped on a desk shelling peanuts and reading Hale's *Handbook on the Law of Torts*. Painted on the door's frosted glass were the words "Chief Investigator, Office of the District Attorney." But in his off-time, which he made certain ran to nearly all his time, Biddle was reading for the bar.

Fair-haired and tall when upright, Biddle had a deliberate, almost laconic, manner that belied an elevated self-confidence. Though not yet thirty, he'd had seven years' experience as a New York police detective when he decided to set out on a legal career. All he would need was an undemanding job and a member of the bar to mentor him.

These two items dropped in his lap when in the late summer

of 1902 the district attorney for Wahtawah County was found in a New York hotel room with a corpse, the late Mabel Kessler. Mabel, who was then appearing in the gypsy chorus of *The Bohemian Girl*, was known to have a strong, if irregular, voice. What hadn't been known until that night was that she had a weak and equally irregular heart. For Biddle, opportunity had knocked. An arrangement was made whereby the district attorney would have his name kept from the newspapers and Biddle his undemanding job and mentor.

Now, however, his reading was interrupted by a perfunctory—though quite literal—knock. A tentative young man entered the room. He handed Biddle a Postal Telegraph Co. envelope and, without uttering a word, sat down at another, smaller, desk. He was still feeling the sting of the last admonition.

Biddle glanced at the envelope and tossed it aside. "Everything go OK?" he asked.

"Seemed to." Two words. No one could call that gabby.

"What do you mean, seemed to?" Biddle queried, reluctantly.

"Well, we got him locked up. But Jeffers and Whitney, the two city men who went with me, they say something doesn't seem right. Danny Lyons didn't recognize either of 'em."

"Huh. But they recognized him?"

"Yeah. They were sure it was him."

Biddle went back to his reading. He'd been speaking with Michael Trim, the deputy he insisted on hiring when it seemed the routine tasks of his job might interfere with his studies. A year older than Biddle, but looking younger, Trim was the sort of naïf attracted to police work where opportunities for graft were limited. They'd been working together for just three weeks. But already Biddle had learned to take his loquacious deputy's frequent claims of inexplicable occurrences with generous helpings of salt.

This time, however, something nagged at him. He set down his book.

"He has a twin, you know."

"Who?" his deputy asked.

"Danny Lyons. Has a twin brother named Pat. I knew 'em in New York."

"So maybe we took in the wrong one?"

"Could be. But why wouldn't he have told you? Did he have anything with a name on it?"

"No, nothing."

"It seems to me there was only one way to tell them apart, something queer.... Send a wire to New York and ask for copies of the Bertillon cards for Danny and Pat Lyons."

Trim took a telegram blank from a drawer and began filling it out. Then stopped. "Pat Lyons. Didn't I come across that name before?" He began looking through the stacks of paper on his desk.

Biddle had just picked up his book when he was again interrupted.

"Here! There's a warrant out of Jefferson County for perpetrating a fraud, collecting money for a nonexistent charity, The Remember the Maine Widows and Orphans Relief Society."

Certain now he had his boss's attention, Trim set down the paper and looked wistfully at the blank wall before him.

"Remember the *Maine*.... Yes, I remember the *Maine*. How could I ever forget it? Men blown to bits, arms an' legs flying everywhere, heads torn right off of bodies. The air thick with the stench of burnt flesh. The whole of Havana harbor red with blood...."

"You were on the *Maine*?" Biddle asked.

"Me? No, I wasn't on it. But just the same, I remember it. I'll never forget remembering it."

Biddle shook his head and went back to his book.

But his deputy had barely gotten under way. "I was in the army. The 203rd New York Volunteers."

"Cuba?"

"No, only got as far as South Carolina. That took six months, and by then the fightin' in Cuba was over."

"Well, at least you all made it home." Biddle returned to his book.

"No, sir. Not all," his deputy said gravely. "Lost nineteen dead, altogether."

"Nineteen dead? In South Carolina? I thought that was ours...."

"Not *in* South Carolina, on the campaign down there. Lost most on Long Island, then a few more in Pennsylvania."

"Unfriendly locals?"

"Typhoid and malaria, mostly. Still, just as dead as the ones cut down at San Juan Hill.... Never knew Hell 'til I spent a rainy July on Long Island."

Biddle made a feint toward his book and Trim took his cue.

"Just the one wounded down in South Carolina.... Shot in a skirmish."

"Skirmish?"

"With the 2nd West Virginia. You see, our provost shot one of their fellows who was taking target practice at a tree beside our camp. When their boy died, they got irritated and came after one of ours."

"Kind of like the Hatfields and McCoys?" Biddle suggested.

"Yeah. But there wasn't much of that sort of trouble. The 203rd had a good record... mostly...."

The deputy seemed to trail off and Biddle went back to his book. But Michael Trim never left a tale partway told.

"Not more than fifty desertions in the whole time we were mustered...."

"Fifty?"

"Sixty, at most."

"Huh. Maybe you oughtta go send that wire?"

When the door closed, Biddle opened the envelope from the Postal Telegraph Co. and read:

Arrived noon Kronprinz Wilhelm
Morning train on third to Byblos

Biddle allowed himself a brief smile, then set down his law book and picked up a dog-eared copy of *The Taming of the Shrew*.

2

It was late on a pleasantly warm, summer-like evening when the express carrying our Greta pulled into Byblos. She and Jack followed the crowd out of the New York Central depot and onto the well-lit street.

"Cab, lady?" a friendly voice called down from his perch.

"No, we don' need no cab," Greta told him.

"Sure? That's a mighty big bag yer carryin'. An the boy's is bigger 'an he is."

"How far ta 410 Meeker Street?"

"Oh, three, four miles...."

"Cut it out, Murphy," a gruff voice called from behind.

Greta turned to find a beefy cop smiling down at her.

"Ain't more than five blocks, missus," he told her. "What's a matter with you, Murphy? Takin' advantage of a poor mother. Youse oughtta be ashamed."

"'Shamed? My wife's in the same condition, an' we got six more besides, an' I don't get a v-spot once a week from every saloon an' fast house on my beat, like some people...."

"Get outta here, or I'll take my stick to ya!"

The cabby drove off in retreat. But his reference to his antagonist's petty graft had hit home. The force's chivalric veneer could stand some burnishing.

"Here, now, I'll walk youse there myself, li'l lady."

He picked up Greta's bag, but was careful not to notice the larger one carried by Jack. A veneer can only stand for so much burnishing. As they walked, he tried to make conversation. But Greta, remembering the warrant out on Pat, played dumb.

She had a natural predisposition for playing dumb. Then Pat had suggested she cultivate the talent further when it became evident that each time she opened her mouth, collections for The

Remember the Maine Widows and Orphans Relief Society fell by thirty percent.

"You new to town?" the cop asked.

"Yeah."

"Come up from New York?"

"Yeah."

"Who you stayin' with?"

"Friend."

"Gotta name?"

"Me? Greta. Wha's yers?"

"Rhody. I meant, what's yer friend's name."

"Him?" Greta asked while nodding toward the boy following behind. "That's Jack. Say hi ta Rhody, Jack."

Jack answered with an unintelligible grunt, then spat on the sidewalk.

"Jack, huh? I'lls remember you, Jack." A fissure had broken through the veneer.

Nothing more was exchanged until they arrived at the small frame house.

"Hey, this's Danny Lyons' place."

"*Danny?*" Greta asked.

"Yeah. Youse won't find no one there, though. They took him away today."

"Who took him away?"

"Us did. The cops."

"I'm suppose' ta meet anutter friend here. Maybe it ain't locked."

They walked to the door and the cop opened it.

No doubt you remember, attentive reader, that it was not Danny the cops had in custody, but his twin brother, Pat. Danny had spent the evening in the darkened house working on a quart of rum while waiting to make a night-time getaway. On seeing the silhouette of a cop in his doorway, he crept further into the darkness.

"I'll be OK," Greta told the policeman. "Come on, Jack."

Jack pushed past them.

"Thanks, Rhody. I'll see ya around."

Greta closed the door just as Jack discovered the button for the overhead light.

"You hungry, Jack? I'm starvin'. Le's see what der is ta eat."

They found the kitchen light and made a brief inventory of the larder: a half bottle of rum, one of soured milk, a can of coffee, and a half dozen eggs.

"Eggs! Goddam, Jack, if I has ta eat another goddam egg I'll pull a croak. What wus that?"

Greta had been interrupted by a noise coming from below. Jack opened doors until he found the one leading to the basement.

The girl came up beside him and called down into the darkness, "That you, Pat? It's me, Greta."

There was another noise below and then a voice called up, "Hit da light, will ya?"

Greta found the button and a figure appeared at the bottom of the stairs.

"Da bull gone?"

"Yeah, he's gone."

As he climbed the stairs, Danny transformed himself into his brother Pat. This was not so simple a task as it might sound. Though nearly identical physically, Pat stood apart in having an acquaintance with the rudiments of the English language. After all, one can't captivate a hired hall's worth of gulls without a refined patter.

"My, my, Greta. Ain't you a sight for sore eyes? How long's it been?"

"How long's it been? Listen ta him, Jack. How long! I'll tell ya how long—a week since you went off—widout a word!"

"Oh, don't be angry, sweetums." Had Pat taken a wife and not told him? He gave her a peck on the cheek and turned to Jack. "An' how's junior?"

Jack looked up at Greta.

"Junior? Whattaya talkin' about, Pat?" she asked. "Dat's Jack."

"Sure, I know he's Jack. I meant the one in the oven, sweetums." He was tapping her belly now. "Say, sit down and let me pour ya a drink."

"No, I don' wanna drink. An' what's wit' dis sweetums?"

"I'm just so glad ta see ya, Greta, baby."

"Well, cut out da apple sauce. Yer makin' me sick. That cop tol' me Danny Lyons lived here. Who's he?"

"Danny's my brother. Da damn bulls pulled him in just a while ago. Dat's why I was hidin' in da cellar."

"Why di'n't ya e'en tell me where you was goin'?"

"Whatta ya mean? You're here, ain't ya?"

"Only cuz Gus felt sorry fer me an' give me da address."

"Why, I told him to give it to ya! What da hell's da matter with dat Gus? But that don't matter now. We oughtta celebrate. Sure you don't wanna drink?"

"What I needs is somethin' ta eat."

"Sure ya do. An how 'bout you, Jack? Rush da duck an' I'll annie up." He nodded toward a lidded pail on the counter. "Gallagher's is jus' two blocks down. An' ask 'em for a half dozen ham sandwiches, with lots of mustard...."

"No mustard," Greta corrected.

"All right, no mustard—but plenty a' pickle. Here's a plunk. You can keep what's left, Jack."

But the boy stood looking at him. Something wasn't right.

"Go on, Jack," Greta encouraged him. "I'm starvin'."

Jack picked up the pail and Danny walked him out to the street to point the way.

In the brief time he was out of the house, Greta opened her bag, unwrapped the love philtre, and topped off the bottle of rum. What had been a translucent golden liquor was now a murky brown cocktail. She'd just hidden the philtre when Danny returned.

"I think I'll have da drink now, Pat."

"Good for you, sweetums."

Danny picked up the bottle and held it to the light. Then he sniffed it and concluded Pat's wife had come to poison her husband. A search of her luggage would no doubt reveal a life insurance policy of recent vintage. He poured out two glasses and handed one to Greta.

"Here's to ya, sweetums!"

He waited while Greta took a sip then sprayed it out over her frock.

"Gee, sweetums. Maybe youse wanna clean up? Let me show you da bathroom. Got towels an' everything."

He led her to the tiny room and closed the door. Then tiptoed to the closet where he'd stashed his traveling bag.

II

It was after eleven when Danny arrived at the Water Street cigar store of his friend and confidant. The business was closed, but a good deal of thumping on the back door eventually brought the proprietor down from his second-floor apartment.

"Hey, Danny. I thought you'd a left town already."

"Dough up, Jess. Gimme what you took in today."

"Hell, Danny, I had to give it all back when there weren't no drawing."

"Ya give it back? Well, lend me a c-note."

"Don't have it, Danny. Took a big delivery today. Here, it's all I got."

"Twenty bucks? How far's dat gonna get me?"

"Sorry, Danny."

A voice called down from the apartment above.

"The wife. You better go, Danny, the neighbors are upstairs playin' cards. An' he's a cop."

Danny glared at him, then slunk off down the alley and took refuge in a tool shed. He needed time to think things through. He knew now that none of his associates were likely to come through with a loan of any size. A fellow on the lam is a poor credit risk. What he really needed was a bankroll large enough to start over in a new town—preferably in another state.

Outside of the banks, there was only one stash in Byblos of

sufficient depth. Timothy Dexter's—the local tycoon who had a well-known contempt for banks. Danny had it on good authority that Dexter kept stacks of hundred-dollar bills hidden in an office of his hotel. The only thing that kept others from raiding his cashbox was the fact that the old hawk was known to sleep with a shotgun. And he had a hair trigger, as the fellow who'd been painting the porch outside the office had learned the year before. But Danny happened to know that at that moment Dexter was in London.

The hotel was situated on a corner in what years before had been one of the choicer neighborhoods of Byblos. The building formed an L, with the smaller wing used by the family. Danny had been told previously which of the second-floor windows was that of the office and he climbed up to the porch outside it.

The window had been conveniently left open. Danny slid inside and was about to strike a match when from out of the darkness came a voice.

"Is that you, Arthur?"

Danny froze. His unseen companion repeated her question.

"Sure it's me, who'd ya think?"

"Why'd you come in the window? So Mother wouldn't hear?"

"Yeah, dat's right."

"Well, come to me now.... I'm ready...."

The voice had taken on a sultry quality that Danny found well-nigh irresistible. He inched toward it. Then when the invisible Lorelei reached out her hand, he took it, and willingly grounded himself on her not-so-rocky shoals.

The siren's Christian name was Felicia. She was the daughter of Timothy Dexter, and had been eagerly awaiting the arrival of her fiancé, Arthur Biddle. It was a match her father opposed, and it was her plan to force the issue by allowing herself to be compromised before his return.

But Biddle, who lived at the hotel, had come in late and then been waylaid by Mrs. Dexter. Her mother had discovered Felicia's plan and was determined to thwart it. She was sitting on the first-floor porch sipping brandy when he arrived.

"Do stop and have a drink with me, Mr. Biddle."

"Sure."

"Beautiful night, isn't it?"

"Yeah, I guess it is."

That was the extent of their conversation until just after their third brandy together, when a noise came from above.

"It's those blasted raccoons, running about on the porch," Mrs. Dexter told her guest.

"Seem to have gone now."

"Yes, thank goodness. Have another brandy, Mr. Biddle."

"Don't mind if I do. By the way, I'll be moving out tomorrow."

"You're leaving us?"

"Yeah, seems people talk, what with us being engaged and sleeping under the same roof."

"Yes, it probably would be for the best. Have another brandy."

They were sipping silently when an eerie mewing came from above. This was followed by a most singular high-pitched chittering. Rhythmically syncopated and melodically repetitive, it gradually swelled into a climactic crescendo of sharp, breathless yelps.

"Baby raccoons," Mrs. Dexter pronounced.

"Baby raccoons?"

"Yes, they make the most atrocious noise. Frightening, isn't it?"

"Sure is. How about another brandy, Mrs. Dexter?"

III

About noon the next day, Timothy Dexter could be found in the smoking car of the Empire State Express dictating a letter to his recently acquired Polish secretary, Tomasz Szczęsny.

"The Kaiser, Wilhelm the Second, his palace, Berlin. Dear Cousin..."

"Cousin?" Tomasz queried.

"That's just how we nobles talk to each other. Dear Cousin, was riding one of your boats last week, the one named for your boy, and lost a pair of silver cuff links—dills, not sweet. I'm chagrined, Billy, and I don't mind saying so. Have your people check the seat cushions. And then have someone check their pockets. I won't tell you how to run your business, Billy, but you've got some shifty-looking birds sailing that boat. Keep an eye on them. Yours fraternally, Lord Timothy Dexter."

Tomasz had given up trying to make sense of his employer's correspondence several days before, when he'd taken a letter instructing a tailor to prepare an admiral's uniform of peculiar design.

A waiter approached. "Time for one last drink before Byblos, gentlemen."

"Then make it a double," Lord Dexter told him.

"None for me, thank you."

"Give him the same. Hell, boy, you can't meet the wife and daughter without a snort."

Tomasz couldn't help but notice that the nearer they came to Byblos, the more subdued became Lord Dexter's snow-white eyebrows. The formerly playful appendages looked today like a pair of leaden storm clouds.

Elsewhere on the Empire State Express were the two other members of Lord Dexter's entourage. Lady Eleanor Marsouin, Duchess of Aquatique and theosopher to the court of Lord Dexter, was in a coach three cars ahead giving instructions to her retainer, Mélisande. Sleeping between them—apparently weaned of her need for the sound of leaky plumbing—was the duchess's child, Eugenia.

"Remember, stay out of sight of the others. I don't want them to see you, or the baby. Here's ten dollars. That's enough to get to a hotel and settle in. A cab driver should be able to recommend one. Check in under your own name, but as *Madame Bodel*. Let them assume the baby is yours. As soon as you have a room, send a message to me at Dexter's hotel."

"Which *you?*" the girl asked in her thick French accent. "You

Lady Eleanor, Miss Duncan... or Mrs. Biddle?"

"For now, I'm Lady Eleanor."

Meanwhile, in the parlor car, his lordship's English valet, one Archie Cobb, picked up an overstuffed wallet from the floor. He stopped the man who'd just passed him and enquired if it was he who had dropped it.

"No," he said, checking his pocket. "I have mine."

"That's too bad. There's $1,300 here." Archie quickly fanned the banknotes.

"$1,300? That *is* a lot of money."

"Well, no way to catch the owner now—let's see where he lives.... Here's something, a letter. Lives in Detroit."

"I'm going to Detroit!"

"My, now that *is* a coincidence."

In fact, it was no coincidence. Archie had chosen his mark carefully. The man he was speaking with was a Dutch business-man going to Detroit whose gullibility Archie had verified earlier in the trip when he claimed ownership of the New York Central Railroad.

"I need to get off at this stop," Archie told him. "But if you were to bring this to the gentleman in Detroit, I imagine he'd be very generous with you. Give you a big reward. And, if you couldn't locate him, well...."

"Yes, yes. I would be honored to bring the gentleman his wallet."

"Of course, I wouldn't be around to get my share in the... ah... reward. Doesn't seem fair, really, does it?"

"I could mail it to you?"

"I'll tell you what, how about you advance me $100 of your own money, and I'll renounce all claim to the... a... reward. Then it's in your hands to do what you think best."

The train had arrived at the depot and Archie still held the wallet. He fanned the banknotes again.

"Yes, yes." The Dutchman took out his wallet and handed Archie a crisp one-hundred-dollar bill—agreeably green, and not at all apricot-toned like those contained in the overstuffed wallet.

Archie gave him the wallet, tipped his hat, and disembarked.

On the platform, Lord Dexter approached him.

"Now, don't forget. From here on in, you're Lord Archibald, Viscount of Abernasty."

"The proper title is Lord *Abernethy*, Your Lordship."

"Just make sure you convince my wife of it. And you better leave off calling me lordship. We're equals now."

By then, Mélisande was already outside the station with the baby in her arms and a porter just behind.

"Cab, lady?" a friendly voice called down from his perch.

"I need to find a *good* hotel."

"Just how good, ma'am?"

"One with a bathroom."

"Got just the place. Hot water in every room."

"OK," Mélisande said as she got in the cab and her bags were loaded. "But we must hurry."

"Go as fast as we can, ma'am, but you won't find the good hotels near the depot. Not with all the noise an' smoke."

"Yes, yes. Just go...."

As the cab pulled from the curb, Mélisande exchanged glances with Tomasz. He and the others had just emerged from the depot.

"Lady Eleanor, wasn't that your friend leaving with her baby?"

"I'm afraid you're mistaken, Mr. Szczęsny. As I told you before, she has gone home."

"Yes. To Pittsbourg, Philadelphia. But that lady looked very much like her."

Under the watchful eye of the chief investigator for the Wahtawah County district attorney, observing from a barber shop across the street, Lord Dexter led his party past the cabs to a wagon outfitted with cushioned seating and topped with a fringed and tasseled awning. His wife—a normally sprightly woman, but today feeling the effects of too much brandy and a restless night spent listening to baby raccoons—climbed down and greeted him.

"My missus," Dexter announced without enthusiasm. "Goes

by Tillie. An' this is Lady Eleanor. I've given her the job of court theosophier."

"I'm very pleased to meet you, Lady Eleanor. I myself am a theosophist."

"How delightful. Then we shall have much to talk about."

"And here's that lord I promised you. Lord Archibald, Viscount of Abernasty."

"Abernethy," Archie corrected while tipping his hat. "I had no idea Lord Dexter had such a young and charming wife. I thought as we approached, there must be the fair Felicia."

"Oh, thank you, Lord Archibald. Felicia woke exhausted for some reason, so I let her wait for us at the hotel. Timothy, you haven't taken to calling yourself a lord again, have you?"

"Why the hell shouldn't I? I come by it as honestly as Lord Archibald here."

"So right," Archie swiftly agreed. "After all, virtue is the only true nobility."

"That's very tolerant of you, Lord Archibald," Tillie told him.

"And this here is Tommy, my secretary. See to the luggage, boy, and you can meet us at home. Tell the driver to get you to Dexter's Hotel and Sanatorium."

"Just Hotel," his wife corrected as the wagon left the depot. "I'm afraid the Sanatorium idea didn't take. That Dr. Kretschmer you hired left us. Along with the silver."

"Damn him! Well, I'll find a new quack. Hell, he was nothing but a horse doctor."

"I don't think that will be necessary. What with the deaths, all the patients have left as well."

"What deaths?"

"Mrs. Bently was drowned taking the water cure, and just a day later, Mr. Carbody choked to death on cook's pudding."

The Viscount of Abernethy caught the eye of the Duchess of Aquatique sitting across from him. He felt uneasy. And her impish grin did nothing to relieve his apprehension.

By now, Mélisande's driver had brought her to the outskirts

of Byblos proper and was looping back into the commercial district on a parallel street. When he saw that both she and her baby were sleeping soundly, he pulled up outside Dwyer's saloon. There was no sense exhausting the mare making endless circuits of the city for the benefit of a sleeping fare.

An hour later, they arrived at the Baggs Hotel. The driver gently shook Mélisande awake, then carried the luggage inside while she followed with the baby.

"That'll be ten dollars, lady."

"Ten dollars? Why is everything so expensive here?"

"Talk to Mr. Roosevelt."

Mélisande held out the ten-dollar bill her employer had given her two hours before. It disappeared in an instant. The Murpheys would not be eating pot pie tonight.

"No tip?" he asked

"*Quelle absurdité!*" She handed him a ten-centime piece, then checked in with the desk clerk.

The driver was still examining the coin when the bellboy took her to her room.

"No pleasing some people," he told the clerk. "Where's my dollar, Jim?"

The clerk pulled a bill from the stack reserved for greasing the palms of cabbies, then offered a wry commentary on the other's business practices. Sadly, as so frequently happened, his best line was lost in a thunderous rumble. The 2:25 from Albany was pulling into the depot half a block away.

A Taste of Biddle

Before continuing with the story proper, I thought I might provide you a sample from Mrs. Biddle's private journal. It will serve the dual purpose of supplementing your familiarity with the city of Byblos and demonstrating the pomposity of her prose. This is the entry dated June 3rd, 1903:

Byblos. May's mud warmed over and Lord Dexter sitting in his wagonette. Unrelenting June weather. As much dust in the streets as in those of long-buried Samarkand, and it would not be wonderful to meet a Bactrian camel towing a canal boat through the dirt-brown waters of the Erie as it bisects the town. Black dust spewed from factories' stacks, grey dust blown from vacant lots, and dung dust dropped by ten hundred horses.

Sun everywhere. Sun up the avenue, where it infiltrates the household and fades the curtains; sun down the avenue, where it peeks into the office and market, forcing an impertinent illumination on the commerce of a mediocre (yet corrupt) city. Sun on the Mohican River, sun on the farms lining its valley. Sun creeping into the cabooses of the freight trains, sun lying out in the rail yards. Sun cruelly piercing the late-rising vaude-villian's lingering inebriation as he stumbles his way to the theatre, which offers a continuous show at ten, twenty, and thirty cents a seat.

The warm afternoon is warmest, and the bright sun bright-est, and the dust-filled streets dustiest near that limestone cita-del of justice, the Wahtawah County Courthouse, at the very heart of which sits the presiding judge of the Court of Special Sessions.

Who happens to be in the judge's court this balmy after-noon? The corporation counsel, defending the city of Byblos against Lord Dexter's suit questioning the accuracy of the city's valuation of a former canal bed which came into his lordship's possession some dozen years before. The suit, brought almost as long ago, has been lost by the plaintiff time and time again, only to be revived via obscure legal loophole.

Dexter v. Byblos drones on. The city wishes it ended. The judge wishes it ended. Even Dexter's counsel wishes it ended. But like so many others, the scarecrow of a suit will not end. Not so long as a nation affords its feebleminded access to its courts.

It is but a glimpse of Dexter's notion of architecture that we want on this same afternoon. But an eyeful we will have. His eponymous hotel and erstwhile sanatorium seems built in fits and starts, each segment in a style independent to itself. One stone, two brick, three clapboard; one underway and one in ruin. Down one street and up another it oozes, submerging inoffensive cottages in a magma of aesthetic dissonance, as the molten vulgarity solidifies into perpetual deformity.

Clever and amusing, perhaps. But its haughtiness, like that of its author, becomes tiresome ere long. Now let us return to the story as properly rendered....

3

After giving her noble guests time to refresh, Tillie Dexter served a well-provisioned tea in the hotel's skylighted palm court. It was only Lord Abernethy and Lady Eleanor who joined her in the cavernous room used solely on days free of precipitation. Lord Dexter himself was off acquainting his new secretary with his novel system of bookkeeping, which incorporated attributes of both accounting and astrology with scrupulous impartiality.

On rainy days the palm court's skylight had a tendency to leak. So heavily, in fact, that it was necessary to have a graveled drainage trench cut across the terrazzo floor. This room, like much of the hotel, was the design of Lord Dexter's former architect and poet laureate, a man named Dempsey, who'd been a canal mule driver before meeting Lord Dexter and was now comfortably ensconced writing doggerel for the *New York Journal*.

Mrs. Dexter was quite pleased to be hosting the pair of aristocrats. Lady Eleanor, a paragon of poise and grace, would provide just the sort of model her daughter was in need of. And though she would have preferred Lord Abernethy a little younger and more fully hirsute, she was not as ready as her husband to write him off as a prospective son-in-law.

"More tea, Lady Eleanor?"

"No, thank you."

"By the way, a boy brought a letter for you." Tillie handed her an envelope and Mrs. Biddle put it aside without looking at it. "Do you have friends in Byblos?"

"Acquaintances."

"Lord Abernethy? More tea?"

"I wonder if that's a decanter of sherry on the sideboard?" After three visits to the buffet, Archie Cobb felt in need of a digestive.

"Yes, of course. I should have offered it sooner. Lady Eleanor, will you join us?"

"Yes, sounds delightful."

"Allow me." Archie served the ladies two of the dainty glasses found beside the decanter, then emptied a water goblet into the graveled trench for himself.

Mrs. Dexter sighed inaudibly, a technique she had mastered during the long residency of Mr. Dempsey. Why was it all her husband's guests, even those who didn't know one end of a canal mule from another, must drink so heavily? She would need to reserve judgment on the matter of the viscount's suitability as suitor. Perhaps the soon-to-be-divorced Arthur Biddle wasn't so flawed a choice after all. He seemed reasonably honest. And it would mean not having to cross her headstrong daughter. If only she could be sure the penchant for brandy he'd displayed the night before wasn't a habit.

At twenty minutes past three, Felicia made her entrance. She first sighted Lord Abernethy, and was both disappointed and comforted to find him just the sort of aristocrat her father could be expected to show up with. Comforted that he'd be easily worked, disappointed that it would hardly be worth the effort.

Archie rose and made a slight bow as her mother made introductions. Then, after she and Lady Eleanor had exchanged superficial greetings, Felicia slumped onto a settee an awkward distance from the others and asked vaguely for a sherry.

While Archie obliged, the duchess entered into conversation with the girl.

"Your father has told me a great deal about you."

Felicia's response was more a challenge than a question. "What, for instance?"

"Well... your plans to marry."

"They're further along than he suspects."

She was not the rival Mrs. Biddle had envisaged. She had imagined Biddle enamored of a woman like herself—handsome, dynamic, and rational. And she was confident no woman could approach her on those terms. But Felicia Dexter was something else entirely.

Measured objectively, it was no contest. Lady Eleanor was a

statuesque beauty who spoke four languages fluently. Felicia Dexter was a plump girl who spoke through her nose. Mrs. Biddle was fair and blonde, Miss Dexter ruddy, with dark, oily hair. While the one had studied art and philosophy, the other was a study in lethargy.

Yet as the afternoon progressed, Mrs. Biddle found herself feeling uneasy. Whatever her faults, Felicia was—damn her—a very attractive girl. What's more, her greatest assets were the very qualities Mrs. Biddle lacked most. And she knew how to display them to advantage. The casual house gown she wore was carefully chosen to accentuate her voluptuous figure. As was her suggestive gait.

She swept the floor with her skirt before sitting down, and in pulling her bare feet up onto the couch, managed to expose one of her shapely legs well past the line of decency and almost to her knee. She then pushed the skirt partway down with a languid movement of her plump hand, doing more to draw attention to the exposed flesh than to conceal it.

Most disturbing of all, what would be seen as flaws in others—the glistening face, the over-large and somewhat asymmetrical lips—only served to enhance her sensuality. And for a girl who hadn't slept well, her face seemed unusually radiant. Or was it due to *not* having slept....

"Mr. Biddle, Felicia's intended, met her while boarding with us," Mrs. Dexter explained. "He was the last of our guests—paying guests, I mean. He just moved out this morning."

"He did?" Her daughter seemed surprised. "He didn't mention it when he left...."

"Told me last night. He thought it best now that you're engaged. And I quite agree. That reminds me, I must remember to tell Timothy to do something about those raccoons. They must have a nest up in the attic. Their babies' squealing went on all night."

When she imitated their various vocalizations for the edification of her European guests, her daughter's face turned a color not unlike that of the amontillado which then slipped from her hand. The shattering of cut glass on terrazzo drew the attention of the others and Mrs. Biddle now made the same assumption Felicia herself had the night before.

"I've invited him to dinner," Tillie went on. "Mr. Biddle, I mean."

It was Felicia who was now feeling uneasy. She had little trouble competing with the other young women of Byblos. But the specimen sharing the sherry that afternoon was a different matter. It wasn't simply that she was handsomer, and more learned, and fairer complexioned. She was all those things. But even more provoking was her knack for undermining witticisms with well-timed gestures. Among the Byblos push—the city's patrician youth she ruled as queen—Felicia had turned her lack of learning into a source of humor, deliberately and extravagantly mispronouncing words she was unsure of, and interposing slang to hide grammatical uncertainty. But what she felt her finest quip of the afternoon—a suggestive pun involving the Persian kitten which had sidled into the room and rubbed against Lord Abernethy's leg—was addressed to the back of the duchess's head as Lady Eleanor pretended to check her hair in a hand mirror.

II

At that same moment, and some two dozen blocks away, Michael Trim was performing his primary afternoon duty of leaving his superior in peace. This he accomplished by wandering about the courthouse looking for others in need of conversation and providing it. Today, he was entertaining the doorman with a riveting account of a daytrip to Albany he'd taken some years earlier with the purpose of visiting his Great-Aunt Aurelia. He'd just reached the threshold of the tale's dramatic climax and had paused to heighten his audience's anticipation when the postman arrived with the afternoon mail.

"Thick envelope from New York for you."

The deputy investigator took possession of the correspondence and then turned back to the doorman. He had just explained how he'd misplaced his return ticket and given a detailed description of the fruitless search which ensued. But the ill-timed interruption had broken the spell.

"I bet it was in your cuff," the other said. "I'm always tucking things in my cuff and forgetting about them."

The thwarted raconteur confirmed the doorman's supposition with a single syllable, then retreated upstairs to his office. An irritated Arthur Biddle looked up from his reading.

"What?" he asked.

"From New York. The Bertolli cards for the Lyons brothers."

"*Bertillon,*" his superior corrected. "Skip all the measurements and look at the remarks."

"Pat's says: *Identical twin of Daniel Lyons. Sole distinguishing feature: omp... halos... protruding.*"

"Let me see it." Biddle took possession of the card and clarified the pronunciation. "Om*phal*os protruding."

"What's it mean?"

"Beats me. What's Danny's say?"

"Same, only om*phal*os depressed. It doesn't mean...?" Trim trailed off, looking at his lap.

"Jeez, I hope not. Who's the doctor they use at the jail?"

"Dr. VanLengen."

"Take the cards by his place. He ought to know his anatomy."

The dutiful deputy was waiting in the doctor's outer office when he lapsed into one of his frequent daydreams. There was a strong thematic consistency to Michael Trim's daydreams. In them, he was prone to acts of chivalry. Malefactors were vanquished, wrongs were made right, and, before long, a comely maiden was offering herself freely in undying gratitude.

He could see himself now bringing the charlatan Pat Lyons to justice and forcing him to disgorge the many thousands of dollars accumulated through his fraudulent charity. Afterward, he would see that the money was distributed to the deserving widows of the lost men of the *Maine*, and, of course, their equally deserving orphaned children. One of the latter—a girl of thirteen when news of her father's fate had arrived, but now a ripe eighteen, not stunningly attractive, but, in her own way, winsome—

"The doctor will see you now."

The deputy took in the cards and handed them to Dr. VanLengen.

"What's this om*phalos* they're talking about?" he asked.

"Pull up your shirt."

"Oh, I'm all right."

The doctor pulled up Trim's shirt and stuck a finger in his navel.

"Your omphalos is depressed. So is mine. So are most people's." The doctor opened the door and called in his wife. "Pull up your waist, dear."

"What? Why ever..."

"Pull up your shirtwaist. Just enough to show the man your navel."

Mrs. VanLengen, well used to the many impositions made on a physician's wife, sighed deeply and complied.

"Omphalos protruding," her husband announced.

"Doctor! Come quick!"

Much to Mrs. VanLengen's chagrin, a second woman had entered the room and was now staring at her protruding omphalos.

"What is it?" the doctor asked.

"Woman... having a baby," the breathless newcomer informed him.

As the doctor picked up his bag, his wife stopped him.

"Dear, don't let the child become an object of curiosity. Make it a proper bellybutton."

As they trotted along Meeker Street, the doctor inquired of the messenger, "One of yours?"

"No. Not one of *mine*."

But the doctor's question was a fair one, for he knew Jane Jebril to be the proprietress of a disorderly house she operated under the trade name of Madame de Trottoir.

"Found her in the house I was renting to Danny Lyons. The cops took him in, so I went by to check on it."

When they entered the house, they found Greta lying on the couch and doing vocal impressions of an acutely annoyed banshee. Her contractions had commenced and Jack was having second thoughts about agreeing to hold her hand. So tightly was she clutching his, it had long since turned blue, and would likely end up amputated once the gangrene set in. Not once, but twice, she'd swung her arm with such implausible strength he'd collided with a nearby coal stove. There was no question but that the boy was in above his weight class.

The doctor took verbal control of the situation, sending Jane to the kitchen to boil water and offering Greta encouragement.

"I see him. He's headed in the right direction," he told her. "Keep pushing."

A minute later, Greta's son began to emerge, and, seconds after that, was found instead to be her daughter. At the doctor's slap, she wailed, and at long last Greta released Jack's numbed hand.

Soon after the proper omphalos had been tied, mother and daughter were lost to slumber.

"I don't know what to do with them," Jane confided to the doctor.

"Where'd you come from, son?" he asked Jack.

"Brooklyn. Come ta find Pat Lyons."

"Danny's brother?" Jane asked.

"Yeah. He skipped on us 'gain."

Jane accompanied the doctor outside.

"I guess I'm stuck with them. And of course she's broke."

"How do you know that?" he asked.

She looked at him, incredulous. "How do you think? I looked through her things. I'm not runnin' a charity hospital for lyin'-in."

"Give her a week."

"All right. Then it's off to the county poorhouse."

"Might be something better.... There're always people in need of a wet nurse."

"Paying what?"

"Oh, if they're well-to-do, and they usually are, maybe five dollars a week. I knew one family who paid ten."

Jane Jebril saw an opportunity. "How do I find these people?"

"Put an ad in the newspaper."

"What time is it?"

The doctor pulled out his watch. "Just after five."

"Still time to get it in the morning editions."

When she left, the doctor went inside and handed Jack four bits.

"Get your mother some milk, son. And eggs. Just what she needs to get her strength back."

III

At the Wahtawah County Jail, a little further out Meeker Street from the nativity portrayed above, Michael Trim finished his examination of the prisoner whose name had been entered as Danny Lyons. As soon as he was asked to pull up his shirt, Pat knew he'd been found out. There's no simple way of hiding a protruding omphalos.

When his deputy returned to the office to report the outcome, Biddle at last gave him the slap on the back he'd been craving.

"So you caught him? That's a big win for you. Means a trip to Watertown."

"Watertown?"

"Jefferson County seat. Someone has to escort Lyons up there. Means a night in a hotel, steak dinner. Tastes better when it's paid for by the county." Biddle's seeming enthusiasm stemmed from his expectation of two days of silent study. "Go wire the district attorney up there. Tell him you'll leave here tomorrow."

Biddle picked up his book, only to be interrupted by the phone. It was Felicia calling.

"Is it you, Arthur?" Her telephone voice was too lacking in

modulation to be called mellifluous. But just the same, the words came out slow and sticky.

"Yeah, it's me."

"I just wanted to tell you, it really wouldn't be a good idea for you to come to dinner tonight."

"Wouldn't have been able to make it, anyway."

"Well, how about later.... It's awfully warm.... My window will be open again...."

Biddle smiled. "We'll see. Gotta go now."

He hung up the phone and returned to his book.

Early that evening, while Mrs. VanLengen carried a covered pail of stew to the new mother on Meeker Street, Lord Dexter met in his office with his court theosopher. He was explaining over cocktails the salient points of law touched on by his suit against the City of Byblos, making frequent, if misbegotten, reference to the Magna Carta, the Mayflower Compact, and the novels of James Fenimore Cooper. By the time the excruciating ordeal was over, Mrs. Biddle had drained three juleps and knew only that it involved a property tax dispute on a former canal bed his lordship had won in a crooked faro game he'd hosted back when his hotel was known as the Dexter Casino.

"In a contest such as this," she advised, "one must make clear to one's opponents the costs involved."

"Costs? Hell, I've cost the city more than they could hope to gain in a year of Sundays. It's that damned alderman, O'Hearn. Runs the machine. Our Tammany Hall. Bleed the rich man! That's his cry."

"I see. Well, there's only one way of handling a man who won't see reason."

"What's that?"

"Voodoo."

Since his return to Byblos and the weighing concerns of both his public and his private lives, Lord Dexter's eyebrows had sat limp upon his forehead. But with this single word came revival.

"New Orleans hoodoo?" he inquired from below mischievously arched tussocks of snow-white thatch.

"Yes, I was taught it as a child by my devoted mammy."

"What's it take?"

"A clump of beeswax to form into the alderman's likeness, and a knowledge of incantations. You may leave it to me."

She left her sponsor and went off to confer with his wife. Still under the impression that Arthur Biddle would be attending dinner that evening, Lady Eleanor asked that a tray be sent to her room. She would need to keep out of view as much as possible, and most particularly that of her husband.

Later, when the others were digesting their meal on the broad porch, Mrs. Biddle slipped out the back entrance and down the alley. A block from the hotel she boarded a streetcar bound for the center of town. When she disembarked, she instinctively looked over her shoulder. She'd been followed.

Realizing he'd been spotted, Tomasz Szczęsny sheepishly approached.

"Lady Eleanor, forgive me. It was only that I was worried for you."

"In the future, I hope you will express your concern in a more forthright manner."

"Yes, yes. You have my word. But where is it you go off to at this hour?"

"That I can't tell you. At least, not for now."

"Are you still in danger? Is it that Oskar, the assassin?"

"I'm always in danger. Whether he is still on my trail, I can't say. But there is another. A man who poses as a policeman here in Byblos. His name is Arthur Biddle."

"Miss Dexter's fiancé?"

"Yes. Learn what you can about him. Visit some barrooms— you'll be sure to find someone who knows him. Then see where he spends the night."

"I need to watch him *all night*?"

"No... No, I ask too much of you...."

"Certainly not! I would be honored to watch this Biddle for you."

"Then, go now."

When she was sure he was out of sight, Mrs. Biddle entered the Baggs Hotel and found Mélisande in her room waiting impatiently.

"Madame, I cannot be locked up in a hotel night and day."

"All right. But whenever you go out, you'll need to take the baby."

"The baby, the baby... You know I love my little sister, but there are times...."

"Don't forget the five hundred dollars."

"Oh, I've not forgotten that. Still...," she shrugged.

"It isn't an ideal arrangement, I know. What we need is a wet nurse... *une nourrice*."

"Ah, *abéqueuse*. Where do we find this *wet* nurse?"

"Check the newspapers. And also look into renting an apartment. I'll give you another thirty dollars."

"You better make it fifty, money goes so fast here."

Early the next morning, Mrs. Biddle returned to her room at the Dexter Hotel. She'd just fallen asleep when she was woken by the tell-tale squeals of baby raccoons. Still under the misapprehension that it was her estranged husband enjoying the favors of the boisterous Felicia, she added them both to the forthcoming congress of wax figurines.

But Arthur Biddle was not with Lord Dexter's daughter. He had rented the second floor of a house catty-corner to the hotel and was sitting on the dark porch observing. He had been surprised to see his estranged wife disembark from a streetcar at one a.m., and spent most of an hour musing on what sort of business she'd been conducting. He was less surprised when at two a.m. he saw a man shimmying up to the porch outside Felicia's room.

A dog barked and the man turned, his face now illuminated by a street lamp. Though he hadn't seen either of them since his time in New York, Biddle recognized him as one of the Lyons brothers. And though his omphalos was concealed, the chief investigator deduced it was Danny, as he knew Pat to be safely behind bars.

4

Mrs. Biddle was just finishing her morning toilette when she was summoned to her door by a tentative knock. She was neither looking nor feeling her best, her sleep having been disturbed by the nocturnal behavior of certain other of the hotel's inmates. But she took solace when on opening the door she found Tomasz Szczęsny looking much the worse. His rumpled jacket was soiled, his damp hair awry, and a colorful bruise was forming on his right cheek.

"May I assume you found Biddle?" she asked. "Where did he spend the night?"

"No, Lady Eleanor. I never found this Biddle."

"You'd better come in." She dampened a towel at the wash-stand and handed it to him. "Hold it to your cheek. And tell me what transpired."

"I did as you suggested. I went into a barroom and asked about Biddle. A man told me he thought he lived here, at Lord Dexter's hotel. So I tried another barroom, and another. There, in the third, I met a fellow countryman. He insisted I drink with him. Many drinks later, I went to another barroom and asked again about Biddle. A man offered to take me to him. When we got outside, he led me into an alley...."

"Yes, I think I know the rest. He knocked you out and took your money."

"I am sorry that I failed you. But do not fear, I will try again."

"I believe he works out of the courthouse. Perhaps you can follow him when he leaves this evening."

"That would seem a much safer course."

"Now let's see what they're offering for breakfast."

Mrs. Biddle opened the door and Tomasz preceded her into the hall.

There were two witnesses to their exit. A shotgun-wielding Lord Dexter had just come down from the attic after a vain search for nesting raccoons. On seeing his depleted secretary in the company of his sleepy-eyed theosopher, he concluded that the night's disturbance would need no further explanation. And his Rabelaisian eyebrows—assuming Tomasz's bruised cheek the result of spirited play in the bedroom—concurred. They exchanged a long succession of knowing nods and insinuating wags.

At the other end of the hall, Mrs. Dexter had just come upstairs to ensure that Lady Eleanor had everything she required. Tillie was a far more conventional sort than her husband, and especially his eyebrows. Nonetheless, she reached a similar conclusion. Her half-uttered greeting was quickly swallowed in embarrassment as she scurried off to the dining room.

A few moments later, Lord Dexter entered with Lady Eleanor on his left arm and the shotgun under his right. The fetching duchess had risen in his estimation. From the very first, her beauty and attentions had charmed and flattered him. But below the surface? Cold steel. This display of warm-blooded wantonness provided a welcome refutation.

When it became obvious that Tomasz would not be attending the breakfast table, Tillie took a tray up to his room, where she ministered to him both spiritually and bodily. She now saw in the boy something she'd not noticed on meeting him, and was more charmed than vexed by his protests of innocence as she dabbed his swollen face with ointment.

It was afternoon by the time Michael Trim had completed preparations for his excursion to Watertown, some four hours to the north by train. He was relieved to find that Pat Lyons had resigned himself to his fate, even making light of his predicament by asking to borrow a pen knife so as to emend his protruding omphalos.

"Too late for that, my friend," Trim told him. "Now we'd better be on our way—it's a long walk to the depot."

A teamster leaving the jail overheard their conversation.

"I'm headed that way. Hop on, if ya want."

Trim was hesitant. The jail breaks he'd read about in the nickel magazines nearly always involved a confederate who'd come on the scene to apparent innocent purpose.

"Why not?" Pat coaxed. "Save some wear on the feet. And we'll be sure to catch that train."

Trim looked at his watch. Though there was still thirty minutes before the 1:20 departure, he was by temperament a man compulsively early. He checked his pocket for the revolver Biddle had trusted him with. Then, awkwardly, the handcuffed pair boarded the wagon.

"Sit up front," Pat offered. "I'll squat down behind you."

Trim looked at him suspiciously. "That's all right. We can both ride in the back."

They'd gone barely a block before the deputy investigator had relaxed enough to launch into a recollection the situation reminded him of. Back in '88 (or was it '89?), he had accompanied his father on a two-day (more or less) trek to the county fair, where their prized (but, due solely to the crooked judging, never prize-winning) steers were entered in the ox pull.

"Poor bastards," Pat interjected.

"How do you mean?"

"No one deserves to be treated like that."

"Like what? My father loved them, like... like sons."

"Yeah? He castrate you, too?"

"Pat? Is dat you?" A small boy was trotting beside the wagon.

"Jack! When'd you get here?"

"Day 'for yes'ta'day. Greta had da baby, Pat."

"Where is she?"

"Yer place."

Jack ran off and into the house a block away. By the time the wagon caught up, Greta was standing in the door holding her baby.

"Whoa!" Pat commanded. "We have to stop, Deputy. You can't take me away without lettin' me see my newborn kid."

Trim looked over at the haggard girl holding the baby. She

seemed nothing at all like the conspiratorial molls of the nickel magazines.

Greta faltered, and Jack led her back into the house.

"Let him see the kid," the teamster said. "I'll wait for ya."

Trim climbed down with his prisoner and then had him lead the way into the house. His hand clutched the revolver in the pocket of his jacket.

They found Greta on the couch.

"Sit down, Pat. An' hol' yer daughter."

The deputy nodded and then moved beside the couch so Pat could sit beside her. Gingerly, Greta handed over the baby.

"Ain't she a beaut?" Pat asked. "What're we callin' her?"

"Gretchen."

"Little Greta, now ain't that sweet."

Jack arrived from the kitchen with a glass of milk. While his keeper watched the woman sip it, Pat swung his arm in a way similar to how Greta had during the birthing scene. But where Jack had managed to avoid being knocked out by the iron stove, Michael Trim was not so lucky.

Pat handed the baby back to Greta and the glass fell to the floor.

"Help me find the key, Jack."

Jack found it in a shirt pocket and removed the handcuffs. A second later, Pat had unearthed the deputy's wallet and was counting the bills when it came to his attention that Jack had discovered the gun.

"Give it to me, Jack."

"Nit. Youse hand over."

"There's only twenty-five bucks, Jack. I need it ta get away."

"Youse better get. Da driver will be comin' in. Leave da green."

Pat dropped all but a five-dollar bill.

"OK," Jack acquiesced. "Now beat it."

Pat stopped to look down at the olive-toned baby.

"Chenango Forks, my ass! It was that Cuban sailor you were with the night I met ya."

"I's tol' ya to beat it," Jack repeated.

Pat made his way to the back of the house and out into the alley.

II

"Hey!" the teamster was calling from the front stoop.

While Jack put the gun in the cold stove, Greta hid the twenty dollars in the baby's swaddling. A moment later, the teamster entered and took in the scene.

"He 'scaped," Greta explained.

"Hell, what I get myself into? Is he dead?" The driver nudged Trim's limp body with his foot, prompting a reassuring groan. "We better get him awake. Give him somethin' to drink. Ya got any whiskey?"

Jack and Greta exchanged looks.

"Is he married?" she asked.

"Don't think so," the teamster told her. "No ring anyways. Why..."

"What's he make a week?"

"I don't know, fifteen, twenty."

"What about you?"

"Me?"

"How much you make?"

"I own my own rig, I do all right. What's..."

"*You* thirsty?" she asked, then quickly added, "That a weddin' ring?"

"Yeah, what's all this got ta do—"

Greta interrupted him. "Dat rum in da kitchen, Jack. Let da cop have some."

Jack went off and returned with the discolored liquor and the least dirty glass. The driver took the bottle and held it up to the light.

"Whatta ya, make it yerself?"

He knelt down and filled the glass, then forced some down Trim's throat. The deputy woke with a start and shook his head.

"How d'ya feel, fella?" Greta asked.

Trim looked up at her, bewildered. He'd just begun to offer some reply when up came lunch and breakfast. Then he passed out.

"Oh, Christ." The driver rose and wiped his shoe on the corner of the couch. "Well, they ain't goin' ta find me here when they start lookin' for someone ta blame. Good luck ta ya all."

The teamster left the house resolved never to mention the incident again. A resolve he held to until later that night when he'd run out of small talk playing two-handed euchre with his wife.

Jack fetched a towel and began cleaning up.

"Was i' 'nough?" he asked.

"Enough what?" Greta asked in ill-feigned ignorance.

"Youse knows what. Your love potion."

"Oh... I... forgot..."

"It's OK, Gret. He piped ya 'fore trowin' it up," Jack assured her. "Fifteen a week ain't bad."

"Maybe twenty," Greta added hopefully.

An hour later, Michael Trim was explaining to his chief what had happened.

"You tell anyone on your way here?" Biddle asked.

"No, thought I should ask you what to do."

"So the only ones who know are the teamster, and the woman and boy who probably helped him escape."

"I don't know if they had..."

"Jeezus. Well, you can be sure they won't be doing any talking about it. And the teamster went off leaving you. Either he was in on it too, or knows we'll think he was. You're lucky."

"How so?" Trim asked, rubbing his head. "Can't say I feel lucky."

"We have time to find him ourselves. First thing, send a wire to Watertown. Tell them there'll be a delay in getting Lyons up there. How much cash did you have?"

"Twenty-five. He took it. And the revolver."

"It might be he'll meet up with Danny. He's still hanging around town."

"How do you know?"

"Seen him. An' I know where he spent last night. You send that wire. After that go up to the freight yards. Find where the jungle is."

"Jungle?"

"Where the tramps camp out waiting for trains. Probably be at least two, one east, one west. Offer ten bucks to anyone spotting Lyons—use Danny's name, don't mention Pat. Talk to the railroad cops, too. Then eat a big supper because you'll need to spend the night watching the back of the house where you were ambushed. I'll report that I saw Danny and get all the beat cops looking for him. Since they can't tell the difference, they'll bring Pat in if they spot him. And don't let your tongue get away from you. You tell anyone your story and it will be the end for both of us. Then you'll have me to deal with."

Earlier that morning, Mélisande had perused the *Byblos Observer* over breakfast. After learning that Mrs. Seymour Whittaker had spent the last week in Rochester visiting her widowed sister Martha, who'd recently suffered a bout of grippe, but was feeling better now, and that the J.B. Wells department store was selling parakeets in the basement for the exceptionally low price of $1.69, she discovered the classified ads. One in particular arrested her attention:

WET NURSE – For family of means. Call Jane after noon. Tel. 4-2761.

Mélisande spent the remainder of the morning lugging Eugenia to various apartments she'd seen advertised. None of them impressed her. At noon, she returned to the hotel and made her call.

A gruff voice answered, and then the phone was passed to Jane.

"Is this the *wet* nurse?" Mélisande asked.

"Who wants ta know?"

"This is Madame Bodel. I am looking for a wet nurse for my baby. Is it you?"

"*Madame?*" Jane asked suspiciously. She certainly had no intention of dealing with any competitors. "Are you respectable?"

"*Respectable?*"

"What's your address, dearie?"

"The Baggs Hotel."

"Hotel? Well, I'll come around there at two. An' we can talk about it."

Mélisande agreed and at ten minutes past that hour welcomed the woman to her room. Jane quizzed the girl about her background while casually surveying her belongings. It wasn't until seeing a menu from the first-class dining room of the S.S. *Kronprinz Wilhelm* that she became convinced that Mme. Bodel was just the sort of comfortably middle-class mother she was looking for.

"Now, Madame, just how much were you expecting to pay for this wet nurse?"

"Ten dollars a month?"

"More like ten dollars a *week*, dearie," Jane corrected. "You going to put her up here?"

"I need to find an apartment."

"You want to rent a place? I can give you the girl *and a house* for twenty a week. An' I'll throw in a boy to run errands for you. No charge."

"Boy?"

"Little tyke, hardly eats a thing."

"When can I see this girl, and the house?"

"I'll take you over right now. Do you have the cash? It will be two weeks in advance."

"Yes, yes. Let us go see."

III

Having inspected it, Mélisande thought the Meeker Street house more than satisfactory. There were two bedrooms upstairs, and downstairs, off the kitchen, a bathroom. There was even the possibility of hot water, provided the boiler in the gas stove was kept lit.

But the wet nurse was something else altogether. She'd been hoping for a healthy peasant girl, well-fed, with rosy cheeks and ample udders. Greta was just the opposite. Pale, almost flat-chested, and looking as if she'd hardly eaten in days. What's more, her hair was dirty and matted and her clothes unkempt.

When she saw the dark-complexioned baby and was told her father was "at sea," she reached the same conclusion Dr. VanLengen had earlier: the young mother was an employee of Jane Jebril's. That entrepreneur's attitude had at first confused Mélisande, but now she understood. She'd known women of her ilk before. Greta was an unfortunate who through bad luck had been impregnated by one of Jane's clients, then probably been starved in an effort to force a miscarriage. Unsuccessful at that, her mistress sought another way to profit from her stock.

Mélisande picked Eugenia up from the armchair where she'd been left sleeping, then turned to Jane Jebril.

"No, Madame, this will not do for me."

"What's the matter?"

"I will not pay you ten dollars a week for your... *gadoue*."

"What *gadoue*?"

By way of answer, Mélisande made a sound of disgust and left the house.

Jack, who'd been observing the exchange from the shadows, followed her out and walked along beside her.

"She took ar' money," he told her.

Mélisande ignored him and he repeated the charge.

"*Who* took your money?" she asked without slowing.

"Jane. Took twenty bucks. Fer two weeks rent. What was you thar fer?"

Mélisande stopped and looked down at him.

"Is Greta your mama?"

"No."

"Does she... work for this Jane?"

"Work fer? Nah. We jus' come ta town. From Brooklyn. What was you thar fer?"

"Do you know *wet nurse?*" Mélisande asked.

Jack was unfamiliar with the term and so she endeavored to explain. The sensitive nature of the subject, coupled with the limited English vocabulary of both parties involved, made for a long, often circuitous, explication. One too tortuous to bear repeating. It concluded with Jack asking the age-old, two-word question which punctuates so many exchanges in a free society.

"How much?"

"Jane, she wanted ten dollars a week."

"Why w'd she get the money?"

"She is a beast. Don't you see?"

Jack was not ignorant of Jane's aggressive commercial nature. But it was so like that of every other adult he'd ever encountered, he hadn't made the same distinction. Business was business, and everything could be reduced to business. So well had he learned this lesson, he now made his own proposal: he'd sublet the larger bedroom for seven dollars a week and Greta's teat for eight.

Mélisande asked for time to consider his proposition and offered to get back to him the next morning. Jack agreed—provided she gave him a two-dollar deposit to hold open her option on the teat.

Meanwhile, at the manse of Lord Dexter, Archie Cobb was making his way to the decanter of sherry which graced the palm court's sideboard. He'd spent a grueling afternoon playing the part of the Viscount of Abernethy, to the delight of Tillie Dexter and the amusement of her daughter. They'd taken him on a round of calls to the well-to-dos of Byblos, where he had no trouble impressing the city's matrons. Many of their children, however—encouraged by Felicia—had toyed with him. Whether she was on to his charade or merely an impertinent hellion was open to question. Either way, the cure was at hand. He filled a goblet to the brim.

"I'll join you, if you don't mind." Mrs. Biddle had entered the room with a similar intent. "How was your coming-out?"

"Just as gruesome as you'd suspect. That girl of Dexter's has it in for me."

"Has it in for everyone, it seems."

"I do have one thing to show for my efforts. I now know who holds the money in town. They certainly make no secret of it. How's the theosophy game playing out?"

"Oh, that's simple enough. We spent the afternoon sticking pins in a wax replica of an alderman."

"Is that theosophy?"

"Shed of its pretense. What bothers me is that I seem to have awoken his lordship's amorous soul."

"Good god. Is it true what they say, that love makes a wit of the fool?"

"No, unfortunately. Only a more tiresome fool."

"Well, I imagine you've dealt with that problem before. Odd he waited until we were under the same roof as his wife."

"I believe the idea was put in his head when he saw his secretary emerge from my room this morning."

"What, *Tommy?* I must say..."

"Oh, not you too. He simply came to talk."

"Yes, of course. More sherry?"

At ten o'clock that evening, Mrs. Biddle was provisioning her daughter at the Baggs Hotel while Mélisande gave a somewhat sweetened account of the house and wet nurse she'd visited that afternoon. She had decided she would exercise her option on the morrow.

"Meeker Street? Is it far?"

"Not far, no. One kilometer, maybe."

"What's the house like?"

"Eh. But big rooms, and hot water."

"And the girl? Has she a husband?"

"Oh, yes. He is a sailor. On a boat."

"A canal boat?"

"Yes. His own canal boat."

"And she still has her own baby?"

"Yes, nice little girl. And a little boy. Very smart."

"Does she look healthy enough for two babies?"

"Sure. I'll make her fat."

"Well, I'll need to trust your judgment. I won't be able to come by for a few days. I can't risk coming out at night like this."

Mrs. Biddle was right be wary. Unbeknownst to her, her husband had observed her boarding the streetcar and followed in a cab. He then saw her go in the rear entrance to the Baggs Hotel. But when questioned, the preemptively bribed staff denied ever seeing her.

For the first time since he'd received the telegram from New York two days before, Arthur Biddle was having second thoughts. He'd felt certain he was at last bringing his shrew of a wife to heel. But these late evening assignations weakened his conviction and begged for explanation.

Now, however, he had his own appointment back uptown.

5

On the first of Danny's visitations to her chamber, Felicia—intoxicated as she was by a heady cocktail of erotic fantasy and fervid anticipation—lay blissfully unaware that the man sharing her bed was someone other than her intended. It stands as testament to Danny's careful handling that she woke the next morning with her fantasies intact and her anticipation burning all the hotter.

On that second night, however, she became aware of certain incongruities. Her fiancé—heretofore clean-shaven—bore an incipient beard. True, his attitude toward facial hair may have altered, but what of the lost six inches in height? For one brief moment, she considered turning on a light. But then, as with so much else that night, Felicia swallowed her doubts.

The next afternoon she devoted to refashioning her ever-evolving romantic ideal. The previous model was meticulously detailed and nicely personified in Arthur Biddle: tall, blond, and blue-eyed; taciturn, yet quick-witted; no better schooled than she herself, but ambitious enough to keep her in comfort.

The new model had but five features, all corporeal, and every one essential. First and second were the two hands, which seemed to know instinctively which expanse of her flesh yearned most for a caress, and how best to coax her yielding figure from one position of advantage to another. Third was the tireless tongue, which transported each of her sensitive peaks and valleys to ecstatic exhaustion before skittering on to the next. Then came the appendage the poet Whitman most aptly named his body's captain, and, more bizarrely, his pond-snipe. This he wielded with unwavering accuracy, and a genuine eagerness to please. (It's Danny I'm referring to, but old Walt may well have done similarly. In his own way, of course.)

The fifth essential feature was the one least expected by Felicia—her lover's scent. It was quite a distinctive odor. And had she encountered it two days before in a crowded elevator, she would have expressed her disgust with an exaggerated cough and a scathing stare. But now that he had scented her as his own, she longed to be marked anew. And one can easily understand her feelings. Such a perfect Don Juan, so unstinting, and so awfully keen to satisfy—and, alas, so soon fated to die. But let's not get ahead of our story....

That night, after Danny had entered her bower of a room for the third time, and her one of bliss for who knows how many, Felicia did some probing of her own. At first, he deflected her queries. But once assured she was ill-disposed to sound the alarm, he came clean and gave his tale freely.

She had never been one of those clueless girls so inattentive to the outlays a life of ease necessitated that she could think it romantic to elope with a penniless outlaw on the run—whatever his endowments. But here she was, warming to the idea. All but the penniless part. Something would need to be done about that.

Her curiosity piqued, Felicia kept her lover by her side until the sun crested the horizon and she caught her first glimpse of Danny Lyons. She found him not so bad-looking as she'd feared, nor so good as she'd hoped. But that scent still gave her a fever....

"Will you come back tonight?" she asked as he dressed.

"Sure thing, sweetums. Where's my socks?"

"There they are, by the plant stand. Come kiss me, Danny."

He obliged, and then sent her one last "sweetums" as he headed out the window.

"Watch after yourself, Danny."

Although he was by then shimmying down the porch post, Danny heard her words of caution. As did Arthur Biddle, standing just below. He had spent a long night waiting, and greeted the agile lothario by knocking him to the ground and kneeling on his back.

"Jeezus chris'!" Danny protested.

"Keep it down, Danny, or I'll box your ears."

Biddle handcuffed him and pulled him to his feet. Only then did Danny recognize his jailer.

"Hey, Art. Heard ya was in town."

"Yeah."

By then, Felicia, roused by the sounds she took to be Danny falling from the porch, came to the rail and called down. "Are you all right, Danny?"

"He's just fine," Biddle told her. "But you might want to put on a wrapper, sweetums."

"Arthur! Oh, no! Please, Arthur! Come back!"

Biddle ignored her appeals and continued with his prisoner toward his own home.

His wife, around the corner of the hotel in the guest wing, had also gone to bed with her window open. She'd finally fallen asleep after another long night serenaded by infant raccoons when she was woken by Felicia begging her lover to return to her bed.... More pins, she decided.

Upstairs in his kitchen, Biddle handcuffed Danny to the stove and made coffee.

"Why ya bring me here?"

"Why not? You known Dexter's daughter long?"

"Few days. Met her by accident. You know her?"

"Not as well as you. A little noisy for my money."

"I like 'em dat way. So's ya knows yer on da right track. Say, you ain't da Arthur she's s'posed...."

"Yeah."

"Damn, Art. I didn't know dat...."

"Forget her. Pat's escaped. Or'd you know already?"

"Yeah. I heard. An' dat you wuz takin' him to Waddertown."

"Seen him?"

"Nah. An' I don't wan' ta see 'im."

"Cuz you set him up?" Biddle asked.

"Maybe dat."

"Well, here's the thing. Him escaping is a problem for me. An' you're the solution. You see, one way or another, Pat Lyons is heading to Watertown."

"You can't pass me off as him."

"Why not?"

"Check da cards."

"The Bertillon cards? I got those."

"Den youse know."

Biddle opened a drawer and took out a paring knife. "That's fixed easy enough. Pull up your shirt."

Danny obliged. "Won' work. See—I'm da one widout it."

"If I make the hole big enough, it won't matter."

"Jeezus chris'!"

"Wanna help me find Pat?"

"Yeah, sure, I'lls help ya, Art. Put da damn knife away."

"Where you been spending your days?"

"Here an' der. Shed down at da ol' brickworks, mos'ly."

"Yeah? Eatin' brick dust?" Biddle cleaned a thumbnail with his knife. "Who took you in?"

"Jane. Jane Jebril. Runs a house down on Jay Street."

"Put you up outta love?"

"Fat chance."

"Dexter's girl been givin' you money?"

"Little."

"Empty your pockets."

Biddle gathered two fresh ten-dollar bills and sixty cents in silver from the table.

"So the girl's been givin' you money each night, then next day you spend it at auntie's?"

"Alls I gets is a place ta hole up. An' couple meals."

"Pat there, too?"

"Pat? Nah, didn' even know Jane."

"Let's go make sure."

II

Biddle handcuffed himself to Danny and they rode a nearly empty car down to Jay Street. It was still before six o'clock.

"What's the address?"

"One toity four."

On reaching the house, Biddle attached Danny to a street-

lamp, then climbed the porch and used a milk bottle to methodi-
cally break each of the panes of the three windows. With the
sound of breaking glass still echoing, he hurried to the back of the
house. A still-dressing alderman emerged from the kitchen.

"Mornin', Mr. O'Hearn," Biddle greeted him.

"What the hell's goin' on?"

"Been harboring a fugitive here. Know anything about that?"

The alderman grunted and continued on his way.

Biddle picked up an iron pan as he passed through the kitch-
en. When he came up behind a large man guarding the front door
of the house, he laid him out. A search of the second-floor bedrooms yielded no unforeseen revelations, and no sign of Pat Lyons.

A livid Jane Jebril followed Biddle downstairs.

"You god-damn son of a bitch..."

Biddle turned on her, grabbed her by the hair, and tossed
her into a chair. After a brief interview, he concluded she knew
nothing of Pat. Outside, he reattached himself to Danny and led
him toward the jail.

"You won't be welcome back there for a while. I'm taking
you in and booking you as Danny—for now. But either we find
your brother or you'll be headed up to Watertown to face that
felony. All I need to do is take a pencil to those cards. Now, think
real hard about where he might be."

"Nowhere here. Unless he goes back ta my place."

"That his wife there?"

"I guess she's his wife."

"If he left town, would he head back to New York?"

"Nah. Outta state."

"Because of the warrant?"

"Sure."

"So give me some names."

Danny told him of a cousin in Philadelphia, and a former
flame of Pat's he'd last heard was residing in Montreal.

"I'll come back for you after supper."

In the alley behind Danny's home, a dew-dampened Michael
Trim was pacing to warm himself.

"Any sign?" Biddle asked.

"No—'course I might'a dozed some."

"Go around front and search the house. I'll wait here."

A minute later, Gretchen announced the deputy's arrival at the room she shared with her mother. Five minutes after that, Trim came out the back door limping.

"No sign. An' I woke the baby."

"Yeah, I heard. The wife kick you?"

"Nah, little boy."

"Go on home and sleep. He won't be moving about in daylight. Meet me back here at eight. You got another long night ahead of you."

Biddle went in to his office and wrote out wires to Philadelphia and Montreal. As soon as the messenger had gone, he put his feet up on the desk and picked up a treatise on the law of contracts.

At nine-thirty that same morning, Mélisande arrived at the Meeker Street house in a cab. As her luggage was unloaded, she went to the door with Eugenia cradled in one arm. Jack greeted her and they finalized the rental of room and teat. From that moment on, the girl took absolute charge of the house. With her blithe nature in abeyance, she began issuing edicts like a czarina.

She set Jack to work sweeping the front while she inspected the larder, then compiled a list of groceries and supplies, using the American vernacular as she understood it.

"This is for you to get," she told the boy.

Jack held out his hand and rubbed his thumb with his forefinger.

"*Marmot!* I gave you already fifteen dollars. Go!"

She'd just started on the dishes when Greta descended with her baby. Ignoring the young mother's protests, she sat her at the table and fixed her an omelet with the last two eggs.

"Now I make you a bath. A nice hot bath."

Greta only nodded. The girl was spent. The birth, the journey to a strange city, the repeated desertions, the endless lies and deceits—all had taken their toll. She was too confused to think, and too tired to bother trying.

While Greta soaked in the tub, Mélisande washed Gretchen in the sink. Then set her in the makeshift crib she'd created for Eugenia by pushing chairs against the couch. Next, she went through Greta's wardrobe, gathering what garments she thought beyond salvage and burning them in the rusted metal drum behind the kitchen.

Finding Greta asleep in the tub, Mélisande woke her, dried her, and dressed her in a nightgown of her own.

"Now you sleep some more. When your lunch is ready, I wake you up. For now, you eat, sleep. No more. Just eat, sleep. OK? I watch the babies."

The program struck Greta as a sound one, and she willingly ascended to her room and dropped into a perfect oblivion.

Mélisande was scrubbing the kitchen floor when Eugenia woke, hungry. Her minder was well accustomed to her schedule and the bottle of warmed milk was at the ready. Then she found Gretchen equally hungry. The bottle was empty when Jack arrived home.

"Da grub bein' 'livered," he told her. "Where ya wan' da pig?"

"Kitchen, *naturellement*."

Mélisande first appreciated the price of her lexical imprecision when Jack went back out to the porch and returned with a piglet and not the slab of bacon she had intended.

"He wuz da runt. Got 'im for a plunk."

"Ah! Out!"

Jack took the admonishment in stride. He went out back and tied his piglet to the porch, then fetched it a saucer of milk.

By dinner that evening, it was Mélisande feeling spent. She'd filled the pantry, cleaned the house, and arranged laundry service in anticipation of the household's ravenous appetite for clean linen. What's more, she'd brought Greta back from the dead. For the first time in days, there seemed to be some color in the girl's cheeks.

Jack took the table scraps and made them into a mush for

his piglet. Outside, he found a stray dog worrying the beast. He whipped stones until the hound retreated, then fashioned a protective sty out of a wooden crate.

III

Earlier that afternoon, his secretary read Lord Dexter the long-awaited communication from his lawyers:

Mr. Dexter,

We are pleased to inform you that at eleven o'clock this morning, Judge Dreiser, the presiding judge of the Court of Special Sessions, ruled in our favor on the question of whether your property which formerly comprised the Chenango Canal bed could be valued as normal commercial property. He agreed with our interpretation that the deeds restricting the land's use to that of a transportation right-of-way decreased its utility substantially enough to necessitate a reassessment by a third party appointed by himself and that that valuation will be used in calculating future assessments. As for the prior tax bills now in arrears, he has ruled that they should be reduced by 60% from the total of $8,490.65, or by $5,094.39, leaving a total due of $3,396.26....

"Ha! Saved myself over five thousand dollars! And those fools told me to drop the case." His lordship's right eyebrow broke into a celebratory cakewalk, much to the amusement of its companion across the way.

Tomasz, by now accustomed to his employer's mercurial nature, chose not to mention for the present the lawyers' invoice for $5,475 which was helpfully included in the same envelope. He did, however, make the mistake of bringing a second letter to Lord Dexter's attention. It was from the City of Byblos notifying Dexter that his former canal bed had been declared a nuisance and that until the mosquito-breeding mire was properly drained, a fine of $10 a day would be levied.

"Nuisance! By god, it's the hand of O'Hearn."

"O'Hearn?"

"A meddlesome alderman, always burrowing under my skin, like a bloodsucking tick. Well, I've got something in store for *him*." It was now the turn of the other, more sinister, of his lordship's eyebrows to perform a venomous tarantella. "Fetch me my theosopher!"

A rattled Tomasz gladly made his exit. After a thorough search of the hotel's public rooms below, he eventually located Lady Eleanor in her chamber. She invited him in.

"His lordship wishes to see you. But be warned, My Lady, he is in a very foul mood."

"He lost his suit?"

"No, he won. But now the city is fining him. And when he sees the bill from his lawyers..."

"All right, I can deal with him. But remember, I'm counting on you to follow this Biddle. He'll be leaving the courthouse sometime after five."

"What does he look like?"

"Tall, sandy hair, no beard or moustache. The important thing is to find out where he spends the night. But don't confront him."

"You need not worry on that point." The fingers of his right hand moved unconsciously toward his magenta-hued cheek.

Once again, they left the room together—and were, once again, observed by Mrs. Dexter. She had followed Tomasz upstairs, rightfully suspecting he was revisiting Lady Eleanor in her chamber. But now Tillie could breathe a sigh of relief. The meeting had been too short for any serious breach to have occurred.

It was almost seven when Tomasz finally saw the tall, sandy-haired man with no beard or moustache leaving the Wahtawah County Courthouse. He followed him to a restaurant, where Biddle dined on chops, while outside, Tomasz ate a pretzel purchased from a man pushing a cart. From there, Biddle led him to the county jail. He came out with a rough-looking man handcuffed to his wrist.

Staying to the shadows, Tomasz followed them down an alley, where they met another man. Biddle transferred his end of the handcuffs to this third man.

"It's up to you two to catch Pat," Biddle told the others. "If he hasn't made his way out of town, odds are he'll show up here to see his wife." Then he poked the prisoner in the chest. "Just remember, if Pat gets away, Trim here will be takin' you up to Watertown."

"What about the key?" his deputy asked him.

Biddle looked at him. "Why don't I keep the key."

Then he nodded toward the house. "I see two women in there—who's the second one?"

The others followed his gaze up to the second-floor bedrooms.

"Dat's Pat's Greta, on da left. Never saw da utter one 'fore," the prisoner told him. "Nice looker."

"She wasn't there when I went through this morning," Trim added.

Tomasz, however, *did* recognize the woman brushing her hair in the right-hand bedroom. It was Lady Eleanor's baby-tossing travel companion.

"See if you can get a name for her in the morning," Biddle told his deputy. "Then you can take Danny back to his cell. I left a key for the cuffs at the sergeant's desk. So long."

Tomasz followed Biddle to his home catty-corner from Dexter's monstrosity. He saw a light go on in a second-floor window, then went to the schoolyard across the street for a better view. Biddle moved about the apartment for some time, then settled into an easy chair with a book. Tomasz sat down under an elm tree and took out the sandwich the cook had prepared for him. He'd barely taken his first bite when the rain started.

The two lookouts stationed in the alley behind the house on Meeker Street were also feeling the first drops of rain.

"Whaddaya say we head inside somewhere?" Danny proposed. "Gallagher's is jus' a couple streets over."

"Nah, we'll be all right here."

Then the rain picked up. Ten minutes later the deputy was reevaluating his decision when there was a commotion at the back of the house. It sounded as if a dog was attacking someone. Both men ran toward the fray, Danny as eager as his escort to catch his wayward brother.

Inside, Jack correctly deduced the dog was back to worrying his pig and shot out the kitchen door. By then the hound had shattered the makeshift sty and was making a lunge for the piglet. Jack bravely jumped on the dog as the piglet sought safety on the far side of the yard. In its panic, it circled the thin trunk of an ailanthus and its lead was now stretched taught across the path of the two lookouts charging at the fellow they saw gripped in the dog's jaws.

When the deputy's foot caught the piglet's perfectly positioned lead, his forward motion was abruptly halted and Danny swung off his feet. Then, at the cost of several layers of skin, the handcuffs slipped from Trim's wrist, and a combination of momentum and bad luck propelled his prisoner head-first into the cellar well just below the back porch.

While the deputy clutched his burning wrist, a bloodied Jack released the yelping dog and spat out its ear. Only the piglet was left unscathed.

6

Mélisande, exhausted by a day spent performing the household tasks she normally preferred to avoid, had gone to her room shortly after dinner and fallen into a deep sleep. As had the two babies beside her. Greta, however, was not so fortunate. She was soon woken by a pressing need to attend to the one essential function left off Mélisande's "just eat, sleep" prescription. She'd gone downstairs and was seeing to the matter when she heard the dog bark and Jack rush out the door. On leaving the bathroom, she saw the silhouette of Jack grappling with that of the dog, and, even more ominously, those of the two men charging the boy.

Invigorated by the emergency, Greta's unassuming mind surprised her with an original thought. She made her way to the cold stove in the front room and returned with the revolver Jack had hidden there the day before. It was during her brief absence that the deputy's foot caught the piglet's lead and Danny performed his dive into the cellar well. She was, however, in time to see Jack mark his triumph by spitting out the dog's ear.

"You all right, Jack?" she called out.

"Da damn hound bit me. Bu' watch it, someone else out here."

The rain having let up some, Greta went out past Jack and stood over Trim where he sat clutching his wrist.

"You 'gain?" she asked, the gun pointed at him.

"Look, Gret. It's Pat. Down here."

"Pat?"

"He's out. Cut bad."

"You help git 'im inside," she told Trim.

He and Jack, both wounded themselves, struggled to lift the limp prisoner out of the well, dropping him twice before finally getting him up into the house.

"Bring him ta da front," Greta instructed.

Once Danny had been placed on the couch, she ordered Trim to sit on the floor.

"Someone had better fetch a doctor," he said.

"Tie the cop up, Jack."

"Nah, no good, Gret. Wha' we gonna do den?"

"He'll take Pat away."

"That's not Pat," Trim explained. "That's his brother, Danny."

"Brother," Greta mouthed with contempt. "Don't feed me that...."

"Pull up his shirt."

"Why wud I pull up his shirt?"

"Pull it up, you'll see. Omphalos depressed."

"What?"

"His bellybutton. Pat's sticks out."

Jack went over and pulled up the unconscious man's shirt.

"He's right, Gret. It ain't Pat."

Greta looked over at the exposed navel, but remained unpersuaded. She was not a keen enough observer to have noted the morphology of Pat Lyons' umbilicus. And she had herself read too many nickel magazines not to recognize the identical-twin-brother gag as nothing but a dodge used by authors who'd written themselves into a corner.

Pragmatism also colored her thinking, for she still thought Pat the most eligible marriage prospect. The Remember the Maine Widows and Orphans Society had brought in a cool hundred a week. And the night before abandoning her in Brooklyn, Pat had assured her that he had another, even more lucrative, scheme in mind.

The cop wasn't good for more than twenty a week. And from the way he'd woken her that morning when searching the house, she surmised the love philtre hadn't taken.

"Long as I got the gun, he's Pat. Got it?"

"Sure, Gret," Jack told her. "I better go fer da doctor now."

"All right," she agreed. "But you stay sittin', cop." After Jack went out, she slumped into a chair, still keeping the gun pointed at the deputy.

"Reminds me of Carla and Bertha," he began.

"Who does?"

"Danny and Pat Lyons. Lookin' so much alike. We had two cows like that. Carla and Bertha. Same white shoulder on the right, same white hind quarter on the left. Or vice versa, was it? Caused no end of trouble."

"What'd it matter?" she asked.

"Carla'd only let you milk her from the left side. But with Bertha, you had to come in from the right. Else they'd kick at you. No, I'm lyin'. It was Carla you had to come in from the right with. Ever been kicked by a cow?"

"Nah."

"Still got the scar from Carla," Trim told her while turning up his pants leg. "See?"

"Nah." Greta was growing sleepy. And the further she relaxed, the cooler she felt. The thin nightgown had gotten damp in the rain and with the heat of the crisis now past, there was nothing to counteract the chill. Suddenly, an involuntary shiver shot through her body and the gun fell from her hand. Trim picked up the revolver and placed it in his pocket, then took a jacket hanging by the door and draped it over her.

"Thanks."

While she dozed, Trim found a coverlet and arranged it over Danny, being careful to conceal the handcuffed wrist. It was ten minutes more before Jack arrived with Dr. VanLengen.

"He should be all right," the doctor said after bandaging the bloody head. "Don't move him, just let him sleep 'til morning. Then maybe give him some brandy. I'll come by when I can. How's the baby?"

"She's OK, upstairs sleepin'," Greta told him.

The doctor treated Jack's bites and Trim's wrist, then packed up his bag.

"We need a priest," Greta told him.

"Priest? For him? I told you, he should be OK."

"Ta get married."

"Oh. Roman Catholic?"

"Yeah."

"Father Timoteo is closest. Just over at Saint Lucy's."

"Thanks," she said. "An' thanks for lookin' after Pat."

Biddle went out on his porch and lit a cigar. He could just make out Tomasz beneath the elm in the schoolyard across the street. He'd twice noticed the man following him that evening and knew him as a new member of Dexter's ever-revolving troupe of hangers-on. What he didn't know was on whose behalf he was working. He left the glowing cigar on the porch and went out the rear of the house, then made a wide circle to just behind the elm tree.

Tomasz was on his feet, stomping to keep warm in the persistent drizzle. Biddle reached out a hand and grabbed him by the shoulder. The astonished Pole's cry was heard throughout the neighborhood, leading some to fear the baby raccoons were at it again. Windows could be heard closing.

"Come on, we've got some talking to do," Biddle told him.

He took Tomasz upstairs and gave him warm coffee.

"Why're you following me?"

"I should better ask you, why are you threatening Lady Eleanor?"

"The duchess?" Biddle asked. "You working for her?"

"My lips are sealed."

"Yeah? Wanna know the truth about her?"

"What makes you think I would believe your lies?"

"She's got you good, hasn't she? Well, suit yourself."

Biddle frisked him, taking his money and papers. Then brought him outside to a police call box. Five minutes later, a roundsman arrived.

"Vagrant. Found him peering in windows."

"Right."

When Biddle entered his office the next morning, his deputy was waiting.

"What happened to your arm?" he asked.

"Tripped over a pig's lead," Trim told him. "Tore the handcuffs off."

"Huh. You turn Danny back in at the jail?"

"Couldn't. He got knocked out."

"Who knocked him out?"

"I suppose you could say the pig, but wasn't his fault."

"Where is he?"

"The pig? In back of the house on Meeker Street. Danny's there too, inside. Doctor said better not move him."

"But no sign of Pat?"

"No. No Pat. Seems the girl there isn't his wife, least not yet."

"Either way, I don't suppose she'd tell us where he is even if she knew."

"No, not likely. Besides, she thinks Danny is Pat. Told her about the omphalos protruding, but she don't believe it. Got the revolver back, though." He rose and pulled the gun from the pocket of his jacket on the coat-rack.

"Why don't I hold on to that for now. How about the other girl?"

"Didn't see her, must have been sleeping."

"Maybe you oughtta get back there and keep an eye on Danny."

The moment his deputy had left, Biddle took a pencil to the two Bertillon cards. When he was done, Pat's was the omphalos depressed.

II

By habit, Trim approached the Meeker Street house from the rear. He passed the piglet sleeping in a patch of sunlight without incident. But when he reached the kitchen door, the girl from the right-hand bedroom greeted him with a butcher knife.

"What is this?" she asked.

"Looks like a knife."

"*Imbécile!* What do you want?"

155

"I've come to check on my prisoner."

"Oh, *you* are the cop?"

"Not cop, exactly. I'm the deputy investigator for the district attorney."

"Eh?"

"Sort of a cop. You see..."

She turned her back on him and retreated into the kitchen, where she was frying a pan of bacon. He followed.

"That sure smells good."

"Tsch. Now I must feed cops, too?"

"Just who are you?"

"Madame Bodel."

"Why're you here?"

"I live here!"

"A friend of Danny Lyons?"

"Who is he?" she asked.

"The fella sleeping on your couch."

"Never saw him before. I have hired the girl, Greta, for my wet nurse. My baby is upstairs."

"Can't give milk, huh? We had a cow like that. Nancy, think it was. Never quite sure what happened to her. My father said it was the grass, gave her to a fellow further down the valley with sweeter soil. Course, we ate a lot of beef that winter...."

Mélisande pointed toward the front room.

Trim took her suggestion and arrived in time to see Jack attaching Danny to the iron stove. Some minutes earlier, he'd discovered that the lock could be opened with the same key he'd taken from Trim's pocket two days before. And by extending Danny's right arm, the opposite end of the handcuffs would just reach the foot of the stove.

"How'd you do that?" Trim asked, still unaware that Jack had abetted Pat's escape, and that all handcuffs used the same key. The boy stood mute, and Trim went on. "Well, however you did it, I suppose I should thank you."

Jack looked at him, puzzled. "Can't leave 'til he's married Greta."

"But he's not Pat, he's Danny."

Jack shrugged. "He ken be Pat 'til dey're married. What's da diff'rence?"

"You her boy?"

"Nit, I'm Jack. Her frien'."

"Jack who?"

"Jack Tigue."

"Where's your folks?"

The boy shrugged.

"You in school?"

"*School?* Nit, I ain't in school, an' I don' wanna be."

"Not a question of wantin'. Danny wake up at all?"

"Nah. Hasn't moved. Still breathin', though."

Mélisande called Jack in for breakfast. Greta, depleted by a long morning suckling Gretchen and her crib-mate, was already at the table. The deputy investigator positioned himself at the doorway to the kitchen and leaned on the jamb looking in.

"You make your eggs the French way. Had a cousin who learned that. Worked at a hotel on Blue Mountain Lake. Before she was married. Fancy place. Burned down a few years ago. No it weren't. That was Saranac. Got three kids now, all boys...."

Mélisande got up and set another place at the table.

"Eat—but no talk."

Mrs. Trim had often felt the same sentiment, but a mother can ill afford to be so direct with her only son and likely pension.

When the meal was over, Greta turned to Jack.

"Time fer da priest, Jack."

"Wha' if he won' come?"

"Tell him a man's dyin' an' he needs da las' rites. Dey'll always come fer dat."

While Greta went up to her room to prepare herself, the deputy helped Mélisande with the dishes.

"Where's your husband? If you don't mind my prying."

"Oh, he is dead."

"Sorry..."

"It's OK. He was a bad husband. I find a new one. Better."

"What'd he die of?"

"Umm... killed."

"Murdered?"

"Yes, they cut off his head. His *gang*."

"Jeez.... Why'd they do that?"

"They find out he was a cop." She picked up the butcher knife and spent an inordinately long time wiping it off, then asked with what seemed like genuine curiosity, "Why do you want to be a cop?"

"Well, like I said before, I'm not a cop exactly. Ya see, the investigator for the district attorney, a fellow named Biddle, he fancied the idea of getting 'chief' in front of his name. So he naturally needed a deputy...."

"Biddle?"

"That's right, Arthur Biddle."

Trim went on for some time, not realizing he'd lost his listener at the name Arthur Biddle. Now she knew why they were in Byblos.

"This Biddle, is he married?" she asked.

"Is, but's divorcing the first wife and marrying a new one. Girl named Felicia. Felicia Dexter..."

"Dexter?"

"Yeah. Father owns a hotel. A crank, sort of... nutty, some say. But rich."

"Yes, I think I know him."

They heard Jack return and joined him in the front room. There they were introduced to Father Timoteo, a plump, dark-haired man of thirty-five. When he saw Danny, he opened the case he'd brought with him and began putting on vestments.

"What is his name?" he asked in a heavy accent.

"Danny Lyons," Trim told him. "But the doctor says he should be all right."

"He's Pat Lyons." Greta had entered the room dressed in one of Mélisande's finer blouses. "An' yer here ta marry him ta me."

The priest's eyes followed Danny's arm to the handcuffs, and those to the iron stove. It wouldn't be the first time he'd married a man knocked insensible and held by restraints. But it seemed unlikely the remuneration would be as compelling as it had been on those prior occasions.

"I'm sorry, but no. A man like this, unconscious..."

"We ken wake 'im up," Greta told him, then went over and slapped her intended hard on the face. He showed no signs of waking. Undaunted, Greta pulled a pin from her hat and sent it into his exposed left arm.

"Saw 'is lips move," Jack reported.

"No, no. You cannot *torture* the man!" the priest protested. "Send for me when he is awake. Or better, set a date for the church. And don't forget, you need a license. And ten dollars."

He put his things back into his case and made for the door.

"Wait!" Mélisande stopped him. "You can... *baptiser?*"

"Bring the child to the late service tomorrow."

"Two childs. But here is better." Mélisande had grabbed hold of his arm and pressed her body against his. "Oh, please...."

She had wanted to have baby Eugenia baptized since her birth. But the baby's mother, recognizing no deity save herself, wouldn't hear of it. Not willing to jeopardize the five hundred dollars promised her, Mélisande couldn't risk a public display at the church. She pressed harder.

"What is your name, child?" the holy father asked.

"Mélisande."

"*Française?*"

"*Oui. Et vous?*"

"*Italien.*"

The two babies were fetched and Mélisande explained to the priest in French that Greta was the mother of both.

"*Jumelles?*" he asked surprised.

Yes, Mélisande assured him, they were twins. The odd difference in complexion she compared to a litter of both brown and white puppies.

"Ah, my holy water," he said. "I forgot to fill it."

"No bother."

She took the vial she wore round her neck and handed it to

him. Then she and Trim stood as godparents for both babies during a brief ceremony which bore only the slimmest resemblance to the sacramental rite.

"Normally, baptisms are five dollars. But we can make it seven-fifty for the two." The holy father's magnanimous spirit had been aroused.

"Yes, yes," Mélisande assured him. "I will come by... some evening. You wait, I pay you."

"All right, my dear. I will await your call."

Meanwhile, Greta had gone to the kitchen and fetched the love philtre. There was precious little of it left. From its scent, Mélisande had mistaken it for a solvent and used it to clean tar from the floor.

The hopeful bride poured a slug down Danny's throat in one last bid to wake him before the priest had gone. Unfortunately, Danny did not revive. In fact, he passed from a contented repose to stone cold death with only the briefest of layovers in the throes of agony.

Trim put an ear to his chest.

"Think he's dead."

The priest went over and confirmed it. "Yes, quite dead. Well, it will save a trip." He set his case back down and now performed the ceremony he'd originally come for. When he finished, Greta broke into sobs.

"Now what's ta become of me?" she asked, tears running down her cheeks.

"It'll be OK, Gret," Jack assured her.

"I need to hurry off," the priest told Mélisande. "Perhaps a second evening? To cover this...."

"Yes, yes," she promised.

III

Though she might not have agreed, it really was for the best that Greta's marriage plans had fallen through. Sisters should not marry brothers. Even half-brothers. To be fair, the poor girl was

ignorant of her pedigree. But as old Mrs. Skowron so often coun-
seled, facts is facts, and there's no reason you, dear reader,
should be left in the dark as well.

Danny and Pat were said to be the twin sons of Danny Lyons, Sr., the infamous leader of the Whyos gang, who earned a
living maiming his brother man and pimping women. His stable
included such well-known tarts as Lizzie the Dove, Bunty Kate,
and Gentle Maggie, as well as several of the more humble variety.
It was one of the latter, Pliant Annie, who gave birth to Pat and
Danny, Jr., just before Christmas, 1875. And it was she who
named Danny, Sr., their father when abandoning them at the
foundling hospital. Years later, when depositing Greta at the
same institution, she gave Danny Driscoll as the father's name.
This Danny was another prominent leader of the Whyos gang.

Whether they were in fact the fathers is impossible to ascertain. Those who knew Annie had come to distrust her attributions
of paternity from the time she insisted Horace Greely had fathered a baby girl born eleven months after his death. And she
had, of course, every reason to lie. What loving mother wouldn't
wish for her children a lineage traced to the Whyos aristocracy?

The truth, alas, had long since gone to the grave. Danny
Driscoll and Danny Lyons, Sr., were both hanged in 1888, each
separately convicted of murder. Pliant Annie had met a more
ignominious end. It seems that Gentle Maggie and Lizzie the
Dove were so moved by their employers' demise they entered into
a quarrel as to just who felt the loss the more. As in all disputes
among gentry, the matter was settled on the field of honor—in
this case a Bowery concert saloon. Pliant Annie, a pacifist by
nature, and therefore not a party to the conflict, had like all the
other spectators been brought to a pitch of feverish exhilaration
by the eye gouging and hair pulling. Then, when Maggie shed her
gentle nature and took a cheese knife to Lizzie's throat, Annie
foolishly joined in the cheering—apparently having forgotten
she'd been gnawing a pickled pig's knuckle. Death by aspiration,
the coroner ruled.

But enough of the family's genealogy. What of the recently

deceased Danny, Jr., still lying on the couch and handcuffed to the iron stove? On leaving, Father Timoteo had suggested a doctor be called to fill out a death certificate. But no movement had been made in that direction. The illogical Greta was in the kitchen, keening over the loss of one she supposed to be the man who'd abandoned her twice over. While in the front, Trim explained to Mélisande and Jack his predicament.

"I'll be in for it now. First I let Pat get away, an' now Danny dies on me. I won't have a chance explaining this."

"It's not your fault," Mélisande commiserated.

"Pat's gettin' away was my fault. An' he was the one wanted on the felony. If only it had been him who cracked his head in that cellar."

Greta entered the room and picked up the bottle holding the last drops of love philtre. She brought it over to the deputy. "Drink."

"After what happened to him? I don't think I will, thank you."

"Well, drink it or not, you're marryin' me. You killed my Pat, so I'll have ta settle for your fifteen a week."

Though the circumstances were appreciably altered from his recurring daydreams, Trim felt the tug of the noble act. True, Greta was not the fetching maiden he'd so often imagined. She was, however, in need of comfort. And dressed for her wedding, she was not entirely unattractive. But nobility compelled honesty.

"It's only fourteen a week. But I won't be getting anything without turning up Pat."

"Pat's right dare, dead!" she insisted.

"Not without a protruding omphalos."

"If dat's all, why don' we give him one?" Jack inquired.

"One what?" Mélisande asked back.

"Da big bellybutton!"

It was easier than you might guess to explain the matter to Mélisande, for she was likewise a member of the tribe marked by a protruding omphalos. The always-game girl embraced Jack's idea wholeheartedly. But not his suggestion that her own umbilicus be transplanted to Danny.

Once Trim and Greta had agreed to the wedding contract, Mélisande and Jack surveyed the corpse for appropriate donor tissue. Eventually they settled on an earlobe. While Jack went to the kitchen for a cleaver, and Mélisande upstairs for her sewing kit, the weak-stomached deputy slipped quietly outside to chat with the piglet, leaving Greta alone with the body. She pulled up a chair and settled in for the show.

7

Luncheon at the Meeker Street house was sparsely attended that Saturday afternoon, as thoughts of the grisly goings on in the front room did much to sap the appetites of the weaker among the conspirators. After making a hash of Danny's right one, Jack conceded that a meat cleaver might not be the ideal instrument for the surgical removal of an earlobe and gladly consented when Mélisande offered to tackle the left one with her manicure scissors. The work had left him feeling queasy.

Not so Greta. As she moved in for a closer view, Jack took the opportunity to leave the room unobserved, then joined Trim and the piglet out back, where the deputy had anesthetized the captive with his meticulous account of the time his mother, quite accidentally, shut him in the root cellar and forgot about him until three o'clock the next afternoon.

While the piglet laid plans for corralling Trim in the basement, Jack hurried to a corner of the yard, where he forfeited his morning meal.

A half hour later, Mélisande called from the kitchen door to tell them her needlework was completed and now on display in the parlor. Both of the menfolk declined the invitation, and declined again when she suggested a lunch of cold meat and cheese. This time Trim joined Jack in the corner of the yard before going off to his boarding-house to wash.

Later, while dressing, the deputy considered how best to explain to his chief Danny's death and subsequent metamorphosis into his brother Pat. It was, he decided, a conundrum for which there was no ready solution. Better to stick to a cursory description of the fatal accident and let someone else make the revelation about the protruding omphalos. Perhaps the doctor? Yes, he would do nicely.

Biddle greeted the news of Danny's demise with his usual equanimity.

"Too bad. Can't say I'll miss him."

"I suppose there's someone who might miss him...."

"Sure, anyone he owed money," Biddle conceded. "Phone that Dr. VanLengen and have him come by the house and fill out the death certificate. And better give him those Bertillon cards so he gets the name right. Make sure he sees them. Then you can send the body to the morgue."

It wasn't until Trim had arrived back at Meeker Street that he noticed the alteration of the cards. Biddle had done a careful job, but a few telltale signs of erasure remained. Trim quickly, and rather clumsily, changed them back to their original state, finishing just as Dr. VanLengen arrived to make his examination.

The doctor voiced surprise on seeing the mutilated right ear.

"I can't imagine how I missed that," he said vaguely, then looked over at the four spectators. "Almost like it happened after death...."

There was a moment of embarrassed silence as the conspirators glanced at one another, and then back at the doctor, until, finally, Mélisande leapt into the breach.

"The pig. He come inside, very hungry."

"Yeah," Greta agreed. "Da damn pig."

"I see. Well, I'll need to do an autopsy to determine the precise cause of death. But I suppose massive head injury will be sufficient for the death certificate. His name?"

"Pat Lyons," Greta told him.

"You family?"

"Almost."

"Here're the cards," Trim said, handing them over. "You remember. Pat's got the omphalos protruding."

"Yes, I remember."

He reached for Danny's shirt, but Mélisande got there first. She flipped it up, and a second later back down—displaying the mock umbilicus for as brief a time as possible.

"All right," the doctor said. "I'll get to the autopsy on Monday."

He picked up his hat and handed the death certificate to the deputy. The others joined Trim in admiring it.

"That's all set then," Greta announced. "Now you an' me got business ta 'tend to."

She took Trim by the arm and they made their way to room 214 of city hall, where a marriage license was procured for the nominal fee of one dollar. Like so many couples headed for the altar, they were now joined in a snarled web of sticky threads: economic necessity, noble intent, bureaucratic sanction, criminal collusion—even, perhaps, some warmth of feeling. But what of concupiscent desire? To be sure, the deputy felt some flickers. Poor Greta, however, seemed a lost cause—her heart too hardened by betrayal, her soul too withered by drudgery, and her body too frayed by promiscuity and its consequences. She was a spent force, both spiritually and physically, and her convalescence would be a long one.

At ten o'clock the next morning, Tomasz was released from his cell. It was his friend Archie Cobb who paid his bail.

"You must be more careful, Tommy. These Yanks are a crude lot."

"One must do one's duty, regardless of the risks."

"What duty?"

"My duty to Lady Eleanor, of course."

"Oh, that. You know, Tommy, I warned you before not to get too attached to her. It's a sad truth, but beauty and honesty seldom agree."

"She is in danger!"

"Seems to me she's quite good at lookin' after herself."

"No, I think not. This man, Biddle, he is very... big."

"Biddle, you say?"

"Yes, Arthur Biddle."

"Same fellow who's to marry Dexter's daughter?"

"Yes."

"What's he got against the duchess?"

"Who knows what motivates fiends like him?"

"Who, indeed...."

Archie had never bothered to learn the married name of this daughter of the man most recently calling himself Albert Dowling. Names in that family were too ephemeral. But he did remember meeting Lady Eleanor's baby on the boat, and her telling him that she had personal business to attend to. And when a young mother returns home to attend to personal business, whom else is it likely to involve?

Back at Dexter's, Tomasz found Lady Eleanor taking the morning sun in the walled garden. She was enjoying the works of Martial, a man whose caustic opinions concerning his fellow humans closely mirrored her own. You may well ask how a volume of Latin epigrams had made it into Dexter's library, just as you may likewise ask how the 1883 city directory for Cairo, Illinois, happened to occupy the shelf beside it: such are the consequences of buying books by the linear foot.

"Where have you been?" she asked.

"Jail—since yesterday morning."

Tomasz hoped for some sign of sympathy, but it was not to be.

"Were you able to learn anything?" she asked.

"This Biddle, he lives in a flat just down the street."

"Does he, now. And he was there all night?"

"I cannot say. He caught me off guard and sent me away with a policeman. But your friend... the girl with the baby..."

"I told you, she is in Pittsburgh."

"No, I am sure now. She is here. I saw her in a house. A house which this Biddle was watching with two other men."

"Are you certain?"

"Yes, quite certain."

"How did he know where she was?"

"I don't think he did. He seemed not to have any idea who she was. It was another girl at the same house they knew. They were waiting to catch some man. All very confusing."

"You must take me to this house at once. Can you find it?"

"Yes, I think so."

As they left the hotel, Tomasz pointed out Biddle's apartment—the porch of which afforded a direct line of sight toward her own. Clearly, her husband had known of her arrival.

They took a downtown car and a little later were in the alley behind Meeker Street.

"This is the house," Tomasz told her.

"Go and ask for her, Mélisande. Tell her I'm waiting here. But make sure no one overhears."

"Very well, My Lady."

II

Tomasz crept to the door of the kitchen. He could see Lady Eleanor's traveling companion washing her baby in the sink. Without making a sound, he opened the door and whispered a greeting.

"It is me, Tomasz...."

Having heard nothing until that moment, Mélisande jumped, sending the well-lathered Eugenia skyward. Once more, the earnest Pole sacrificed himself to cushion her fall—this time by diving on the hot stove.

Having herself recovered, Mélisande took the baby and placed her beside Gretchen in the large basket now serving as cradle, then treated Tomasz's burn with butter.

"You should be more careful," she told him.

"And you should not throw your baby about that way."

"Pissh. *You* should not sneak up on people.... How did you know I was here?"

"I saw you from outside, the other evening."

"Looking into windows? You naughty boy."

"No, certainly not...."

"It's OK. I forgive you."

She kissed his forehead and he blushed.

"Lady Eleanor is waiting for you outside."

"Her? Why?"

"I told her your house was being watched. By a man named Biddle. He means the duchess harm."

Mélisande's mind turned quickly. She had deliberately refrained from telling her mistress about the household's connection to her husband, and even given serious consideration to contacting him herself. Partly because she wanted to determine what was in baby Eugenia's best interest. And partly because she wanted to determine what was in her own best interest.

But it was too late for that now. She left Tomasz with the babies and went outside to make her report.

"*Madame, Dieu merci!*" Mélisande exclaimed. "I have much to tell you."

"Why didn't you send me a note of some kind?"

"So much has happened, so quick."

"What, exactly?"

You may believe, steadfast reader, it would tax the patience of us all for me to repeat the girl's account in full. She began in broken English, then lapsed into a personal patois of vernacular French and American slang. And what began as subtle embellishment soon gave way to gross exaggeration. For the practiced jongleur, verisimilitude can never be allowed to stand in the way of presentation. The girl knew her best line, and she was determined to set it up properly. [Editor's note: The four examples of French argot contained in the following can be roughly translated as: thrust; my tongue; his pond-snipe; is excited. But please, for propriety's sake, don't assume cause and effect.]

"...I know *then*, I must find out *who* sends this Trim. So, I do a clutch swing into the slow and the dreamy, and I, ah... *carfouille... ma lavette,* and sting him in all the eight places, and when, eh... *son sansonnet,* it ... ooh... *godille,* and he is happy to eat my front fence, I ask him, 'Who, who sends you here? Tell me!' He falls down, all weak. Then, looks up at me, 'Biddle. Arthur Biddle sent me!'"

"He knew you were here?"

"No, no. As I say, Trim comes to catch Pat Lyons, who used to be Danny Lyons, now dead...."

"So it is mere coincidence?"

"*Apparemment.*"

"And this Trim has no idea who you are, or the baby?"

"No, no idea."

"I think I would like to meet him."

"That is easy. Today he will be married, at three o'clock."

"Where?"

"Here. It is a secret. His mother would not like him to marry a Catholic girl. And not one with a baby."

"Married to *you?*"

"No, *pas mon gniasse. L'abéqueuse*, Greta."

"I thought you said she was married to a canal boat captain?"

"Well, I make a little mistake. A *Cubain*, a sailor—only not married."

"What sort of place did you bring my child to?"

"Remember, madame, if I didn't, we would not have this Trim in our *very hot* tentacles."

Mrs. Biddle smiled briefly, then suppressed it.

"Send out Tomasz, and I will see you at three o'clock. Tell the others I am a friend, Miss Custis."

"Tcha! *Another* name to remember?"

Mrs. Biddle's return to chez Dexter in the company of the sedulous Tomasz did not go unnoticed. Felicia had just come out to her porch. She still had not learned what motivated this faux duchess. But unlike her mother, then sitting on the porch below, she was sure it didn't involve her father's secretary, or anything so unremunerative as romantic love.

At ten of three that afternoon, Mrs. Biddle knocked at the front door of the Meeker Street house and was greeted by Jack, clothed as respectably as was possible given that his wardrobe consisted of seven articles of clothing in toto, three of them being socks.

"Who're you?" he asked.

"Miss Custis, a friend of Madame Bodel. You must be Jack."

"Tha's right. Ya come for the weddin'?"

"Yes, but first I was hoping to have a word with you, Jack. Come, sit with me for a moment."

As she led him to the wicker loveseat which graced the porch, Jack surveyed the richly dressed and well-proportioned woman. He decided she looked OK. And though her face was obscured by the veil suspended from her wide hat, he could feel her intense blue eyes looking back at him.

"I'm worried for my friend, Jack. Worried for her, and her baby. I need someone I can trust—someone capable—to watch out for her."

"Wha's she have ta worry 'bout?"

"I can't explain all that just now. But you may believe me, the need is real. I wonder, Jack, would you be willing to help me?"

"Maybe.... How much?" Jack may have been beguiled, but not to the point of lunacy.

Mrs. Biddle smiled. She knew then she'd found a like-minded spirit.

"Five dollars a week, two weeks in advance. Plus carfare. You will report to me twice a day. I will give you the address." She took a ten-dollar bill from her chatelaine purse and held it out. "Do we have a deal?"

"Yeah."

Jack took the bill and she rose.

"One more thing, Jack. I don't want Madame Bodel to know about our agreement. There's no need to embarrass her."

"Awl right."

As she entered the house, Jack held the banknote to his nose. It smelled of her.

Father Timoteo arrived a little past three and performed the ceremony with his customary brevity. He skipped over much of the prescribed service and omitted the Mass entirely.

Both bride and groom were much impressed with Miss Custis. Try as he might, Trim couldn't help thinking that she would have in many ways been a preferable grateful maiden on whom to bestow his noble act. Not only was his new wife not nearly so comely, she suffered from the additional handicaps of being neither a maiden nor noticeably grateful. Greta, too, was impressed by the woman's handsome form. But what impressed her more was the envelope holding the brief note of good wishes and fifty dollars in cash.

When the holy father drew Mélisande aside in order to arrange for his compensation, he was, unfortunately, overheard by her employer.

"I find it refreshing," Mrs. Biddle told him, "that in this world of perpetual change, the Church has remained constant in adhering to its base precepts."

"Miss Custis, you wrong me," he replied. "It is with no carnal intent that I propose to share an evening with this girl. Rather, the contrary. It is only by confronting temptation directly that we can prove ourselves worthy of the Lord, our Father."

"I see. You practice a casual form of syneisaktism: you lie with women, but do not avail yourself of their charms."

"Just so! You are very learned, Miss Custis. It is a rite dating from the early days of the Church. Come morning, the girl leaves my side as much a virgin as when she arrived...."

"Provided she was no virgin."

"Surely the temptation is all the greater with a woman of experience. You may think it forward of me to suggest, but with a woman such as yourself, the temptation would be all but unbearable. What glory there would be in it."

"Subsequent to the girl? Or are you proposing the two of us together?"

"Why not? It's purported that the Blessed St. Aldhelm of Malmesbury would often lie between two maidens, doubling the... eh..."

"Glory? No, no thank you. I've no desire to serve myself up in your libidinal sandwich."

A celebratory buffet was set out and Mrs. Biddle and her newfound ecclesiastical friend both fascinated and confused the others over cake and cheap wine by conversing in Italian, French, and Latin, with occasional forays into Greek and Sanskrit. The incomprehensible jabbering took Greta back to her sixth birthday, when a supposed uncle took her and her supposed mother to the Central Park Zoo. It was well past five when Father Timoteo excused himself to return to his church and prepare for the late mass.

III

Having secured the goodwill of the rest of the house, Mrs. Biddle now set her sights on Trim. While Greta attended to her charges, Mélisande the dishes, and Jack his piglet, she led the deputy investigator to the wicker loveseat on the front porch.

"I understand you've had quite some excitement these last few days."

"A little too much excitement," he confided.

"And now married. Just how did you meet your wife?"

The question was an awkward one, but one which Trim had prepared for since the afternoon before, when he and Greta had encountered a high school classmate at city hall. He had managed to evade the matter then, but later he concocted a tale based loosely on his daydream of saving widows and orphans of the war with Spain, which would explain the olive complexion of his bride's animate trousseau.

"I suppose you remember the buffalo soldiers who went up San Juan Hill with Colonel Roosevelt? President now, of course. The colored fellows?"

"Yes, I do remember reading about them."

"Greta was married to one. After the fact. Name of Ezekiel, Ezekiel Kingsley. Took a bullet to the eye."

"How awful. Did he die quickly?"

"No, that's just it. Hung on for four more years. Even fathered the baby in there...."

"I see. Greta and he...?"

"Greta'd been nursing him. Out of kindness, mostly. Well, they married last year, an' a week later, he died. Left the poor girl with nothing but a baby."

"My, whatever did she do?"

"Well, seems there was this fellow, name of Pat Lyons, who

was collecting for widows an' orphans of the war. He promised her three hundred dollars. Said he'd set her up as a shop girl. But he was nothin' but a humbug. Was wanted, even."

"Good lord!"

"She followed him here just as I was apprehending him. He got away from me once, but I ran him down and found him trying to sneak in the back door here. He tripped over Jack's pig and cracked his skull. Died in the parlor there yesterday morning. Right where we were married."

"My, what an extraordinary story...." Mrs. Biddle paused to look him in the eye. "...And so unlike the one Mélisande told me."

"Yeah? How'd she have it different?"

"She imagined there was a Cuban sailor involved somehow... and a twin brother of Pat's named Danny. And it was he who died yesterday in this house. Then there was something about a protruding omphalos...."

"I think your friend Melanie ought not to talk so much. 'Specially since it was her who clipped his ear."

"Oh, you can trust it will go no further. It was all done for the best of motives. Greta now has someone to look after her, and a father for her child. And what harm came to anyone? The man is just as dead whatever the name."

"I'm glad you see it that way. An' now, you being in with us, I think maybe I ought ta 'fess up. We all got our secrets, don't we?"

Trim winked, and Mrs. Biddle was unaccustomedly knocked off her pins. As with nearly all her exchanges, she'd entered into this conversation with a firm objective and well-planned strategy. She wasn't used to others, particularly yokels, meeting her on equal terms.

"I'm not sure what you're speaking of. Has Mélisande told you something?"

"Not directly. Only, yesterday, when I mentioned my boss's name, a fellow named Biddle, it seemed to strike a chord. Made me wonder a bit."

"What did you wonder?"

"Well, all sorts of things. I knew his wife went to France, an' here was this French girl that seemed interested in him...."

"You think she is Biddle's wife?"

"No, but I figured she might know his wife. See, I knew she couldn't be his wife."

"How?"

"I've seen her photograph. Didn't make the connection at first, what with the veil.... But now, up close..."

"Ah. Well, I must admit, you've caught me off guard. I'm surprised to learn he even has a photograph." Mrs. Biddle took some time to remove a piece of nonexistent lint from her sleeve. "So, now you know my secret, and I yours. I suppose that's the safest situation for us both."

"I suppose. But just why are you here? The way he tells it, you abandoned him, going off to France."

"One could just as easily say he abandoned me, coming here."

"You expected him to come after you?"

Mrs. Biddle shrugged.

"But now you've come after him."

"No. No, certainly not. I came to see this girl, the girl he's planning to marry."

"Don't see that happenin'."

"What do you mean? He doesn't care for her?"

"Can't say about that. Not the type of fellow who shares his thoughts. But that fellow who died in there, Danny Lyons. He told me something...."

"What?"

"Well, told me he's been payin' nightly visits to Felicia's room. An' Biddle told me he knew where Danny was spending the night."

"That's very interesting."

"Yeah, lot to think about."

"What did this Danny look like? Was he so attractive?"

"No, least not like Biddle. Why haven't you told him about the baby?"

"The baby?"

"You were gone nine months, come back with a French girl

who can't give milk, and a baby. I saw you holdin' her while we was married."

"You're very perceptive."

"No, just grew up on a farm. You get to notice things like that. Why don't you tell him about his girl? He'd give in to you then."

"Yes, no doubt he would."

"Oh, I see. That's it. Too proud. Just like Tubs Kinney."

"Tubs Kinney?"

"Fellow I was in the army with. Real name was Jake, I think. Didn't like it when I was made corporal over him, me bein' a farm boy and him a grocer's son. Not Jake, Fred. It was durin' the Pennsylvania campaign."

"Pennsylvania campaign?"

"No, that's not right, 'twas the Long Island campaign. I said, 'Fred, I wouldn't pitch my tent at the bottom of a slope like that.' He just laughed. Rained that night... and the next one. But he was too proud to admit I was right and move it. Ended up in the hospital.... Didn't die, though.... Not like his brother.... Judd was his name. Typhoid... or was it malaria?"

"Tell me, Corporal Trim, do you have a brother in Lisbon who married a Jewess?"

"No, but that's funny you should ask. I've got a brother-in-law in Port Jervis who married a Dutch girl."

"Greta's brother?"

"Don't know if she has a brother."

"Then the Dutch girl is your sister?"

"No she isn't. My sister's in Syracuse. It's her husband's brother that married the Dutch girl. A bit of a nag."

"The Dutch girl?"

"No, my sister. Never met the Dutch girl...."

"Well," Mrs. Biddle interjected, "perhaps I'll spend some time with the baby." She rose, then took his hand. "I have one last request to make, Corporal Trim. Please don't tell the others my secret. Not even Greta. At least, not yet."

"Sure. But I'm not *Corporal* Trim anymore."

"I'll try to remember that."

8

Mrs. Biddle spent the evening with Eugenia, mulling the day's revelations. It was clear now that she'd been too cavalier. Her husband was playing a more complex game than she'd originally imagined—or even thought him capable of.

That Biddle had known she was in town had come as no large surprise. After all, she was staying at the home of his fiancée. But had he anticipated her arrival? Why else had he moved that very day to a flat almost across the street if not to spy on her? And now Trim's revelations led her to a far more intriguing question: had Biddle ever really intended to marry Felicia Dexter? She couldn't imagine him attaching himself to a girl so fickle as to carry on with some other man. He was far too conceited for that. What's more, she found it improbable that a woman expecting soon to share a bed with Biddle would settle instead for Danny Lyons.

No, chary reader, you need not fear that our heroine has shed her essential narcissism. Rest assured, Mrs. Biddle's faith in her husband's supremacy was not based on any intrinsic characteristics. Yes, he was tall, fair, and fit. And quick-witted. But what truly set Arthur Biddle apart from other men was that *she* had deigned to take him as her husband. The fact that she had never set eyes on Danny Lyons was immaterial, the contest decided a priori.

So, she concluded, the engagement had been a sham. But to what end? Ah, the answer now seemed obvious. Especially when she remembered how she had heard of the betrothal. A school friend had written her in France. A woman she had not corresponded with since she'd left New York, and therefore would not have been expected to know her whereabouts. A woman who knew, and liked, her husband.

Mrs. Biddle had been set up; worse, she'd taken the bait.

Now she felt the barbed hook in her cheek. Only by gaining the upper hand could the wound be salved. The question was, how?

She returned to Dexter's hotel, and after a long, restless night—free of baby raccoons, but not of her preoccupation—she had her answer. At ten o'clock that morning, a veiled Mrs. Biddle was in the law offices of Messrs. Goodelle, Nottingham & Rafferty swearing out an affidavit in which she admitted to the abandonment of her husband. If Biddle's engagement was merely a ruse to get her back in the country, the story that the divorce was holding up the wedding was also a fabrication. He never wanted a divorce. So she would call his bluff.

"You realize," Mr. Rafferty told her, "once your husband's lawyer has this in hand, he will have no trouble attaining a judgment in his client's favor. There will be no chance of alimony."

"Yes, I understand."

"And that your affidavit will be part of the public record."

"The more public the better."

"Fine, then, if that's what you wish. I will see that this is filed this afternoon."

"Thank you."

Mrs. Biddle returned to the hotel wondering how she could ensure that news of the affidavit would reach Felicia and her parents. But she need not have concerned herself on that score. Biddle's engagement to Felicia and impending divorce had been a topic of conversation for some time. And when Mrs. Biddle told Mr. Rafferty she preferred the matter to be public, he had obliged her by telephoning his wife. By three that afternoon, there was no one in Byblos society left unaware.

Earlier that morning, Biddle had arrived at room 312 of the Wahtawah County Courthouse to find his anxious deputy waiting.

"Some peculiar news about Danny," Trim reported. "Seems he was Pat. Doctor confirmed it from the Bertolli cards."

Beyond a perfunctory "huh," Biddle made no attempt at feigning surprise. "Works better for us."

"Yeah, I figured that too."

"Why don't I let you write something up for the newspapers. 'Pat Lyons dies from fall during attempted escape.' Just don't let it get too far from the truth."

Trim took up pen and paper and Biddle a case book on the law of admiralty.

It was nearly lunch time when a knock interrupted them. Trim answered and accepted delivery of a wire.

"From Detective Chabrol, Montreal Police."

"Read it," Biddle told him.

"'Have located Pat Lyons and have him under observation. Do you wish to undertake extradition? Please instruct.'"

Biddle's "huh" sounded more genuine than usual. While Trim stood by silently, his superior gazed out the window. Then, inspiration.

"Wire him back," Biddle instructed. "Pat Lyons is dead, body positively identified. The man you are observing must be Danny Lyons. Please inform him that all charges have been dropped and he should return at once to arrange the funeral of his brother."

His deputy transcribed the message and then picked up his hat.

"When I finish with this, I'll stop by the papers."

"Yeah. And don't hurry back."

As Trim went out to send his wire, Dr. VanLengen was completing the autopsy of Pat Lyons in the basement morgue of the hospital. As he'd expected, the cause of death was severe head injury, likely caused by a fall against a hard surface. And though he doubted the damage to the ears was caused by a piglet, he considered it irrelevant, as it clearly occurred after death.

But when the protruding omphalos was suddenly shot aloft, his curiosity was roused. He picked up the small flap of flesh off the floor and examined it. Little bits of rose-colored silk thread extended from it—apparently insufficient to the task once the buildup of gases in the abdomen had progressed.

The doctor went over to where he'd set out the Bertillon

cards. The notation under "Remarks" had obviously been erased and written in by another hand. He could see the remnants of the prior notation incompletely erased. From this, he deduced that it was *Danny* Lyons who had the protruding omphalos. And that the corpse had been altered to make him believe it was Danny who had died. He was relieved that the death certificate had been correctly filled out with the name of Pat Lyons.

The news of Mrs. Biddle's affidavit was expected by her friends to bring cheer to Felicia Dexter. Alas, it did not. She'd been having second thoughts about the engagement since the moment she'd noticed her obliging lover was six inches shorter (in height) than her intended. She spent the later part of the afternoon sulking in her room. And few knew how to sulk as well as Felicia. Not only did she refuse visitors, she even forwent her habitual afternoon course of pastries. That evening, however, when her sometime social ally Celia Rafferty sent up a note implying she had secrets to bestow, Felicia relented.

As it happened, Celia had stopped by her father's law office to touch her sire for twenty dollars and been waiting in the outer room when Mrs. Biddle made her exit. What's more, Celia had been one of the few to have encountered the reclusive Lady Eleanor. Though the woman leaving her father's office was veiled, Celia had no trouble recognizing her voice, stature, and gait.

She accompanied Felicia to the porch outside her bedroom and divulged her news. Felicia looked at her dumbly, and Celia repeated it more slowly.

"Don't you see, Lady Eleanor and Mrs. Arthur Biddle are one and the same."

"I heard what you said, dear."

"What does it mean?"

"I'm not sure. But someone seems to be playing me for the fool. I must think. You better go now. But not a word about this to anyone else."

"All right."

"I mean it, Celia. *Not a word.*"

"I *said*, all right."

"And on your way out, stop by the kitchen and ask cook to send up some pastries. Something with lots of butter."

Felicia sat down and tried to focus her indolent mind on the problem at hand. She was not a stupid girl, but her brain was not used to being put to such rigors. It was only then that she noticed the newspaper her friend had absentmindedly left behind. It was folded, exposing only the top left-hand quadrant of the front page.

Lyons Brother Dies in Escape Attempt

Pat Lyons, brother of Danny Lyons, died Saturday from wounds he suffered during an attempt to escape the custody of the deputy to the chief investigator for the district attorney. In his efforts to free himself, he fell and badly injured his head....

The story went on at some length, explaining that the two were identical twins who could only be told apart by their omphali. It also noted they'd recently exchanged identities.

Was this the man her fiancé had taken into custody below her porch? And was the wound he died of merely Arthur's retribution for having been beaten to her bun? Felicia tried to remember the nature of her lover's omphalos, but that was the one appendage she had no memory of.

Not ten feet from her, but occluded by a partition of woven laths, Tomasz had been sitting on the porch outside Lord Dexter's office trying to decipher his lordship's accounts. He had heard both iterations of Celia's report, and though he had hitherto steadfastly believed in Lady Eleanor, and summarily rejected all accusations against her, he felt himself wavering. And once allowed to enter his mind, the doubts multiplied. Why had Lady Eleanor denied the presence of her baby-tossing friend? And thinking back, why had she accused the assistant purser of the *Kronprinz Wilhelm* of being an assassin and then greeted him warmly when they were disembarking? And why had she missed each of the assignations they'd arranged? Tomasz, too, was at last realizing he had been played for a fool.

It has been said that heaven has no rage like love to hatred turned. And while this would not be an accurate assessment of the attitude harbored by Tomasz, who was by disposition incapable of hatred, there can be little doubt that he was feeling *very* indignant.

Felicia, on the other hand, was a very capable hater—with or without the antecedent love. She relished the sweet taste of revenge and liked nothing better than to feed on the vanquished. If she could only come up with a plan....

For the first time since her arrival, Mrs. Biddle went to bed with an easy mind. She was reassured to learn that her husband had schemed to draw her back home. And confident that she was, at last, a step ahead of him.

But have a care, Mrs. Biddle. Dark forces are at work....

Dames Engaged

The Third Novella

1

When news of his wife's affidavit reached Arthur Biddle, and the casebook he was reading slipped from his lap, the ensuing thud was barely noticed in the courtroom below. But a moment later, when Hale's *Handbook on the Law of Torts* was purposefully dispatched in the same direction, the somnolent judge was reminded of an occasion during the Siege of Petersburg when a misdirected mortar sent a 64-pound shell into the breastworks not twenty yards from where he was similarly engaged.

Biddle was perplexed. After nearly eighteen months of marriage, the only thing he had learned for certain was that shrew taming was a good deal more difficult than that punster Shakespeare had let on. To be fair, the modern shrew was appreciably more complex than the sixteenth-century variety. Using the bard's play as a guide to contemporary wife husbandry was a little like trying to repair a steam-powered automobile with advice gleaned from a manual on the care and feeding of the dray horse.

When he'd heard of his wife's arrival in New York, Biddle had been confident the hook was firmly planted. Before long, she would come to him and admit her error, allowing him the satisfaction of magnanimously forgiving her. But if that were her intention, why would she now confess to having abandoned him and thus hasten the divorce?

On the other hand, if she had wanted the divorce to go forward, why did she bother coming to Byblos at all? She could just as well have sent an affidavit from France.

Superficially, her actions appeared illogical—but that was one thing she was not. Biddle could think of two possible explanations. The first was that she only decided to accede to the divorce *after* her arrival. Seeing him again, as he assumed she had, and Byblos for the first time, she had determined she could do quite nicely without either. Perhaps she'd already set her sights on someone else. It wasn't that he thought it likely she'd found someone in any way superior to himself. That seemed quite impossible, especially in a town the size of Byblos. Rather, she may have simply decided she'd prefer someone more easily worked. Someone weak-willed enough to do her bidding. Someone like that Polander, so obviously enamored of her.

The second explanation was far more troubling, and worse, far more in keeping with his wife's character: she had come with no other purpose than to make his life miserable. We may well ask ourselves, as Biddle did then, was she really so vindictive she'd travel 3,000 miles to the sort of jay town she despised with no purpose other than to inflict pain and misery on one she felt had wronged her? Oh, yes, was his answer—10,000 miles... on hands and knees... and still arrive glad about making the trip.

Now, Biddle's thoughts continued, suppose she had somehow found out that Danny Lyons had been dipping regularly in and out of Felicia's various chambers—literal *and* euphemistic— while the girl was betrothed to Biddle. Why, naturally, she would seize the opportunity to facilitate the divorce, thus condemning her former husband to life as a cuckold. He could picture her smiling as she planned it. Biddle had seen his fair share of wicked smiles in his day, but none matched that of his wife. Even he found it unnerving—unnerving, and yet strangely erotic. It's that which had spelled his doom.

"Danny Lyons came in this morning." Biddle's garrulous deputy, Michael Trim, had entered the room. "McCreedy saw him at the depot. Funeral's this afternoon. Pat's funeral, I mean."

Biddle, of course, knew that "Danny" Lyons was in fact his brother Pat traveling under an assumed name, and the man to be buried as "Pat" Lyons was the authentic Danny. As did Trim. What neither was sure of was what exactly the other knew. So both played it safe and abided the subterfuge.

"Huh," his chief replied. "I'm going out. Watch the store."

Biddle was too distracted by his wife's machinations to give much thought to either of the Lyons brothers, the quick or the dead. There was one stone he'd left unturned. He had never gotten to the bottom of the duchess's late-evening visit to the Baggs Hotel. Now he'd go back. And this time he wouldn't leave without answers.

He asked the clerk again about the statuesque blonde who'd come to the hotel late on June the fourth, and again was told no one had seen her. He had the night clerk called down from his room and was told the same story. Biddle grabbed the guest cards and flipped through them, separating out three single women, all long-term residents, and all listing their occupation as "modiste."

He handed the three cards to the clerk.

"Wake 'em up and bring 'em down."

"What do you mean...?"

"And any others doing turns upstairs. Right on the depot, must be a dozen more."

"Now, see here..."

"I find out about that blonde, or I tear this place apart. Either way suits me."

The first clerk mumbled an expletive, then gave a nod. The night man pulled a card from the stack.

"She saw this Madame Bodel. Checked out the next morning."

"Describe her."

"Madame Bodel? French girl, young, nice looking. On the short side. Brown hair."

"I'd call it chestnut," the day man added.

Biddle looked at the card, only now noticing the prior residence listed as Étaples, his wife's recent address in France.

"How long was the blonde with her?"

"Couple hours, maybe. That night, and the one before."

"This Madame Bodel, did she leave in a cab?"

"Assume so, didn't see it."

"What about a forwarding address?"

"Didn't leave one. Wasn't here long enough to get any mail."

"And you haven't seen either of them since?"

When both men shook their heads, Biddle pocketed Madame Bodel's card and walked out.

"What a bastard," the day man said.

"Maybe we should have told him about the baby? Wasn't listed on the card."

"Let him find out for himself, if he wants to know."

It had been raining most of the day, but the sun finally made an appearance when "Pat" Lyons' funeral party assembled at the Cedar Grove Cemetery. There were five in the party: the corpse's brother "Danny," Arthur Biddle, Father Timoteo, and two men leaning on shovels exchanging critiques of the priest's rapid-pace service.

"Done already? Ain't that consid'rate of 'em?"

"Don' know I like it. Keep that up and they could get through a couple dozen a day. An' who'd be doin' the diggin'?"

"Hadn't thought of that."

The service over, Father Timoteo pocketed his ten dollars, whispered the perfunctory platitudes, and then hurried off to an appointment at the rectory with the admirably pious and adequately well-preserved widow of an Italian saloon-owner.

"Too bad about Pat," Biddle said without intonation.

"Yeah, he was quite a fellow," the supposed Danny agreed.

"Let's cut the bunk."

"Whaddaya mean, Art?"

"Want me to pull up your shirt?"

"So's you know?"

"What the hell do you think?"

"Then what's the game?"

Biddle shrugged. "I needed a Pat Lyons, and once he was croaked, Danny filled the bill."

"I get it. Now it might be awkward if another Pat showed up?"

"Awkward for me maybe. A lot worse for him. Ever do time up at Dannemora? That's where they'd send ya."

"No, never north of Blackwell's. You've got no worries from me. Will it suit you if I take over Danny's route? I'll cut ya in, of course."

"Yeah, that'd suit me. Think you can pass for him?"

"Why not? I duded up my wardrobe before coming down. Now I just need to rough up the patter some. Not too many big thinkers playin' policy."

"No, suppose not. You might take a shot at his girl, too."

"Yeah? Is she a looker?"

"Seen worse. Danny was hot for her."

"Course, she gotta've seen him with his shirt off.... Might be hard to fool her."

"Might be she wouldn't mind bein' fooled."

"That kind, huh?"

"Yeah. An' no big thinker either."

"Maybe I'll give her a spin. What's her name?"

"Felicia. Felicia Dexter."

"Felicia? I like the sound."

"Sleeps with her window open. An' her old man's loaded."

"How come you don't give her a try?"

"Not my type."

"Well, nice talkin' with ya, Art. I better get goin', or someone else will be takin' over the family business. See ya."

"Yeah."

When Pat reached the edge of the cemetery, he was approached by a young boy—an unseen sixth party attending the funeral. Pat pretended not to recognize him.

"No go," Jack told him. "I knows it's you, Pat."

"Yeah? What makes ya t'ink so?"

"Was us put da bellybutton on Danny, dat's why dey t'ink yer dead."

"Oh. You and Greta did that? For me? Ain't that sweet...."

"Nit. Not fer you. So she could marry da cop."

"What cop?"

"Ferget it. But she's set up OK now. You ain't gonna bother her, are ya?"

"Me? What for? I'm tickled ta death for her. Tell her I'll send her a weddin' present soon as I get something goin'. This cop don't mind about the pickaninny?"

"Name's Gretchen."

"Yeah, I remember. Little Greta. Say, Jack, you want work?"

"Doin' what?"

"Runnin' numbers, an' such."

Jack shrugged.

"I sure could use someone I can trust."

What Pat meant was that he'd feel better trusting Jack with his secret if he were on the payroll. And Jack was willing to oblige—provided...

"How much?"

II

A mere ten blocks away as the crow flies—but eleven for his desultory cousin, the jay—Archie Cobb was keeping what had become a regular afternoon tryst with the sherry decanter which graced the sideboard of the Dexter Hotel's palm court. He'd drained his third beaker when Lady Eleanor entered the room.

"Join me? I was just about to have a second."

"Make it two, and I'll catch up," Mrs. Biddle replied. "I've spent a trying afternoon entertaining our host. He's taken to wearing a uniform he imagines used by Lord Nelson at Trafalgar, and insists that now he be addressed as *Admiral* Lord Dexter." She made short work of the first glass, then paused before moving on to the second. "And how are you getting along with the Byblos bourgeois, Lord Abernethy?"

"The board's certainly up to snuff. I've got dinner engagements through to the end of the summer. And one of my new friends has kindly offered to put me up in Saratoga next week."

"You'll like that. Unfortunately, the horses won't be running until August."

"So I'm told. But the casino is open and the financiers will be running. Should be plenty of ripe opportunities. In the meantime, I've set up a venture peddling pedigrees. For a hundred dollars, I trace your family back to its inevitable juncture with one of the Saxon monarchs."

"Quite reasonable."

"Yes, perhaps too reasonable. I may risk flooding the market. For two hundred, I was allowing them to name the monarch. But they'd all pick Arthur."

"Why not a mythical monarch for their fairy-tale family tree?"

"It's all right for them, but what's it do for my credibility? In the future, I may limit myself to claimants of specific titles. That's where the big money is. I have one fellow willing to pay $1,000 if I can prove he holds the title to a mere baronetcy. Now, how hard can that be? Should be able to get five thousand for an earldom, maybe ten for a dukedom."

"I don't see how you'd get away with that. A visit to any good library..."

"I thought of that. What if I publish my own version of *Debrett's*? Take most of the original verbatim, but stick in a handful of additions."

"Could work, I suppose." The Duchess of Aquatique finished her second sherry and gestured for another. "These customers of yours—you must be learning quite a bit of family lore."

"Oh, yes. I've taken to keeping notes."

"Would you be willing to share? I've been asked to conduct a séance and it would help if I could name a few dead relatives."

"I suppose an arrangement could be made."

"A good family secret would be better still."

"I came across one of those today, involving a Mrs. Rafferty."

"The lawyer's wife?"

"Yes, and mother of Felicia's playmate Celia, a child almost as noxious as she is."

"What was it you learned?"

"It's a fine one, and one I hope to profit from for a good long while."

"I don't need to reveal it, just allude to it. It can only help you to put a little fear into her."

"Yes, that's true enough. An' truth is, I'm aching to share it."

Before beginning, Archie took a long preparatory draught, then set down his beaker and ritually dabbed his face with his handkerchief. "After luncheon today Mrs. Rafferty drew me out to the garden. I was afraid she was making advances, but it was only that she wanted to be discreet. 'Tell me, Lord Abernethy,' she says. 'Suppose a girl's father was not her father. What I mean to say is, suppose an earl were visiting the same hotel in, say, Trouville, as a young American bride whose husband spent too much time in the casino? What then? I mean, what about her daughter?'"

Mrs. Biddle emitted a little laugh. "How priceless."

"Literally so, I hope."

"What did you tell her?"

"What she wanted to hear. 'The daughter,' I assured her, 'would be a Lady-in-fact, even if discretion demanded her parentage be kept mum.' Mrs. Rafferty was beside herself. That's when I mentioned Saratoga, and how nice it would be to spend some time there."

"*You* mentioned it?"

"Why not? She that tells a secret is another's servant."

"Poor Mrs. Rafferty. I hope she knows what she's in for."

"Oh, I doubt she minds. Or her daughter."

"You think she told Celia?"

"I do. When I arrived, she was the typical spoiled American child, rude and coarse. When I departed, she was speaking with a stage accent and held her hand out for me to kiss."

"Oh, that *will* be useful. I'll owe you something in return."

"Will you be around long enough for me to collect?"

Mrs. Biddle shrugged, and Archie went on.

"Tommy told me about Biddle."

"Told you what?"

"Only that you had him watching the fellow. Is he why you decided to come along as theosopher?"

Mrs. Biddle looked away, ignoring the question.

"All right," he said. "Pretend I didn't ask."

Upstairs, in Lord Dexter's office, his Polish secretary was typing another in a long series of nonsensical letters. This one was addressed to William Howard Taft, Governor General of the Philippines, asking if any of the smaller islands were still free for the taking. His lordship was hoping to establish a Pacific outpost. It was in anticipation of this grant that Dexter had donned his naval garb and title.

Tomasz had just completed his task when Felicia entered the room. He rose and stammered out a greeting. The girl made him nervous, in much the same way Lady Eleanor had before she was revealed to be an impostor. Unfortunately for Tomasz, Felicia enjoyed making young men nervous. As she reached for a stack of writing paper, she made a point of brushing her bountiful bosom against his back.

Tomasz turned toward her, his face reddened, just as she'd expected, and his breathing irregular, just as she'd aspired.

"Do excuse me," she said.

"Yes... yes, of course."

She afforded him a fleeting smile, then turned to leave.

"I was hoping for a word, Miss Dexter."

She leaned against the doorway and looked back coyly. "Were you?"

"Yes. It concerns a matter of mutual interest."

"What does?"

"The matter I wish to discuss."

"I think you've been spending too much time with my father. What is the matter you wish to discuss?"

"I fear, to answer that, I must admit to an indiscretion. The other day, when you were visiting with your friend, out on your porch, I was on the porch off this room."

"You were eavesdropping?"

"No, certainly not. At least, I had no intention..."

"What did you hear, exactly?"

"What your friend told you about Lady Eleanor being Mrs. Biddle. You see, I too was deceived by that woman. When I think of what a fool she has made of me..."

"Oh, so that's it. And now you're hoping for a little revenge?"

"I wouldn't put it quite like that."

"Why not? It will do you good, trust me."

"I don't want to be cruel, only, I think she should be exposed to all. Don't you?"

"Yes, I certainly do. And I know just when to do it. She's planning to hold a séance, and I mean to show everyone just what a fraud she is. Care to help?"

"Of course. What is it you wish me to do?"

III

Jack, having contracted out his services at seven dollars a week, was making the rounds of policy game retailers with his employer. These were the same grocers and cigar stores Pat had visited the day he was mistaken for Danny and arrested. This time, however, he was intentionally playing the part of Danny. He found it came quite easily. Pat was a natural showman, and knew well all his brother's habits and idiosyncrasies, from the colorful choices of attire to the unique manner of spitting tobacco between syllables whenever he wished to emphasize a conversational point, usually one concerning female anatomy, or some procedure involving it.

It wasn't until they reached the cigar store on Water Street that things went off track.

Jess, the owner, greeted "Danny" warmly.

"Hey, that was some trick you played on that brother of yours."

"Yeah, weren't it?" Pat agreed.

"Too bad about him gettin' his head cracked open. You think the cops croaked him?"

"Who da hell knows, Jess? Say, youse ready ta start up again?"

"Sure. Whenever you give the word. Indian's all oiled up and workin' good."

Pat knew nothing about the aboriginal in question, but there seemed to be a contradiction in the stogie peddler's description.

"Yeah? Dat's swell! Where's he at?"

"Where's he at? In the cage, like always."

"Sure. Da cage. Whaddaya say we show Jack ar Indian?"

Jess led them into the store. In the middle of the room was a platform, surrounded by a sort of giant bird cage, and inside this, a brightly painted replica of an Indian smoking a pipe.

"Yeah, he's lookin' good, Jess."

"Ain't you goin' to try him out?"

"Sure I am."

While Jess eyed him suspiciously, Pat circled the platform, looking for some means of initiating an action. After three fruitless trips around, he reached in between the bars and gave the brave's ill-fitting left foot a twist. It came off in his hand.

"Hell's bells, you ain't Danny!" Jess exclaimed.

"Well, maybe I ain't Danny. What's it matter to you?" Pat had dropped his brother's playful tone and adopted one he'd mastered years earlier during his tenure as chief of protocol for an East Side social club.

"Don't get hot about it. Makes no difference to me—just so youse remember your friends."

"I always remember my friends, ain't that so, Jack?"

Jack spat into the sawdust that carpeted the floor and Pat turned back to the tobacconist.

"So how's it work?"

Jess walked behind the counter.

"It's all steam—little gas boiler just below it. Then a valve back here, you just press it with your foot." He did so and the Indian's mouth opened and released a white plume.

"Danny used this to call the numbers?"

"Yeah. Kind of like smoke signals."

"After the mugs made their bets?"

"Sure, after they made their bets. How else?"

"Jeez, never get away with that in New York."

"Danny was smart about it. Has half a dozen women he makes sure win regular. They bet their dimes and win a plunk or two every week. So how can it be crooked if these dippy dames come out winners? They talk it up for him. Better than an ad in the newspaper."

Pat was impressed, both by his brother's appreciation of the need for theatrics when shaving the rubes, and by the gullibility of the rubes. No doubt about it, the enterprise held out great potential. Only one thing troubled him: he'd been in town less than a day and already had three people in on his secret and on his payroll.

He and Jack were walking back toward his hotel when a woman rushed across the street and blocked their way.

"Eighteen bucks, Danny!"

"Eighteen bucks?"

"Don't play dumb. You brought that damn cop aroun', an' you kin' pay for the winda's he broke."

"Sure, I'lls pay. Jeez, d'I ever welch on ya yet?"

Pat gave her two tens, the last of the money he'd won playing his cold deck on the train down from Montreal. She slipped them in a small pouch she wore on her waist.

"Youse can keep the change, sweetums," Pat told her, once it was clear none would be forthcoming.

"Sweetums? Christ..."

The woman stomped off and Pat turned to Jack.

"Wonder who the hell that was?"

"Jane. Owns da house we're in on Meeker Street."

"Danny's landlady? Wonder if he had something goin' with her...."

Jack spat. "Runs a parlor house on Jay Street."

"What's a little fella like you know about parlor houses?"

"Jus' what I hears."

"Buy me supper, will ya, Jack? Auntie cleaned me out."

"Sure."

Jack could afford to be generous. He now had money coming in from two employers, the pseudonymous Danny and the ersatz duchess, plus what he made selling the city's most popular morning paper on its most lucrative corner—a post he'd won by right of conquest a few days before. Though he hadn't been in town a fortnight, the glass jar buried in the dirt floor of the basement already contained nine dollars and thirty-five cents—all in silver. Jack preferred a currency with heft to it.

I wonder, amiable reader, if we might pause here and come to some agreement in regards to nomenclature when referring to the surviving Lyons brother? It seems—from what I've read of my sources—that he will be with us for some time, and repeated explanations of his predicament will quickly become tiresome. So let us lay down one simple rule. In conversation—excepting when alone with others in on his secret—he shall, of course, be referred to as Danny. At all other times, such as when I impart some intelligence about his actions, he shall be Pat. If there has been a lengthy gap since our last meeting with him, I may offer some slight elaboration. But otherwise, you may rely that when I say "Pat," I mean "Danny." And when I have someone else say "Danny," he, or she, will be referring to Pat, who he, or she, believes to be Danny. Unless, as I mentioned previously, he, or she, happens to be in on the secret. Simple, isn't it?

2

It's difficult to explain what exactly motivated Tomasz to re-visit the house on Meeker Street that evening. To himself, he claimed it was to warn the young baby-tossing mother from Pittsbourg about the deceit perpetrated by the so-called Lady Eleanor. But not even our dreamy Pole was so guileless as to believe Mélisande had spent six days sharing a steamship cabin without learning her companion's secret. Perhaps, he wondered, he only *hoped* she was innocent of involvement. But why would it matter?

Tomasz felt the temptation to examine his innermost feel-ings—yet he resisted. He knew from experience how distracting an endeavor that could prove. In one such case, while still at university, he had bumped into a girl on the tram. When he apologized, she smiled, then got off, never to be seen again. Tomasz spent the remainder of that term exploring his feelings toward the girl. It was all-consuming work, and inevitably led to his failing each of his classes. He did, however, manage to work it up into an impressively thick manuscript. An indulgent friend who got as far as the forty-ninth chapter told him it resembled Tolstoy's *War and Peace*—were that novel reduced to two charac-ters and shorn of all dialogue, action, and plot.

When Tomasz reached the alley behind Meeker Street, he saw Mélisande upstairs, once again brushing her hair. She was wearing a sheer nightgown which highlighted the contours of her body, the sort which left little to the imagination. But no night-gown, however sheer and revealing, could still Tomasz's imagina-tion. Just how long his reverie lasted is anyone's guess. How it ended is another matter.

Jack was returning home after an evening spent pitching pennies with idle newsies outside the depot. He'd just bitten into a worm—an inhabitant of the apple stolen from an Italian fruit vendor's cart—when he noticed a figure standing not five feet from his piglet's reconstructed sty.

"Ge' 'way from my pig!"

Tomasz, wrenched brutally from the connubial couch, turned toward the interloper—just in time to catch the speeding core with his right eye. While Jack raced to the sty, the wounded Pole made his escape.

Back at Admiral Lord Dexter's, Lady Eleanor was consulting with his lordship over the matter of the former canal bed. The city's declaration that a fine of ten dollars a day would be levied until the "mosquito-breeding mire" was drained had taken the wind out of his sails. The two of them had stuck countless pins into a dozen wax incarnations of Alderman O'Hearn, but had nothing to show for it beyond calloused fingers. Mrs. Biddle could sense that Dexter was losing faith.

"Logically, there can be only one explanation," she announced. "The alderman is himself a master of the black arts."

Dexter's eyebrows unfurled themselves and billowed, like topsails loosened upon a brig's masts. This thought had not occurred to them, nor had it to their ship's master.

"Beelzebub!" he cried. "I might have suspected he was in league with Old Nick! What now, theosopher?"

"That would depend on what's more important to Your Lordship: reaping a profit from your property, or galling Alderman O'Hearn."

For the admiral, this was no dilemma. Dexter felt the same healthy affection for capital as all successful men of commerce. But for him, to live was to vex. Nothing pleased him more than to provoke an opponent into an apoplexy of exasperation.

"Gall, gall, and gall again! Go forth and gall!" he shouted. And his eyebrows signaled their concurrence by billowing all the more, very nearly popping their stays.

"Then what I suggest is that you donate the canal bed to the city...."

The covetous topsails deflated—this was not to their liking. But Mrs. Biddle had not finished.

"...donate it to the city, *with the proviso* that it be turned into parkland and named forevermore 'Dexter's Green.' Given that it nearly bisects the city, Alderman O'Hearn can hardly avoid encountering it. And each time he will be reminded of the honor bestowed on his rival."

Lord Dexter's theosopher had scored a direct hit amidships. Her solution not only stoked her employer's burning desire to annoy his fellow man, it fed his insatiable vanity. The topsails inflated and lifted his lordship from his seat.

"Diabolical, my dear! Utterly diabolical! I'll put the plan in motion forthwith."

Though the hour was by now late, Lord Dexter proceeded upstairs to the room of his secretary. He found the door ajar, and from inside, he heard the soft voice of his wife. He peered in and saw the boy in an armchair and his wife leaning over him. His lordship cleared his throat and his wife started.

"Oh... Timothy... I was just tending to Mr. Szczęsny's... eye. The poor boy has been struck again, and his cheek still not healed."

Tomasz rose and corrected her. "Not struck this time—an apple, I believe...."

Thinking his wife incapable of infidelity, Lord Dexter accepted her innocent explanation. His less credulous brows, however, reserved judgment.

"Never mind that now, the boy has work. One eye will do, if he's still got a finger or two that moves."

The next morning, Trim's chief surprised him by uttering the words the deputy had given up all hope of hearing.

"Come on. I need some help."

Trim had longed to gain his superior's confidence and was determined to make the most of this chance. And he no doubt would have. If only prior commitments hadn't made that impossible.

As they left the courthouse, Biddle told him about Madame Bodel and needlessly gave his deputy the French girl's description. Trim could have given him a far more detailed one, or even have pointed out that Biddle himself had seen the girl in the second-floor window of the house on Meeker Street a few days before. But he held his tongue. There was much Trim had neglected to tell his chief. Of his own marriage, for instance. And that he was in alliance with Biddle's wife. And shared his new home with Eugenia, the baby daughter his chief knew nothing about. But why spoil a perfectly pleasant morning by opening that can of worms?

"She left the Baggs Hotel last Friday morning. I'll talk to the cabbies outside the hotels, you go to the Central Depot and talk to the ticket sellers and anyone else who might have seen her leave. I'll work my way down there and meet you in an hour."

Trim went off to the depot on what he knew would be a fruitless quest. He was growing increasingly uneasy. Biddle was the dogged type who would keep looking until he found the cabbie who took Mélisande from the hotel. And soon after, he'd find out what his deputy had been keeping from him.

Michael Trim wandered the depot, desperate for a solution. Then, as the morning express made its departure, it came to him. He raced out and met Biddle coming down Hudson Avenue.

"Took the express into New York, last Friday."

"Ticket seller remember her? Show me, I want to talk to him."

"No, porter on the train. Gone now. Even remembered her bein' French."

"How'd he notice that?"

Trim hadn't quite thought that point through.

"Well... Saw her speakin' with a Frenchman. Even mentioned the freckles on her nose."

"What freckles on her nose?"

"Didn't you say she had freckles?"

"Uh-uh."

"Maybe I just assumed so on account of the chestnut hair.

Ya see, I knew a girl in school. Covered in freckles...."

"An' chestnut hair?"

"More red than chestnut. Name was Margaret. Meg we called her...."

II

Later that morning, Lady Eleanor telephoned the Rafferty residence and asked to speak with Celia.

"I was wondering if you might be free for luncheon?"

"I should tell you now," the girl warned, "I know all about you."

"What do you know?"

"Who you are. And about your affidavit."

The insolent girl had caught Mrs. Biddle off guard. But, as in all such cases, she soon regained her composure.

"What a coincidence. You see, I had a dream last night, and you were in it."

"I was in it?"

"Yes. Though your mother featured more prominently. She was quite a handsome woman in her younger days, wasn't she, Celia? Or should I say, *Lady* Celia?"

The line went quiet for a long moment.

"Where do you want to meet?"

"I thought you might suggest someplace. Someplace we're unlikely to be seen."

"Maxwell's, on James. There's a small room in back."

"Sounds delightful. One o'clock?"

"Yes, all right."

Celia hung up the telephone and pondered. She was a girl prone to pondering. The smallest decisions weighed on her. Five-story buildings, complete with steam heat and elevators, were erected in the time it took her to choose a hat.

On this day, she set aside the question of headgear and pondered how the would-be Lady Eleanor had learned her secret. There were two possibilities. The first, and the more probable, was that her fellow guest at the hotel, Lord Abernethy, had indiscreetly let slip the intelligence. The second and, to Celia's thinking, more desirable solution, was that Lady Eleanor had indeed dreamed of the affair.

Though she had until then doubted the theosopher's credentials, she now hoped to be proved wrong. For, if Lady Eleanor was what she claimed, and had dreamed the dream she claimed, it would confirm a story which heretofore rested solely on the testimony of her mother—a woman with strong tendencies toward exaggeration. It wasn't that she suspected her mother had lied about the infidelity, only about the social standing of the other party involved. What Celia feared most was that she was not the fruit of an English earl's loins, but rather that of a suave French waiter or, worse still, a smooth-talking bell-boy.

She arrived early for the rendezvous and spent the time formulating a strategy: she would test Lady Eleanor's powers by inquiring on some matter Lord Abernethy could know nothing about. It was a sound strategy, and one her friends would have been surprised she was capable of conceiving. Mrs. Biddle, however, gave her more credit than her friends.

She expected to be examined by the girl and had planned accordingly. She knew she couldn't depend on Celia asking about one of the dozen or so anecdotes Archie Cobb had divulged. So she would need to take control of the conversation.

"How good of you to accept my invitation," Mrs. Biddle told her.

"I'm looking forward to... chatting with you."

After they'd exchanged small talk and given the waiter their orders, Celia leaned across the table.

"I was wondering... if you could tell me... Oh, I hope you won't find it impertinent if I..."

"Test me? Not at all—it's a cross every practicing theosopher must bear willingly."

"All right. Since you don't mind. Let's see.... Yes, that will do.... No, I've a better one...."

While Celia pondered, Lady Eleanor broke into a laugh.

"Oh, forgive me. It's just that last night, later in the same dream I spoke to you of earlier, I came upon a scene with you as a little girl. A very attractive girl, I might add. I'd guess you were about twelve."

"Really? What happened?"

"Well... Oh, dear... sometimes it's so difficult to share these things. People can so easily become embarrassed."

"Embarrassed? What was it that happened?"

"Are you sure you'll forgive me? It's really quite normal... most children, at one time or another..."

"Oh, you *must* tell me now! *Please!*"

"Well, since you insist." Mrs. Biddle leaned across the table until their faces nearly touched and whispered, "As I said, you looked to be about twelve. A boy, about the same age, was in the kitchen, unloading a box of groceries. A blond-haired boy."

"Jimmy Forester, the grocer's son."

"Yes, I remember now, you called him Jimmy. 'Hello, Jimmy,' you said. Then you hopped up on the table and, well, I couldn't quite hear what was said next... but somehow it turned into a game.... Oh, do forgive me.... It turned into a game of 'I'll show mine, if you show yours'—if you follow my meaning." Mrs. Biddle took the girl's scarlet visage as confirmation that she did indeed follow her meaning. "Nothing to be embarrassed about. Perfectly normal...."

Celia had stopped listening. The episodes she'd planned to use were of a different sort. They involved secrets she'd shared with a favorite doll. Try as she might, she could imagine no means but the occult for Lady Eleanor to have learned of her clandestine encounter with the grocer's boy. His family had moved away soon after. And Celia had never mentioned it to a soul. What she hadn't known was that the longtime family retainer—a woman Lord Abernethy found to be both full of resentments and readily bribable—had been outside hanging laundry and thus witnessed the prepubescent tête-à-tête through the kitchen window.

Though Celia was relieved to learn that the story her mother had told was true, and that she was a Lady-in-fact, even if discretion necessitated the truth remain a well-guarded secret, she was at the same time seriously concerned. Her tone during the telephone conversation earlier that day may have offended Lady Eleanor. And it was now obvious that she was not a woman to be trifled with.

Celia pondered what course to steer now. The evening before, she had assured Felicia she would help in the unmasking of Lady Eleanor. And if she broke that pledge, she knew Felicia was quite capable of making her life miserable.

Once again, Lady Eleanor led the way for her.

"I imagine Felicia has spoken with you… about me. I suspect she has something planned for the séance tomorrow evening. She hopes to expose me as a fraud. Isn't that so?"

"Well, yes. I'm afraid she does have those plans…. But once I tell her…"

"But how could you reveal what you have learned without exposing your own, quite innocent, secrets? No. No, please. Don't compromise yourself on my account. Do what she asks, by all means. But that doesn't mean we can't be friends, does it?"

"No—as long as she doesn't catch on."

"And why should she? After all, we're entitled to our secrets," Mrs. Biddle said, then broke into a giggle. "I'll bet she has her share…."

Celia laughed now, too. "Oh, more than her share, believe me…."

"Oh, I do believe you, Celia. I do. Waiter? More wine, please…."

III

In her room later that evening, Felicia chaired a conference with Tomasz and Celia in attendance.

"I've found a book that explains all about the tricks these spiritualists use."

"What does it advise?" Tomasz asked.

"Well, to tell the truth, I didn't get far.... I thought you might read it through. You like books, don't you?"

She tossed him the paper-bound book, *Revelations of a Spirit Medium, or, Spiritualistic Mysteries Exposed*, by A. Medium.

"From what I *did* gather," she went on, "the most important thing is not to reveal anything about yourself. The mistake most of these fools make is that they let little things slip. *Don't tell her anything!* Is that understood, Celia?"

"Why... why are you looking at me that way?"

"I just want you to remember, keep your trap shut! Don't tell her any details about yourself, no matter how trivial they seem."

"Honestly, I haven't said two words to her since she came. Honestly."

Felicia had been inclined to believe her sometime ally—but that final "honestly" gave her pause. She eyed the girl suspiciously, and then went on.

"The other thing to watch for is raps."

"Raps?" Tomasz asked.

"Yes, you know. The medium tells us she's speaking with a dead relative and asks the corpse to respond with raps, once for yes, twice for no, three times for... ah.... Well, you get the idea. What we need to do is keep her from making the raps. One of us needs to be on each side of her, holding her hands... and her feet. And watch out for knuckle cracking."

"Knuckle cracking?" Tomasz asked.

"Yes, apparently that's how the Fox sisters did it, cracking their toe knuckles. I'll tell you what. Celia will be on one side of her, and I'll be on the other, and you'll keep watch under the table."

"Won't it be dark?"

"Yes, I suppose it will be. Well, grab hold of her feet."

"I'm not sure I..."

"Look, you want to expose the woman, don't you? Do be a man about it!"

"It isn't a question..."

Realizing her expression of contempt had failed to sting, Felicia reached for another arrow in her quiver. She went over to where Tomasz was seated and fell into his lap, then stroked his unbruised cheek.

"Won't you do it? For me?"

She shifted, and ever so slightly pressed downward with her right thigh. When she sensed the predictable reaction, she rose—slowly, and while running her fingers across his mouth.

"There, I knew you'd come around."

Though she tried her best to exhibit her disgust, Celia couldn't help but look on in awe.

At eight o'clock the next evening, the Dexters and their guests were assembled around the large table in the hotel's dining room. The lights were dimmed, then a muffled gong sounded and Lady Eleanor, dressed in an elaborately embroidered gown, noiselessly entered the room. She took her seat, then bent her beturbaned head as if in prayer. The others watched in silence.

To her right was Felicia, and to her left, Celia. Their respective mothers sat beside them and at the far end sat Admiral Lord Dexter, his regalia newly augmented by a jumble of medals and ribbons acquired from a dealer in second-hand clothing—souvenirs of various conventions his lordship had not attended, his particular favorite being the bronze medallion commemorating the Knights of Pythias' 1897 assembly in Wilkes-Barre, Pa.

A dozen other members of Byblos society—some skeptics, some believers—filled in the table. And beneath it was Tomasz. At Felicia's insistence, he'd taken his post an hour before so as to avoid detection and his bowed spine was beginning to feel the effects. Anticipating he might waver, the girl had slipped off a shoe and periodically stroked him with her shapely, but not entirely pleasant-smelling, foot—the twin traits alternately lulling and vivifying her hidden confederate.

She suggested they go around the table, beginning with Celia, and each pose questions to Lady Eleanor. Not surprisingly, given the girl's complete conversion, the results of Celia's interview much impressed the others. Mrs. Biddle knew her favorite doll's name, and the cause of its cracked left foot, and the many intimacies shared with it. When she had trouble guessing the color of a treasured Easter bonnet, she told the girl that "a boy named Jimmy has appeared to me... he suggests the bonnet was lavender."

"Yes, that's it. Lavender."

"Peach, wasn't it?" her mother interjected.

"I should know which was my favorite bonnet, Mother."

"Yes, yes, of course, dear."

As they continued around the table, Mrs. Biddle had as many misses as hits. But whenever she missed, she explained—quite delicately—it was the fault of the interviewer for not being receptive to her thought waves. And when she hit, she hit home. So obscure was the family arcana provided by Archie Cobb that even among the skeptics few still harbored doubts.

Finally, it was Felicia's turn. She'd been frustrated by the fact Lady Eleanor had made no use of rapping spirits and so began by prompting in that direction.

"It's a pity none of us can hear these spooks you're talking with. Could you get one of them to give us some sort of signal?"

"I can only try.... Wait, I see an image... a strange image.... It looks like... it seems fantastic, but it looks to be one of your raccoons, *but in human form!*" She relaxed for a moment and turned to Tillie. "I wonder, Mrs. Dexter, if you might perform one of your calls for us? The baby raccoon you imitated so perfectly. It might compel its anthropomorphic cousin to speak with us."

Tillie complied, and two of the young men in attendance broke into uncontrollable titters. Felicia, it seems, had spread her favors wide.

"Oh, animal spirit," Lady Eleanor went on, "will you speak with us?"

Under the table, Tomasz took this as his cue and reached for the medium's feet. He tried touching them as lightly as possible, so he could feel any untoward movement yet remain undetected.

But an involuntary twitch caused him to squeeze the left foot. Above the table, Mrs. Biddle gave no appearance of having sensed the intruder. But down below, she kicked outward with the pointed toe of her right shoe. Tomasz's previously unbruised left cheek took the brunt of the blow, with the balance of the force sending his head into the center of the table.

Hearing the loud knock, and feeling the spiritual reverberations, the congregants looked from one to the other in wonderment. But there remained one doubter in their midst, a doctor and man of science. He pulled up the edge of the tablecloth and looked below. He saw nothing in the darkness, so got down on his hands and knees.

Tomasz looked desperately about for a safe haven. Just in time, one appeared before him. Felicia, having grasped the emergency, lifted her plentiful skirt and Tomasz took refuge. Then she tightened her thighs around him, and he was soon lost in a delirium born of erotic asphyxia and erratic hygiene.

The doctor, who'd crawled to the center of the table and found nothing, regained his seat a believer.

Lady Eleanor then proceeded. "O bestial being, what is it you wish to bestow upon us?"

Tomasz, now released, but suffering the combined effects of concussion, oxygen deprivation, and frustrated tumescence, slumped back into his assigned position.

"Is it of our dear friend Felicia you wish to speak?" Lady Eleanor asked her ethereal messenger.

The still-disoriented Pole reached out for the medium's feet. But this time, he would remove the risk by taking firm hold of her ankles.

"Speak, spirit!" Mrs. Biddle commanded. Again she kicked out her foot.... But her target had moved, shifting two places to her right.

"Ooooh!" cried Tillie. "I feel the spirit!"

Realizing his error, Tomasz retracted his hands and huddled beneath the center of the table, now fearful of moving in any direction.

From then on, the apparition addressed Lady Eleanor alone.

"What is it you wish me to tell Felicia? Sam, a still-living spirit, sends his greetings? Yes, yes, now I see Sam. From the manner of his dress, and the tools he carries, it would seem he lays track for the railroad. Do you remember Sam, Felicia? The layer of track? Oh, he remembers you. What a smile. I can see how... Well, perhaps we should move on.... There... there is another rugged-looking man. This lively spirit lays pipe for the city. Frank, I believe, is the name I see...."

And so the parade continued: two bricklayers—brothers Carl and Eddie; a linesman for Western Union known only by the nickname Big Red; and a roustabout for the Forepaugh & Sells Brothers Circus who wished to remain anonymous. When it was over, the guests were aghast, his lordship's eyebrows electrified, Tillie mystified, and Felicia's humiliation complete.

Oh, let us hope, sympathetic reader, that our heroine has not bitten off more than she can chew. I caution you again, Mrs. Biddle, do have a care!

3

Felicia was the first to exit the dining room that evening. Her cunning adversary had thwarted her plans and now she retreated to her lair to lick her wounds—at least, that is, until someone better suited to the task presented himself.

The others lingered, heaping accolades on Lady Eleanor and reveling in the demolition of her rival. Lord Dexter's daughter had been queen of her circle, but her haughty attitude engendered feelings in her minions not unlike those of the friends who greeted Caesar outside the senate on the occasion of his final visit there.

When at last her guests had departed, Mrs. Dexter dallied just outside the scene of the séance. She had experienced the requisite ecstatic charge when the spirit had seized her about the ankles. Yet she couldn't help but notice that his clasping appendages had felt more like the warm-blooded hands of a human than the fore-paws of an ethereal raccoon. Curious, she watched and waited. It wasn't long before a bedraggled Pole stumbled out from under the table.

When he saw his hostess observing him, Tomasz froze. Tillie, equally embarrassed, spun about and walked directly into the path of her husband, then passing through the hall. The admiral stopped to take in the scene.

"Oh, Timothy…," was all that his wife could manage before skittering off to the kitchen.

Then Tomasz approached his employer, his left cheek already a darkened blue. He held up a fountain pen as he passed. "I believe it must have slipped from my pocket at dinner last evening. I found it under the table."

What conclusions his lordship drew remain to be seen. Even his normally emotive brows gave no sign of their opinions.

Well after midnight, Felicia heard a voice at her window.

"Ya in dare, sweetums?" Pat whispered.

"Danny!"

Felicia rushed to him, not supposing even a twin brother could recreate Danny's tortured diction, or possibly know the endearment he'd chosen for her and her alone. She stripped him naked, and, to Pat's great relief, showed not the slightest interest in the protuberance above his waist.

Some hours later, as she lay beside him, exhausted, and thoroughly moistened—many were the wounds that needed licking—Felicia found she was, once again, having doubts. The pleasing hands, the insatiable tongue, and the blessedly resilient pond-snipe had all performed as advertised. But something was missing.

Whether it was due to some minor genetic variation or merely to the fact that he bathed with greater regularity, Pat lacked the essential scent of his brother. It was only now that she slid a hand over his abdomen and confirmed his deceit.

"You're the other one!"

"Whaddaya mean, sweetums?"

"You're your brother! I read about the bellybuttons."

"What's it matter, sweetums? Made you sing, didn't I? That was quite some noise, too."

Pat laughed, but laughed alone.

"I ought to call my father."

"Now, don't get sore, sweetums. It ain't my fault Danny's croaked. Really had a thing for him, huh?"

"What business is that of yours?"

"How do you think I feel about it? My own brother."

"It was Arthur who killed him, I'm sure," she said, addressing herself. "I don't care what the newspaper says. He saw him leave my room and killed him out of jealousy."

"You mean Art Biddle?"

"Yes, Biddle."

"Well, it might be he killed Danny. But 'tweren't out of jealousy."

"How can you know that?"

"Well, I jus' know, that's all."

"What do you know?"

"Well, it was Art who told me about you. Even mentioned you sleepin' with the window open."

"What!"

"It's the truth, sweetums."

"That son of a bitch!"

"Yeah, he's a son of a bitch, all right. Always has been. But why're you so sore about him puttin' me on to you?"

"Because *he's* engaged to me!"

"That right?"

"Yes! The deceitful bastard!"

"Does seem a little queer. Wonder what he's up to?"

"Thinks he can toss me aside. Well, I'll get back at him. Him *and* his damn wife!"

"Art's married already? Ain't that going to be a little awkward?"

"They're divorcing. She's actually staying here, in the hotel. She's been pretending to be a Lady Eleanor, one of those spirit mediums."

"Her? Tall blondie?"

"You've seen her?"

"I was havin' lunch in a place. Yesterday, or day before that now. Max's, or something."

"Maxwell's?"

"Yeah, that's it. I was at the counter, an' this tall blondie comes out of the back room with a girl, another blonde, but not so impressive. After they go out, I hear the girl sittin' next to me tell her friend, 'There goes Lady Eleanor, the one who talks to the spooks.'"

"The girl with Lady Eleanor, was she about my size?"

"Well, I ain't seen a lot of you standin' up, but I'd say about. The girl sittin' next to me called her Cecily, or Ceecee."

"Celia! That little bitch. I knew it had to be her."

"Yeah, might a' been Celia."

"Her too, then."

"Her too, what?"

"I need to get even with her."

"Looks like you got a full plate there, gettin' even with 'em all. Let me know if you need some help. Maybe we can work somethin' out."

He tried to slide atop of her, but she anticipated his move and flipped him onto the floor, then rolled over and peered down at him.

"I'll make you a deal," she told him. "You help me, and I won't let on that you aren't Danny."

"No need to get threatenin', sweetums. You can count on me."

"Now you better go."

"It's still early...."

"My father sleeps with a shotgun."

"Yeah? He oughtta take a wife."

"Go!"

"OK, sweetums. See you tonight."

Felicia chose not to disabuse him of his assumption and even assented to a kiss which began on her lips but then slowly migrated to the back of her neck, where it ended in a bite.

"Go," she whispered. And he did.

She was physically drained, but sleep was out of the question. Pat's revelations had caused her mind to spin. Not like a top exactly. More wobbly. Still, it spun.

Thinking he'd done in her Danny, she'd been planning to dump her fiancé. But hearing how he'd passed her on to an acquaintance like a worn shoe, a shoe he himself had never deigned to wear, she was inclined to do the exact opposite: marry him. Marry him out of sheer spite. After all, was there any better vantage for making a fellow human miserable than that of spouse? She thought not.

She went to a drawer and retrieved an azure tie. It was a favorite of Arthur Biddle's and she'd playfully taken it from him one evening on the porch. Now she placed it on the floor outside her door. Then crawled back in bed. With visions of bloody retribution dancing before her, she soon slipped into a blissful slumber.

Some hours later, Mrs. Biddle was passing the girl's door after having been summoned to her father's office. The sight of the azure tie stopped her in her tracks. As well it might. She picked it up and read the label of the New York emporium where she had purchased it. Then returned it to the floor.

Trim had told her that it was Danny whom the girl had taken to her bed. But here it was, some days after Danny's death, and again she wakes to the squeals of baby raccoons, and now finds a tie she'd given her husband outside the slut's door.

Mrs. Biddle's thoughts towards her spouse were no longer conflicted. The only thing left to be decided was the precise form of his protracted and painful death. As for the third-rate city he'd drawn her to, something along the lines of General Sherman's revels in Atlanta seemed in order.

II

When she entered his lordship's office a brief moment later, Lady Eleanor found him in a mood as foul as her own.

"Read," he told her. He held out a letter written on the mayor's own stationery.

Mr. Dexter,

Your offer of the former canal bed for use as a city park is a most generous one. But after consulting with the Board of Aldermen, I'm afraid I must decline the gift on your terms.

I've also been asked to remind you of the fine now accruing at ten dollars per diem.

Yours....

"The little weasel! He's in the pocket of that jackal, O'Hearn. What now, theosopher?"

Mrs. Biddle had no answer for her employer, but felt some

demonstration of her sympathetic sentiment was called for. She picked up the ceremonial dagger used as a letter opener, lifted her arm to its full height, then brought it down with such force that the wax replica of Alderman O'Hearn was cleaved in two and the blade of the dagger embedded in the desktop nearly to its hilt.

Dexter was impressed by his theosopher's show of vigor, but he had lost faith in her hoodoo powers.

"Your mammy," he said.

"What's that?"

"We need your old mammy. You must have something wrong. Can you find the woman?"

"Well... I suppose I can.... Yes. Yes, I'm sure I can. But I should warn you, it won't come cheap."

"How much can a mammy run?"

"Oh, we aren't speaking of some simple-minded old nurse-maid. But a true mistress of the occult, quite comfortably ensconced in her Bourbon Street mansion. It will take some doing to coax her to travel all the way up here. I suggest sending her an offering.... Yes, an offering... of at least two thousand dollars."

Admiral Lord Dexter pulled a cardboard box from under the desk, counted out twenty apricot-toned banknotes, and then handed them to Lady Eleanor. She shook her head.

"No, I'm afraid that won't do. If Mammy were as much a fool as that, there'd be little point in contacting her. Perhaps if you were to write a check...."

"No checks," Dexter snapped, then considered the need. The image of a gloating O'Hearn decided the matter. "Turn around."

When she had, he peeled back a corner of the carpet and opened the safe hidden in the floor beneath. He removed twenty one-hundred-dollar bills, then re-concealed his stash.

"Wire her this and tell her there's two thousand more if she solves my problem."

"Very well, I'll attend to it immediately."

"Five if she brings about O'Hearn's demise."

On leaving, Mrs. Biddle passed a preoccupied Mrs. Dexter in

the hall. Her hostess had just found the azure tie. She brought it into her husband's office and closed the door.

"Oh, Timothy... Look what I found, just outside Felicia's door. It's Mr. Biddle's. Now they must marry soon."

His lordship's mood turned fouler still. "He that gots wife and kid hast given hostages to fortune, for they're imped'ments to great entraprises!"

"What's that?"

"Something Lord Archibald told me. Should have put aldermen in there with them."

"I don't know what you're talking about.... Oh, and those raccoons seem to be back."

His firm's coffers having been replenished by a string of profitable signals emanating from the prophetic Indian, Pat Lyons hosted an extravagant luncheon in his rooms at the Butterfield Hotel for his staff—i.e., Jack.

"I told you we'd make a go of it. An' I was right, wasn't I, Jack?"

Jack was staring at a Little Neck clam lying limp on the half-shell and trying to work up the courage to down it as Pat had two dozen of its fellows.

"Suck it down! You better get used to slippery things if ya want to make it with the girls, Jack."

Though he held no particular desire to explore the slippery parts of girls, Jack nevertheless closed his eyes and did as his mentor suggested. Thus initiated, he swallowed a dozen more before moving on to the duckling in olive sauce and asparagus Hollandaise.

"I got plans, Jack. This policy racket ain't big enough. 'Specially in a jay town like this. Now, bucket shops. That's where the spondulicks is."

"Wus' a bucket shop?"

"It's where the rubes can bet on the stock market without havin' to go to the trouble of buyin' the stock!"

"Wus' that?"

"Eh, well, never mind that for now. You'll pick it up. But what I was thinkin' was that you got the policy racket down cold. Right?"

The boy shrugged. "Sure, guess so."

"Well, how 'bout I let you take over doin' the rounds in the afternoon? Pickin' up the slips an' the bets? Then I can start work on the bucket shop."

Jack looked at him coolly. "How much?"

"Ha! Always down ta business, that's what I like about you, Jack. No beatin' about the bush. Whaddaya say to ten percent! How's that sit with ya? After expenses, 'course—payin' the shop-keepers, the cops, an' all that."

Jack considered. Then made his counteroffer: "Twen'y."

"Twenty! Now, look here, Jack. You're just a kid. An' it's my family legacy we're talkin' about."

Jack took a bite off the duck breast he was holding. Then, without looking up, and through a full mouth, he spelled out his position. "Too bad if dey foun' out you ain't Danny. Greta t'inks so, too."

"Jeez, Jack. Comin' from you? I'll just make like you never said that. An' we'll say twenty, just to keep things friendly. An' we'll give Greta her weddin' present from tonight's take."

Jack nodded and picked up another sticky drumstick.

Pat wasn't upset with how the negotiations had gone. Now he'd eliminated his risk of getting picked up with a pocketful of slips. And cutting Jack in for twenty percent worked out to less than paying someone less trustworthy ten percent after he'd skimmed fifteen off the top.

When they'd eaten their fill, Jack went off to make rounds and Pat took out a cigar. The bucket shop scheme needed careful planning. He'd have to attract a fancier crowd, and that would require the proper accoutrements. No mechanical Indians need apply.

There was a knock, and he found Jane Jebril at the door.

"Just thought I'd stop by," she told him. "Make sure there were no hard feelings."

"Hard feelings? With old friends like us, sweetums?"

"For chrissakes, cut out that damn sweetums."

"Whatever you say, kid. Have a drink. Brandy?"

"Sure, why not." She sat down and took the glass. "You know, I heard a funny rumor. 'Bout you, an' your brother."

"Who from?"

"Don't matter who from," she told him. In fact, it was the owner of the mechanical Indian, Jess, who paid regular visits to her Jay Street establishment. Jane paused to sip her brandy. "I suppose I should be callin' ya Pat."

"Can't prove nothin'."

She reached over and stuck a hand under his shirt.

"My, what a little pecker! I hope the other one ain't so small."

"Stick around, maybe I'll show it to ya."

"We got other business to 'tend to."

"It's funny you sayin' that, Jane. I was just goin' to look you up."

"Yeah? What about?"

"Bucket shop."

"Bucket shop?"

"It's a place..."

"I know what a damn bucket shop is—what's it got to do with me?"

"I'm startin' one up."

"Won't you be goin' after the same ginks as the policy graft?"

"Nah, a bucket shop's up the ladder. In New York, even the swells go in for it—the thick-headed ones, anyway."

"Not too many swells in this burg—but plenty a' thick-heads. How do I come in?"

"Here's the thing. You get two clienteles comin' to bucket shops: fellas who don't want the missus ta know what they're doin' with the pay envelope. An' the wives, who don't want their husbands ta catch on ta what they're doin' with the house money. Of course, neither one will go someplace where their other half might show up. So, I was thinkin', why don't I open two joints, one for the ladies, an' one for the gents. Now, what ya need is a draw. For the women, that's easy. You just give 'em a place where they can gamble, an' drink, an' not be seen by the neighbors. For the men..."

"Girls."

"Sure...."

Pat had impressed himself by coming up with a ready answer to Jane's threat of blackmail. But the list of individuals in on his secret was beginning to rival that of those ignorant of it. And it included just the sort of people he'd rather not be beholden to: Biddle, the corrupt cop; the abandoned and resentful Greta; Jack, her loyal ally; Jess, the shifty owner of the mechanical Indian; Felicia, the fickle girl with a taste for vengeance; and now Jane, the parlor house madam with a sideline in extortion.

III

He and Jane spent a lazy afternoon consummating their contract. Pat really hadn't felt much interest in sampling her wares, but he feared she'd be insulted were he to decline. Much as a proffered drink can't be refused at the conclusion of a business deal without offending the other party.

"Been back to Danny's place?" she asked while dressing. "Saw you with the boy."

"Nah, Jack's just doin' some work for me. I hear you're the landlord."

"Yeah. Wasn't that your girl that had the baby?"

"Nah, just worked a graft with me. The kid belongs to a Cuban sailor she met workin' in Brooklyn."

"They got a cozy set-up. What with the French girl, an' her baby. An' I hear there's a cop hangin' around."

"Probably was lookin' for me."

"Maybe, but even after you was croaked he's been comin' by."

"Not Biddle?"

"Not him. That bastard an' me got a score to settle. Some rube that works for him."

It then dawned on Pat that this might be the same cop Jack spoke of, the one who'd married Greta. But that left another mystery.

"How'd a French girl get hooked up with Jack an' Greta?"

"Needed to rent a tit for her baby."

"She sick?"

"Don't look it."

"Chippie?"

"Ain't workin' now."

"Why would a French girl come up here to rent a tit?"

"Can't say. But I got a guess."

"What's that?"

"It ain't her kid. She stole it, an' then lammed up here."

"Could be, I suppose. Got money?"

"Dresses like it."

"Huh. So we got an arrangement?" Pat asked. "I mean, settin' up the bucket shop?"

"Sure. But don't fade me, or you'll be damn sorry."

"Fade ya? Not me, sweetums."

"An' Jeez, quit callin' me that!"

That evening, after the steaming brave signaled yet another successful session for the syndicate, Jack escorted Pat to his hotel.

"Hey, maybe I'll walk to the house with you, Jack. Give Greta that weddin' present."

"Give ta me. I'll hand it over."

"Sure, Jack, but where's the joy for me? I want to see her face when I hand her twenty bucks."

"She ain't gonna wan' a see yours."

"For runnin' off? What choice did I have?"

Jack, assuming rightly that the price Greta put on her pride was something less than twenty dollars, ceased protesting. They arrived to find the young mother sitting on the wicker loveseat beside Mélisande.

"Hey, Gret! Ain't you lookin' swell!"

"What're you doin' here?"

"Took over the family business. Didn't Jack tell ya?"

Jack slunk into the house.

"No. He didn't tell me. Ain't you afraid of gettin' caught?"

"Hell, no. Everybody seems to like it that I'm Danny an' it's Pat that's dead. An' I never thought it was fair he got to be named for our pop. Say, hear you got hitched up!"

"What's that to you?"

"No need to talk that way, I just brought 'round your weddin' present."

He held out twenty crumpled dollar bills. Greta stared at them.

"Go on, you're gonna need it, settin' up house with a cop. What's he make?"

Greta grabbed the money and went into the house.

"No pleasin' some people," Pat said after her. Then he turned to Mélisande. "*Parlez-vous?*"

"*Oui. Et vous?*"

"*Petit.*"

"*Un peu,*" she corrected. "Greta, she told me about you. Left her alone, with baby, in Brookland."

"Hey, just look at that kid! She ain't my doin'."

Mélisande exhaled a vague sound of indeterminate meaning.

"You come all the way over from France?"

"Sure. Why not?"

"No reason. Just kind of far to come to find a girl with a spare nipple. Got friends here?"

She shrugged. "Greta, and Jack."

"But didn't come lookin' for them, did you?"

Mélisande felt the interrogation had gone on long enough. Pat needed distracting.

"Why won't you sit down?" she asked.

"Ain't been invited 'til now."

He sat close beside her.

"You should be nice to me," she told him.

"Yeah, why's that?"

"It was me that sewed Danny's ear on his... *ventre.*" She tapped her tummy.

"An' without even knowin' me? That was sweet of ya. Say, what's your name?"

"Mélisande."

"Ooh, that *is* French, ain't it? Mélisande. I like it."

"Danny is OK, too."

Pat had taken her hand and casually brought it to his thigh. From then on, she took control of proceedings, bringing them to a satisfying conclusion just as a church bell rang for the tenth time and Trim came bounding up the steps. It wasn't until he was on the porch that he noticed them.

Pat hopped up, not recognizing the newcomer. Trim, however, had no problem identifying the prisoner he'd allowed to escape.

"Didn't expect to see you here. Should have left yourself dead."

"Did. That's why I'm Danny now. Say, you're the fella... Gee, no hard feelin's about the crack on the head?"

"Just so you leave Greta alone."

"Sure thing."

Trim went in and Pat turned to the girl.

"Greta's husband?"

"Yes."

"He knows 'bout you pinnin' Danny's ear to his belly?"

"Sure. It was so he wouldn't lose his job."

"Ain't he the fella that works for Biddle?"

"Biddle? What Biddle?" Mélisande's sang-froid had abandoned her. "What time is it? I must go...."

She gave him a peck on the cheek, then hurried inside. Intrigued, Pat stood a minute staring at the closed door, then started back toward his hotel. A hundred yards on, a veiled woman passed him on the sidewalk. He looked back over his shoulder and saw her enter the house he'd been visiting.

Inside, Mrs. Biddle found Mélisande and Trim in the kitchen.

"We're leaving here," she told the girl.

"When?"

"A day or two."

"What about my five hundred dollars?"

"When we get to New York, I'll give it to you."

"What changed your mind?" Trim asked.

"You were wrong about Dexter's daughter."

"How so?"

"Biddle was with her last night."

"No, he weren't."

"How could you know that?"

"Because I was with him, watchin' a house in Rome. Didn't get back here 'til an hour ago."

"You're sure he was there all night? You must have slept some."

"Not much. I don't suppose I need tell you about the snorin'."

Mrs. Biddle smiled. An odd sort of smile, nearly free of cynical suggestion. But she didn't like the feel of it and soon gave it up.

"Does that mean we stay?" Mélisande asked.

"Yes, I suppose. You're not disappointed?"

The girl shrugged. "For now, OK."

While they were chatting, Pat had circled around to the back of the house. He saw Greta pass the window of the left bedroom, and the others sitting in the kitchen. The woman had removed her veil and he recognized her as the spook compeller he'd seen at the restaurant. He couldn't imagine what connection she had to the house and was still mulling the matter when he saw her leave the room. Then a light went on in the right bedroom. A few minutes later, Mrs. Biddle paced by the window with a baby at her breast.

His curiosity contented, Pat hurried home. A cool breeze had reminded him of a dampness in his nether regions....

4

Ostensibly, it was concern for the wounded boy's health which drew Tillie back to the room of her husband's secretary that evening. He'd not shown himself since emerging from beneath the dining room table the night before. Nor had he accepted any of the half dozen offers of sustenance she'd carried up to him.

This time she was determined. It was well past eleven when she knocked bearing a plate of cold meat, bread, and cheese, and a bottle each of claret and iodine. Thankfully, her resolve would not be tested. Tomasz's hunger had at last gotten the better of his mortification at being discovered by his hostess as having taken liberties with her ankles.

Sheepishly, he opened the door, thanked her, and reached for the tray.

"No, dear boy. I insist on coming in and seeing to your cheek. My word! You do look a fright."

She set the tray on the small desk and allowed Tomasz to focus on his meal while she prepared a moistened towel, then sat on the bed and watched him. Even now, when starving, he ate with such grace. So very unlike her husband and his usual company.

When he'd finished, she had him sit on the bed. She daubed his cheek and applied iodine to the small cut. Tomasz winced at the sting, his head involuntarily swinging away and knocking the bottle from Tillie's hand. Fearing a stain, she lunged across him, grabbing the bottle a split second before it reached the patchwork quilt her Great Aunt Charity had made to celebrate the Union victory at Gettysburg.

Though not a drop of the blood-red liquid was spilt, the two now found themselves intimately entangled. Tillie, lying face down across Tomasz's lap, was afraid to move lest she risk blemishing the exquisite polychromatic portrait of General Meade's horse crafted from minute bits of chintz. And Tomasz—his hands having instinctively gone to work steadying the load, the left supporting her bosom from below, and the right resting on her derriere for no reason other than that it had presented itself—sat immobilized by a surge of conflicting emotions. Terror being the most prominent.

It was upon this knotty tableau that the increasingly suspicious Lord Dexter now gazed through the keyhole. He maintained his vigil until the couple disengaged, then made a silent exit. He was lost in thought. So thoroughly lost that he was at first unaware his sardonic eyebrows had launched into a gleeful schottische. Their suspicions had been confirmed.

It wasn't until the wee hours of the morning that Pat finally arrived at the window of his lordship's daughter. He had needed time to recuperate from the rigors of the day. And he hoped the delay in the licentious girl's gratification might serve to weaken her will and make her a more agreeable companion. But that hope was soon laid to rest.

"Where the hell have you been?"

"Miss me, sweetums?"

"When you keep me waiting half the night? You're lucky I don't call my father."

"Maybe I should leave. That what you want?"

"Do whatever you like," Felicia snapped—then turned on her back while flinging the sheet aside in a dramatic show of pique, having calculated precisely where to position her formidable breasts so the crescent of light emanating from the streetlamp would catch them in all their heaving glory.

Pat, instantly rejuvenated, did what he liked. And, if the subsequent complaints about baby raccoons are taken as indicative, Felicia also found it to her liking.

But at the first sign of sunlight, she slid away from him.

"You'd better go—and don't keep me waiting tonight!"

"Maybe I'm not ready to go."

"You're not ready to go? *I'll* tell you when you're ready."

"Say, you need to sugar up to me, sweetums. Otherwise I might not feel like tellin' ya what I found out."

"Found out about what?"

"About who. Your spook lady, that's who. Biddle's wife."

"Tell me!"

"That's no way to get what you want."

Felicia, knowing she was licked, returned the favor. This alternate methodology brought quick results, and within moments, her lover gave forth.

"Damn, sweetums. You sure know the ropes."

"Don't dither, you got yours. Now what was it you found out?"

"Your Lady Eleanor didn't come to town alone."

"I *know* that! She came with my father."

"No, I mean, she brought some baggage.... An' she's hidin' it over at my brother Danny's old house."

"What sort of baggage?"

"The kind that cries an' wants to suck at her tit."

"A *man?*"

"Damn, sweetums, you got a one-track mind," Pat chuckled. "A *baby*. Brought it over from France an' stashed it away with a wet nurse."

"How do you know all this?"

"Well the wet nurse and me used to be... business associates."

"And she told you it was this woman's baby?"

"No, I figured that out for myself. Saw her in there with her shirtwaist open an' the baby takin' its supper."

"I don't get it. What's she up to?"

"Well, I did some thinkin' about it. She wants to keep someone from knowin' about this baby. Someone who might not be happy about it."

"Arthur?"

"Sure."

"But she just signed an affidavit to let the divorce go through."

"You said Biddle wanted a divorce so's he could marry you?"

"Yes."

"Well, sweetums, I don't think that's what he has in mind. Maybe she figured that out too."

"So?"

"So she signs the affidavit just to make him admit it."

"Why does she care?"

"She wouldn't, unless she has plans to get back together with him. Why else would she show up here? So now he knows she's here, an' she knows he knows. But the one thing she don't want him to know about is that baby. Only one reason I can think of...."

"Because it isn't his...."

"Sure. An' she's afraid of what he'd do if he finds out, which means she must want him back."

"Then that's it."

"What's it?"

"That's how I get even with her. Take the baby and show it to him. I'll need your help."

"I don't know, sweetums. Stealin' babies ain't really in my line."

Felicia reached down and tugged at his outsized umbilicus.

"Your line is doing what I ask!"

"All right. But we'll need someone else in on it."

"I've just the person. He's looking to get even with the duchess as well."

"Duchess?"

"Lady Eleanor, 'Duchess of Aquatique,' she calls herself."

"Bet there's money in a con like that."

"Yes, I wouldn't doubt she's wheedled a nice bit from Father. Fooled him, easy enough. And Mother, of course."

"But not you, sweetums."

"*Of course not me!* What do you take me for?" Pat, relieved her inquiry was a rhetorical one, waited for her to continue. "We'll need to meet later. To make plans. Where are you staying?"

"You want to come around to my place?"

"*What's wrong with that?*"

"Nothin', sweetums. Nothin' at all. The Butterfield. Room 209."

"I'll be there at three this afternoon."

"All right, sweetums. Three o'clock it is."

"Now go, quickly."

Oh, Mrs. Biddle, you *poor thing*—your own deceptions may prove your undoing. Well, you can't say I didn't warn you....

II

On the advice of Celia, Mrs. Biddle attended services the next morning at the Methodists' outpost in Byblos. These bland sects of Christianity, practiced in their bland little churches, were not to her taste. If she were to go in for some religion (other than the self-worship she practiced so devoutly), it would be of the classical pagan sort. Zeus, Aphrodite, Athena—these were gods she could identify with. And whose visitations one might look forward to with some feeling other than guilt, or fear. *She* certainly had. When still a romantic young girl—sometime after her introduction to *Bulfinch's Mythology*, yet before the onset of menses—she made frequent visits to Central Park, where she practiced her powers of seduction on the resident swans. (Rest assured, modest reader, nothing came of it.)

Mrs. Biddle's reason for enduring the Sunday ritual was a purely practical one. When asked, Celia could think of only one woman living in Byblos who was of the proper age and complexion to play the part of her New Orleans mammy: Josephine Miner, a former school teacher and devout Methodist.

While that lady exchanged meaningless twaddle with fellow parishioners and complimented the pastor on a sermon only moderately less mind-numbing than that of the previous Sunday, Mrs. Biddle awaited her at the bottom of the steps. Reflexively, Mrs. Miner offered her hand as she approached.

"So good to see you, Mrs. Miner."

"Have we met before?"

"No, I've not had the pleasure. A friend told me of you."

"Told you of me?"

"Yes, it's a rather... complex situation."

"What situation?"

"The one I wish to speak to you about."

"Do you always speak in riddles?"

"No, forgive me. But I wonder if there's someplace we might go to talk?"

"You can come back to the house, if you like."

"Very kind of you. I understand you were a school teacher. Now retired?"

"Retired? No, let go. We were both teaching, Mr. Miner and I, at one of the colored schools in Brooklyn. Then, when the state ordered the schools to desegregate, we were let go. Most white parents didn't want their children taught by coloreds. Now Mr. Miner works as a porter on the Pullman cars."

"How dispiriting."

"Oh, can't allow yourself to become dispirited. Still, I do miss Brooklyn."

The conversation moved on to more prosaic topics until they arrived at the small house on a street just two blocks below the Erie Canal. Mrs. Miner made coffee and served her guest a slice of pecan pie.

"Tell me, Mrs. Miner, what do you know of Timothy Dexter?"

"Only that he's rich... and odd... though some say worse.... Has wheels in his head, they say."

She laughed, and Mrs. Biddle laughed with her.

"Well, I have come to know him. And I can attest that he is, indeed, a batty old coot. But it's equally true that he *is* rich. And taken together, those can be very endearing qualities."

"I've heard how all the charlatans have managed to exploit the old man.... Oh, dear, please don't be offended.... I'm sure you..."

"Sadly, Mrs. Miner, I must confess to being yet another charlatan exploiting Mr.—or, as he prefers to be called, *Lord* Dexter."

"Yes, I've heard that too. Well, I suppose it's not as if his wife and child will go to bed hungry. And who am I to judge.... But why is it you've come to me?"

"I've set myself up in his lordship's service as a soothsayer."

"Oh, so you're Lady Eleanor? Yes, we've certainly heard about you."

"I'm flattered. But it seems Lord Dexter has lost faith in my hoodoo powers."

"Hoodoo powers?"

"Yes, I told him some nonsense of having come from New Orleans, and having been taught by my.... Tell me, Mrs. Miner, have you done any play-acting?"

"Some, at college."

"Do you think you could adopt a southern vernacular?"

"Oh, lord. Not that black-face gibberish Mr. Clemens uses? No, that *would* be dispiriting. Besides, I've never been south of Philadelphia."

"No, that won't be necessary. Did you take French at school?"

"Some. Oh, I see what you're getting at. New Orleans... Something like Palmyre, the philosophe."

"Palmyre?"

"In Mr. Cable's book. What was it called? *The Grandissimes!*"

"Yes. That's it exactly. Just work in that you were my mammy."

"I'd need to study up some. It's been years since I've read it. But what are we talking about? I could never do something like that. What would my husband say? Or the pastor, for that matter."

"Mrs. Miner, if you can forgive such a personal question, how much did you earn as a teacher?"

"Well... six hundred dollars that last year."

Mrs. Biddle opened her chatelaine purse and pulled out a roll of banknotes. She counted out six one-hundred-dollar bills and slid them across the table.

"This is in addition to whatever Lord Dexter might send your way."

Mrs. Miner eyed the stack covetously.

"The roof does need fixing."

"And I'm sure the pastor, if he were to find out, would not look amiss at a contribution derived from so harmless a charade. Then, too, you must think of the time when Mr. Miner is no longer able to perform such demanding work. Carefully nurtured, Lord Dexter's largesse could see you comfortably through your twilight years. And with very little effort."

"I'll visit the library first thing in the morning."

"Wonderful. And I will tell his lordship that Mammy has replied in the affirmative."

"Must I call him Lord Dexter?"

"Well, it does grease the skids."

"What if I were to bestow on him some hoodoo-sounding name? Something French."

"I suppose..."

"I have it! Tartuffe!"

"Oh, Mrs. Miner, how perfect!"

"Not too transparent?"

"Well, not for Dexter, or his wife. And certainly not for his dim-witted daughter. And I doubt anyone getting the joke would want to ruin it. It seems Lord Dexter is a cherished source of amusement for what passes as the literati of this benighted city."

Mrs. Biddle rose and held out her hand. "I'm so relieved you've entered into the spirit of the thing, Mrs. Miner."

"*Madame Palmyre, s'il vous plaît.*"

Pat, meanwhile, sat in his room and considered his options. He was appreciably less than sanguine at the prospect of kidnapping Mrs. Biddle's baby. She looked to be the sort of woman who would make a fuss. And if they were mistaken, and it *was* Biddle's baby, there would be hell to pay.

On the other hand, if he balked, there was little doubt that Felicia would follow through on her threat to expose him. He was going to need to thread a very fine needle. He was still contemplating this dilemma when he heard a soft knock at the door.

"Hey, there! Ain't you lookin' swell!"

It was Mélisande, dressed for church. She hadn't been quite sure what to make of Greta's former accomplice. He wasn't anything like handsome. But his *joie de vivre* had provided a welcome diversion from the monotony of domesticity. And now she was in the mood for another helping.

"*Bonjour, mon chéri*. I think maybe you like to come to Mass with me?"

"Mass?"

"*Oui*. Are you not Catholic?"

"Yeah, I suppose so. But how 'bout we stay here? I can tend to your spiritual needs...."

Mélisande made a noise. "No, *mon chéri*. Come, I must go."

"Tell you what, I'll walk you there."

As they left the hotel, she took his arm in hers.

"Are you sure you won't come with me?"

"Sorry, I get hives just passin' those places. Where's Greta? She usually goes in for the mumbo-jumbo."

"She watches the babies, then later I watch them and she goes to late Mass."

"Yeah? What time's that?"

"Six o'clock. You want to come by?"

"Sure. But does her man go with her?"

"He is gone today. To Syracuse. To see his sister."

"So it'll be just you and me?"

"Sure."

"And Jack, I suppose..."

"Jack, he almost never is home in daytime. Always off somewhere..."

"Well, then, I'll see you at six o'clock."

He tried to kiss her, but she pushed him off.

"Later... maybe."

III

At three o'clock, Pat was woken by a far more determined knock at the door.

"Hey there, sweetums! I was waitin' for you."

"Then why did I need to pound on the door for five minutes?"

Felicia pushed past him, then Tomasz, standing behind, made a slight bow and followed.

"This is Tommy. My father's secretary. He needs to get even with Lady Eleanor too."

"Well, I wouldn't..."

"Oh, do stop your whining," she demanded. "It's too late to back out now. Sit down. Both of you. Wait," she told Pat. "Call down and have them send up something. How're their pastries?"

"Doughnuts are OK."

"*Doughnuts?* See if they have a tart of some sort, a strudel would be better. And coffee."

Pat did as commanded.

"Now," the girl went on, "all we need to do is get the baby from this house.... Where is it exactly?"

"Meeker Street, just a few blocks away."

"We get the baby and bring it around to Arthur's apartment. He'll be there all day. Reading his damn law books."

"Which baby?" Tomasz asked.

"*I already told you!* This Biddle woman has a baby stashed away at this house."

"There are two babies there," Tomasz informed her. "One is that of the young widow who traveled on the boat with Lady Eleanor."

"Then it must be the other one, mustn't it?" Felicia asked, exasperated.

"The dark one?"

"The dark one? What are you talking about?"

"The other baby, she looks much darker."

"Yeah, that's the one," Pat confirmed. The Pole had made a serendipitous error.

"It's strange, isn't it, that I never saw it on the boat," Tomasz said.

Felicia looked on him with pity. "*I've told you*, she's been hiding it!"

"No wonder why," Pat added. "Little pickaninny."

"What?" Felicia asked. "Her baby is *black?*"

"Not black. More like milky coffee."

"Then it couldn't possibly be Arthur's! Why didn't you tell me that before?"

"Must've slipped my mind."

"This is wonderful," she announced. "We take the baby to his place, and send a note to her saying the baby's been kidnapped and to come to his address. She'll show up to rescue it... and there'll be no denying the baby's hers."

"But how do we take a baby without someone calling for the police?" Tomasz asked.

"I got that all figured out," Pat told them. "At six o'clock, the French girl will be home alone."

"How do you know that?" Felicia asked.

"She told me. Met her the other night. Remember, I got some friends staying in the same house. Well, like I said, at six o'clock, she'll be there alone. I told her I might stop by."

"Stop by? What's she look like?"

"Oh, plain-looking little thing, not quite homely."

"She is not at all homely," Tomasz insisted.

"Well, each to his own. But the fact is, she's got a thing for me. So at six o'clock I go over and get her out on the front porch. While I got her occupied, you can go in the back way and grab the brat."

"Can you find the house from the alley?" Felicia asked Tomasz.

"Yes, but..."

"Quiet! I'll have my runabout—that way we can take the baby to Arthur's without having to take the trolley."

"Runabout?" Pat asked.

"Electric. It can go fifteen miles in an hour."

"Speedy. Well, looks like we got ourselves a plan. Give me half an hour to get her settled on the porch."

After emptying three plates of pastry, Felicia rose and sauntered over to where Pat was standing.

"Remember, I'm counting on you." She'd put her hand under his shirt and was rubbing his stomach—then gave his umbilicus another sharp pull. "*Don't let me down!*"

"Never dream of it, sweetums!"

"Good. Come on, you." She followed Tomasz out the door, but as was her custom, neglected to shut it.

Pat did so himself, then had a private laugh. The misguided Pole's error had come as a stroke of luck. Later, he might need to settle with Greta for the temporary loan of her baby. But five dollars would probably be enough. Whereas an angry Biddle might cost him five years.

At six o'clock he showed up at the Meeker Street house with a dozen blue irises and a well-refined patter. Mélisande greeted him in a house dress of the same color, carefully fitted to make the most of her humble bosom. She put the flowers in an empty pickle jar, then sat him down on the couch in the front room.

"*Mon chéri!*" She flung off his hat, then pinned him to the couch, her knees planted on either side of his lap.

Her aggressiveness had caught Pat off guard, and it took some time before he managed to refocus his mind on the pressing matter of the kidnapping—longer still for other segments of his anatomy.

"Say, kid, why don't we move out to the porch? Get some air."

"The porch?"

"Yeah. It feels kind of... close in here."

"Close?"

"Yeah. You been eatin' a lot of cabbage?"

"Cabbage?"

"Well, I hate to bring it up..."

Mélisande rose and looked at him, not sure if she should be offended.

"Ah, I see. You are the type who likes it outside."

"Well, it's a nice day...."

"Sure. You want people to see.... Well," she shrugged, "it's OK with me."

She led him out to the porch, and once they had sat down she stretched her legs across his lap. It being a Sunday evening and the street full of strollers, more than a few heads turned their way. But to her surprise, and the spectators' regret, Pat made no attempt to take advantage of the arrangement.

"I was hoping to have a chat," he told her.

"Chat?"

"Sure. Say, tell me something about France. Been to Paris?"

"One time. With the *Abbesse*."

"*Abbesse?*"

"Eh, the head sister. Ah... a nun. Do you want me to tell you about it?"

"Sure."

"Well, one day, long ago..."

And so began Mélisande's tale of the abbess who had an itch.

(As it would disrupt the carefully crafted pacing of the current work, the abbess's tale itself has been left out. But fear not, devoted reader! It can be found in *The Fly Maiden's Book of Virtues,* which you have no doubt already availed yourself of at the *BybloslForetold.com* web site.)

At six-thirty, Felicia drove her electric runabout slowly up the alley.

"That is the house," Tomasz said.

"You know what to do," she told him. *"Now, get going!"*

Tomasz crept carefully by the sleeping piglet and into the house. He heard the faint sound of a waking baby upstairs and followed it to the chamber where the two infants were lying side by side in their cradle. It was Eugenia who was awake, and she didn't look pleased about it. Tomasz picked her up and swung her gently in his arms while humming the same Polish lullaby he'd used on her to good effect when they were earlier aboard the

Kronprinz Wilhelm. When her eyes closed, he set her down and picked up the sleeping Gretchen, then hurried downstairs and out into the alley. He had to leap onto the moving auto—Felicia having helpfully set it in motion on sighting him—and nearly dropped the baby when his knee clipped the side.

Jack, then on his way home for supper, spotted them just as they emerged from the alley. He recognized the would-be pig-napper from their previous encounter and quite naturally assumed the bundle the miscreant held was his piglet.

"Hey, you!" he shouted, before giving chase.

5

Two blocks on, Jack nearly caught up to the electric runabout when it was held up by a streetcar. But then the apparent pig-nappers were given six blocks unimpeded and it was all he could do to keep them in sight. Two quick turns, and they had vanished.

Jack ran frantically up and down parallel avenues, scanning the cross streets as he passed. There! The auto had stopped and the original pig-napper was limping off. Jack charged him from behind, stopping briefly along the way to pick up a stout branch.

When he and Felicia had arrived a few moments before, Tomasz declined to go with her to visit Biddle. He told her how his previous encounter with said Biddle had ended in an unpleasant sojourn in the city jail and that he wasn't altogether keen on a reprise. She called him a coward, of course, and worse. But when it was clear he could not be swayed, she took the baby and went up alone.

It wasn't until Jack was within two yards of him that Tomasz realized he was being pursued. The precise meaning of Jack's invective—"Pu' dawn da porker, or I'll soaks youse good!"—was not clear, but the boy's blistering intonation made apparent his general frame of mind. He was not pleased about something. And, Tomasz noticed as he turned, he was wielding a large stick. The two, taken together, spelled danger. If only they had spelled it a little sooner.

This time, it was the area around Tomasz's left eye which took the blow—the sole quadrant of his face so far left unscathed. Though not *permanently* blinded, he was knocked silly. When Jack attempted to interrogate him, the pig-napper could only stare off into the distance, emitting a stray groan whenever the pain's intensity pierced his stupor. Eventually, he stumbled into the schoolyard and collapsed beneath the same elm he had supped under on another disagreeable evening the week before.

Jack searched the auto for signs of his piglet, but saw none. The malevolent accomplice must have taken the bundled booty. Where, he didn't know, but surely it had to be someplace nearby.

And it was. Just across the street, in fact. As she had foreseen, Felicia's knock had interrupted Biddle studying one of his deathly dull law treatises. When he opened the door, she pushed her way in and placed the still-sleeping baby on the couch, then pointed at it dramatically.

"There! What do you think of that?"

"Nice. But I'm not in the market. Where'd you pick it up?"

"Where indeed!" she shouted, then slumped into a chair. The execution of the crime had exhausted her, and she wasn't up to maintaining so theatrical a pose for any length of time. "I need a brandy."

Biddle provided her a glass, then stood looking down at the serenely somnolent, and seemingly imperturbable, Gretchen.

"What's this about?"

"Do you know where I found the child?"

"No idea."

"A house on Meeker Street. A house frequented by the woman staying with us under the name of Lady Eleanor. Though you know her by another name...."

"Found out about her, huh?"

"Yes, I found out about her. But not from you. Playing me for the dupe...."

"Don't get sore, sweetums."

"Don't call me that!"

"Look, you got no worse than you gave. Takin' in Danny Lyons while I was downstairs on the porch with your mother. You oughtta be ashamed."

"Don't play horse with me! You know it was you I was expecting."

"I got delayed. But that's all water under the bridge. Let's get back to the bundle of joy. Whose is it?"

"Whose?" Felicia asked through a sneering grin. "She should be here soon. I'll let *her* tell you...."

By blackmailing the cook—who she took for granted was stealing from the loosely documented household accounts, just as every other domestic had before her—Felicia had arranged that a note would be delivered to Lady Eleanor along with her soup. But the duchess was not there to partake of it.

Lady Eleanor had been called away to conduct an emergency séance. The Persian cat of a mill owner's wife had passed away that morning and it was imperative that communication with its spirit handlers be established before the feline was served her evening meal. (*No fish* was the message. The persnickety puss had once choked on a salmon's rib and since then the mere smell of fish sent her into a week-long pout.)

Archie Cobb, thankfully, suffered from no such phobia. He was partial to seafood, and most especially to lobster. Since the soup that evening was a bisque featuring that very arthropod, he took the liberty of exchanging his soon-emptied bowl with that set out for the absent duchess. When he performed the maneuver, Felicia's note flittered to the floor. Discreetly, Archie picked it up and read:

Your baby has been taken to 27 Louisa Street, 2nd floor. You may retrieve it any time after seven. Knock three times.

He had met Lady Eleanor's child fleetingly when they were aboard the *Kronprinz Wilhelm*—then been sworn to secrecy. What happened to it on their arrival, she had not divulged. But he had taken it as a given that it was nearby.

Archie had developed a certain avuncular affection for the cunning young woman. True, there was an element of the devil about her. And yes, she had swindled her own father, *and* engineered his arrest. But she had always—as far as he was aware—been square with Archie.

Not knowing when she would return home, he felt disposed to act on her behalf. And had the next course been anything other than a sumptuously prepared spring lamb, he would have done so posthaste. As it was, after just two helpings his compassionate spirit took hold and shook him to his feet. He begged the pardon of his hostess, then slipped into the kitchen.

"I wonder, Gladys," he asked the cook, "who it was who transmitted this note to Lady Eleanor?"

"Oh, I had no choice, Lord Abernethy. That evil girl gave it to me and told me if I didn't send it in to Lady Eleanor, she'd... well, make trouble for me...."

"I see. I don't suppose there's any need to inquire as to which evil girl."

"Only one I know that evil...."

"Then I take it you've never visited Lambeth?"

"Lambeth?"

"Well, I'll attend to this. And no one need know your part in it."

"That's very white of you, Lord Abernethy."

"Not at all. Tell me, would it be possible to set aside the remainder of my meal...?"

"Oh, absolutely."

"And tomorrow, might we have some of your delicious bisque again?"

"Well... Yes. Yes, of course."

When a few minutes later Archie rapped three times on the door of Biddle's apartment, Felicia, quite uncharacteristically, leapt to her feet.

"Now we'll see!"

Biddle opened the door and Archie removed his hat.

"Archie Cobb. Or Lord Abernethy, if you fancy. I've come to represent the interests of Lady Eleanor. Though I expect you might know her by some other name."

"What are you doing here?" Felicia demanded.

"Lady Eleanor wasn't at home, and I happened upon your note. As the situation seemed to demand immediate action, I thought it best to come in her stead. Is that the child?"

"It's *her* child," Felicia said.

"*What?* Are you saying this kid belongs to... Lady Eleanor?" Biddle asked.

"Of course it does! It belongs to your scheming wife!"

Biddle looked at Archie for confirmation. Cobb walked over and looked down at the sleeping infant.

"Well, it's not quite as I remember it, but I only saw it for a moment. On the boat over."

"That's right! She brought it with her from France," Felicia added, whilst donning what she considered the most devastating of her wide repertory of sneers.

II

On the porch of a certain house on Meeker Street, Mélisande had just finished telling the story of the abbess who had an itch. Pat was not normally drawn to fiction, but he felt obliged to compliment her on her prowess as a fabulist.

"You sure know how to keep a story interestin'. I'm spent. Wonder if we have nuns like that here? I sure never met 'em."

Mélisande rose and suggested that she fetch some refreshment from the kitchen. Fearing this might include a visit to the nursery, Pat offered an alternative.

"Let's stretch our legs. Tell you what, step over to my place and I'll stand you a drink."

"Leave the babies?"

"Aw, come on. They're sleepin', or else you'd hear them squawkin'."

"No. We must stay."

As she sat back down, Trim came up the steps.

"Becoming reg'lar company...." he said to Pat. Then he inquired of Mélisande if Greta was at home.

"No, not 'til late. Mass, then vaudeville. With Mrs. Emerick, from next door."

"How was Syracuse?" Pat asked, hoping to delay the deputy's entry.

"Better than the last time."

"Your sister is OK?" Mélisande asked.

"Weren't there. Might be why it went better than last time. Her husband was. Went fishing. Ever fished Onondaga Lake?"

"Not that I recollect," Pat admitted.

"I have." It was Mr. Emerick, from the porch next door. He'd been listening to Mélisande's tale most attentively while pretending to read the newspaper. "What you catch?"

"Sturgeon. But 'tweren't no ordinary sturgeon," Trim told him.

"Weren't any sort of sturgeon. Not in Onondaga," Mr. Emerick corrected.

"Might be it wasn't sturgeon. But you haven't heard the strange part. My brother-in-law..."

"Musky, maybe. But not a sturgeon."

"As I was saying... my brother-in-law cast out a fly, one he tied himself, and he reels in a musky, let's call it."

"A musky? By casting a fly? That wasn't no musky. You're talkin' through your whiskers."

"Well, rainbow trout then. But a big one. An' not just that— it's got *two heads!*"

"Rainbow trout? In *that* lake?"

Trim and his neighbor continued their ill-omened colloquy for some time. Mr. Emerick, who fancied himself an authority on the piscine inhabitants of the Empire State, refused to allow the discussion to veer from what he saw as the nub of the matter: the species of the fish. To his mind, idiosyncrasies of its individual anatomy were irrelevant.

Mélisande at last agreed to go for a stroll when Trim in his frustration was reduced to shouting, *"Two heads! Two heads! Two heads!"*

"Whar's my pig, lady!" Jack was standing in the still-open door at Biddle's apartment.

"What pig? Arthur, get rid of the urchin."

Jack saw the bundle on the sofa and went over to it.

"Gretchen! Why'd ya go an' steal Gretchen?"

He picked up the baby. "Don't none of youse get in my way."

"No one's going to get in your way," Biddle told him. "That your baby sister?"

"Nit. Greta's baby."

"You little liar!" Felicia shouted. "Tell him. It belongs to a woman named Biddle. Calls herself Lady Eleanor."

"Calls herself Miss Custis, too," Jack added. "But this ain't her baby."

"Miss Custis?" Biddle recognized the name as one of his wife's former aliases.

"This is absurd. Are you going to believe *me*, or this little... delinquent?"

"Well, sweetums, he seems to know more about it than any of us."

"Oh, damn you all!"

Confounded, Felicia stormed out of the apartment and retreated to her home. She often became confounded when complex situations presented themselves, and this one had left her feeling like a prospective conqueror challenged to undo a diabolical knot by King Gordius. Back in her sanctum, she brooded. She knew that it would be a waste of time for her to try to unravel the tangle of truths on her own. Better to simply slice through the knot and get on with more pressing matters. In this case, that meant setting aside questions of parentage and ordering up a plate of blueberry turnovers.

Biddle, meanwhile, invited Jack to sit down.

"Nit. Need ta get back, 'fore Greta finds 'er baby gone."

"All right, we'll bring back Greta's baby. First, maybe you can tell me about this Miss Custis."

Jack stared back at him.

Biddle took out a quarter and handed it to him.

"She gives me a V a week."

"*Five bucks a week? For what?*"

Jack shrugged.

"Look, I don't know what she told you. But she's my wife and I'm goin' to get to the bottom of this."

"I know. You're Biddle... a cop."

"Yeah. So don't make me have to get rough."

Jack was three-quarters of the way to spitting on the carpet, but checked himself for fear of endangering Gretchen. His expression, however, made clear his contempt, even if the hastily recalled spittle dribbling down his chin somewhat mitigated the effect.

"Well," Archie announced, "if I'm no longer required, I think I'll go back and finish my dinner."

"Sure," Biddle said. "Go and finish your dinner. But don't say anything to Lady Eleanor."

Archie left the room and descended the first half-flight of stairs. Then he stopped and listened.

Biddle turned back to Jack. "Look, I'm not puttin' the screws on anyone. But I've got to know. What's she payin' you for?"

"You won't try and take her baby?"

"Her baby? What baby?"

"Calls her Eugeenya."

"You're sure the kid is hers?"

"Yeah."

"Take me to it."

"You won't try and steal her?"

"No, I'm not goin' to try and steal her. Just see her."

"An' you won't tell it was me who told you."

"Hell, no."

"All right."

Archie hid behind a cupboard and went unnoticed as the two passed him. Outside, they crossed the street and came to the runabout.

"Ever ride in one of these?" Biddle asked.

"Nah. It's hers. That lady that stole Gretchen."

"Yeah, I know. What ya say we save some time and ride over to your place?"

"Sure. How's it work?"

"We'll have to figure that out. Get in."

Biddle offered to hold the baby while he boarded, but Jack

managed himself. After some fumbling, Biddle set them in motion.

"Where we goin'?" he asked.

"Meeker Street, 410."

"410 Meeker Street?"

"Yeah."

"Danny Lyons' place?"

"Yeah."

"An' this Greta, she's with Pat?"

"Pat's dead."

"All right, so she's with Danny?"

"No. Married someone else."

"Why's my wife got her baby there?"

Jack shrugged.

"She hidin' it from me?"

The boy shrugged again. "We can go in da back. Down da alley."

Biddle did as he was told and stopped behind the house he recognized.

"Come on," Jack directed. He led Biddle past the piglet and into the house. They could hear Trim on the front porch.

"*Two heads! Two heads! Two heads!*"

Biddle looked at the boy quizzically.

"Greta's husband," Jack whispered. Then led the way up the stairs and into the chamber where Eugenia was still sleeping. He set Gretchen in beside her and Biddle came up behind him.

"That her?"

"Yeah. Wanna hold her?"

"Sure."

"Sit down. Ever hold a baby before?" Jack asked.

"Sure."

Jack picked up Eugenia and brought her to Biddle on the bed.

"Careful of her head," he instructed. "Ain't hooked on good yet."

"All right."

Biddle sat quietly, looking over the baby for signs of a re-semblance.

"What you gonna do?" Jack asked.

"Not sure yet. What would you do?"

Jack shrugged.

"Yeah. Me too. That fella we heard yellin' downstairs…"

"Greta's ol' man."

"Yeah. Name wouldn't be Trim, would it?"

Jack smiled.

"You know he works for me?"

A shrug.

"So this Greta helps Pat get away from Trim, then he marries her? An' my wife just happens to come by with her baby?"

"Nit. Mel'nie brought the baby. Said she needed a nurse. A wet one."

"Who's Melanie?"

"Girl. From France. Friend of Miss Custis."

"What the hell's she up to?"

Jack thought of shrugging, but gave it up when he heard the voice of the woman in question downstairs.

"Where's Mélisande?" she asked Trim, who'd apparently ceded the field to Mr. Emerick and retreated with her into the kitchen.

"Hide!" Jack whispered.

III

Though she had agreed to go off with him, Mélisande de-clined Pat's invitation to visit his hotel. Instead, she suggested that they perambulate together about the neighborhood. As you may have surmised, she enjoyed the company of men. She found them amusing. And Pat particularly so. He was lively, and smooth-talking, and of questionable character—the holy trinity of qualities for a romantic girl who'd spent her formative years holed up in a cloister.

But there is one area where even you, keen reader, may have

surmised incorrectly. I know I did. Even Mrs. Biddle, her mistress and traveling companion, labors under this misapprehension. I'm referring to the present status of the girl's maidenhead. It is, contrary to all indications, intact.

How can this be, you wonder. With what had she bribed the police sergeant in Cherbourg if not her virtue? And what of M. Bouc, the mayor's cuckold, with whom she spent a long night in that same city?

It seems that sometime before her thirteenth birthday, on a very cold January morning, a thoughtful priest suggested she join him on his side of the confessional, where there was a coal brazier. Having by then made the excursion to Paris with the itch-prone abbess, she had a fairly clear idea of what the cleric had in mind.

She had two choices, she decided: attempt to shy away from him—a near-impossible task for a small girl in a convent—or remove the threat. She opted for the latter. She reached under his robe and felt her way about. In no time at all, she'd brought him to a fever-pitch of excitement... then... release. The girl crossed herself and went off to breakfast—being sure to rinse her hand in the baptismal font on her way.

Over the years she had refined her technique. M. Bouc had been taken in hand in the café where they met, and then again on the landing on the way to his room. Even before she closed the door, he was fast asleep. Then once more when he woke at dawn, and back asleep—just in time for her to empty his wallet and make off with his watch.

This evening was a warm one, so Pat, who'd had his itch scratched at precisely the same moment as the abbess had hers, felt none of the discomfort he had the night before.

By chance, their aimless walk had brought the couple abreast the entrance to the busy alley. Pat happened to glance down it and saw the runabout parked behind the house. His normally tranquil heart began to palpitate. Why hadn't Felicia and the Pole made their escape? Something had gone wrong—but what?

"Wait here," he said, then slunk down the alley. There was no sign of his fellow conspirators.

He could think of only one solution that fit the facts: they had gotten a late start and Trim, having ended his debate with Mr. Emerick, caught them in the act of stealing his stepdaughter. They'd be hard-pressed to talk their way out of that. Especially two so dim-witted. And he could hardly count on the vindictive Felicia to keep his name out of it. The only course open was to lie low until he could determine the level of risk.

He got in the runabout and, after a minor set-to with a neighbor's henhouse, drove it quickly out to the street. When he reached the girl, he stopped—lying low without the right company quickly becomes tedious.

"Get in, kid. Let's go someplace."

Mélisande did as instructed without making any query as to the provenance of the electric auto, or their destination. It was an adventure, and she was sorely in need of an adventure.

Upstairs, Biddle had just hidden behind the door when his wife entered the room. She found Jack sitting on the bed cradling her daughter.

"I think she's hungry," he told her.

"Jack, where's that damn girl gone off to?"

"Mel'nie? I told her I'd watch 'em 'til Greta got back."

"Thank god I can depend on you, Jack. You're the only one in this house with any sense. I arrived to find Trim screaming at his neighbor about a two-headed fish."

"Two-headed fish?" Jack's curiosity was piqued.

"He's in the kitchen—I'm sure he'd be glad to tell you all about it."

He handed her the baby and went downstairs, then led Trim into the front room, where he willingly held forth on his excessively endowed catch.

Mrs. Biddle put Eugenia down while she unbuttoned her blouse, then brought her up to feed while she made her way to Mélisande's room. Her husband had seen nothing of this from behind the door. But now he crept out to the landing and spied on his wife while she fed his daughter in the room beyond. It was then that he heard Pat backing into the henhouse. The spell broken, he went quickly downstairs and out the back door. Luckily, his wife took no notice of the crash. And Trim was too far along with his fish story to be drawn away by any transitory goings-on outside.

Biddle made it to the alley in time to see the runabout stop at the street and a girl get in. Who the driver was he couldn't tell, but the girl he recognized. He'd seen her previously brushing her hair in the second-floor window. No doubt the girl Jack called Melanie. And, almost certainly, the Madame Bodel his wife had visited at the Baggs Hotel the week before. Just as he suspected, Trim had lied to him about her boarding an express to New York. Now he knew why.

Biddle had much to think about. Several questions needed to be settled. The first, and most obvious, was whether he was in fact the father of the child. This he settled quickly in the affirmative. Not simply because he'd felt an immediate attachment to the infant, or because he'd seen in her a shared resemblance. But because had she *not* been his child, it was far more likely his merciless wife would have announced the fact publicly than that she would have hidden it out of shame or embarrassment. She was incapable of feeling either. But she'd be more than happy to serve up large portions of both to her somewhat less hardened husband.

6

It was Mrs. Biddle's custom to leave the Meeker Street house just after midnight, once Eugenia had had her second, late supper. But on this night, that hour passed with still no sign of Mélisande. This annoyed her mistress, as you may well expect. At two o'clock, when the girl still hadn't shown, Mrs. Biddle, quite naturally, began to consider that she might have suffered some misfortune. But rather than turning sympathetic, she merely redoubled her annoyance to include the anonymous second party.

The next morning, she found Trim hosting Jack's piglet in the kitchen.

"Breakfast?" he asked. "Just made some hash."

"No, thank you. But I will have some coffee."

She poured herself a cup and watched as Trim set the plate he'd just offered her before the piglet.

"That damn girl never came home," she told him. "Do you have any idea where she might've gone?"

"Off with Pat Lyons, I suspect."

"The dead man's brother? What's she have to do with him?"

"He's been hangin' round, eyin' her. An' she don't seem to mind."

"The foolish little tart."

"Oh, he's a smooth one. Knows how to turn a girl's head."

"And she's the type always willing to give a turn."

"No sign of Jack, either."

"Isn't he out selling his newspapers?"

Trim led her into the front room, where Jack made his bed on the couch.

"Didn't sleep here. That hat layin' there. It's Pat Lyons'. Been there since I came home yesterday."

"Do you think the boy's all right?"

"Generally takes care of himself pretty well. But maybe a little too fond of a fight."

"Well, I need to be going. Let Greta know the baby's alone in Mélisande's room."

Mrs. Biddle hurried back to the hotel in time to be seen at breakfast. An hour later, Lady Eleanor was with Admiral Lord Dexter in his office. He'd asked her there to help him determine the most theosophically auspicious composition for the ever-growing amalgam of souvenir medals that graced the chest of his uniform.

As she pinned and unpinned, she could feel his warm breath, even at this early hour smelling of cigar and bourbon. Somehow, she resisted the urge to stab him with the needle-sharp spike extending from the posterior of an elk (a memento of the 1901 B.P.O.E. convention in Worcester, Mass.) she was currently positioning over his left breast.

"I have wonderful news," she told him. "I just received a wire from my dear old mammy, Madame Palmyre. She has consented to help us, and intimated that she had already formulated a course of action. She'll be catching an afternoon train and should arrive sometime on Wednesday."

"Ha! O'Hearn should be dead by Friday!"

"I wouldn't set my hopes too high. These things take time. I remember it was years before Mammy finally did in her old master."

"*Years?*"

"Yes, but in the meantime she ensured his life was what might fairly be termed a living hell. And isn't that far more satisfying? Dead by Friday and what's to look forward to next week?"

"Dancing on his grave!"

"True. There would be a certain satisfaction in that, but an ephemeral one. Try to imagine the alderman suffering an endless plague of woes—kidney stones, swollen joints, feet blanketed in painful corns, chronic headaches, not to mention the worst of all...."

Lord Dexter's eyebrows were intrigued, but neither they nor the admiral could decipher her meaning. "Better mention it," he told his theosopher.

"What the English call the French gout, and the French *le mal de Naples*, while the Germans, I've heard, use *Türkische-musik*. The Turks, no doubt, blame the Persians, and they the Medes. Where it began, nobody knows."

"The pox?"

"Yes, that very thing."

"If he doesn't already have it."

"Perhaps he does, but the list of potential torments is without limit," Mrs. Biddle assured him. "Of course, there will be costs involved...."

"How much?"

"That's difficult to say. But I suggest you do whatever's necessary to accommodate Mme. Palmyre. If she finds her position here congenial, you can expect years of faithful service. But do be careful. If you should cross her... Well, my advice is, see that you don't."

"Mean?"

"No, not mean. But very thorough when it comes to settling scores. Just make sure that she's comfortable and without complaint."

"I'll go and tell Tillie to prepare the finest room."

"I thought I'd been given the finest room?" Lady Eleanor teased.

Dexter's eyebrows shared a laugh at his faux pas. But the man below was not amused. Too often, this theosopher's quips had come at his expense. What's more, she had slapped aside his playful advances with a finality which gave lie to her protestations of having found them flattering. Why was it he could never find courtiers who lasted?

The conference over, both went off—his lordship to find his wife, and Lady Eleanor to make an unusual morning visit to the sherry decanter. She, too, was tiring of their arrangement. Dexter's eccentricities had long since lost their capacity to amuse.

In the palm court, she found Lord Abernethy making what was for him a not-at-all-unusual morning visit.

"This seems to be the only place we meet with any regularity," she said.

"The only safe haven in the madhouse."

"And one which seems to tap into an inexhaustible supply of sherry."

"That's my doing," Archie confessed. "I've dubbed his lordship's vintner the Earl of Perfordshire."

"Perfordshire? Sounds made-up."

"It'd better be. Anyway, he finds it to his liking."

Archie poured Mrs. Biddle a beaker and handed it to her.

"I wonder if you could satisfy my curiosity?" he asked.

"On what point?"

"That child of yours..."

"What became of her?"

"Yes. I take it she's nearby?"

"Yes. Quite nearby."

"And safe?"

"Yes. What are you getting at?"

"Well, I believe, from something I've overheard, that Felicia, dear girl, has somehow caught wind of the child."

"I see. Well, I was with her last night. She's quite safe. What was it you heard?"

Lord Abernethy was reluctant to cross Biddle's instructions on keeping mum about the events in his apartment. Jack might not have found the policeman's threats of violence a matter of concern, but Archie found them wholly credible. Having ascertained that the child was secure, he felt his duty to Lady Eleanor fulfilled. Now, safety demanded he dissemble.

"Felicia was on the telephone. I heard her say, 'I've just learned she has a baby. Hidden away someplace.' And I thought, from her tone, that she might have been referring to you."

"Perhaps I underestimated her. She seems so thoroughly dull."

"Dull, no doubt. But wicked. And as they say, the more wicked, the more lucky. I imagine it was by chance she found out. A friend, perhaps, saw something."

"I'd hoped I'd freed her of friends."

"Oh, a girl like that—rich and domineering—will always find sheep to do her bidding."

At that same moment, Lord Dexter had located his wife. He was spying on her from the hall as she yet again ministered to the injury-prone Pole in his room. This time, at least, they were both upright. And there seemed nothing improper about the way she was applying ointment to the newest of his secretary's wounds. If only she'd left off the motherly kiss, which struck her husband as too prolonged and involving too much muscular action to be thought entirely devoid of lascivious intent.

His voyeuristic brows, however, were left in the dark. Before venturing into the guest wing, Lord Dexter had donned his admiral's hat and pulled it low—what noble wishes to appear the cuckold before his vassals?

Not far away, in his office at the county courthouse, Arthur Biddle telephoned the attorney who had filed his divorce papers.

"Phelps? Biddle. Listen, I've decided to withdraw my application for divorce."

"*What?* I hope you're joking. I was just about to call you. The judge has a couple hours free tomorrow and asked me if I'd be ready. I told him I would be."

"I thought you said this would go on for months?"

"Not once your wife admitted to abandoning the marriage. What changed your mind?"

"Can't say. But maybe this will work out for the better. What time's the party?"

"Four o'clock."

"Will my wife be there?"

"No need for it."

"Could you subpoena her?"

"I suppose the judge would be amenable to that. But why?"

"I've got my reasons. She's staying at Dexter's hotel. Under the name Lady Eleanor."

"Yes, I heard all about her. All right, I'll see you at four tomorrow."

II

No sooner had Biddle gotten off the phone than it rang.

"Arthur? Is that you?"

It was the gelatinous drawl of his onetime fiancée.

"Yeah, it's me."

"I'm calling to invite you to dinner this evening."

"Don't think I can make it."

"Oh, you'll want to be there. I have an announcement to make. Seven o'clock."

With that, she hung up.

Biddle was still staring at the phone when Trim entered the office several minutes later.

"I got somethin' of a problem," he told his chief.

"Just one?"

"One that's pressin'. But I can't get to that one without gettin' past a bigger one."

"You want to tell me about it?"

"Well, can't say I *want* to tell you, just no choice...."

"Go on."

"It starts back with Pat Lyons' protruding omphalos. You see, it wasn't Pat that cracked his head and died. We only made it look that way."

"*You* made it look that way?"

"By givin' Danny a protruding omphalos."

"How'd you do that?"

"I can't claim any credit for it, but a friend took a piece of his ear and sewed it to his belly."

"But I switched that bit on the cards."

"Yeah. But I didn't notice about that 'til after the omphalos was sewed on, so I switched 'em back."

"Huh. Guess we would've saved ourselves some trouble if we'd come clean."

"Yeah, reckon so. Next thing I oughtta mention... You remember how that girl followed Pat Lyons up here?"

"You married her."

"How'd you hear about that?"

"I was by the house yesterday. Jack brought me by."

"You know Jack? 'Cause it's about him."

"What's about him?"

"The more pressin' part of it. Seems he had a run-in with the beat cop at the depot. Fellow named Rhody Dolan. Says Jack spit at him. I tried gettin' him to drop the charge, but no go. Thought maybe you'd..."

"All right. But first you'd better tell me the rest. I met both babies yesterday."

"Did? Cute, ain't they?"

"Uhuh. Now sit down and tell me everything you know about my wife and her baby."

"Well..."

"And don't be long about it, or Jack'll grow old waitin'."

Needless to say, Trim *was* long about it. And since the facts are well known to ourselves, let's catch up with Pat and Mélisande, whom we left the previous evening as they were heading out of town in Felicia's electric auto. After a brief stop for provisions, they made for Sylvan Beach—reaching it just as the runabout ran out of power. Pat had chosen the small resort town because it was a popular port for the steamboats that plied Lake Oneida. Unfortunately, it being nearly midnight when they arrived, the last boat had long since sailed. And when the couple inquired at the local hotels, they were sent away. A gaudily dressed man, accompanied by a young girl, arriving late at night, and with no luggage—it was all a bit too obvious, even to innkeepers used to turning a blind eye.

Pat suggested they go for a late-night swim and then sleep on the beach. But Mélisande doubted he would be as easily distracted as the fat, middle-aged cuckold she'd spent the night with in Cherbourg. And that lying on the sand with him—half-dressed, damp, and chilled—she'd have the resolve to even try.

Especially if they partook of the brandy Pat had procured on the way.

As they walked, they came upon a small boat tied to a dock.

"Ah! We can still go on the lake," she told him. "Take me, and I will tell you about the... *porteur*...." She pantomimed carrying a load.

"Porter?"

"Yes! The porter, and especially the three girls...."

"*Three?*"

"Yes, sisters. And all very, very beautiful."

Pat needed little convincing. Taking her was just what he had in mind. And a dinghy didn't allow a girl many places to hide. He helped her aboard and loaded their provisions, then rowed them out onto the lake. There was a bright, gibbous moon, and the scene seemed set. But by then she'd launched into her story and he thought it entertaining enough to let her finish.

Early the next morning, Mélisande maneuvered them to a dock at the hamlet of Jewell on the north shore of the lake—Pat having been rendered incapable by a long night of drinking and... well, we needn't go into that here. (Devoted readers wanting a fuller explanation of the night's goings-on, including a bulletin on the status of the girl's maidenhead, are advised to consult "The Maiden on the Lake," the fourth tale in *The Fly Maiden's Book of Virtues*.)

Through a quick exchange of telegrams with an acquaintance on a morning newspaper, Pat determined it was safe to return to Byblos. It took two trains, and most of the morning, but just before noon they arrived back in town. Pat walked the girl to the Meeker Street house and there they found Greta on the porch, sunning the two babies.

"Why you takin' up with him?" she asked Mélisande. "You know how he left me."

"Now, Gret. That's no way to talk," Pat told her.

"An' where's Jack?" she shot back.

"Jack? He don't answer to me."

"He runs numbers for ya. Never come home last night."

"Wasn't runnin' numbers yesterday. Not on Sunday. Me and the good Lord got an understanding. He don't intrude on my racket, and I don't intrude on his."

"Here's Jack." Mélisande nodded toward the street, where Jack and Biddle were approaching.

"Where ya been, Jack?" Greta asked sharply.

"Dat cop frien' a yers, Rhody. Pulled me in for flippin' pennies."

"Pulled you in for spittin' at 'im," Biddle reminded him.

Jack instinctively spat on the sidewalk.

Biddle grabbed him by the shirt and spun him around.

"Look, Jack, it's all right bein' tough. But not bein' dumb. I fixed it this time, but don't count on me pullin' you out every time you get yourself in trouble. Not if you're goin' at it like that."

"Listen to him, Jack," Pat added. "No sense pickin' fights you don't need."

Jack broke free and went inside. Then Biddle watched as Mélisande and Greta followed with the babies.

"He'll be OK," Pat told him. "When you two get acquainted?"

"Yesterday. When Felicia brought a baby by my place. Know anything about that?"

"No use lyin'. Come by the hotel and I'll stand ya a drink."

"All right. You can tell me on the way."

"Well, I knew she had somethin' planned, but I led her to thinkin' the pickaninny was your wife's. Some joke, huh?"

"Yeah. But how'd you know my wife had her baby here?"

"Came by for a visit. Just happened to see her."

"Visiting the French girl?"

"Yeah. Nice kid. But the kind who leaves you feelin' short-changed."

"No problem on that score with Felicia?"

"Nah. Never met one like her. Long as you keep her lyin' down. Outta bed, she can get kind of unpleasant."

"But rich. An' I think she'll be in the market for a husband real soon."

"Yeah?" Pat considered the prospect. "How rich, ya think?"

III

Felicia had surprised her mother when she announced she was arranging a dinner for that evening. Tillie found the girl's enthusiasm encouraging, she so rarely took an interest in the family's social affairs. In addition to Arthur Biddle, Lady Eleanor, her father's secretary, and Lord Abernethy, invitations were issued to Mr. and Mrs. Rafferty, their dear daughter Celia, and, lastly, the district attorney and his wife.

An odd group, her mother thought, particularly since only two days before Felicia had given her the impression she no longer counted Celia among her friends. But perhaps "wring her neck until her eyes pop out" had an ironical meaning among young people. So often they seemed to say the exact opposite of what they meant.

The Raffertys, of course, were invited in their roles as town criers. Felicia had a revelation to make, and she wanted to ensure that it made the rounds as soon as possible. Between Celia and her mother, that would be accomplished in short order.

The district attorney, Roscoe Stilwell, was one of the few elected officials not in the pocket of the O'Hearn machine, and hence in Lord Dexter's good graces. But that was not why he and his patrician wife, Cornelia, were invited. He was there as Arthur Biddle's superior, someone responsible for his underling's character. And she, to remind him of it.

What was Felicia's plan? Fortunately—or unfortunately, depending on your allegiance—yet another misguided one. In her frustration, she had impulsively stomped out of Biddle's apartment moments before Jack revealed the existence of a second baby. When she later considered the question, as best she could, she concluded that Pat had misled her about Mrs. Biddle having a child. Still hoping to marry Biddle—out of spite, if you recall—she fixed on a new strategy. She would let slip, in as subtle a manner as she was able, that he had impregnated her.

He would be trapped. The Rafferty women would see that all

of Byblos knew of it by the next morning. And the district attorney could be counted on to make sure his chief investigator "did the right thing." Or, at least, his wife could be counted on to make sure that he made sure.

The first disruption of her plans came that afternoon when her father abruptly announced that he needed to travel to Schenectady and wouldn't be returning until the next day. But no matter, she reasoned, he would hear the news soon enough. Then, at seven-thirty, when all the other guests had arrived and were becoming restless, she was forced to accept that Biddle, true to his word, would not be attending. This annoyed her a good deal more, but she decided his presence was not nearly as important as that of the others. They sat down to dinner, and throughout the first three courses Felicia bored the guests with her elaborate plans for her wedding. It would be held in late July, she said.

"A month isn't much time," Mrs. Rafferty told her. "I mean, for what you have planned."

"True," Felicia agreed. "But there are other considerations...."

"What other considerations?" Celia asked.

"Well, as you know, Arthur and I have spent quite a lot of time together. And..."

"And?" her mother asked.

"Well, you know how impatient men can be...."

"But surely, not with you, dear," her former friend said through a saccharine smile.

"What are you getting at, Felicia?" her mother insisted.

"I think she's implying that Mr. Biddle has knocked her up," Celia elucidated.

"Celia!" Mrs. Rafferty was shocked—but rapt.

"The cad!" Tomasz shouted. This was his first utterance of the evening, and Mr. Rafferty needed to be reminded by his wife who exactly the boy was.

It was Lady Eleanor who broke the ensuing silence. "Can you be certain it wasn't Sam, the layer of track?"

"Oh, I'm certain, all right," her adversary snarled.

"I think perhaps we should be going," Mrs. Stilwell said to her husband.

"Yes, I've some work at home. Lovely meal."

Mr. Rafferty's thoughts ran along the same lines, but he had a much harder time prying his wife and child from the performance.

Though things had not gone exactly as she had hoped, Felicia felt sure she had achieved her primary goal. Arthur Biddle would have no choice now but to marry her. She went off to share with him the happy news.

He was out on his porch, reading by an electric lamp, when she came upon him unannounced.

"We're to be married," she told him.

"Yeah? Who to?"

"To each other! I've just announced that I'm bearing your child."

"Huh. No chance it's someone else's?"

"It's immaterial who it belongs to. It's who people *think* it belongs to. And by morning, everyone will think they know it's yours. It's a pity you couldn't come to dinner. The district attorney was there. And his wife."

"Yeah?"

"Yes. And *your* wife."

"How'd she take it?"

"Seemed to think it amusing."

"It is, sort of. Second immaculate conception."

"Joke if you want. But now you'll have to divorce her and marry me."

"Can't do it."

"Why not?"

"Seems I got a real kid with her. Trumps your make-believe one."

"I thought that was someone else's child?"

"That one was. Its crib-mate is mine. You should have stuck around last night."

"You'll lose your job. And be forced to leave town."

"Think so? That would be tough. Still, can't be helped, sweetums."

"Don't call me that!"

"Maybe Danny'll marry you."

"Pat, you mean. You *killed* Danny."

"No, he really did fall and crack his head. If I'd killed him, I'd've made sure they never found the body. By the way, Pat says great things about you."

"Like what?"

"Well, you're rich... and accommodating...."

"Damn you!"

Felicia once again stomped out of Biddle's apartment confounded, this time having the forethought to stop by the kitchen on the way to her room. But even after finishing the three leftover desserts not previously taken by Lord Abernethy, she remained unsettled. Self-indulgence wouldn't be enough tonight—she needed someone to lend a hand. Two hands would be better. Throw in an obliging tongue, and the pond-snipe could do as it pleased.

A fervid fantasy played out in her mind and she had soon worked herself into a heat. She went out on her porch for air. Her father's secretary, the silly Slav, was typing beside an open window in the office. He wasn't a bad-looking boy. And, perhaps, not so ineffectual as he seemed. It was while giving him this mental audition that she remembered her lover had failed to visit her the night before. Fearing a reprise, she called out, utilizing the tone she reserved for signaling availability.

"*Tommy.*"

The typing stopped, and Tomasz came out on the neighboring porch—mere inches away, but separated by the woven laths.

"Miss Dexter?" he whispered.

"Oh, Tommy," she moaned. "That brute has abandoned me."

"Biddle?"

"Yes. Now I'm all alone."

"You poor girl. The man should be shot."

"Yes, that *would* be nice. But in the meantime... I don't feel up to being alone...."

"Would you like to come over here? There's coffee, and brandy."

"I was thinking you might come over here."

"Oh. Now?"

"*Yes,* now." Felicia's impatient libido had shoved the coy seductress aside.

"All right. Just let me finish this letter. I told his lordship it would go in the early mail."

"Oh... *Finish* the damn letter!"

No longer feeling charitable, she packed a small bag and slipped out of the house, then took a streetcar to the Butterfield Hotel.

As you might expect, the events of the evening had upset Tillie, so much so that she'd gone to bed soon after dinner. She was somewhat surprised at her daughter's behavior, even more so at that of Mr. Biddle. He'd seemed so decent. This was one occasion when she almost wished her husband was there with her.

Alas, Lord Dexter *was* in the room with her. He was hiding in his wardrobe. His suspicions about his wife and secretary had become all-consuming, and his business trip was a mere ruse to provide them opportunity.

It was a large wardrobe, and he had fashioned himself a comfortable perch with stacks of Confederate currency and odd bits of apparel. But by ten o'clock, he'd been in position for four hours. Feeling cramps in every limb, he rearranged himself to provide some relief.

As he did so, the scraping on the sides of the wardrobe produced an eerie noise. Reminiscent to Tillie of scampering raccoons. She was not fond of wildlife, and most particularly not in her boudoir. Quietly, she put on her dressing gown and tiptoed out of her vermin-beset chamber, just in time to hear someone descending the stairs, then leaving by the front door.

7

From the hall window, Felicia's mother watched as she disappeared into the night. Off to Biddle, Tillie assumed. Oh, what did it matter—that horse had left the barn. And at least now there was another bed made up and available.

As she passed her husband's office, Tillie heard typing. She stopped awhile and observed Tomasz from the open door—her thoughts at that moment such private ones it would be unseemly even to conjecture. Baring nothing beyond a faint, melancholic smile, she proceeded on to the bedroom of her daughter.

Twenty minutes later, lying in bed, sleepless—her thoughts now even more demanding of privacy than those I mentioned earlier—she heard a knock, then a voice, too soft to make out.

"Who... who is it?" she whispered.

"I, Tomasz. Shall I come in?"

How Tillie answered is a matter between her and her maker. But you may be assured, curious reader, we'll be afforded some revealing hints on the morrow.

In the meantime, let us pay a visit to room 209 of the Butterfield Hotel. Pat is pouring a brandy for Felicia, she having just recounted her declaration at dinner and subsequent conversation with Arthur Biddle.

"You're to blame," she told him. "How could you put us on to the wrong baby?"

"Honest mistake, sweetums."

"So you say."

"Think you can corral Biddle into marryin' you?"

"What do you mean, *corral?*"

"Well, it ain't his kid yer carryin', is it? I suppose it's Danny's?"

"What makes you think it isn't yours?"

"Don't see there's been time for that. Haven't known ya a week, sweetums."

"Well, if he wiggles out of it... someone will need to take his place."

"*Me?*"

"Why not?"

"Nothin' I'd like better, sweetums. Sure. Suit me fine. We got somethin' goin', all right. Of course, not sure you'd like it. Bein' on the lam."

"On the what?"

"The lam. The run. Biddle knows all about me, an' he can't be too happy about that baby business. Any minute, he could give the word and it's off to Dannemora."

"Well... it doesn't matter. If I married you, my father would be sure to cut me off."

"Wouldn't want that. Still, doesn't mean we can't be friends."

Based on the complaints lodged the next morning by the guests staying in rooms 207 and 211, we may fairly infer that Felicia was of a similar mind. The nesting raccoons had found new quarters.

Sometime after his wife's silent departure, Lord Dexter located the bottle of bourbon he kept hidden in his wardrobe and was thereby able to drink himself into insensibility, thus gaining a modicum of relief for his cramped limbs. From then on, he drifted in and out of a restless sleep—listening in vain for sounds of infidelity while awake, but nonetheless haunted by visions of its consummation each time he dozed.

When he woke for the last time, he held his watch in the sliver of light which seeped in between the doors of the wardrobe. It was nearly nine o'clock. He listened, but heard nothing, then came out and saw that his wife had already risen. After a careful examination of the bed linen, even his prurient eyebrows were forced to concede that nothing indecent had occurred.

After donning a fresh change of clothes, Dexter crept quietly downstairs and outside, only to return noisily a few seconds later. He shouted a greeting to his unseen wife, then went up to his office, where the telephone was ringing.

In the room next door, Tomasz began gathering his clothes. He'd heard the bellow of his master and thought the time ripe to make his exit.

"Dexter," his lordship grunted into the mouthpiece.

"Constable Donleavy. Sylvan Beach. You own a little electric runabout?"

"My daughter's. Why?"

"It's sittin' beside the pier here. Got left there the other night. Seems maybe your daughter was here with a fellow."

"What fellow?"

"Ain't got a name. But he was a fancy dresser. An' they were actin' pretty friendly, I'm told. Hotel sent them on their way."

Lord Dexter could sense his eyebrows snickering inaudibly at his predicament.

"Whaddaya want me to do with the auto?" the constable asked.

But Lord Dexter had already left the phone to summon his daughter. Thus it was that he came upon Tomasz just as he emerged from her room.

The admiral took the boy by the ear and pulled him into the office, then closed the door.

"I'm away for one night, just one night! And what do I find on coming home? You having your way with my daughter!"

Tomasz's feelings at that moment were mixed. His first impulse was to defend himself from the charge. But that misbegotten idea was quickly repressed.

Though the cold reality of the situation was now easily discerned, he preferred the warm embrace of the fantasy he'd inhabited the night before. By tapping into his vast powers of imagination, he'd managed to persuade himself he was enjoying the favors of the voluptuous Felicia. And he wasn't prepared to upset that psychological apple cart with any revelations to the contrary. There was also the reaction of her father (husband) to think of. After all, his *daughter's* virtue was already a thing of the past.

"Yes, Your Lordship. I fear I have been weak. But you may

rest assured, I, Tomasz Szczęsny, will do the honorable thing!"

"Shoot yourself?"

"Ah... No. I was proposing to marry your daughter."

"Wife's set on a duke."

"I have not mentioned it before, but I am of aristocratic blood."

"Pfft."

"It is true! Though it was some time ago that our lands were taken away by the insatiable Prussians."

"Germans?"

"Yes. I believe so. Though perhaps it was the Austrians...."

"What's this about Sylvan Beach?"

"Sylvan Beach? I lay no claim to any beach...."

Lord Dexter returned to the telephone. "What night was that?"

"Night before last, Sunday." Then the line went dead.

Dexter remembered that his daughter had not appeared at dinner that day. His secretary, however, had, and then spent the later part of the evening recording his lordship's draft constitution for the Pacific island he was certain would soon be coming his way. What's more, the Pole was in no way a colorful dresser. Ergo, the girl had spent two nights with two different men. Then he remembered the azure tie.... *Three* nights with *three* different men!

Based on this erroneous evidence (and supplemented by the myriad allusions made at the séance), Dexter correctly concluded that his daughter was far from her virginal state. A trip to the altar was in order, but with whom? Biddle was still married, and flashy dressers were out of the question. That left one entrant.

"You'll do," he told his future son-in-law.

Tomasz tilted his head by way of a bow, then managed to evince a stoic half-smile.

Crestfallen, his lordship's eyebrows made no attempt to mask their disappointment. They'd had their hearts set on gunplay.

By now, Tillie had tiptoed out of her daughter's room and

down the hall—but not without being seen. At that same moment, Felicia was slinking up the stairs. They greeted each other like two members of the altar guild, one surprised by the other with her hand in the collection box and the other taking a slug from the sacramental wine jug. After exchanging mumbled explanations, they hurried to their respective rooms.

II

When the summons arrived for her that morning, it was Mrs. Biddle's turn to feel perplexed. She had assumed that her affidavit would force her husband to withdraw his sham suit for divorce. Had she been wrong about his intentions? And if that was the case, could Felicia have actually been telling the truth about him impregnating her?

The first order of business was to determine if the girl was, in fact, knocked up. She could, she supposed, learn the name of the girl's doctor and see if the pertinent facts could be wheedled from him. But that would be a time-consuming and quite likely fruitless endeavor. Doctors so often make an affectation of discretion.

But not so laundresses. Lady Eleanor found Mrs. Killkenny in the steamy room in the basement which constituted her domain. Having been one of the few guests with enough sense to anoint the palms of those privy to their secrets, Mrs. Biddle had no trouble gaining the woman's confidence.

"I don't know if you've heard, Mrs. Killkenny, but last evening at dinner, Miss Dexter as much as said she was carrying a child."

"I heard, a' course. Wouldn't be surprisin' if she were, way she carries on. Sheets don't talk, but jus' the same, they tell a story.... An' under her father's own roof! But don't see how she could know yet. Havin' been in flowers."

"How recently was that?"

"Neow, le' me see. Miss Felicia... Three weeks ago, it was, the captain was a visitin' her."

"The flag was up?"

"Oh, yes. No mistakin' that."

"Well, thank you, Mrs. Killkenny." The duchess offered her hand, only partially concealing a folded five-dollar bill.

Mrs. Biddle next telephoned Celia and arranged to meet her for a late luncheon at Maxwell's. Then she hurried off to Meeker Street, where she found the household dining in the kitchen. At the sight of her, Jack hopped up from his seat and shot out the door like a hare on fire.

"I should be gettin' back, too," Trim said.

"*You just sat down,*" his wife scolded him. "What's goin' on?"

"Yes, what's going on, Corporal Trim?" Mrs. Biddle added sharply.

Trim looked up at the formidable woman and realized resistance would be futile.

"Well, don't suppose there's any use keepin' quiet—it will all be out soon enough," he told her.

"Never knew ya ta keep quiet 'bout anythin'," his wife of a week observed.

"Seems Biddle found out about Eugenia. Met her, even."

Mélisande made a noise like escaping steam, then watched for her mistress's reaction.

"Damn you, Trim!" she shouted. But then surprised her retainer by not taking a skillet to the deputy investigator's skull.

"Wasn't my fault," he protested. "I only found out after the fact. Maybe I should tell you about it outside."

"*Why?*" asked his wife. "Don't I have a right ta know what goes on in my own house?"

"All right," Mrs. Biddle told him. "Come on out back. I'm afraid you ladies will need to remain here."

Once safely away from the house, Trim repeated the story of Gretchen's kidnapping as Jack had relayed it the evening before. It wasn't until she smiled at his second-hand account of the scene in Biddle's apartment that Trim was able to breathe freely.

"That girl is nothing if not entertaining," she remarked.

"And so Jack felt compelled to show Biddle my baby?"

"His baby, too."

"Yes, his baby, too."

"All came out OK. No harm to Gretchen. But you can see why I thought it better not to tell Greta."

"Yes, no need to set her on edge. All right, Corporal, go finish your lunch. But send out Mélisande."

After a brief conference with her servant, Mrs. Biddle went off to her luncheon date—confident she had anticipated and checked her husband's next move.

Once seated at Maxwell's, she shared with Celia the news of Felicia's recent menses.

"How did you learn that?"

"It would be indiscreet to say, but from someone who would know...."

"Her doctor?"

Mrs. Biddle smiled enigmatically. There was no sense endangering Mrs. Killkenny's position at the Dexters'. An observant laundress might prove useful in the future.

"So not pregnant at all?" Celia asked. "I assumed she was lying about knowing who the father was, but the pregnancy seemed too likely to doubt. If she can't produce a baby, she'll look a complete fool."

"Yes, I foresee a wedding announcement imminently."

"To Biddle? Your husband?"

"No. But whoever it is, you can be sure she'll set him upon the task of substantiating her claim as soon as she can get him between the sheets."

"I don't suppose she could wait and claim a miscarriage."

"I think once her father hears of her announcement, he'll insist on a wedding."

"I wonder who the unlucky fool will be?"

"I have a guess."

"Yes, so do I. Danny Lyons. She's been visiting him the last couple days at the Butterfield Hotel."

"And before that, he was visiting her in her bedroom."

"Seriously?"

"Oh, yes. How her father managed not to learn of it is a wonder. But I don't think he's the right candidate."

"Who's yours?"

"Her father's secretary."

"The man who spoke up for her? Calling your husband a cad? He seems rather docile."

"Yes. Just the type for a girl like that."

"Poor soul."

"I should be on my way. I understand you and your family are heading to Saratoga this week."

"Yes, with Lord Abernethy. Mother finds him very amusing. Do you think you'll be staying in town?"

"Perhaps."

"With your husband?"

"That's what I need to find out this afternoon. Au revoir, Celia."

"Au revoir, Mrs. Biddle."

It was twenty minutes past four when the judge finally made his entrance in the courtroom where *Biddle v. Biddle* was expected to be resolved that afternoon. Biddle the complainant sat with his lawyer at a table on one side of the room, and on the opposite side sat Mrs. Biddle, alone. The only others in the room were the stenographer, the bailiff, a bored courthouse reporter, and Mélisande cradling a bundle.

"I assume we can dispense with this matter quickly. I've read Mr. Biddle's complaint, and the affidavit of his wife. There seems no reason not to enter judgment immediately. I see you aren't represented by counsel, Mrs. Biddle. Do you wish now to voice any objection?"

"No, Your Honor. I think it best to free my husband."

"Fine...."

"Your Honor," Biddle's lawyer interrupted. "Your Honor, my client has just informed me that the circumstances of the case have changed."

"Which circumstances? Didn't his wife abandon him?"

"If it please Your Honor," Mrs. Biddle interjected, "there is no contesting the fact that I *did* abandon him."

"That's not the circumstance I was speaking of, Your Honor. It's come to light that a child was born of this union. Heretofore unknown to my client."

"Is that true?" the judge asked Mrs. Biddle.

"Well, Your Honor, a child was born to *me*."

"Are you suggesting your husband is not the child's father?"

"There is some evidence to the contrary."

"Your Honor, my client is willing to admit paternity, and asks to withdraw his petition for divorce."

"Can he do that, Your Honor?" Mrs. Biddle asked.

"Of course he can do that."

"Well, then can I petition for divorce?"

"You can, if you have cause. What evidence is there that the child is not your husband's?"

"Well, Your Honor, perhaps you'd like to judge for yourself."

Mrs. Biddle motioned for Mélisande to come forward, then smiled over at her husband. She had anticipated his move, nobly withdrawing the petition for the sake of his child. But the thought of being on the receiving end of a noble act made her ill.

Yes, clever reader, as you've probably guessed, during their conversation earlier that afternoon, our heroine had directed her servant to bring the coffee-hued Gretchen into the courtroom. *Then* let her husband claim paternity!

My, what a ruthless woman. One can't help but admire her cunning—and fear for those nearest her.

III

It seems there was a petite flaw in Mrs. Biddle's plan, and that was Mélisande. The girl was a consummate sentimentalist, and an unrepentant papist. She simply couldn't bring herself to be party to the dissolution of a marriage over such trivialities. It was Eugenia she held and triumphantly displayed to the court.

The icy glare of her employer sent a shiver down her spine—and then back up for an encore. But this time she would not be cowed. Five hundred dollars or no five hundred dollars.

"Is this your baby?" the judge asked Mrs. Biddle.

"Yes, Your Honor," she conceded, then took her daughter from the girl.

"It's his baby!" Mélisande exclaimed.

"She knows nothing of it, Your Honor."

"I do," the girl insisted. "She told me herself." It was a lie, but a white lie.

"I don't know what your game is, Mrs. Biddle, but I don't appreciate your using my courtroom to play out your family drama. The petition is withdrawn and the matter closed."

His wife was trying to hail a cab when Arthur Biddle caught up with her.

"I'll flip ya for the kid."

"No. No, I think I'll keep her—as a memento."

"Fair enough. I still have that tie-pin you gave me a year ago Christmas."

"But not the tie that came with it."

"It will turn up. Where you heading?"

"New York, I imagine."

"I mean just now."

"To gather our things."

"Already done."

"What's already done?"

"Your things. Yours and the baby's. While we were havin' our fun inside, I had Trim bring 'em round to the house I rented."

"How typically presumptuous. But I'm afraid I have other plans."

"Sure? It's a nice place. Furnished. Best available in town."

"Best available in By-blows?" Mrs. Biddle used the natives' pronunciation of the city's name to accentuate her opinion of its housing stock. "I'll try to make do with something on Manhattan."

"Too bad. I was countin' on you to come up with the dough

to pay for it. Guess I'll have to let the maid go."

"You hired a maid?"

"Sure. But I figured you could do the cooking."

"It sounds like a comfortable arrangement for you."

"Yeah, I thought so. You can spend the night if you want. Plenty of room. Then get an early start in the morning."

"How generous."

A cab stopped.

"One night," she told him, then boarded while he held his daughter. When he'd sat down beside her, she took back the baby. "When was it you decided to read for the bar?" she asked.

"Back in August."

"Before I left? Why didn't you mention it?"

"It's when you were tellin' me I needed to quit the cops. I didn't want it to look like I was givin' in."

"How typical. So what are your plans now?"

"Well, a lot depends on if I still have a job."

"You're afraid the district attorney will believe Felicia's story?"

"He doesn't care one way or another, but he's a politician. And he has a wife with ambitions. I got somethin' I've been usin' on him, but if I tell it, I'll just make things worse for both of us."

"You've been blackmailing your boss?"

"Don't play the duchess with *me*. I knew you when you were doin' the doxy in a divorce ring. Besides, it's more of an agreement. A gentlemen's agreement. On account of him bein' caught in a hotel room with a chorus girl who had a weak heart."

"I see. It seems Dexter's dim-witted daughter may have gotten the better of you after all. Maybe you *should* marry her."

"Think so? Kind of hard to trust a girl like that. I wonder if she's even knocked up?"

"She's not."

"How do you know?"

"The laundress."

At dinner that evening with his family, secretary, and the

Viscount of Abernethy, Lord Dexter announced the engagement of his daughter to Tomasz Szczęsny.

"Weddin's to be held on Saturday," he told them.

"I would think I might have some say in the matter," Felicia interjected.

"You had your say, just picked the wrong or'fice to do it with," her father noted.

"How crude!"

"*I* can afford to be crude, girlie."

"Is it really what you want, Tommy?" the bride's mother asked the boy.

"What *he* wants?" her husband shouted back. "He took what he wanted, and now he'll have a plate full of it."

"Yes, Mrs. Dexter," Tomasz said. "It is the only way."

"You make it sound as if you're headed to the gallows," his fiancée told him.

She herself had quickly come around to the idea. She didn't mind the town thinking she was promiscuous, but she would resent them knowing she'd lied about being pregnant simply to trap a husband. And Tommy—diffident and obliging—was just the sort of man she could get along with. But he would need training. There seemed little doubt he was still a virgin.

For her mother, the night before had been revelatory. Previously, she had held the conventional condemnatory view toward infidelity. Now she saw no reason to be so dogmatic. She knew, of course, she couldn't hold on to the boy. Nevertheless, the loss would have been easier on her if he wasn't married to her daughter. Easier on him as well, she expected.

For Tomasz, who'd spent his adult life conditioned to think of marriage as a means to an end, the arrangement had both its pluses and its minuses. He found Felicia's coarse manner off-putting. But there was no denying that her arousing likeness had participated in some of his most convincing sexual fantasies. What's more, he'd be able to tell his father he had married the daughter of a lord. His friend Archie had even offered to authenticate the claim.

For Lord Abernethy himself, one thought above all else occupied his attention. Why was there so little lobster in his bisque?

On arriving at the newly rented house, Mrs. Biddle fed her daughter. Then later, she allowed her husband to partake of the meal she prepared and served herself, the maid not yet in residence. When they had finished, she led him into the kitchen.

"I need to go out, so you had best get started cleaning up. And by the time you're done in here, the baby's diaper will need changing."

"Diaper?"

"Just follow your nose. And don't wait up."

Mrs. Biddle went off to the railroad depot with every intention of leaving town the next day. She looked forward to being back in New York, especially since she'd be arriving with a full purse. Her one abiding regret was that Dexter's damn daughter would think she had succeeded in driving her from town and destroying her husband's career. And, she feared, the image of the loathsome girl's gloating would soon come to dominate her thoughts.

Sometime after she'd visited the depot's ticket counter, but before she'd wired the Netherland Hotel in New York, it occurred to her she might be able to at least prevent her husband from getting the sack. Not for his sake, of course, but merely to show Felicia, and all the other rubes, what she was capable of.

At the information counter, she asked to consult the city directory. Then she took a cab to a small mansion on one of the finer blocks of Hudson Avenue.

8

On the occasion of Felicia's dinner, the district attorney's snobbish spouse had made two remarks our heroine thought useful to remember. The first was the name of her alma mater. The second, that of her favorite author of classical literature. Mrs. Biddle did not say so at the time, but she was intimately familiar with both.

"Please tell Mrs. Stilwell a fellow alumna would like to see her," she told the maid who answered the door.

"And the name?"

"Mrs. Biddle."

The girl left, then came back a few minutes later and led Mrs. Biddle into the library. It was another half hour before Mrs. Stilwell entered.

"I apologize—we were still at dinner," she lied. In truth, she'd been in her garden, enjoying the evening air and the thought of keeping the faux duchess waiting.

"No matter. I was admiring your collection."

"So you went to Smith?"

"Yes, class of '99."

"I suppose that's what comes from..." She trailed off, but her supercilious tone gave a strong hint as to her intent.

Mrs. Biddle made no sign of having felt the barb.

"Comes from weakening the criteria for admission?" she asked.

"Eviscerating is the word I'd choose. As if they want to bring back the seminary for girls. Is it too much to expect of a female scholar that she have some grounding in both the classical languages?"

"Not in my case. And I in large part agree with your sentiment."

"You came in having learned Greek?"

"I did, yes. I was just admiring your Aristophanes. Beautifully bound."

"I became enamored of him while at school. I wanted to name my daughter Praxagora."

"From *Ecclesiazusae*. A fledgling subversive. That *would* be rich. And all the better since almost no one would know the reference."

"But you, apparently." Mrs. Stilwell's inflection made clear she was not voicing any admiration for the duplicitous woman who stood before her. Lady Eleanor could quite easily be fabricating both her curriculum vitae and a prior acquaintance with the father of comedy. Her use of the Greek title of the play, however, was more difficult to explain.

"Unfortunately, my husband insisted she be named for his recently deceased mother, Lela," she said almost pleasantly.

"Not a bad name. Will she be going to Smith someday? Class of 1920?"

"You flatter me. And her, I'm afraid. She'd be going off this year. But even with the loosening of standards, she'd have trouble getting in."

"Not capable, or not inclined?"

"Certainly the latter..."

"And you fear, perhaps, the former."

"She's quite intelligent. But without the desire, it matters little."

"Perhaps in need of a tutor."

"It's been tried."

"I suppose you know why I came?"

"Not really. To explain your behavior? Or that of your husband?"

"As for my husband, the girl was lying. Arthur never bedded her. You can be sure of that. Nor is she even pregnant."

"How can you know that?"

"Catamenia. Just three weeks ago. I have it on some authority."

"What a silly girl."

"Yes. As for my own behavior, posing as Lady Eleanor, *et cetera*, well, I have no excuse to offer. Nor do I feel any great need to do so. I'll be leaving here tomorrow, and glad of it. I'm not even sure why I ever came."

"Aren't you? Isn't it because your husband summoned you?"

"Summoned *me?*"

"Or had your father."

"My father? What do you know of my father?"

"Well, since you ask.... It's rather an involved story. I only found out when I confronted my husband over some correspondence he was keeping secret. It seems this spring your father was taken into custody by the police in New York for working some confidence game. He contacted your husband, hoping he could intercede. And your husband then made a similar request of my husband. Eventually, your father was released. But there were two conditions. First, that he make restitution. And second, a purely oral agreement, that he find a way to get you back over here from France."

"Arthur sent my father to *fetch* me?"

"Well, it seems there *is* something you don't know. Your husband told your father about Dexter, and his being in London, and suggested he could be... *persuaded* to cover the cost of the voyage."

"So Arthur set the whole thing up...." A broad smile came to Mrs. Biddle's face. "I can't wait to tell him I've found out."

"To take him down a peg?"

"Something like that. As it is now, it looks as if I came running back to him."

"I suggest keeping the secret. I should be satisfied with what lengths he went to in order to have me back. But I suppose that's moot if you're leaving."

Mrs. Biddle made no reply. She was lost in thought. That Biddle had gone to some effort to effect her return put things in a different light. He might not have followed her to France, but he *had* made the first move toward a reconciliation, or, at least, a return bout.

"You *are* still planning to leave?" Mrs. Stilwell asked. Her thoughts too were conflicted. The charlatan Lady Eleanor and her deft manipulations represented all she found most contemptible in the human species. On the other hand, a learned Mrs. Biddle could prove a welcome interlocutor in the cultural backwater that was Byblos.

"I've bought the ticket," Mrs. Biddle told her. Then there was a long pause before she continued. "And even if I were to consider changing my plans, there's the matter of my being received here."

"You certainly made a name for yourself. Hardly appropriate for the wife of a county official."

"Yes. A valid point."

"Were I to assist you, there would be risk for me—and my husband's career."

"Well, I can't bring myself to plead. But I will offer you a bargain."

"With what will you bargain?"

"I'll see that your daughter attends Smith in the fall."

"I think you may be biting off more than you can chew. It *might* be possible were she willing, but sadly…"

"A boy?"

"Yes. A young writer, currently living in New York. His penniless, bohemian existence strikes her as idyllic. And now she has a ridiculous notion to go on the stage."

"I understand. And I know just how to handle it. Leave it in my hands—but don't mention anything to her. I will see that we meet in the right way."

"Very well."

"Good night, Mrs. Stilwell. And thank you for seeing me."

"You're welcome. And perhaps later I'll be thanking *you*."

"Oh, you may be sure of it."

The next morning, Arthur Biddle prepared breakfast while his wife sat nearby reading the newspaper.

"How serendipitous," she commented.

"It is cozy, isn't it?"

"For god's sake, don't go all maudlin or I *will* have cause for divorce. I was speaking of this notice, 'The League of Thespians will hold an open meeting Wednesday afternoon at 3 p.m. in the ballroom of the Odd Fellows' Hall.'"

"Ball players? Inside?"

"A theatre group, you dolt. Last evening, Mrs. Stilwell informed me her daughter aspires to go on the stage."

"The one you plan to teach Greek and talk into going to college?" he asked, while slow-cooking her fried eggs into rubber. Of all her gibes, the ones incorporating the word *dolt* irked him most.

"Yes. And this last line makes certain the girl will be there: 'Be forewarned, the League does not shy from tweaking bourgeois sensibilities or thumbing its collective nose at the Puritan ethos.'" She let loose a short laugh. "And I know just the thing to take along. Did you bring up my books and papers from New York?"

"In those crates in my study."

"I think you mean *my* library."

The front bell sounded, ending the round before either side had landed a blow. Biddle served his wife her vulcanized breakfast, then went out to answer it.

"Hey, Jack. Want some eggs?"

"Nit. Got any sausage?"

"Sure. Come on."

Mrs. Biddle set down her newspaper and greeted her young operative.

"I'll need your help this morning, unpacking some things."

"I figured we was all through, now you an' the baby is stayin' here."

"Oh, no, Jack. There's much to be done."

"I come ta tell ya, Melanie's goin' off t'day. Ta New York."

"Without saying a word?"

"Figures you woun't wanna see her."

"What time's her train?"

"One o'clock."

"Foolish girl."

II

Having turned her trunk over to a porter, Mélisande arrived at platform two of the New York Central Depot that afternoon weighed down by nothing but her anxieties and a small carpet bag. She was going to New York far sooner than she had expected, alone, and with barely fifty dollars to her name. But the timing was unavoidable. Remaining in Byblos after having betrayed her mistress, a woman she knew to have both a fondness and a talent for getting even, was unthinkable. She must go. Go, without even bidding adieu to her beloved baby sister.

At least the Trim family had come to see her off, so she was spared the ignominy of a lonely departure. She kissed Gretchen and had just handed her to her stepfather when a familiar voice called from behind.

"Going off without saying good-bye?"

Businesslike, Mrs. Biddle handed the girl her baby sister, then reached in her bag for an envelope.

"There's a hundred dollars in this. Don't lose it."

"I suppose I must be thankful...."

"The five hundred is waiting for you at the Hanover National Bank—the details are in the envelope. It's been there since we landed in New York. Be very careful with it. I just wired Miriam Springer to tell her you're coming. Her address is also in the envelope. Be sure to write when you've settled in someplace. Now bid your sister au revoir."

Mélisande kissed the baby and then leaned over to do likewise to her benefactor—the latter barely able to suppress an involuntary urge to recoil. What made it worse for Mrs. Biddle was that the mawkish display was witnessed by Archie Cobb, then approaching in the company of Tomasz.

"On to Saratoga, Lord Abernethy?" she asked. "The two of you?"

"I am. Tommy's just come to see me off. You must congratulate him. He's to marry Felicia Dexter on Saturday."

"You're marrying?" Mélisande asked the Pole. "Why?"

"It was the only honorable thing to do."

"Oh, dear," Mrs. Biddle interjected. "As bad as that?"

Mélisande handed Eugenia back to her mother, then reached down to retrieve something from her carpet bag. Mrs. Biddle turned back to Archie.

"I've a question for you. Your friend who sold Dexter the mired steamship..."

"Len Bailey?"

"Yes. He told you about Dexter?"

"Well, truth is, your father alerted *us* to the opportunity, but insisted I not tell you that part of it. Why? What does it matter?"

"Oh, just satisfying my curiosity," she claimed, but in truth feeding her ego. "Happy hunting in Saratoga."

By then, Mélisande had found what she'd been searching for in her bag. She rose and put her closed hand in Tomasz's.

"Wear them on your wedding day."

She kissed him, the Trims, and finally Jack, then boarded with Archie Cobb.

As the train pulled out of the depot, Tomasz suddenly noticed Eugenia.

"She's forgotten her baby!"

"It's my baby, you idiot."

"Oh, I see.... That explains a great deal."

"I wonder, Greta, if you wouldn't mind watching her this afternoon?"

"All right, I suppose."

Mrs. Biddle quickly diagnosed the cause of the implied reluctance.

"Don't worry, you're still on the payroll." She handed her baby to the wet nurse and then turned back to Tomasz. "Come along, there's someone I want you to meet."

Moments later, they were headed off in a cab.

"I must offer my apologies for my behavior the other evening," he told her.

"Yes, I should think so. But perhaps they should be addressed to the mother of the child you took from her crib."

"You see, I was led to believe the other baby was yours."

"So you thought it all right to kidnap her?"

"No, not kidnap... I was angry. You made me feel a fool."

"Never mind about that. I'm taking you now to meet a woman who will be coming to Dexter's in my stead."

"Another theosopher?"

"Yes, something like that. It's important you two should be on good terms. She may need your help. And, in turn, she may be able to help you."

"Help me how?"

"Who can say? But surely you must recognize your life with Felicia will not be an easy one."

"She is very headstrong."

"Yes, and greedy, and a simpleton. It's the three together which will likely make your life with her something akin to what poor Prometheus went through."

"An eagle eating my insides?" Tomasz shuddered at the thought of perpetual disembowelment. "Might we talk of something else?"

But by then they had arrived at their destination, a small house on a street just two blocks below the canal.

The exotic woman who greeted them bore little resemblance to the former school teacher Mrs. Biddle had met three days before. She was wearing a bright scarlet blouse over a black skirt, and her normally repressed hair had been teased out into a tangled ball which nearly surrounded her face.

She laughed at their astonished expressions, then held up the necklace of chickens' feet and pigs' knuckles lying across her bosom.

"The butcher didn't have any bear claws or alligator teeth."

"Many are the privations one endures when living in a provincial backwater," Mrs. Biddle sympathized. "This is Tomasz Szczęsny, Lord Dexter's secretary. I thought it important you two be allies. He can make sure you see Dexter's mail before he does. That should enhance your powers of prognostication."

"*Bonjour,* Tomasz," Mrs. Miner greeted him, using what she imagined as the drawled plantation French appropriate to her part.

"*Bonjour, Madame...?*"

"*Madame Palmyre, philosophe.*"

Tomasz carried Mrs. Miner's bags to the cab and soon they were on their way.

"It's interesting you brought up the mail," he told Lady Eleanor. "You know that old canal?"

"Lord Dexter somehow acquired the bed of an old canal which passes through town," she explained to Palmyre, philosophe.

"Yes, we know all about that. More of an elongated cesspool these days."

"It seems a railroad wants it to make a new route into the city," Tomasz told them. "They're offering him *$25,000.* I picked up the letter just as I left."

"So Dexter is unaware of it?" Mrs. Biddle asked.

"Yes, we were in a hurry to catch the train. I expected to tell him on my return. It will, I hope, make him very happy."

"It will make him just as happy tomorrow," she told him. "Palmyre, do you think you have a spell to conjure up such an outcome?"

"Palmyre knows many spells," the philosophe answered. Then Mrs. Miner posed a question. "How gaudy a display would suit his lordship's taste?"

"Oh, the gaudier the better."

"Ah! Palmyre will perform the voudou rite at midnight... at the Congo dancing-ground!"

"Just the thing. The old coot will eat it up."

"You're both invited, of course," Mrs. Miner told them.

"Congo dancing-ground?" Tomasz asked.

"I know the perfect spot, an abandoned tannery about a mile out of town," she explained. "Some decrepit shacks, cattle bones scattered about, and the faint stench of rendering. It'd give anyone the creeps."

"I can see you will get on famously in your new occupation," Mrs. Biddle assured her.

"Not too famously, I hope. If my husband hears of it, there'll be the devil to pay."

"When his lordship learns the happy news tomorrow, hit him for a thousand dollars. Better yet, don't ask for it. Just vaguely hint at it. I told him he should be wary of crossing you. That should be enough to satisfy the devil and your husband both."

A few minutes later, they arrived at the Dexter manse and introductions were made. Then Palmyre announced that she and the admiral should go into private conference.

Meanwhile, aboard the 12:52 express, Archie Cobb had an inspiration.

"I wonder if you'd consider stopping off in Saratoga for a week or so," he asked the comely French maiden sitting next to him.

Mélisande looked at him dismissively, then made a noise that nicely summarized her opinion of his proposal. "*Merci* no, not with you."

"Sorry. I should have made my intentions clearer. You see, there's a good deal of gambling that goes on there. And that means a good many fools arriving with their pockets over-flowing in gold and silver. I plan to relieve them of some small portion of it. And it would be much easier if I had an accomplice. Say, a young French countess?"

III

From Dexter's hotel, Lady Eleanor hurried on to the Odd Fellows' Hall, where the League of Thespians was holding its summit. She arrived some thirty minutes late, but the anarchistic crowd was only just being brought to order. In the front of the ballroom, three men sat at a table facing a dozen others of both sexes. The immensity of the room accentuated the sparseness of the assembly. The man seated at the center of the table—the only one in the room over the age of thirty—rose to speak.

"To begin with," he needlessly began, "we of the League of Thespians practice what we call subversive theatre. We *want* to upset people."

The tiny audience applauded his pronouncement. All but Mrs. Biddle.

"You wish to undermine the comfortable complacency of society?" she asked.

"Yes, that's it exactly."

"And yet the League itself is run by a typical bourgeois hierarchy. The oldest male presiding."

"What does that matter?"

"Nothing, I'm sure. Just thought I'd make note of it. Do carry on."

"Thank you," he said, but without seeming to mean it. "Now, our first order of business is to choose a work for our summer production."

"To be performed *here?*" Mrs. Biddle asked in disbelief.

"Yes, here. Why not?"

"Yes, why not this hallowed hall of a fraternal cabal? I only wonder if someplace lacking the stigma of a paternalistic society might not be more in keeping with the League's pretensions? Or, should I say, philosophy?"

"The lease rate is very reasonable."

"Lease rate? Yes, let us, by all means, make sure the rentiers get their due." Mrs. Biddle's voice bubbled with sarcasm—a pot of which she always kept simmering on a back burner.

"What would you suggest?"

"Why not an outdoor venue? Free of societal stuffiness—not to mention the stale smoke of cigar."

"I suppose we could consider that." The self-appointed presiding officer glared at her until he felt sure she was properly cowed. "Now, may I go on?"

"By all means, do."

"There are three works we're considering. Henrik Ibsen's *Hedda Gabler*, George Bernard Shaw's *Mrs. Warren's Profes-*

sion, and August Strindberg's *The Father*. The last is a bit of a coup, as I've been able to secure a copy of Miss Erichsen's recent translation. But all three are works which expose the hypocrisies inherent in our society."

"While that's true," interrupted Mrs. Biddle, "they do so in the very codified vernacular *of* that society. A theatre of the avant-garde should aim higher, don't you think? I believe what it comes down to is this: do you wish to merely tweak the bourgeoisie, or to pull the rug out from under them?"

"And by what means would you suggest we might accomplish the latter?"

"Alfred Jarry's *Ubu Roi*," she answered. Then added the sweetener, "There were riots when it was performed in Paris."

"Are you suggesting we perform a play in *French?*"

"It may be worth considering. But there is an English translation available."

"By whom?"

"By me." Mrs. Biddle reached into her bag and pulled out a sheaf of papers bound in ribbon.

"But the committee hasn't had time to study your work. And we must choose this afternoon."

"Then I appeal to the committee of the whole."

"But how can we make a decision regarding a play we haven't read?"

"My argument is a simple one. If we do a production of *Hedda Gabler*, the local newspapers *might* give it a brief mention on page 11, opposite the railway timetables. But if we do something truly revolutionary, bring Byblos to a boil, the *New York Sun* will give an account of the unrest on page three. The *Tribune*, on page one. And the *Journal* can be depended on to devote an entire spread to photographs of the ensuing conflagration."

"Conflagration?"

"Well, we needn't take it that far. But the point is *to be noticed*. Isn't that what we all want?"

Yes, insightful reader, as you've anticipated, Mrs. Biddle won the vote—and the admiration of all those not sitting at the table in the front of the room. Particularly the young woman whose profile she recognized and who introduced herself as Lela. Mrs. Biddle drew her new friend aside.

"I'm rather hoarse from all that debating," she confided. "I wonder if there's someplace quiet the two of us might go for some refreshment?"

"I know just the spot."

Ten minutes later, they were seated in the back room of Maxwell's, sharing a bottle of the sweet Rhine wine Mrs. Biddle knew to be a favorite of ingénues the world over.

"You really made that pompous George look a fool," Lela said.

"Oh, he was nothing. A woman must be prepared to meet much worse if she wishes to be anything other than a hausfrau."

"A fate worse than death. That's why I plan to escape to New York soon."

"Excellent choice. Provided you're prepared."

"Prepared how?"

"Well, in a city like New York one must always be able to anticipate, especially a woman. Learning how to discern which of those one might trust takes time."

"I'll be all right. I have a friend there."

"A boy?"

"Young man."

"From here?"

"Yes. But he's been in New York almost a year."

"I see. And he will take you under his wing?"

"Yes."

"He will introduce you to his friends?"

"Yes, certainly."

"Make sure you note, *his* friends. And, no doubt, he'll very helpfully offer advice on what to read, what shows to see, even what clothes to wear...."

"I suppose some of that...."

"Well, if you'll pardon my saying it, you might as well be a hausfrau."

"That sounds rather harsh." Lela took a long drink. "You've lived in New York, I assume."

"Most of my life."

"Then it was easy for you. I mean, no adjusting to it."

"Easy at times. At others more difficult than you could imagine."

"Were you abused by a man?"

"What woman hasn't been? But it's far more sordid than just that. I've rarely divulged my story. But you may find it illuminating. Would you like to hear it?"

"Yes, I would."

And who amongst us wouldn't?

9

"I have no memory of my mother," Mrs. Biddle told the girl. "Nor love for my father. He's a confidence man, and has spent all his life running various buncos—selling bogus stock certificates, passing counterfeit banknotes, things of that sort."

"Sounds rather colorful."

"Sounds that way to a girl of—what? Nineteen?"

"Eighteen."

"But living it is far more wretched than it is romantic to a young child."

"He involved you in these swindles as a child?"

"Though I was unaware of it at the time, I later learned how he used me even as an infant. For him, a baby was simply a means to deflect the suspicion of his mark."

"His mark?"

"The person whose attention he wished to misdirect and so enable him to get hold of the dupe's wallet. He kept me with him until I was seven. But by then I had developed some will of my own and he couldn't accept that. So he farmed me out."

"Farmed you out?"

"Yes, to a vicious old woman who wanted a slavey to look after her needs."

"That sounds horrible."

"Oh, you can be quite sure it was. She was blind, made her living begging. And she was rather fond of beating me with her cane—though always careful not to do so within the sight of others. It was a hellish two years, but I learned a few things from that hag. She was the epitome of cunning. I watched her once cheat a *butcher,* of all people. And she never failed at detecting deceit herself. On one occasion, someone dropped a dime into her cup and I tried replacing it with a penny, simply to buy some bread to eat. She took up her cane and beat me black and blue. I realized then that she'd learned to tell the denomination of each contribution by the sound it made falling into the tin cup. There was no getting the better of that old beggar."

"It sounds like something from the brothers Grimm. And no one came to your aid?"

"Eventually. A young school teacher lived in the same tenement and she took me in. The old witch threatened, claiming she paid a hundred dollars for my services. But my patron stood firm. And, a little later, she enrolled me in school. I was far behind the others. But with her help, I soon caught up, and from then on, excelled at my studies. When I was fourteen, she married. There was no place for me in her new family, so she arranged for me to go to a private academy for daughters of the well-to-do."

"How could she afford that?"

"She couldn't. It was agreed I would perform certain tasks in exchange for tuition and room and board. I soon learned those 'certain tasks' encompassed everything from tutoring the youngest children to scrubbing floors. My own studies languished. That is, until a new classics instructor came on the scene and took pity on me. It was from her I learned Latin and Greek."

"How extraordinary."

It is rather extraordinary, isn't it, chary reader? And what makes it all the more extraordinary is that—at least from what I've been able to gather—it's not too terribly far from the truth.

"What came next?" Lela asked, having been led by the nose to this very point.

"College, of course."

"Why 'of course'?"

"I would have thought it obvious, simply from how I dispatched that gink at the meeting this afternoon. I didn't learn that from a blind beggar-woman. Only a fool would miss the opportunity to attend college. Though I know it is out of the reach of many."

"How were you able to afford it?"

"Well, I had learned a thing or two from my life as a mendicant, and—may God forgive me—still did occasional work with my father while at the boarding school. So I had a little nest egg set aside. And the classics instructor who'd befriended me had herself attended Smith, so she contacted..."

"You went to Smith?"

"Yes."

"My mother went there."

"What an odd coincidence. Yet she's not willing to send you?"

"Well, she'd like nothing better...."

"I'm sorry. So it's a matter of not being able to send you?"

"No, that isn't a problem either...."

Good lord! Is there no one this woman can't twist around her little finger? I don't know about you, scrupulous reader, but there are times when I find her Machiavellian ways more than a little off-putting. Alas, it is the great misfortune of the literary herald that she is rarely given the heroine she deserves.

That evening at dinner, the district attorney for Wahtawah County nearly spat out his consommé when his daughter introduced the topic of attending her mother's alma mater.

"If that's what you want, dear," his wife said with feigned restraint. "It may take some work on your part. Perhaps a tutor?"

"I think I may have found one. Though it will mean paying her something."

"Yes, of course. Your father will write you out a check for whatever's necessary."

"She invited me to her house this evening. May I go now? I'm not really hungry."

"Absolutely."

"Oh, and I may be late coming home. She offered to take me on an outing later."

"What sort of outing?" her father asked suspiciously.

"Nothing improper. Mr. Dexter will be there."

"Of course, dear," her mother told her.

Lela went off and Mrs. Stilwell informed her husband he was by no means to consider dismissing Arthur Biddle.

"I hadn't intended to," he said. "Do you know who this tutor is?"

"Biddle's wife, the erstwhile Lady Eleanor."

"And that's all right with you?"

"In less than twenty-four hours she has turned the girl's head around about college. From now on, whatever she does is all right with me. And with you."

By the time the meal was over, Mrs. Stilwell had completed plans for a series of social events to ease Mrs. Biddle into Byblosian society. Included were four dinners, three teas, and a tennis party for the younger set.

After a long evening spent conjugating Latin verbs—interspersed with her tutor's seductive depictions of college life, where she'd earned a tidy living selling her fellow students ponies (of the linguistic, rather than the equine, variety) and reading them selections from the Marquis de Sade at a dollar per head—Lela accompanied her new mentor to the home of Lord Dexter.

The admiral had his carriage prepared and then drove her and his administrative staff (secretary, theosopher, and philosophe) to the old tannery, i.e., Congo dancing-ground.

Palmyre had the men build a bonfire with wood from a collapsed shack, then produced several small jars of powders from her ritual haversack. She poured some powder onto her palm and blew it into the fire, producing a quick flash of green light. Then she had the others repeat an incantation. Tomasz found the plantation French of the opening too obscure to translate, but he did manage to make out the patois of the final couplet: "If you want to work the voudou, you will have to shake your tutu."

Another powder, and this time a magenta-colored flash.

"Now, Miché Tartuffe, you must run round and round the fire, with your arms held high!"

His lordship, caught up in the spirit of the affair, voiced no objection. His eyebrows, however, made their mutual mortification apparent by attempting to crawl up under their admiral's hat. But by the third circumnavigation, they could hold themselves aloof no longer, and launched into a sprightly, yet carefully synchronized, bourrée—thereby offering a welcome counterpoint to the spasmodic goings-on below.

The orgy went on until well past two, and it was an exhausted Lela who disembarked from the carriage at the home of her parents. As they parted, Mrs. Biddle slipped her a book wrapped in brown paper. Exhausted she may have been, but Lela nevertheless found the energy that night to make it through *Gamiani* in its entirety, igniting simultaneously a lifelong interest in the French language and a deep affection for erotic literature. By morning, the hitherto pristine French and English dictionary her mother had given her on her fourteenth birthday was in need of a new spine.

The next day, Lord Dexter received the unexpected news that the New York, Ontario & Western Railroad was offering $25,000 for his ribbon of malarial swamp. Convinced of her powers, and fearing to offend her sense of worth, he straightaway promised his philosophe a fee of ten percent. Mrs. Miner, in turn, promised five hundred to her theatrical agent, Mrs. Biddle, and another five hundred to his lordship's obligingly indiscreet secretary as a wedding present.

On the day appointed, when he found himself too nervous to execute the procedure himself, Tomasz asked the help of his soon-to-be father-in-law in donning the silver cuff links Mélisande had placed in his hand on her departure. Engraved on each of them was an ovate image he found suggestive of something unpleasant, but which Lord Dexter and his eyebrows recognized as the family totem. What's more, his lordship knew from experience that pickle-emblazoned cuff links were unavailable without a custom order, and these bore a striking resemblance to the dills he'd lost on the S.S. *Kronprinz Wilhelm*. But for once in his life, Dexter set aside matters of possession. If the boy was fool enough to take on his spoiled (in both senses) daughter, he could have a cigar box full of silver cuff links—with or without the relish.

The ceremony—performed according to the Catholic rite at Tomasz's insistence, but with the alacrity habitual to Father

Timoteo—was a mercifully brief one. The celebration afterward, however, was a painfully protracted one. Though prodigious quantities of wine were consumed, the mood remained as chilled as the pheasant with truffle aspic which adorned the buffet. There were no speeches, or even a token toast. And no one seemed the least bit inclined to make merry—or even meet it halfway. In the end, it was left to the admiral's tireless brows to perform the obligatory charivari as the couple made their way to the conjugal chamber.

Throughout that summer, Pat Lyons raked in large profits as his sexually bifurcated bucket shop prospered during a long bear market. When the market's tide showed signs of turning, he sold his interest to Jane Jebril and invested in a new enterprise—a restaurant with a theatre annex. The opening production was a musical version of *Ubu Roi,* with the all-female cast dressed in flesh-colored tights. There were no riots, but the police nevertheless closed the show on the fourth night—thus providing Pat's venture front-page treatment in every newspaper in the county. It was full houses from then on.

During the subsequent bull market, always a bad time for bucket shops, Jane quite nearly lost everything she had. All that saved her from ruin (just the one sense) was the influx of railroad men constructing the new line for the New York, Ontario & Western. These lusty itinerants visited her Jay Street establishment with an almost religious regularity—the lustiest of all being a layer of track named Sam.

The evening before leaving for college, Lela Stilwell recited in Greek a short passage from *Ecclesiazusae.* Her rendition was halting, and full of mispronunciations, but that went unnoticed by her mother. And her father, without even needing to be told, wrote out another check.

That fall, having conquered Byblosian society just as she had the Dexters, the Stilwells, and countless others, Mrs. Biddle opened a business tutoring the children of the well-to-do. Her specialty was the problem child—a species the modern couple spawns with unerring reliability.

It was in many ways a fine house that Arthur Biddle had secured for his family. Even his difficult-to-please wife was challenged to find fault with it—until, that is, their seventh night there. Just after midnight, the town was drenched in an unusually heavy rain and the true cost of the builder's error in giving his wine-loving French brother-in-law the roof contract was laid bare. But as her parents rushed about with buckets and pans, Eugenia slept like a lamb, lulled by a familiar, rhythmic sound...

plic... plic... plic....

~~~ ~~~ ~~~
The End
~~~ ~~~ ~~~

Thus ends our book. If it provided you but a few hours of pleasure, I will rest content. Though honestly, I've always found it easier to rest content after enjoying a hearty helping of adulation, so please, don't stint. As thoughtful reviews are the bread and butter of the book business, if you can leave one for me at Amazon, it will be greatly appreciated.

Glossary

apple sauce : sweet talk, often disingenuous

aunt, auntie : procuress, madam of a brothel

Blackwell's : Blackwell's Island in the East River, where the New York City penitentiary was located

bower of bliss : [see note below*]

bull : a cop

cold deck : a crooked deck of cards

Dannemora : prison located in town of same name in far northern New York state

doxy : a woman of questionable character

expectorial : involving spittle

fade : to cross; to put at a disadvantage

fast house : a brothel

fly : street-wise; hip

gadoue : French slang for a low prostitute

genetrix : a woman who has given birth

jay town : hick town

marmot : French slang for an urchin; literally, little monkey

Miché : used in place of "Monsieur" in the patois of George W. Cable's New Orleans novels

nit : no

parlor house : a brothel of a higher class

play horse with : tease

plunk : a dollar

pony : a prepared translation, usually of Latin or Greek, given (or in Mrs. Biddle's case, sold) by one student to another

queer : counterfeit

thing : [see note below*]

*Note: Modesty prevents me from naming this most private of all a woman's concerns. Those partial to it have been known to use the term *divine monosyllable,* while the more practical-minded, and somewhat misogynistic, Elizabethans preferred *a woman's commodity.*

The Great Novaplex

Most cherished reader,

If you would like to learn more about the Byblos Foretold Novaplex, please visit: **BlyblosForetold.com**

Amongst other treasures, you will find there Mélisande's own book, The Fly Maiden's Book of Virtues, *which includes a tale recounting her adventures in Saratoga, not to mention her first night in New York, her trip to Paris with the itchy abbess, and her time on the lake with Pat—a gift to my most devoted readers!*

Yours, with undying gratitude,

M.E. Meegs